After the Climb

AFTER THE CLIMB

RIVER RAIN SERIES

KRISTEN ASHLEY

After the Climb

A River Rain Novel Book 1

By Kristen Ashley

Copyright 2021 Kristen Ashley

ISBN: 978-1-952457-85-2

Published by Blue Box Press, an imprint of Evil Eye Concepts, Incorporated

BOOK DESCRIPTION

After the Climb
A River Rain Novel, Book 1
By Kristen Ashley

From *New York Times* bestselling author Kristen Ashley comes the new, extended version of the first book in her River Rain Series, *After the Climb.*

With many new chapters, and introducing a new series character, this re-released Special Edition version of After the Climb *is the book you have, but it's also so much more!*

They were the Three Amigos: Duncan Holloway, Imogen Swan and Corey Szabo. Two young boys with difficult lives at home banding together with a cool girl who didn't mind mucking through the mud on their hikes.

They grew up to be Duncan Holloway, activist, CEO and face of the popular River Rain outdoor stores, Imogen Swan, award-winning actress and America's sweetheart, and Corey Szabo, ruthless tech billionaire.

Rich and very famous, they would learn the devastating knowledge of how the selfish acts of one would affect all their lives.

And the lives of those they loved.

Start the River Rain series with After the Climb, the story of Duncan and Imogen navigating their way back to each other, decades after a fierce betrayal.

And introduce yourself to their families, who will have their stories told when River Rain continues.

ABOUT KRISTEN ASHLEY

Kristen Ashley is the *New York Times* bestselling author of over eighty romance novels including the *Rock Chick, Colorado Mountain, Dream Man, Chaos, Unfinished Heroes, The 'Burg, Magdalene, Fantasyland, The Three, Ghost and Reincarnation, The Rising, Dream Team* and *Honey* series along with several standalone novels. She's a hybrid author, publishing titles both independently and traditionally, her books have been translated in fourteen languages and she's sold over five million books.

Kristen's novel, *Law Man*, won the *RT Book Reviews* Reviewer's Choice Award for best Romantic Suspense, her independently published title *Hold On* was nominated for *RT Book Reviews* best Independent Contemporary Romance and her traditionally published title *Breathe* was nominated for best Contemporary Romance. Kristen's titles *Motorcycle Man, The Will*, and *Ride Steady* (which won the Reader's Choice award from *Romance Reviews*) all made the final rounds for Goodreads Choice Awards in the Romance category.

Kristen, born in Gary and raised in Brownsburg, Indiana, was a fourth-generation graduate of Purdue University. Since, she has lived in Denver, the West Country of England, and she now resides in Phoenix. She worked as a charity executive for eighteen years prior to beginning her independent publishing career. She now writes full-time.

Although romance is her genre, the prevailing themes running through all of Kristen's novels are friendship, family and a strong sisterhood. To this end, and as a way to thank her readers for their support, Kristen has created the Rock Chick Nation, a series of programs that are designed to give back to her readers and promote a strong female community.

The mission of the Rock Chick Nation is to live your best life, be true to your true self, recognize your beauty, and last but definitely not least, take your sister's back whether they're at your side as friends and family or if they're thousands of miles away and you don't know who they are.

The programs of the RC Nation include Rock Chick Rendezvous, weekends Kristen organizes full of parties and get-togethers to bring the sisterhood together, Rock Chick Recharges, evenings Kristen arranges for women who have been nominated to receive a special night, and Rock Chick Rewards, an ongoing program that raises funds for nonprofit women's organizations Kristen's readers nominate. Kristen's Rock Chick Rewards have donated hundreds of thousands of dollars to charity and this number continues to rise.

You can read more about Kristen, her titles and the Rock Chick Nation at KristenAshley.net.

ALSO BY KRISTEN ASHLEY

Wildest Dreams

The Golden Dynasty

Fantastical

Broken Dove

Midnight Soul

Gossamer in the Darkness

The Honey Series:

The Deep End

The Farthest Edge

The Greatest Risk

The Magdalene Series:

The Will

Soaring

The Time in Between

Moonlight and Motor Oil Series:

The Hookup

The Slow Burn

The River Rain Series:

After the Climb

Chasing Serenity

Taking the Leap

Making the Match

Fighting the Pull

The Three Series:

Until the Sun Falls from the Sky

With Everything I Am

Wild and Free

The Unfinished Hero Series:

Knight

Creed

Raid

Deacon

Sebring

This book is dedicated to Kathy Sizemore and Kristin Harris.

Whose unwavering support of my writing, and the underlying friendship we share, prompted me to drop everything and give this story time.

Straight up...
I love you gals.

SHOUT OUT

TO MY KA FACEBOOK POSSE.

In the beginning, I used to be able to connect with my FB crew on all sorts of things. Then life got crazy. And I didn't have the time to have as much fun with you. So I changed my life and made the time. Now, we wouldn't have this book without you.

Specific shout outs need to be given to Stephanie Neyerlin, who allowed me to borrow her cat, Cookie, to give to Genny, as well as Sharon Koole, who offered up Shasta, her husky, so she could be with Duncan.

As well as Camsi Roy (and all my French-speaking readers) for giving me guidance for Chloe.

And last, Katrina Barker Scott, for giving this book such a freaking perfect title!

Thanks, Chicklets!

PROLOGUE

THE MEET

Corey

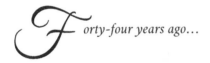 orty-four years ago…

HE STOOD beside Duncan and watched her go.

And as he watched her flounce away, all mad because Duncan was being a jerk, he knew he could watch her forever.

But she was walking away. They didn't have forever. He knew that because, even though she was way down the creek before she made that turn into the woods, it seemed like it was all of a sudden that she was gone.

That was when he looked to his side and up, at Duncan.

Yeah, up.

Because Duncan was taller than him.

It wasn't just being tall.

Duncan was a lot more "ers" than him.

And when Corey's eyes got to Duncan's head, he saw his best friend was still staring at the spot where she last was, like she was still there.

And Dun's face was all weird.

Corey knew that weird.

He *felt* that weird.

Deep in his chest.

Like it'd been there all his life, even if he'd never felt it before.

It was a good weird.

Corey didn't get it, but maybe it was the best weird ever.

No.

Duncan couldn't feel that same thing.

Not for *her*.

Not for her.

"Why'd you have to do that?" Corey grumbled.

Dun didn't even look at him when he replied, "I don't know. I don't know."

He didn't have to say it twice.

Why did he say it twice?

And why did he keep watching that place where she'd gone?

"She's just a girl," Corey muttered.

That was when Duncan finally looked at him.

And he knew.

They both knew.

Imogen wasn't *just a girl*.

And she never would be.

CHAPTER 1

THE BOX

Imogen

y head came up when the Rolls made a turn and the road got bumpy.

We'd been following a mountain path for so long, the twists and turns, I'd been lulled. We were at least a half an hour, maybe longer, from the center of town.

Truth be told, to keep my mind from this upcoming meeting, I wished I didn't get car sick when I focused on something while riding in a vehicle. I'd have been all over marathon texting one of my kids. Getting caught up on Insta. Playing that game I downloaded which I seemed to be able to get lost in for hours.

Hell, just last week, before I found out what had happened with Corey, my phone had warned I was at 10%. I'd looked at the time and it was two in the morning. I'd started playing when it was 8:30.

But then life changed.

I got the call.

Corey had killed himself.

Then I got other calls.

From my agent.

My publicist.

I needed to make a statement.

Corey Szabo, self-made tech billionaire behind Corza computers had committed suicide.

Corey.

Corey.

And, of course, being one of his dearest long-time friends, Imogen Swan, America's sweetheart, had to have something public to say about it.

What to say about my beloved Corey?

My childhood friend.

The boy, and then man, who'd been in my life the longest.

There weren't enough words in all the languages of the world to share how shattered I was that he'd taken his own life.

I closed my eyes tight, before I opened them and stared out the window at the thick trees we were (very slowly on this gravel road) passing.

Because this would be what Corey would do.

What was happening right now.

Me, on my way to visit Bowie.

Bowie hadn't come to the funeral. I had no idea why. And I thought the worse of him for it.

Then again, it didn't take much for me to think the worst of Bowie.

In grade school, all through high school, they'd been the best of friends.

Duncan "Bowie" Holloway and Corey "The Stick" Szabo.

The jock and the nerd.

Impossible.

But there you are.

Then, when Bowie got shot of me, he got shot of Corey.

I had no idea why.

On both counts.

Though, Bowie had told me, rather explicitly, if completely, tortuously and heartbreakingly erroneously, why he was done with me.

Therefore, it was only for Corey's sake I would be in the back of that car right now, heading to Bowie's house.

I knew he lived in Arizona, like I did.

I knew this because somehow, the fates had made him impossible to avoid.

Like Corey.

And me.

Knowing Duncan was that close, it had honest to God been the only reason why I hesitated moving my family from LA to Phoenix.

But he didn't live in Phoenix.

And I was done with the industry, the traffic, the mudslides and fires, and it bears repeating, the industry, but I did not want cold, snow or the possibility of days filled with fighting what humidity did to my hair.

I'd talked Tom into it.

Then we moved to Phoenix.

Suddenly, the landscape opened up, and I wasn't the only one in the car that gasped. Rodney, my driver did too.

Good Lord.

Was that...?

I clenched my teeth as my heart squeezed.

This would be what Duncan would pick if he had the money.

And he had the money.

So there he was.

That lake.

God.

And that house.

Sheer sprawling, rustic, monied perfection.

Even with the lake surrounded by the trees and mountains being such a breathtaking vision, I couldn't take my eyes off the house as the Rolls rounded the graveled drive and came to a stop at the bottom of the steps that led to the carved-wood front door.

Wrap-around porch. Pine-green tin roof. Log cabin style. Multiple stone chimneys.

Outbuildings, several of them.

It was like I drove two hours out of Phoenix and found myself on the set of the *Yellowstone* series.

But with better scenery.

As Rodney got out, my stomach pitched, not with nerves, but with fury.

Why did Corey, as one of his last wishes, decide to put me through this?

Seriously.

I pushed open my own door and folded out, just as Rodney got to my side.

"Can you get the box, do you mind?" I asked him.

"Of course, Ms. Swan."

I nodded. Smiled.

And braced.

I looked up the steps.

As the years passed, I tried not to pay attention. He wasn't like Corey. Me. You couldn't escape Corey or me.

But he looked how he looked. And he did what he did.

Therefore, he was in the public eye and he got photographed.

And I figured he lived up here in the middle of nowhere to do what he could to avoid it.

Duncan "Bowie" William Holloway, founder and CEO of River Rain Outdoor stores. Where you go for your every outdoor need.

Duncan William Holloway, ardent environmentalist, giving and raising millions to save any and every species, our wetlands, our rain forests, anything from fracking. You name it, he was on the front lines to save it.

Bowie was and always would, in some way, be the hero.

Except to me.

And there he was, standing at the top of the steps, wearing jeans. A lighter-colored denim shirt. A down vest over it.

Dark hair too long, messy.

Legs long and shoulders broad.

Features that were a jumble of perfect and imperfect, making them extraordinary.

Hawk nose.

Perfectly angled cheekbones.

Small eyes, but they were hooded.

Square jaw, almost always covered in stubble or a beard.

Like now.

A beard.

He seemed bigger than before.

Younger, he'd had the long, lithe, muscled body of a linebacker.

Now, he looked like a heavyweight boxer.

But of course.

Of course Duncan would only get better.

There was a woman beside him. Diminutive. Casual dress. Older than him.

She was practically wringing her hands as she stared down at me.

By the look of her, the age of her, she was a *Rita's Way* fan.

Maybe *All Roads Lead Here*.

But more likely a fan of Imogen Swan, the actor who played Bonnie in the insanely popular, award-winning, critically acclaimed television series *Rita's Way*.

If they didn't have the Rachel cut, back in the day, they had the Bonnie.

In that show, my love interest Devon and I were both the stand-outs. And fortunately, the veteran actors were cool about it.

Devon and Bonnie, finding their way through young love, committed to each other through thick and thin. The thin being Bonnie coming up pregnant, so they discussed it, at politically correct length, with a good deal of angst, and in the end, decided to keep the baby and get married. More thin when young Devon fought cancer.

Poor Bonnie and Devon didn't have a lot of thick. They lived mostly through thin.

And the American people (and eventually those around the world) rooted for them the entire way.

Nine seasons.

We should have stopped at seven.

But by the end, the residuals meant my children's children were not going to have to worry about anything monetary.

So there was that.

I looked from the woman back to Bowie.

He was staring down at me, hands on hips, face registering no emotion.

Not surprising, it had been a long time since he blew us apart.

Sadly, I could not say I felt no emotion being there, seeing his home, *him*.

Fortunately, I was an award-winning actress, so I was pretty certain I was hiding it.

Rodney returned to my side, holding the heavy box that Corey's lawyers had been instructed to give to me. It was sealed. And it was not meant to be opened unless both myself and Bowie were present.

Only Bowie and myself.

I'd had my assistant Mary make the arrangements. I had no idea if he'd balked and had to be talked around.

I just knew I was now right there.

Rodney and I walked up the steps.

"Duncan."

"Imogen."

Well then.

Right away, I knew.

All these years, and he could still cut me.

Even just that took a slice.

He never called me Imogen.

Gen.

Genny.

Beautiful, gorgeous, babe, baby, darlin', sweetheart...

Love of my life.

Never Imogen.

"Before Bettina loses her mind," he went on and shifted slightly, taking a hand from a hip to indicate the woman beside him. "This is Bettina. She takes care of the place." Hesitation. "And she's a big fan."

It wasn't snide, that last bit.

Not overtly.

It was still mocking.

It said Bettina was a big fan, but he was absolutely not.

I turned to the woman and offered my hand. "Bettina. Lovely to meet you."

She took it, that familiar light shining in her gaze. Excitement. Open indication that in shaking the hand of a perfectly normal individual, she could not believe her luck.

"Sad circumstances," she said, her voice trembling, probably with nerves. "But it truly is an honor to meet you."

"That's very sweet," I replied.

"Let's get this done," Duncan grunted. "Is that it?"

I released Bettina's hand and looked to him just in time to see him jerk his head to the box Rodney was carrying.

"Yes," I replied.

Duncan moved to take it from him, but Rodney turned away.

"I got it," Rodney said.

Duncan looked to me. "It's my understanding this nonsense is supposed to be done, just you and me."

"Rodney, you can give him the box," I said to my driver.

"Ms. Swan," he demurred.

Somewhat surprised, I took a second to study him.

He didn't like Duncan.

Something about that made me ridiculously happy.

"I'm fine," I assured.

I didn't have a full-time driver. The days where I could go nowhere without people doing everything from fawning to accosting me were long gone. Over the past seven years I'd lived in Phoenix, I'd even done my grocery shopping repeatedly without being recognized.

It was like a liberation.

Rodney was one of two the agency sent when I ordered a driver, but he was the one I had most often.

I didn't know if it was just because I was nice or because he admitted his mother was a big fan, and I didn't share it with him, but I went to visit her in her nursing home, though it was clear his mother had told him I'd popped around.

Whatever it was.

He took care of me.

Right now, he was taking care of me by handing over the biggish, and definitely heavy box to Duncan, but obviously not liking it.

"We'll do this in my office," Duncan decreed.

The man was then on the move.

I followed him.

Duncan didn't hesitate to share even further that he wanted this done. He did this by walking very quickly.

And I didn't want to admit (but I did), that I found this disappointing.

Mostly because, upon entering his home, I wanted to stop and take it in.

Instead, I sensed vastness…and lots and lots of wood as I scurried on my heels behind him.

It wasn't lost on me that I could drive myself and I owned a considerable array of casualwear.

So I didn't need Rodney.

And I didn't need to wear these winter-white silk gabardine slacks with the long-neck, soft-taupe, slouchy, lightweight sweater with interesting ribbing and (one of my pairs of) Prada slingbacks.

But there I was, putting on a show for Duncan Holloway.

Apparently, old habits did die hard.

He entered a room and I trailed him in.

But he stopped, and holding the relatively heavy and unwieldy box one-armed, once I was fully inside, he threw the door to.

This made me uncomfortable.

There was no reason the door needed to be closed. It wasn't like Rodney followed us like a guard dog.

I was left with no opportunity to question this.

Duncan was heading to his desk.

However, this offered the opportunity to at least look around his office.

I saw instantly it was heavily decorated in the motif of "I have a penis!" with not very subtle nuances of "I could survive *Naked and Afraid* for an entire season, no sweat. And I wouldn't even need a match or a knife."

I considered that perhaps I was being unkind in this assessment.

Bottom line, the office was very Bowie.

It was very much what I would have expected from the man who grew from the boy who took Corey and me on long hikes as often as he could, no matter how much Corey complained about mosquitos biting him or his feet hurting. The boy who could name the wildflowers or sense a deer even before the deer sensed us. The boy who forewent birthday parties in a deal with his folks so they'd take him and his two besties horseback riding instead.

But the gods' honest truth was that it was also very much the office of the man who accused me of cheating on him, refused to listen to my denials, told me he had it on "good authority," even though he would not share who that authority was no matter how much I begged.

Because, "Genny, *you know.*"

I did not know.

And oh, how I'd begged to know.

Groveled.

Completely humiliated myself in an effort to get him to just *listen to me.*

However, whoever it was, Duncan trusted them more than me. Because he walked out of our apartment, and thus my life, breaking more than my heart. He broke my soul, my innocence, and my stalwart dedication to my view of the world through love-hazed, sex-hazed, *I've got this, whatever it is, whatever may come, because I've got this man* glasses.

I never saw him again.

Until now.

When he left me, he didn't just avoid me and change his number.

He moved to Utah and disappeared for a while, emerging as the CEO of an up-and-coming outdoor store where all the cool kids wanted to get their camping, climbing and kayaking gear.

It had taken me years to get over him.

Years.

It took less time to become a mega-star in Hollywood than it took to get over Bowie Holloway.

But it wasn't like I didn't have forewarning.

He'd scraped me off in high school too.

It had started his glorious senior year, when I was a sophomore, and he'd come clean after all our years of friendship that he was into me.

And I had told him what had been burning in my heart what seemed like forever.

That I felt the same.

And then it was us.

Us. Us. *Us.*

My every thought. Both of our every moments. Even apart. It was *us.*

And that summer after he graduated, I knew he was the man I'd marry. I didn't mind one bit I found him so early. I was all the way *down* with him being my one and only until the day I died.

As such, I'd given him my virginity and he'd treated accepting it like it was the greatest gift God had ever created.

That was a memory, even with all that had come in between, that I still treasured. Every girl should have that experience. And in all that had happened between Duncan and me, there was no taking away that he'd given it to me.

Then he'd dumped me the day before school started my junior year.

He'd gone then too, but just to move to the city in order to continue his promising career of being a mover.

And right then, as I watched him commandeer a letter opener, raring to get this done, I remembered other things too.

That he wasn't as confident and cocksure as everyone thought he was. Those good looks. That body. His prowess on the gridiron. Everyone knew Bowie Holloway was *the guy*. Popular. He could get any girl he wanted (and this was true). He could best any challenge (this was not true).

They all bought into the ideal.

Except Bowie.

I remembered, too, that there was a reason he and Corey got along so well.

Because under that hot guy exterior was a nature nerd, but the relationship Bowie had with his father meant he had to keep that buried way down deep.

I also remembered that the first time his father made him kill a deer, and gut it, earning the nickname "Bowie," he'd come to my house that night. He'd climbed through my window and cried in my ten-year-old arms his twelve-year-old tears, declaring he was never going to do that again, "Even if Dad hates me."

He didn't do it again.

And his father grew to hate him.

I had wondered, and as I ended up being his girl, twice, but I was his friend what seemed like forever, so I did not hesitate to ask why he'd kept the name Bowie.

"To remember...never again," was his answer.

It was implacable.

He could be an intensely stubborn kid.

And I'd lived the nightmare of him being that same kind of man.

But there was more to him that I had not allowed myself to remember, until now, as I watched him standing behind his large, handsome, masculine desk, slitting open that box that he'd set smack in the center.

This was what sent me to stand opposite it, and say, "You look well."

His head came up. His hazel eyes locked on me.

And his mouth moved.

"Let's not."

Well then.

"Of course," I murmured.

"I don't know what Corey was thinking," Duncan stated. "And as usual, I have no goddamned clue what's goin' on in your fuckin' head," he continued. "But for the kid I knew who was my brother, I'm doing this. With you."

He would obviously not know what was going on in my head because he didn't ask, and if I spoke anyway, he wouldn't listen.

I did not get into that.

I was right then just as keen to get this done. See what was in that box. And get the hell out of there.

I nodded.

Duncan slit open the box.

I took a step closer to the desk.

He folded open the flaps.

I leaned, peering in.

And I did not understand what I was seeing.

It looked to be filled with reams of paper, computer printed, and there was one lone #10 envelope on top, sealed, with something hand-written on the front.

Though as my eyes processed what I was seeing, I could make out what the papers said.

And my blood ran cold.

Over and over...

And over and over...

I'm sorry.

Three tall stacks, side by side, the box filled, the top pages all covered in the same thing.

I'm sorry. I'm sorry.

Duncan's large, veined hand reached in, nabbed the envelope and then shifted some papers aside, exposing the same underneath.

If it was all like that, it was thousands and thousands of *I'm sorry*.

"This says..."

My eyes darted up to Duncan, who was reading from the envelope. His voice was quieter.

And I was very aware that I was incredibly disturbed by the literal thousands of apologies when I had no idea what Corey would need to apologize for—to Duncan *and* me—and I did not think that was a joke.

I still saw that Duncan had lost some of the color under his healthy outdoors-man tan.

"...I'm supposed to read this out loud with you here," he carried on. He looked to me. "I'm not allowed to read it myself. He says he wants us to hear it first at the same time."

"Duncan—" I could not hide the disquiet in my voice.

"Let me just read it, Genny," he whispered.

There he was.

There was my Duncan.

My Bowie.

Mine.

Minemineminemineminemine.

I couldn't stop my head ticking, which made his eyes narrow in concern he didn't hide, before I again nodded.

He didn't hesitate to slit the envelope open. Pull out the tri-folded letter that was on such fine-quality stock, I could see it without feeling it.

Duncan unfolded it, and through a dead man's hand, delivered a blow neither of us was prepared to absorb and neither of us would recover from.

Ever.

"Dun and Genny, I can't say it enough. I'm sorry. It was me. And it was me because I loved you, Genny. God, you never figured it out. I thought I was so obvious. But you never figured it out. And you picked him."

"What?" I asked softly.

Duncan didn't even look at me.

"So I told him. I told you, Dun. I told you Genny and I slept together. And I told you because I knew you'd believe me. And I loved Genny so much, I was willing to sacrifice you to have her. So I lied and told you we'd had sex."

The chill of shock slid over my skin, forcing me to take a wooden step away from the desk.

"And I was married. God, what a fuckup. I did it to myself, giving up on Genny and marrying Samantha. Of course, both of you would come to my wedding. Of course, both of you would remember how into each other you were. And of course, you would hook up and be inseparable again. I couldn't even get either of you on the phone because, if you weren't working or sleeping, you were fucking. And every day it kept going on, turning to weeks, months, an entire year. It was torture. It made me crazy. I had to make it stop."

I was trembling.

Duncan stopped reading, I knew he did when he said gently, "While I finish this, why don't you come over here?"

I tore my eyes from the letter in his hand and looked to him.

I should have kept them on that despicable, foul, *hideous* letter.

Because Duncan looked ravaged.

Not pale.

Not stunned.

Not angry.

Destroyed.

I knew why.

His best friend had betrayed him.

Not in the way he thought. In a much more selfish, vicious way.

And he'd done that by convincing him that the woman he'd loved had done the same.

Corey was that good authority.

I got it then. I understood.

I even understood why he didn't tell me who told him.

He didn't think he had to.

But he'd believed Corey beyond doubt.

Because there was one person on this earth at that time that

Duncan would trust more than me, even if that person was betraying him at the same time, something that would never in a million years occur to him.

Corey.

"Just get it done," I said.

"Genny—"

"Just read the damned letter, Duncan," I snapped.

It took a moment, and I knew why.

Duncan despised his father and all he stood for.

But he could not escape his blood, and in having Burt Holloway's blood, he did not like to be told what to do.

And he did not like it when he was denied something he wanted.

In this instance, he beat that back and returned his attention to the letter.

"*I told Sam the same thing so she'd leave me, and she did. I had no idea she was pregnant.*"

And that explained that.

Goddamned *Corey.*

At the end of them, Sam had cooled to me, significantly.

It hurt, because I had no idea why she suddenly disliked me so much, outside the fact their marriage was ending, I was Corey's friend, her not-even-two-year-old-marriage was over, and she was carrying a baby.

We hadn't been close, but we'd liked each other and were becoming friends.

And she'd never let that go. Not in all these years. Not even after her son became a part of our family so we could take care of him when Corey didn't.

Now I knew why.

"*But that was the end. She didn't forgive me, and Dun, you didn't forgive Genny, and I got part of my way, you two were over. But then Gen, you moved to LA, and Duncan, you went to Utah, and all I managed to do was make certain no one had what they wanted.*"

He certainly did that.

"*I knew, way back then, I should say something. I knew way back then, I should come clean. I should tell you, Dun. Or you, Genny. Make it right, at least between the two of you. But I didn't have the guts. I told myself I was working up to it, but—"*

"You can stop now," I interrupted. "I don't really care to hear Corey explain why he betrayed the both of us, and his pregnant wife, in order to have something it was not his to have."

Duncan tossed the paper to his desk and looked across it, into my eyes.

It was very bad form, and moot at this point, not to mention childish, to tell him *I told you so.*

Therefore, I refrained.

It wouldn't matter.

He knew it. I could read it on his face. In fact, it was written on every inch of him.

But that was not my problem.

"Well, there you go," I stated. "Corey proving indisputably that Corey was what the media alluded to repeatedly. Socially awkward. Single-minded. Driven to extremes. And willing to do absolutely anything, walk over people, tear them down, annihilate them, to get what he wanted."

It was just, I never believed that.

That wasn't *my* Corey.

I was very wrong.

Duncan had no response.

At least not verbally.

But Duncan was not a man of limited emotion and he fought hard not to be like his father. A man who hid the fact he was the same because having emotions was not what a real man had.

And now, Duncan was processing.

He did this by reaching into the box and taking a sheaf of the papers out. He sifted through the *I'm sorrys.* Then he tossed them on the desk beyond the box.

Out came more papers, which Duncan inspected while I watched.

And again, he tossed them, most of these sliding to the floor at my feet.

There were many things I had loved about this man beyond reason.

One of them was what I was witnessing now.

It might seem weird, but I'd thought it was incredibly mature, especially back then, when we were so very young.

Because Duncan had a temper. It was explosive. He let it loose, and if you were not used to it, it would be terrifying.

But he knew enough about himself to do it. Even in his early twenties. Enough to know those feelings had to be let go and he had to control them to the point he didn't hurt anyone or himself.

But that was all the control he wielded.

Best of this, it was then done. He flamed bright and searing.

Then he flamed out.

And this was going to happen now.

"Du—" I began.

Too late.

The box was up, and with a powerful heave, it flew across the room, hitting a winged-back chair. The box tipped, the apologies flooding the seat of the chair and the floor, the box wedging itself between the arms.

I did not move through this maneuver, or after.

He then turned burning eyes to me.

"You told me," he said softly.

"I—"

"*You fucking told me!*" he roared.

Yes, his temper was terrifying.

Though I knew him, even though the years had been long since I'd witnessed it, so I was not terrified.

I remained silent.

"I didn't believe you," he stated. "I didn't believe you because he told me. He told me the two of you got drunk, and you fucked him. Because you weren't sure of the future I could give you. But you were sure of him."

Well, hell.

Apparently, Corey was socially aware enough, or humanly aware enough, to know just how to dig right into those soft, vulnerable spots.

And then shove the blade deeper.

Because even then, Duncan was a mover.

By that time, he was foreman of a crew, but he was "only" a mover.

But Corey had been hired out of college on a six-figure salary, was on a rocket trajectory, and even at the time, I thought it was strange (not to mention, it annoyed the hell out of me), not just more of Corey's overcompensating and lack of confidence, how much he didn't let Duncan forget it.

Though, perhaps what Corey didn't know was that Duncan already wasn't ever going to forget it.

Or perhaps he knew that all too well.

"And you were. You were so sure of him," Duncan continued. "So proud of him. '*Corey's gonna rule the world someday, wait and see.*'"

My words of yore coming back to me in this instant made me feel nauseous.

"He was remorseful," Duncan informed me. "He told me he'd understand if I never forgave him. It was a moment of weakness. You were beautiful and he thought the world of you and admitted he had a crush on you and the booze made him stupid. He'd take that hit, of losing me. But I had to forgive you."

Which, of course, would lead a man to think, *Yeah, he was drunk, it's a guy thing. I get losing control. But her? She's a slut out for the best thing she can get.*

Not to mention the reverse psychology.

Boy, Corey had this down.

At age twenty-six.

However, this water was so far under the bridge, it had evaporated, rained down, flowed back under that bridge, and repeat.

Therefore, it was no matter.

"There's no point going over this," I declared. "What's done is done. Corey's dying gift was a one final fuck you. However, I'm taking it as finally having the understanding he was who he was and the relief that my grief at losing a lifelong friend will not last as long as I thought."

"No point?" Duncan asked.

"Sorry?"

"No point going over this?"

"Well…no."

"You were the love of my life."

My stomach folded in on itself so powerfully, I thought I would vomit.

"And you were that from the minute I met you when you were eight," he carried on. "I knew it when I threw that frog at you and you marched up to me, shoved me and said, 'Gentlemen don't throw frogs. You'll hurt *the frog.*'"

God, I remembered that.

And I also remembered how disappointed I was he threw that frog, because he was so cute, but he was also clearly a jerk.

It didn't take him long to reverse that opinion.

"It was little kid love, but it never died," he finished.

"Yes, it did," I pointed out.

He flinched.

My heart hurt.

Time to go.

"I'm sorry I pressed this. I should have just opened the box without subjecting you to—"

My preamble to my departure was interrupted by Duncan.

"You wouldn't want me to know? You wouldn't want me to know that you didn't cheat on me with my best friend?"

"It hardly matters now. You haven't seen Corey or me in over two decades."

"It hardly matters?"

"Yes."

"You ride around in that Rolls everywhere, Genny?"

Damn.

I forgot.

I knew Duncan.

And Duncan knew me.

Duncan didn't let up.

"Hollywood's down-to-earth female Tom Hanks throws on some heels and folds into a Rolls to take a two-hour trip up to a mountain house in the middle of nowhere?"

His tone was dripping disbelief.

"I think we're done here. Goodbye again, Duncan."

And with that, I turned on my Prada kitten heel (when normally, for the most part, I went barefoot, and if I *needed* to put on shoes, they were slides or T-strap flat sandals, and yes, the slides were Valentino and the T-straps were Chanel, but neither were Prada slingbacked kitten heels), and I started to the door.

I stopped when Duncan cut around me and barred it with his big body.

"We're not done," he declared.

"We're very much done," I stated.

"Genny, we need to talk this out."

"What is there to talk out?"

His head jerked, violently, and angry lines formed between his brows.

And his answer was, "Everything."

"Everything what, Duncan? Seriously, *what*? There is nothing to salvage from this. You've been out of my life more than half the time I've been living it. And if Corey has not just demonstrated to you that he is not worthy of your time or emotion, he has *to me*."

"I fucked up."

"Yes, you did, twenty-eight years ago."

"And we need to talk that out."

"I disagree."

"Gen, you're single. And I'm single."

He had to be joking.

I felt my eyes grow wide. "Are you *mad*?"

"If you mean angry, fuck yes. Blind with it at Corey *and* me for fucking up so colossally."

"I didn't mean angry, I meant crazy," I explained.

"Then I'm not that. I'm very sane and I'm very serious." He took a step toward me. "And you know it."

"I actually think you're crazy," I contradicted.

"You couldn't get enough of me," he declared suddenly.

It took all my talent, of which many were convinced I had a great deal, to force nonchalance.

I waved my hand between us. "I was twenty-four years old and—"

"I'm the love of your life too," he bit out.

"You were *then*, Duncan, but my life went on without you at your choice."

"I had no reason not to believe him."

Oh no.

I shook my head. "We're not doing this."

I tried to step around him.

He stepped in front of me.

I snapped my head back. "Let me out of this room, Duncan."

"It destroyed me, walking away from you."

I threw my arms wide. "And yet here you stand, healthy, living your dream."

"Yeah, you'd know about my dream, Genny, wouldn't you?"

Goddamn it.

But he wasn't finished.

"And here *you* stand, tricked out, showing at my cabin in a Rolls."

"This isn't a cabin, Duncan, how many square feet are in this house?"

"Six thousand."

Oh my God.

Was this the stupidest conversation in history?

"Seriously?" I asked.

"He wanted this, Genny." He jabbed a finger at the chair with the box and flood of paper on the floor. "Those apologies mean dick. That is not his final message for us. What he really wanted was you standing in a room with me, knowing what would happen if we did."

"Nothing's going to happen, Duncan."

"Nothing *never* happens between us, Genny."

This was frighteningly true.

And thus, I was at my end.

I changed tactics.

"I cannot describe how little I care that Corey maneuvered this nearly thirty years down the line," I shared. "He doesn't get to explain away tearing the man I loved from me with the proverbial thousand apologies and the lame excuse of, 'I didn't have the guts to right my wrong.' He's not fifteen anymore where we covered his awkwardness for him, and he wasn't fifteen back then when he drove us apart."

"Gen—"

"I'm not done," I clipped.

Duncan closed his mouth.

"And I'm not going to stand here and listen to you try to explain why you didn't believe me."

"It was Corey."

I touched my hand to my chest. "And *I* was *me*."

That again shut his mouth.

"We can't go back, and not only because I don't wish to go back, because we can't. I have a life, a career, and three children—"

"All grown and no man."

"After what you put me through, and what Tom put me through, do you think I want a man?"

There was a subtle but distinct rumble to his, "What'd that guy put you through?"

And again, there was my Bowie.

Protective, almost to a fault.

I shouldn't have brought Tom into it.

I shook my head. "It's none of your business."

"Genny, for Christ's sake—"

"It really turns on a dime like that for you?" I demanded.

"It never turned the other way," he shot back.

Oh my God.

I felt those words through every cell in my body.

And so, I had to do it. I had to pull her up.

Bonnie.

Sweet and kind and funny.

But more importantly, strong and smart and able.

"Well, I'm very sorry, Duncan," I said quietly. "Truly, I am. But it did for me. And there's no turning back."

We stood there, staring at each other.

And it was with no small measure of pain that I took him in, knowing the last time I saw him in person he was twenty-six and glorious.

And now he was fifty-four and no less glorious. Silver in his hair. Also his beard. Lines on his forehead, around his eyes. And maybe part of that heft he had was some weight in his middle, because Duncan was always active, but he loved his food.

And oh, how much I would have treasured being beside him along the way to see him become the man who stood before me.

But that was gone.

Corey took it away.

And Duncan let him.

Yes, most importantly, Duncan had let him.

And that was the Duncan I had now.

Because he was going to do it again.

He stepped out of my way.

But this time, he allowed *me* to walk out of *his* life.

And that was what I did.

CHAPTER 2

THE OPERATION

Chloe

Sitting in her car, she watched her mom walk into the hotel.

And her mom could fool a lot of people.

But she couldn't fool Chloe.

Therefore, once Mom disappeared inside with Rodney, Chloe put the bright red Evoque in drive and slid out of the parking spot.

Driving while hitting the buttons on the dash, she called Mary.

"Oh God, I knew it," was Mary's greeting.

"Instigating Operation Happiness," Chloe replied.

"Your mother is going to fire me."

"She is not."

"If I interfered in *your* love life, would you continue to be my friend?"

"If you reunited me with a serious hot guy who stood for everything I stand for who I'd pined after for years, yes."

Mary didn't have an answer to that.

"There's no time to waste," Chloe told her. "And anyway, you're hardly on the front lines with all of this."

"You're always so dramatic."

"Someone in this family has to be."

"You compensating for your parents' absolute dedication to being down to earth always gets *me* into trouble."

"Now who's being dramatic?"

"I have things to do."

"Yes, you do. Byeeeeeee," Chloe signed off.

After she'd disconnected, she made her second call.

"Oh shit," her baby sister Sasha answered.

"It didn't go well."

"Poor Mom," Sasha whispered. Then, "Is Mary on it?"

"Totes."

"Mom's gonna be pissed."

"Yep. Then eventually, she'll be happy."

"You know..."

Sasha trailed off and didn't start up again.

"I don't know unless you tell me," Chloe prompted.

Sasha sounded like she was sharing a guilty secret when she said, "Uncle Corey, he always gave me a bit of the heebie-jeebies."

Sasha was not alone in that estimation.

"He was into her," Chloe stated.

"*So* into her."

The sisters were silent.

Sasha broke it.

"Okay, take good care of her, okay?"

"You know I will," Chloe assured.

"Should I fly home this weekend?"

"No. I got this."

"Are you going to tell Matt?"

"Absolutely not."

Their brother, annoyingly upright, responsible and protective, would ruin everything.

"Right," Sasha muttered.

"It's going to be okay, *la petite amie.*"

"Yeah," Sasha said.

"Stay cool."

"Stay smart."

"*Au revoir.*"

"You're such a goof. *Ciao*, sis."

Chloe disconnected that call, and then hit more buttons.

"Did you talk with her?" her dad asked in greeting.

Not exactly, she did not answer.

"Well…"

That was all she was going to give him.

For now.

"Tell me. How'd it go, kiddo?" he pressed, knowing mother and daughters had always been close, but once she and Sasha grew up, Mom shifted, and Mom-Mom became Mom-Friend.

Chloe could not say they told each other everything.

But they shared.

A lot.

And Mom had shared this, maybe because she was hurting and fragile after Uncle Corey died.

But mostly because they were tight, and honesty had always been encouraged in their family.

In fact, as far as she knew, it was only Chloe who played fast and loose with that last, occasionally roping her sister in on the act (though never her brother—solid, dependable, do-the-right-thing Matt was apparently working toward sainthood, and it was *vastly* irritating).

And, it couldn't be avoided, in one terrible instance, her father had done the same.

"Not too good, Dad."

"Hell," he whispered.

"She went right to the hotel."

"Hmm."

Hmm was right.

After whatever happened, happened, Mom not asking Rodney to

take her right home was telling.

At least Chloe thought so.

In fact, it was lunacy (and also telling), that before she even headed up, she had Mary make arrangements so Mom could hit that hotel and book a facial for this afternoon, while Mom made plans the next day with friends who lived up in Prescott, all of this after taking that box into the mountains.

If Mom was over that guy, she'd just come up and do what Uncle Corey wanted done and go back down.

And after they'd done whatever Uncle Corey wanted, if Mom was pissed and over it, Mom would cancel everything and drive right back down the mountain and be done.

But she wasn't.

She was sticking close.

In Prescott.

To him.

All right, so it was less telling and more Chloe twisting it to what she needed to be.

But she didn't think she was too far off the mark, if not hitting the bullseye.

"You're not to get involved," her father said in Dad Voice.

Uh-oh.

"Dad—"

"Chloe, I know you. If there's no drama, you create it. And losing Corey, especially him taking his own life, now whatever happened with this, she's had enough drama for a while, don't you think?"

"There's good drama and bad drama, Dad."

"Says only you."

Chloe could debate that, but now was not the time.

"I'm driving, so maybe now isn't a good time to have an annoying conversation with my dad."

"Honey, leave it alone."

She was not going to lie outright to her father.

But she was not above a sin by omission.

Thus, she said nothing.

"Chloe, did you hear me?"

"I heard you, Dad."

"Christ, I could have skipped a generation of another one of your grandmother. It'd be cute, having a granddaughter who was a pain in her parents' ass. A daughter, not so much."

Chloe fake gasped and said, "I'm wounded, *mon père bien-aimé* calling me a pain in the ass."

"Stop speaking French at me."

"If you didn't want me to speak French, you shouldn't have sent me to France."

"We didn't think you'd stay there for three years."

"I can't imagine why, you'd both been to France, repeatedly. And you both know me, through and through. You knew, once France met me, and I met France, if I didn't love you so much, which necessitated me returning home occasionally, I would never leave."

"The worst part about that is, I can't argue it."

Chloe grinned.

"Honey, seriously," he said, and he did it sounding serious, "think hard about whatever it is you're doing."

She already had.

So she felt it wasn't (exactly) even a fib to say, "I will, Dad. Love you."

"Love you more."

That was their usual sign off, so she disconnected.

She then drove the rest of the way out of town, eventually turning into a gravel drive.

She hadn't gone this far when she'd followed Rodney up. She'd driven past, turned around, and waited for their exit.

She didn't actually need to do this sleuthing stuff; Mary had given her his address.

But she couldn't track her mom's movements real-time if she didn't.

Now, by the time she'd stopped in front of that *magnificent* house beside that *stunning* lake she oh-so-*totally* saw her mom loving, and loving to live there, and she got out of the Range Rover, he was standing at the top of the steps.

She'd Googled the hell out of him when her mom shared all that was going down, so it was not lost on Chloe that Duncan Holloway was a looker.

But even if he wasn't her type, and he was old enough to be her dad, IRL, he was *gorgeous*.

She rounded her car and he called, "Can I help you with something?" as she headed toward the steps.

Nice voice too.

She kept going and stopped two steps down from him. "Hi, I'm Chloe Pierce."

She sensed a pang of not-quite-recognition, maybe because she had some of her mom's features, maybe because he knew the name Tom Pierce.

But he did not know her.

Beautiful, super-famous Imogen Swan and talented, hot stud tennis player Tom Pierce suffered the paparazzi and fans like the pros they were.

But both morphed straight to feral when it came to their children.

In other words, she, nor Sasha nor Matt, had been paraded around as accessories.

Her parents' public life was public.

Their private life, especially family, was vehemently private.

To the point the world went apeshit when they broke up, thinking that they were solid and always would be.

But after some time, they got it (or got used to it), when Mom and Dad did it in a way they actually fulfilled the usual lie of "we remain the best of friends."

They were, to this day, the best of friends.

Chloe had struggled with it at the time of the split. Her relationship with her dad took a hit.

She might be a drama queen, a personality trait she nurtured gleefully.

But she was still her mother's daughter.

And in that, the lesson of, "People do things for a myriad of reasons, darling. Just because you don't know what it is, or you do and you don't like it, doesn't mean it isn't valid. But at the end of the day, you have the power to forgive and move on. It's the most selfish thing you can do, letting go of that weight so you can move forward in life without carrying it. It just happens that it's the most compassionate thing you can do too."

Chloe had a feeling she was going to need to count on this.

"I'm Genny Swan's daughter. And we need to talk," she finished.

Instantly, he gave her precisely what she needed in order to know she was doing the right thing.

His middle swayed back like she'd delivered a gut punch.

And his handsome face went haggard.

He also did not move to hide this last.

And the kicker?

He drank in her features like he'd been a man straggling through the desert for days and she was his oasis.

And then he asked, "You drink beer?"

"I'd prefer a martini."

"I'll see what we got."

He then moved to the side in invitation.

Chloe proceeded up the steps.

And she did this fighting a smile.

CHAPTER 3

THE HOTEL

Imogen

*S*haken after the events at Duncan's home, and because of
that, and the necessity to box it up, set it aside, and move
forward without falling apart (until I could do that alone), I was going
through the motions as I walked into the hotel.

Since Trisha and Scott (my friends who lived in the condo next to
mine but had moved up here permanently three years ago) had shared
that this property had been purchased in order for an extensive reno-
vation that would end in it being an exclusive boutique hotel, we'd
wondered if the owner was a lunatic, or a visionary.

And I'd wanted to visit since it had its grand opening.

Thus, I decided to take that opportunity on this trip, as well as
spend some time with Trish and Scott, not to mention Heddy.

Therefore, after I'd given Corey his final wish for me (and now, the
fact I'd done it for that man infuriated me) I'd planned to stay the
evening, booked a late facial in their spa, and after, intended to get
room service, relax and read that night.

The next day was all about Heddy, shopping, tapas at El Gato Azul for lunch, and dinner with Trisha and Scott at Farm Provisions.

In fact, I always enjoyed a visit to Prescott, even knowing Duncan lived close.

It wasn't exactly a remote, low-population town. It was relatively large in and of itself, and a favored destination for Phoenicians to go for a day, or a weekend, to avoid the heat in the summer. And others to buy properties up there, again to avoid the heat (something, once Trish and Scott moved up, Tom and I had considered...but then...Duncan).

But it wasn't Flag. It didn't have ski slopes to attract greater masses.

It had lakes. Hiking trails. The Dells. Shopping. Whiskey Row. And for a week in the summer, Frontier Days.

Mostly, it was pretty sleepy, and partly because it was beautiful, but undoubtedly because it was laidback, slower-paced and the people less harried and more friendly than in the city, it was enticing.

I should not have been enticed.

Not this time.

I should have headed home, to the condo, holed in, made myself a pitcher of gimlets, and contemplated how I'd gone so very wrong for so very long when it came to Corey.

Instead, I took in the interior of the lobby of the hotel, which was decidedly Victorian in a rather close, heavy, dark, fabulous way, with its green-and-gold scroll wallpaper. And the tall desk behind which stood a stylish young woman wearing a slim-fitting, dark-pink dress that had an attached scarf artistically tied at the side of her neck.

I unconsciously braced as her eyes fell on me, ready by rote to handle however this proceeded.

Fortunately, as I stopped in front of her, Rodney unnecessarily at my side, rolling my Tumi that I could roll myself, but also cutting me off from view of the bar that was also on this floor, she simply smiled before she spoke.

"Ms. Swan. We're delighted you're staying with us at The Queen. And I'm happy to report, your suite is ready for you."

"Thank you," I replied.

Her eyes shifted to Rodney, and back to me, and she asked, "Would you like us to help you upstairs with your bag, or—?"

Rodney butted in. "I have it."

"Of course," she said to him. But to me, "Your PA's instructions for check-in have been understood."

Translation: I was booked under the name Virginie Forbes.

Even now, semi-retired, precautions had to be taken.

"And the manager of the spa has been alerted to your appointment," she went on. "Just so you're aware, when you arrive at our facilities, a member of staff will escort you to the locker room, and make sure it's cleared so you can change. And phones have been banned in the lounge, though we encourage that anyway. Regardless, you'll be escorted straight to your treatment room, once your valuables have been secured."

"That wasn't necessary," though it absolutely was, "but thank you."

"Ms. Sinclair believes it is," she replied, referring to the owner of the place. Having been fiddling with things at her desk, she handed me my key card. "You're on the top floor. Room four-oh-one. With a view to the square. We have your cell number on file in case of emergencies, and your credit card in case of incidental charges, so all is well. The elevator is behind me, to your right."

"Again, thank you."

"My pleasure, and should you need anything else, please don't hesitate to ask any member of staff."

I nodded.

After she gave me a thankfully non-obsequious smile to end the equally thankfully non-obsequious check-in process, she busied herself with something at her desk.

Rodney continued to shield me from the bar as we moved beyond it toward the elevators.

When we'd stopped at them, and he'd shifted in order to shield me from the lobby, I looked up to him.

"Honestly, I can take it from here."

"I'll see you to your room, Ms. Swan."

I was sensing from his demeanor that he would.

I gave in. We entered the tiny elevator. And we were silent on the way up, the short walk to the door to my suite, and through it after I touched the key card to the pad.

Rodney moved directly to the sizable, antique, free-standing wardrobe as I looked around.

The room was large, as it would be, considering it was their deluxe suite, taking half the top floor and spanning the entire front of the hotel.

Six arched windows (I suspected two more in the bathroom). Black-backed wallpaper adorned with gold and blue and cream with purple-edges flowers. Camelback settee with scrolled arms covered in an ivory brocade damask. Tufted armchairs angled across from it in brown velvet. Heavily carved, oval coffee table in between that held an attractive urn stuffed full of fresh peonies, dahlias and trailing greenery that looked tipped with berries.

The king bed up against the wall to the right was high, huge, dizzyingly carved, padded and radically covered with pillows.

There was a writing desk at an angle beside one of the two fire-places, facing the room. It had delicately swooping legs and was accompanied by a Belvedere oval-backed chair.

There was also a small bistro table with two chairs in front of one of the windows, the better to enjoy morning coffee and a croissant with a view to the bustle of the square.

And oddly, since it was situated all the way across from the bed, double doors opened to an extravagant Victorian bathroom with gold wallpaper, marble-edged copper basins, a sunken tub, intricately carved wainscoting painted coin-gray, all of this topped with an opulent chandelier.

Last, there was a silver bucket containing a bottle of champagne, a napkin precisely folded and draped over it. And beside the floral arrangement was a plate of what looked like homemade chocolate chip cookies under a glass dome.

It was extraordinary.

I loved every inch.

So much, I could stay in that space for weeks.

But honestly, they had me with the cookies.

My son called me the Cookie Monster.

And there was reason.

Rodney's voice took me out of my admiration of the room and thoughts of my second born.

"Are you sure you don't want me to take you home?"

I turned to him to see him at the door, but on my way, I noted he'd erected the luggage stand, and laid my suitcase on it. "I'm fine."

"Are you sure?"

I licked my lips and felt my face soften.

Even the best of actresses could not pull one over on the kindest of souls.

He knew nothing, and yet, having sat often behind the wheel with me in the back, or me in the back with one or both of my daughters and/or my son, he sensed everything.

"Truly, I'll be all right," I lied.

He knew I was lying and did not hide that fact.

Even so, he said, "I'll be back tomorrow at eight to take you home."

I nodded.

He moved to the door.

He then gave me a long last look, dipped his chin, and left the room.

I stared at the closed door and my eyes started stinging.

"No, no, no, after the facial," I said to myself, and then got busy.

Unpack first, since I hated living out of suitcases, even only for a day, and hated more not having my toiletries and toothbrush at hand when I needed them.

Check.

Go to the floral arrangement and read the note sticking out. Heavy stock. Folded once. And at the front, an embossed SIENNA SINCLAIR.

Handwritten inside,

Ms. Swan,

We're honored you selected The Queen.

If there's anything my staff or I can do to make your visit more enjoyable, please do not hesitate to ask.

Yours,

Sienna

Nice.

Classy.

Read.

Check.

Peruse room service menu and call down to order, giving them a time to deliver, so it'd be ready when I was. Then ask them to refresh the ice in my champagne bucket so I could enjoy it with dinner.

Check.

Change from fancy outfit I never should have worn when confronting Duncan into dove-gray pleated joggers and slightly see-through, V-necked, long-sleeve tee and pull out gray Valentino slides to wear down to the spa.

Check.

Text Chloe and share I was good, and I'd call her later.

Check.

Text Mary and share that I'd arrived, the hotel was fabulous, and I was going dark for a bit so I could enjoy my facial and some downtime.

Check.

Turn off phone.

Check.

Slip on the slides, grab keycard, lock my purse and valuables in the in-room safe, and head to the spa.

Check.

"HEY, MOM."

Hearing Chloe's voice, all was well in the world.

At least for now.

"Hey, honey," I replied, stretching out my legs and leaning back in bed with my champagne.

The room service tray was in the hall.

The cookies were up next after I talked with my girl.

And now, I'd just turned on my phone and called my Chloe.

Unsurprisingly, it had immediately binged with a text from Mary.

I ignored that to focus on my daughter, who I knew would be worried about me.

"How'd it go?" she asked.

"It went," I answered, just as my phone binged with text two, also from Mary, and it started with nothing but *!!!!!!*.

My brows inched together as I took a sip of champagne in preparation to set it aside and swipe.

"That's it, 'it went?'" Chloe pressed.

I paused before swiping.

Because this was a situation that Tom and I had created.

That being drilling into our children's heads the concept that honesty and transparency was the most important thing in any relationship.

And when they were little, if they came to us with an issue, or if they'd done something wrong or bad, and confessed it, we were very careful to temper our reactions, and if there was any punishment, to allow for their honesty.

We'd done it with the goal that they would feel open when the issues became serious, like sex, contraception, possible bullying, plans they wanted to make for their futures. And then we could tackle them before we had such things as unplanned pregnancies or cutting.

However, to teach, we also had to demonstrate.

This was something I began doing with much more openness when they got older, to the point that, since Chloe was living in Phoenix now, meant I'd shared with her about the box...

And Duncan.

Not in detail.

But I felt it safe to explain he was my first love, and how it had ended, and where (I thought at the time) Corey fit in all that.

Now, this life lesson didn't seem so good and not because I didn't want to talk about it due to the fact that, when I did, there was a very real possibility I would break down.

It was because she had a relationship with Corey.

To the kids, he was Uncle Corey. He'd been in their lives since they could remember. He'd loved them, and they'd loved him.

But to have kids who did, indeed, approach when kid stuff got serious, this kind of situation occurred.

And at least what I had on my hands now was far better than what Tom dealt with when we'd decided to divorce, and why, and then we'd had to tell the children.

Tom didn't lose his girls. They were daddy's girls, for one, and although they were disappointed and things were tense and upsetting for a good while, they were also momma's girls.

They came around.

Matt's relationship with his father, however, still needed a good deal of healing.

"*Mom.*"

Chloe was getting impatient.

I sighed.

And I made the only decision I could, considering.

Then I asked, "You know how I told you that Duncan broke things off with me because he thought I'd cheated on him?"

"Yeah."

Now she sounded hesitant.

I thought I knew the cause, considering what her father had done.

"I didn't, honey," I assured. "But what was in that box was a letter explaining that Corey told him I did." God, could I say it? I guessed I could. "With him."

I fancied I heard a wooshing in my ear, considering all the sound left the world in that instant of her silence.

Then, my oh-so-beautiful diva Chloe shrieked, "*What?*" But before I could say anything, she asked wrathfully, "*With him?* Like, *with* Uncle Corey?"

"Yes."

"*You* and dweeby, gawky, skinny Uncle Corey?"

"Yes, Chloe, and a person is not just what they loo—"

"This guy's best friend?"

"Yes."

"*Your* best friend?"

It was harder to repeat it on that.

But I did.

"Yes."

"You've got to be fucking kidding me."

"A lady doesn't—"

"Mom, this is a fuck moment for certain."

I didn't argue and not only because I didn't have the chance.

"What now?" she demanded.

"Sorry?"

"What now? With you and this Duncan guy?"

Another text came through from Mary, but I sat motionless on the bed, staring at the phone lying on my thigh, speechless at her question.

Because there was no "now" with this Duncan guy.

But damn, how my heart had skipped a beat when she'd said that.

"*Mother,*" she hissed.

"Nothing now, honey. It ended years ago," I forced out.

"Okay, so, you guys were like, in love. Like, the way you described it, *really* in love. And you can't think you told me about him, and I didn't Google the shit out of his ass. He's *way* hot, for a dude that could be my dad. He's rich, maybe not as loaded as you, but with all those stores, he can't be hurting. He's also divorced. And so are you. So what now?"

"Chlo—"

She didn't even let me finish her name. "What did he say about all this?"

"Well, I mean, it's not like he's unaware that there's a great deal of water under the bridge," I hedged.

"That isn't an answer to my question. What did he say when he found out Uncle Corey did something that whacked?"

"He was understandably upset."

"And?"

"And…we both were. Upset that is. We shared some words. But there's nothing we can do about it now."

"Why did Uncle Corey do that?"

"He, well, he had a crush on me."

"Yeah. *Duh.* He was totally in love with you."

This stunned me.

Was I the only one who didn't see?

"But I'm in love with Ryan Reynolds," she ranted on. "And I'm not going to do something psycho to break him up with Blake."

"You don't know Ryan Reynolds, darling."

"The point stands, *Mom.*"

It did.

"Okay, honey, the truth is, I'm having a real tough time wrapping my head around why Uncle Corey would do this to me. To me and to Duncan, but real honesty, especially to me. He was like a brother to me. He knew how I felt about Duncan. And he knew I did not feel that for him. So I have a bottle of champagne, courtesy of the owner of this lovely hotel, and a plate of chocolate chip cookies that look divine. Not to mention, Mary is texting with a goodly number of exclamation points, so I need to find out what's happening with her. To end, I can understand you're upset, because he was like an uncle to you. But I really cannot process this with you now."

Her tone was much calmer, and definitely tender, when she said, "Right, Mom. I was just freaked."

"I understand that feeling."

"Yeah, I bet you do. I'm so sorry, Momma."

I was too.

It was like he'd died all over again.

But worse, because I didn't even have the memory of him to sustain me anymore.

"Me too, darling. Now, you'll come over for dinner when I get back. I'll make something you love."

"No way. Beckett's Table. My treat. I'm jonesing for their short ribs."

My girl, dramatic.

And driven.

She'd come back from France, took her trust fund, and to her father's despair, and my concern, opened a boutique in the Melrose district of Phoenix.

But she had style. She had flair. And she was, as her brother described her, *baller*.

That boutique was a year old, it was turning a tidy profit, and she'd already made the cover of *Phoenix* magazine, their cover model for an article on up-and-coming female entrepreneurs.

And during their interview, they'd only asked her one question about her father and me.

In other words, she could buy me dinner.

Though, that was not happening.

"It's a date," I agreed.

"Great," she replied. "Now, are you going to be okay? Do you want some company?"

"I'm two hours away, it's getting late, and I'm fine. I mean, not *fine*-fine. But I'll be okay. I have a great day planned tomorrow. And then I'll be home."

"I'll come over tomorrow night."

"I won't be home until the earliest ten."

"So? I'll mix up some gimlets and we'll binge *Glow* or something."

"We've already binged *Glow*."

"Yeah, that's why I added *or something*."

"Smart aleck," I teased mock-severely.

"Momma, you love me just as I am, so don't even try to pretend you don't."

And again, I felt better.

My daughter knowing that with that kind of certainty?

Yes, all was well in the world.

"Love you, darling."

"Love you more, Mom."

"Thanks for chatting."

"Anytime, and Mom?"

"Right here."

"Don't think you got around the talk about this Duncan hottie."

I said nothing, because she disconnected.

I took a fortifying sip of champagne to get me past her parting comment, and another one before I opened my texts.

I didn't get to read them.

The screen came up with Tom's picture telling me he was calling.

Damn.

I answered because I knew he'd be worried too.

"Hey there."

"Hey, Genny, honey, you okay?"

"I've been better, but I'll survive."

A moment of silence, and then, "Gen."

On his knowingly saying my name, I had the rare thought that perhaps our decision to be adult and get beyond his betrayal and my inattention to salvage the friendship part of our relationship in order to keep our family strong was the wrong one.

And then I said, "It was Corey. The box had a letter sharing that Corey told Duncan that I'd slept with him. Corey, that is. He told Duncan that I'd slept with his best friend. And he also shared he'd been lying in order to break us up, because he was in love with me."

Another moment of silence, and then, with what after years I knew instantly was barely controlled rage, "Why would he do such a thing?"

"He was in love with me."

"And I'll repeat, why would he do such a goddamned, motherfucking, obnoxiously selfish, insanely damaging *thing*?"

"Tom, calm down."

"Calm down? Seriously? How can *you* be calm about this?" he asked in disbelief.

"I'm not. Though it's not brand-new news to me."

"Jesus Christ," he bit out.

"I'm processing now with champagne and chocolate chip cookies, homemade. And tomorrow I'll process with Heddy. Then Trish and Scott. And Chloe is coming over for gimlets when I get home tomorrow night."

"Thank God you have the cookies."

I nearly laughed.

Because he was serious.

"Tom, I'll be okay," I told him.

"It's good that asshole is dead, because if that geek punk was alive, I'd kill him."

"Tom," I whispered.

"You know, you had history with him, so I had to assume you knew something I didn't. But I cannot tell you how relieved I was when my thirteen-year-old son came to me, obviously uncomfortable, and shared he didn't like his mom being around his Uncle Corey, because he thought his Uncle Corey was a creeper. Until then, I thought it was only me."

I was stunned.

"That happened with Matt? And you felt that way too?"

"Absolutely."

"Why didn't you say anything?"

"Because you adored the guy. And then he'd do shit, for you, the kids, that made me, and since Matt and I eventually started talking about it, also Matt, feel like assholes for thinking the way we thought. But I should have listened to my gut. And my son is no fool, *his*. Last, as a father, witnessed how Corey treated his own son, and know to my bones his soul was black."

I wasn't there yet, to see Corey as having a black soul.

Perhaps mentally ill in some way.

But not that.

However, bringing Corey's son Hale into the conversation—a young man who was really mostly our son, because of the way Corey was, and frankly, also the way Samantha was—Tom had a point.

"Tom, I really can't—"

"I know you can't," he said tersely, not angry at me, frustrated there was nothing he could do to help.

That was Tom, my second love, the father of my children, and that was also part of the reason we remained friends.

Because he hurt me, and he did it badly.

He was still a good man.

"But I'm here if you need me," he finished.

Yes.

A good man.

"Thanks, honey."

"Take some melatonin so you can sleep," he advised.

"Right."

"Champagne won't do it, Genny. People think wine is a sleep aid, and it absolutely is not."

What to do when your years as a top-ranked professional tennis player were behind you?

Well, if you have abundant personality and good looks, you get into commentating, like Tom did.

And as a side hobby, you train to become a sports medicine doctor.

Like Tom did.

Overachievers, both of us.

And we watched our children like hawks, terrified our shadows would shrivel something in them when we wanted them to plant the roots of their lives and grow strong.

So far, we hoped, so good.

"I'll check in," Tom said.

"I'd appreciate it," I replied.

"Love you, Genny."

"Same back, Tommy."

We hung up.

I looked to the ceiling and gave that call some time.

Then I returned my attention to my texts.

At what I read, even if my glass was not even close to full, I nearly spilled what was left of it.

I then called Mary immediately.

"Finally!" she cried.

"What's going on?" I demanded.

"First, Cookie is safe with me."

Cookie. My cat. A rescue. Pintsize body, big ears, white with black splodges, some brown, and fur that felt better than mink.

The sweetest feline on the planet.

And the best company.

"There's a flood in the condo?"

Even her tone said "euw" when she replied, "Sanitation."

"Oh my God," I breathed.

"From the top unit. They've been on vacation and they didn't know things were backed up. Building management as yet doesn't know the extent of the damage. I've removed your valuables. Given them access to your unit. I had a look around and I couldn't see anything wrong in your space, I think it happened on the other end. It's just the smell. Right now, they're estimating it's going to take at least a few days, probably a week, possibly even longer, to get it all cleaned up and contain the smell. So I phoned the hotel, booked you in for that week. I'll talk to Chloe, between her and me, we'll get your car up there so you can get around."

I sounded strangled when I asked, "What hotel?"

"The Queen."

"*Here?*" I squeaked.

"Yes, I spoke with them and they said I can bring Cookie."

"Mary—"

"I've called around. Something must be happening in town, and not just a mass exodus from your building. There isn't a suite available for you at the Phoenician, or the Royal Palms, or the Biltmore—"

"I can take a simple room."

"Why, when you have a suite in a cool boutique hotel in Prescott? I mean, it's fall, so you're not avoiding heat, but...*Prescott. Awesome.*"

Prescott was awesome.

But I could not stay here a week, and that wasn't about Prescott.

I opened my mouth to tell her that (or part of it), but my with-it Mary got there before me.

"I'll pack a bag. Or two. I might have them couriered up there so you'll have some selections, just in case it takes me a while to coordinate getting the Cayenne to you."

"Mary, I'd rather be down in Phoenix."

"Okay. I'll get you a room. But I'm going to have to keep Cookie. Those hotels don't take pets."

I hesitated.

I wanted to believe Cookie could not do without me, but in truth, she probably could.

However, she wouldn't like it.

She loved her mommy.

"So which one? The Phoenician? The Biltmore?" Mary prompted.

"They don't take pets?"

"Well, not cats."

This never failed to annoy me.

Dogs always got preferential treatment.

Not that I didn't like dogs. I loved them.

I just didn't like them getting preferential treatment.

"Maybe I can stay with Chloe," I murmured.

She snorted.

Actually *snorted*.

Yes, that was not a good idea.

Chloe loved and adored Cookie like Cookie was her actual blood, except feline.

She also loved and adored me.

But she lived in a small, trendy condo in a downtown, trendy neighborhood that was covered from morning brunch, until nightclub-hopping night with hipsters.

She didn't have an extra bedroom, for one.

And just leaving her place, I'd be covered in millennials fresh off a *Rita's Way* Netflix binge.

It had happened.

It wasn't pretty.

"I'll stay here," I allowed.

"Cool," she said breezily.

"But please, stay on top of the situation at the condo. I'd like to be home as soon as possible."

"Do you want Cookie going with the courier or—?"

Had she lost her mind?

"No, no strangers. But if Chloe can't come up with you very soon with the car, I'd like you to come up with Cookie. Or we can hire the service to follow you up and you can drive my car, then they can take you back down."

"You got it. And I'll cancel them for tomorrow."

"Thanks, as ever, for taking care of things."

"That's my job, boss. As you know."

I rolled my eyes.

I had Mary as my snappy assistant.

I had Chloe as my dramatic daughter.

I had Matt as my in-his-father's image (though I'd never say that right now, but it was all the *good* parts, and my boy would remember soon there were a lot of them) sweet, funny, protective son.

And I had Sasha, my beautiful boho brat, camping at Coachella and up to her knees in mud at Glastonbury.

I downed the rest of my champagne.

After that, I said goodbye to my assistant.

I then got off the bed, put my phone on to charge, filled my glass, and took the dome from the cookies so I could take the plate to the bed.

One of the many wonderful things that came from semi-retirement born of financial and career freedom, and being at an age where they didn't care much about me, and I no longer cared about them, but having a name that gave me endless clout, was the fact that I didn't have to starve myself to meet the ideal of every producer, director and studio head who had control over me and whether or not I would work.

This was the thought I had before I bit into the first cookie.

Sadly, the loveliness of that faded when my thoughts turned to the fact that I was, in a sense, stuck in what was now Duncan's hometown.

He didn't strike me as a man who lunched on tapas or browsed through art galleries and boutiques. He had a business to run, likely trails to hike, perhaps horses to ride, etc.

Therefore, it was improbable I would run into him.

And I ate my way through two cookies, attempting to convince myself that was a good thing.

But there were not enough cookies in the world to beat back the emotions when the box I'd been holding Corey's treachery in burst open.

And the pain, when it came, was acute and very, very real.

So real, I had to set my champagne aside and double over to fight it.

Twenty-eight years, we'd had dinners, lunches, even holidays together.

Twenty-eight years, he'd spent time with my husband, my children...*me*.

Twenty-eight years, he'd allowed me to show him love, friendship. He'd come to me to support him when he broke up with girlfriends, come to me to listen to him rail about his enemies, come to me when his dad died, when his protégé left and set up his own company.

Ah, the betrayal!

He'd taught that guy everything.

How could he do that?

How could he do that to poor, billionaire, perfidious Corey?

"How could you do that, Corey?" I whispered to my thighs, beginning to rock in the bed. "How could you do that to Bowie?"

Yes, rocking, rocking deep.

"To me?"

At that, the sobs came.

And such was my heartache, much like when I lost Duncan...

No, *exactly* like when I lost Duncan, and wouldn't Corey be so proud he'd accomplished this?

The tears never consciously abated.

Because it took hours.

And I cried myself to sleep.

CHAPTER 4

THE LEAF

Corey

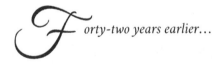 *orty-two years earlier…*

HE HATED it when they got too far ahead of him.

But Duncan couldn't wait to get to wherever he was taking them, and whenever Dun was excited about something, Genny was.

And anyways…

What *was* it with them?

How was he the only one who got eaten up by mosquitos?

He had spray on everywhere, including his clothes. Genny had even sprayed his back.

And it seemed the things were biting him *everywhere*.

Sometimes Corey would see Dun and Genny swat at their arms or their legs, but it never bugged them. They just slapped their arm and then kept going.

And going.

And going.

Walking *forever*.

And where *were* they going? Where was Duncan taking them now?

They were off trail (*again*).

Deep in the woods (*again*).

He didn't get it (though Genny always did).

Dun would show them a path in the grass and say, like he discovered life on Mars, "It's a *game trail*."

And Genny would be all, "*How cool, Bowie*."

It was just a path in the grass.

Grass was not cool.

Some path wasn't cool either.

Gulk.

The worst.

It was more *the worst* when she called him Bowie.

That was new, and Corey hated it.

Hated it.

Because Duncan's dad was a *huge dick*.

And he gave that name to Duncan and Corey knew why.

He knew, when Mr. Holloway made Duncan do what he did, and Corey knew it cut him up inside, cut Duncan deep, he gave that name to Duncan.

And there was Genny, calling him that.

They'd look at each other when she did, like they had a secret.

Corey knew something else.

They did have a secret.

Dun went to *her* after Mr. Holloway made him go hunting.

He went to Genny.

Not Corey.

They'd been best friends *forever*.

And he was going to Genny?

Especially after something his dad did?

His dick dad, like Corey's dad was a huge *dick dad*.

They both had *huge dick dads*.

And Genny's dad was awesome. She didn't know what it was like to have a *huge dick dad*.

And Duncan was going to *her*.

He saw them up ahead.

No, he saw Genny's hair up ahead, the sun shining off it, making it look all gold and stuff, and they'd stopped.

Obviously, since the sun was shining on her, they were in a clearing.

Genny was looking at something and Corey could only see the side of her face, but whatever it was, her mouth was open like she'd never seen anything like it before *in her life*.

And Dun was staring at Genny like he'd never seen anything like *her* before in his entire life, even though they were all together *all the time*, and even though she was two years younger than them and it made them goobers that they were hanging out with a third grader.

They were in fifth. No one in fifth hung out with someone in third.

Especially *a girl*.

Corey stopped approaching them, though, when Dun got a weird look on his face and then Cory watched as Dun lifted his hand and pulled a leaf out of her hair.

She looked at Duncan and all Corey could see of her now was that fall of sunshiny hair.

"A leaf," Duncan said, and Corey saw his face was all red, which made it a good call when he lifted it up between them to show her, so she'd look at the leaf and not at Duncan's stupid red face.

"Okay," Genny whispered.

However Genny was looking at him made Duncan go even more red.

But he was smiling.

Big.

Corey was going to puke.

He pushed through the last of the trees to reach the clearing with them.

They both turned to him like they forgot he was even there.

No, yeah…

That was actually the worst.

But then Genny smiled, like, *massive*, and it lit everything up for miles around. Shinier than the sun on her hair. Shinier than anything.

And she jumped his way, grabbed his hand, and urged, "Look."

Then she turned her head, still holding his hand, and he thought it was crazy, how her hand was both warm and cool at the same time. He felt clammy. Hot. All that walking in the summer.

But she was cool.

And she didn't let go of his hand.

He looked.

And…yeah.

There was a stream cutting through the woods. It wasn't super big. It crooked this way and that. The water was so clear, you could see the rock and mud on the stream bed. And up a ways, there was a hill, which meant the water fell down this tiny waterfall that Corey didn't want to admit (but he had to) was real pretty. But with the sun shining on it, the water twinkled here and there, like little glimmers of magic, which made it more than pretty. It was like it was enchanted.

And the grass all around it, plus the moss on some rocks, plus what looked like two thick but small fields of clover on either side were a jumble of greens that were just…*so green*. There were like, no words for how green they all were. It was wild.

And with the big, tall trees with their dark bark and the tall grass that grew up between them for as far as you could see with the patches of deep brown dirt.

It was like something from *The Fellowship of the Ring* books or something.

Corey began to move toward it.

Duncan reached across Genny to stop him.

"Let's not even leave a footprint," Dun said, all manly like.

Corey felt something strange inside him, like, a burning kinda thing.

This was a deal for Duncan.

When they were out, he was always saying, *Take nothing but a picture. Leave nothing but a footprint.*

They didn't even have a camera.

Duncan's dad said it was an old Indian saying, but when he did, Dun rolled his eyes and later told Corey, "They didn't have people wandering around the Wild West with Polaroids. General Custer wasn't like, 'Grab my Canon!' I don't know who said it, and maybe it was a native, I just know they were smart, and I wish Dad would do as he mouths off about doing, but he doesn't."

Dun was right.

He didn't.

Burt Holloway would stomp all over this place, for sure, killing some rabbits, birds, whatever he could aim his gun at.

And that was what made Corey stop, even if he really wanted to get closer and he wasn't real big on Duncan stopping him.

He was real big on the fact that Genny was still holding his hand.

She tugged it hard because she was falling to her butt and taking him with her.

He sat next to her and she leaned into him and Corey was suddenly totally okay with sitting all the way over here, not close to that twinkling stream or moss or clover.

"I can see fairies flying through here," she said.

See?

Totally enchanted.

"I can see trolls hiding under those rocks," Corey replied.

She pushed her body into his in a *shove it* gesture but then leaned away from him throwing him a big grin.

She might be a third grader, but she was super cute when she smiled.

"This is definitely a fairy place," she pushed.

"Trolls," he pushed back.

"*So* fairies."

"*So* trolls."

"Both," Duncan decided, sitting down next to Genny.

Corey wanted to shout at him.

Or punch him in the face.

Why couldn't he go lean against a tree or something?

Genny pulled *Corey* down to sit beside her, not Duncan.

And now...

Yup.

There she went.

She was tapping the side of her bent leg against the side of Duncan's.

Duncan found the rhythm and started tapping back.

Yeah.

Corey...

Wanted...

To shout.

Duncan gave her clover and a little waterfall and sparkles and knew she loved it.

Duncan got to give her that.

He couldn't let Corey have something?

Just a little something?

Without butting his stupid nose in?

God, Corey might start hating him.

Having that thought, his chest clogged up so bad, whatever that was shoved up his throat, and he immediately felt sick.

Never.

Never.

Not ever.

Everyone thought Corey was a loser.

But not Dun.

Duncan thought he was awesome.

Kids would say things. Be nasty.

Duncan was always there.

Not just telling them to go spit.

But telling them they'd be so lucky to be friends with Corey.

"When he's old enough to buy and sell you and you want to shove your nose up his butt so he'll give you a job, come back to me and tell me why you're being such a dope right now."

Yeah.

Dun had said that about him.

So he hated to walk all over everywhere, get bit by bugs and slip on mud and have to stand real still because Duncan saw a big cat or a snake or something and Corey did not want to get bit by some gross snake or have to try to outrun some cougar (or whatever).

But Duncan spent *way* more time over at Corey's house playing tournaments with him on his Mattel football game or watching Captain Kirk do awesome stuff on TV.

If he didn't have Duncan…he wouldn't have anybody.

And if he didn't have Genny…he would only have Duncan.

And Genny did *all* guy things with them. She also never moaned about it. Even getting into tournaments with them on his Mattel.

No Barbies or any of that crap for Genny.

So now, she dropped her head on Corey's shoulder and he felt like he'd grown as tall as Duncan.

But she was still bumping her knee on Dun's.

Okay.

Whatever.

He had both of them.

She had both of them.

Dun had both of them.

Even if Corey wanted more, he didn't know why.

He had both of them.

So he had it all.

CHAPTER 5

THE BREAKFAST

Duncan

"*H*oly shit, my man."

Duncan was curled over his coffee at their table at Zeke's, his eyes aimed to the java, his hand rubbing the back of his neck.

He'd just told Harv the story.

All of it.

From meeting Corey when they were six. To throwing the frog at Genny when he was ten. To slowly falling in love with her and finally doing something about it when he was seventeen. To cutting her loose because he was such a loser when he was eighteen and hooking up again when he was twenty-four because he'd turned into an asshole.

And last, what had happened yesterday, from her showing like she'd showed, what had come of that, to her daughter's surprise visit and even bigger surprise message.

And that was Harvey's response.

Which didn't touch the half of it.

"And now the woman's daughter wants you to make a play for her mom?" Harvey continued.

Duncan dropped his hand, lifted his head, sat back in his chair and looked at his friend.

He'd met Harvey twenty years ago when Duncan had moved to Prescott. They were friends first, and Duncan recruited him later.

Now Harv was COO of River Rain.

Big guy. Burly. Lots of hair everywhere. So much it covered his arms and ran up to the base of his neck, thick and now graying.

Also a good guy. Loved his wife. Doted on his girls. Doted on Duncan's boys. And even after the divorce, which had gotten messy before he and Dora (and he was not being a dick in saying especially Dora) got their shit together, Harvey doted on Dora.

Duncan definitely got Harv and his wife Beth in the divorce.

But functions where there was necessary mingling weren't uncomfortable anymore.

And that had a lot to do with Harvey.

"She doesn't want it, man. She *ordered* me to do it."

Harvey's face contorted with trying to beat back his smile.

"I'm not sure I'm feelin' a lot of humor in this situation," Duncan pointed out.

Harvey got serious. "I can imagine, Bowie. I still can't believe Corey Szabo did that shit to you guys. I can't even believe you were that tight with Corey Szabo. I mean, you mentioned you grew up with him and used to be friends, but Jesus. However, suffice it to say, I'm pretty stuck on the fact your ex-girlfriend is Imogen Swan. Something, I'll note, you never mentioned."

Duncan wrapped his fingers around his coffee and took a sip before saying, "It wasn't something I wanted to talk about."

"I get that. And I'd heard her and Szabo were tight since childhood, so I shoulda put it together but, Jesus again."

Mm-hmm.

Jesus.

Harvey kept talking.

"You know, I mean, Beth's list includes Antonio Banderas, Javier

Bardem, Benicio Del Toro, and she's got two more I've blocked out, but I think you can get from that she's got a type, and it is not me."

Duncan couldn't stop his lips from twitching.

"But full disclosure," Harv went on, "I got a type too. My list includes Cate Blanchette, Anna Torv, Robin Wright, but I do not need to go on because I'll point out something you already know, they all look like Beth."

Duncan wasn't feeling amused anymore.

And he told his friend why.

"And Genny," he grunted.

"She's the top of my list, bud," Harvey confirmed.

His list.

Duncan knew what he was talking about.

The list of fake freebies you could fuck even if you were committed to another person.

"Christ, Harv, why would you tell me that?"

"Because you should know, straight up, since you're gonna go for it, that that's the case before Beth blabs it. Which she will. But I'm the best friend who *isn't* a horse's ass. Who'd never go there. And no offense to you and my deep abiding love for you, but my love is deeper and more abiding for my wife, so that's a non-starter."

"This isn't funny, Harvey."

Harv ignored him. "And just to say, I'm still reeling that you call Imogen Swan 'Genny.' Though, more importantly, when I meet her, if I act like a fool, just ignore me. I'll eventually get over it. And I figure that'll happen around the time we're fully gray and our RVs are parked beside each other somewhere and Beth and *Genny* are fryin' up some tots while you and me grill the burgers."

"You're not going to meet her because I'm not going to make a play for Genny," he declared.

Harvey's thick eyebrows shot up. "You're not?"

"Hell no."

"Why not?"

"Harv, I told you, she was pretty firm about not wanting to go there."

"She also showed at your house all dressed up, wearing heels. And trust me, you got two sons, but to my everlasting dismay and wonderment as to what I did that God wished to punish me so severely, I got three daughters. And I can tell you, when a girl is done with a guy, she's *done*. She doesn't care anymore. Case in point, Mandy was at Costco with me the other day, and she was what they call 'day three' in her shampoo regimen, and don't ask, they've explained it, I still don't get it. I just know it's important. No makeup. Hoodie. And Robbie strolls up to her, and two months ago, this kid had her in vapors. He talked to her and she spoke words back, but I still don't know if she knew he was there. When they were done, he looked crushed. She just turned to me and asked if we could get a shrimp tray."

"Genny isn't a high school girl."

"Bowie, with the dating you been doin' since you and Dora split, have you not figured out they're never *not* girls? Try buying a woman a vacuum cleaner for her birthday. That's a mature, adult, 'hey, we're doin' this, makin' a life together' gift. It's not like you're declaring she's the only one who's going to use it because she's the little woman and you got football to watch, not rugs to vacuum. But Christ, she'll act like you just called her ugly and went out and killed her dog. Buy her somethin' pink, and it doesn't matter what that something is, it could even be a pink goddamn vacuum, she'll kiss you all over and remember that shit when it's bedtime."

"Harv—"

Abruptly, Harvey leaned across the table as far as he could get, and his face had turned to granite.

"Fuck him," he whispered. "And Bowie, this is the best way to *fuck him*. And I'm not advocating this just for revenge. Lord knows, what Dora put you through, I wanna see you happy. And from what I can tell, Imogen Swan is a stand-up gal. It'd be good she's got some happy too, and I know you'll break your back to give it to her. But take back what he took from you. I can't imagine what this feels like for you. But as your friend, it burns in my gut, way down deep, that a man you called friend did that to you. Reverse the damage, Bowie. You got a chance. Don't blow it."

Duncan could not let his friend's words get in there.

He wanted to.

But this was about Genny.

He had to look after Genny.

"You did not see her back then, Harv. You did not see her when she was begging me to listen to her. When she was swearing she'd never do that to me. When she was telling me she loved me, she'd never love a man like she loved me. I was it for her, I was her future, she'd *never* step out on me. You did not see her, buddy. She was *wrecked. I wrecked her* because I didn't listen to her. I listened to Corey."

Harvey leaned back a little, shook his head and replied, "Okay. I get that had to be rough, for both of you, and you're in a bad spot because you didn't listen. But honest to Christ, Bowie, this came out of the blue. Even she has to admit that if Szabo came to her and told her he knew beyond a doubt you were cheating, she'd take a minute on that."

Duncan did a slow blink.

Because he hadn't thought of that.

She would.

Genny absolutely would take a minute.

And he'd have had to talk fast, shout, beg, plead, crawl to get her to listen.

That was who Corey was to them.

The both of them.

"This guy was your guy. Both of your guy," Harv spoke Duncan's thoughts. "Neither of you could have any clue he'd purposely, with evil intent, and premeditation, inflict that kind of damage on you."

Jesus.

"Country fried scramble," the waitress stated, dumping a plate covered in food in front of Harv, who moved back from the table to receive it. "Green chile and cheese omelet." And Duncan had his food. "Be back 'round for a top up. Anything else?"

"No, Shirl," Harvey replied.

"Thanks, honey," Duncan said.

She winked at him, shot Harv a sassy smile and said, "Don't mention it."

Then she sashayed away.

Duncan went for his cutlery.

So did Harvey.

They started eating.

Harv was the one who took them back to it.

"You know, I've met the man, and truth is, a man like that is no man at all."

Duncan lifted his eyes from his food to give them to his friend.

"Sorry?"

Again, it was like he didn't talk.

"And you are not the man you were back then," he kept at it.

Duncan had a sense he knew what this was about, and it was no longer about Corey.

"Harv—"

"Your father was a jackass, Bowie."

Yep, that was what he'd sensed.

Harvey raised one of his big mitts and waved it before he carried on talking. "Sorry, but you know it's true way more than me. He fucked with your head. And Szabo was a genius and proved at his end that came in a variety of ways. He fucked with it too. You're beyond that now, and she should know the man you became, despite those two."

"My weakness destroyed us," Duncan pointed out.

"Brother, you were twenty-somethin' years old. You barely knew your ass from a hole in the ground."

"That still happened."

"You know, I had a dad who was proud of me from the minute Ma pushed me out. And he made no bones about it. And growin' up, that was everything to me, Bowie, everything."

Duncan said nothing, pleased as fuck Harv had that.

And to that day, fifty-four years old, missing it like a lost limb that he did not.

Harvey kept going.

"I know moms alone can raise good sons. But there's somethin' about a boy and his father. When I met him, that dude, your dad, was past it, looked a million years old, and could barely get around, and he was still swinging his dick like anyone gave a shit how big it was. You are respected and successful, you know it, he knew it, and he still treated you like you were a bum. Nothin' woulda been good enough for him, Bowie. You told me you didn't wanna play football, but you did it anyway, because he wanted you to. You made All-State, he gave you shit because he was a plumber, but you didn't get a full ride to *his dad's* alma mater. That is not a father, man. That's a jackal whose only sustenance to keep himself feelin' steady is feeding on his young."

"I got two boys, Harv, I know this."

"Well, shouldn't she know it too?"

Duncan ate a forkful of egg, chiles and cheese and didn't answer.

But that also got in there.

"Now tell me if I got this wrong," Harvey kept at him.

But Duncan had had enough.

"Listen, Harv—"

"She's her, pretty, talented, wants to make it big in Hollywood as an actress, and you're the man your father convinced you that you were. How relieved were you when you had a valid reason to cut her loose?"

Duncan's throat closed.

What he was feeling inside must have showed on his face, because Harvey nodded once, decisively.

"Just what I thought," Harvey muttered, and shoved eggs, biscuits, gravy and country fried steak in his mouth.

But Duncan was thrown.

Because this was something he'd never told anybody.

He'd barely admitted it to himself.

But as obliterated as he was, thinking Genny had done that to him, as time went on, he could not deny he'd felt relief.

Not at losing her, never that. He wasn't even certain he'd breathed the same again after she was gone.

Until yesterday, when she stood at the foot of his steps.

But they'd been gearing up to move. Possibly to New York, but she preferred the idea of LA, because of the weather, and there were more opportunities there that interested her.

She'd been the lead in all the high school plays. The drama teacher adored her, said she had something, said she had what it was going to take, and encouraged her at every opportunity.

She'd gone to college, double majoring in drama and education, in case acting didn't work out, she could teach and have a fallback position.

But she had dreams, goals, and a plan.

And they were on the cusp of executing that plan.

But Duncan could not deny he had concerns about it.

Because he could get a job doing anything, if it was manual labor.

But she was going to be someone.

And he'd had his own plan, and at that time, it seemed a more distant dream to reach than Genny's dream of making a career of being an actor.

And that was when Corey struck.

Fucking hell, that guy had known precisely what he was doing.

Further, from that very night he slept without her for the first time in over a year, to what he had to admit was now, it had haunted him, like the ghost of a shackle cuffed to his ankle, one he had no hope of losing, that what had actually happened was what Harvey just said.

He'd jumped right on what Corey told him so he could set Genny free.

Free of the burden of him.

Free so she could be all she was supposed to be.

"Am I gettin' in there?" Harvey asked with mouth full.

"You're an asshole," Duncan replied, and shoved more food in.

"In this instance, I'll take that as a compliment."

Duncan's phone vibrated in his breast pocket.

He reached in, pulled it out and saw it was a text from Chloe.

She had his number because she'd confiscated his phone, demanded his passcode, and she was Genny's girl.

For the life of him, he could not refuse her.

He didn't and she'd texted herself from his phone.

So now he was open game.

He sighed before he read the text,

Plan in place. Noon thirty, El Gato. Our partner in crime knows what to do.

"Shit," he murmured.

"What?" Harvey asked.

"Chloe, she's full steam ahead."

"And?"

"She wants me at El Gato at twelve thirty."

"I could use some beef pinchos," Harvey declared before shoving more food in his mouth.

Duncan stared at him a beat before he stated, "If I go, you are not going with me."

"I totally am," Harvey declared in return.

"Bud—"

"And you're going."

"Har—"

Harvey put his hands, still holding fork and knife, to the table and gave Duncan his full attention.

"Jesus, Bowie, you know I'm gonna tell Beth all this shit and you know she's all romantic and you know she loves you like a brother and you know she's gonna lose her shit if she finds out I didn't get your ass to El Gato at twelve thirty. And last, you know she's gonna ride *my* ass if you balk and keep ridin' it until I get your shit together. So throw a man a bone, please. I don't need her nattering in my ear, and *you* don't need Beth wading into this situation."

One thing in all of this Duncan did know.

That was the truth.

With less bullshittery, Harv asked quietly, "Seriously, my man, what will it hurt?"

"It might hurt her," Duncan said.

"I see this as a concern," Harvey allowed.

"I think Corey and I have done enough, don't you?" Duncan asked.

"Corey, yes. You…"

Harvey looked him straight in the eye.

And lowered the hammer.

"Not even close."

Doing what he did to Genny.

Walking away from her.

Not reaching out for twenty-eight years, if only to reestablish some connection after all they'd been to each other.

What Harvey said was another thing in all of this Duncan knew.

His friend was right.

CHAPTER 6

THE LUNCH

Imogen

"*A*re you *high?*"

Heddy's voice was rising.

"Keep it down," I hissed, not a fan of any scene, but definitely not one that involved me.

Already, I'd noticed one person not-quite-surreptitiously holding their phone pointed our way.

One thing in this life I knew for certain.

The advent of phones with cameras *sucked*.

"He told...the man...you loved...the man... you grew up with...as your best friend...the man...who you gave...your virginity to...the man..."

She was stuttering all William-Shatner-like, I could tell it pained her, it was paining me too, thus I had to stop her.

"Yes, that man," I confirmed. "And yes, he told him what I told you he told him."

And sitting on the patio of El Gato Azul, I was seeing that Corey's final fuck-you was going to have long-lasting effects.

I was also debating whether or not I'd tell Trisha and Scott that evening.

Scott would blow his stack.

Trisha would lose her mind.

They would both be hurt if I didn't share, because I knew they were already more than their usual keen for this visit, seeing as they were worried about me due to the fact Corey committed suicide.

But I was done living Corey's latest betrayal.

I'd had long enough of that, thank you very much.

Even if, until recently, I didn't know it was happening.

"And *that* man barricaded you into his office with his body saying you needed to talk things out, and you *left?*"

"Heddy, what he wanted to talk out was a long time, a career, a husband, and three kids ago," I pointed out.

"Ohmigod," she breathed. "Again, are you *high?*"

I sat back in my metal chair on the crowded patio and sighed, all while reaching to my rosé wine in order to take a fortifying sip.

"You know, I've seen him around, and I will preface this next by saying, when it happened, I had utterly no clue that he was yours, but I've seen him and I've had some very lustful thoughts," Heddy declared.

I wished this did not affect me.

But even way back when, Duncan being a fifteen on a scale of one to ten and the amount of female attention he got because of it always stuck in my craw.

And as ridiculous and nonsensical as that feeling was to have now, I was having that feeling.

I did not share this with my friend Heddy.

At least I thought I didn't.

But she hooted and then stated, "You're jealous."

"I am not jealous, and he is not mine," I retorted and finally took my sip of wine.

"Okay, I'm a tertiary character on a huge-ass television show, my character has a short, but heartbreaking story arc as the friend Bonnie makes at the hospital while Devon is fighting cancer. The friend who bites it, because…duh, she's got cancer. My career tanks because I tell *one* director to shove it because I was tired of people telling me my ass was fat, even though my ass is fat. I get the hell out of that demon industry, only to have that super-famous chick I made friends with on the set have superhuman dedication to keeping friends. Therefore, she kept me as a friend, no matter the time or distance. I then find myself fated to live in the same town her ex-boyfriend, first-love, keeper of the gift of her cherry lives. I lust after him and share that. She gives me the look of death. And he's not yours?"

Obviously, after my crying episode last night, and too much alone time over croissants and coffee at the bistro table in my suite, by the time I'd made it to the restaurant, I was ready to unload.

Something I did.

So much of it, we'd managed to order wine, but not any food.

And it was something I wished right then I did not do.

"Your ass is not fat," I snapped.

Heddy grinned largely. "Babe, this is demonstration of your super-human dedication to keeping friends, that in all of that, not only do you pick the thing to address that would make me feel better, you do it subtly dropping the hint I should let this Duncan Holloway thing go. PS. I'm not letting this Duncan Holloway thing go."

"I don't have superhuman dedication to friendship, Heddy. My best friend in all the world accused me of cheating on him. He then disappeared from my life. After that, I became famous and learned very quickly the wealth of ways people can, will and do use you or screw you over because you're famous. So I put a fair amount of effort into keeping the good ones."

She looked remorseful, but just said, "Babe."

I picked up the menu, tipped my gaze to it and requested, "Can we just select our tapas and stop discussing this?"

When it dawned on me she didn't answer, I looked her way and saw her attention was to the doorway out to the patio.

She must have felt my gaze, because she belatedly answered, "I'm thinking yes on both, since it'd be rude to discuss someone when they're sitting right there and it's time for us all to have some lunch." She then raised her hand, waved, and called loudly, "Yoo hoo!"

My skin tightened, my eyes flew to the doorway and yes.

Snaking through the many tables was a big, handsome bear of a man.

And behind him was Duncan.

Good God.

Too late, I reached for Heddy's raised arm, but even if the damage was done, and Duncan and his friend, as well as everyone else, were looking our way, Heddy leaned so far to the side, her chair almost toppled over, and she kept calling out while waving.

"Yes. Here. We know them. And we have two extra seats! Save a table! They can sit with us!"

"I swear to God, Heddy," I hissed under my breath.

But to no avail.

"Yo!" the big man boomed, smiling so wide, *my* face hurt, and adjusting their course to head our way.

Duncan, studying me closely, followed.

Someonekillmesomeonekillmesomeonekillme.

#SecondWorstDayEver

Okay, maybe third, after Duncan dumped me, then yesterday.

What was I thinking?

Fourth.

Because the day I found out Tom was cheating on me absolutely vied for the top spot.

Nope, fifth.

Seeing as the day we told our children our marriage was over was totally up there.

"Hiyeeee!" Heddy said brightly as they made the table.

"God. Jesus. Will you look at this," the big man with Duncan said, staring down at me.

Then he moved, and with an ugly metallic scraping sound, my chair was back, and I was hauled out of it and into two arms that had closed around me in a tight hug.

What was happening?

He jostled me rather mightily before he loosened his hold enough to pull back and look down at me.

"Whaddaya know, you're Genny, Bowie's girl," he decreed.

I didn't know what to make of any of this, but the crazy thing about it was, I mostly didn't know what to make of *that*.

I'd been Imogen Swan for so long, I forgot what it felt like to be just Genny at all.

Bowie's girl or not.

"I—"

He let me go, but only partially. He took my hand and pumped it, vigorously.

"Harvey. Harvey Evans. Friends call me Harv. Bowie's my boy," he introduced himself.

"Harv, man, you think you might wanna not tear her arm off?" Duncan suggested.

He let me go. "Right. Sorry." He turned to Heddy. "Yo. I'm Harv."

She stuck an enthusiastic hand his way. "Heddy. Long suffering friend to this tall, gorgeous drink of water." She jerked her head my way.

"Heddy—" I tried.

"Sit down, sit, sit, sit." Done shaking Harv's hand, Heddy was gesturing magnanimously to the table.

Harv did not hesitate to make motions to take a chair.

Duncan did.

"Hi, you're Duncan, right?" Heddy called. "I'm Heddy. And I'm *so* glad to meet you. Sit!"

She practically shouted the last word.

I was acutely aware all eyes were on us.

I sat and stated somewhat urgently, "Yes, please. Sit. Just sit."

I felt Duncan's attention as he shifted his body to do as I asked, but then I heard, "No. You. There by Gen. You by me, Harv."

Oh God.

Since Heddy and I were sitting kitty-corner, her words meant, at the small square table it was going to be boy, boy, girl, girl, with Duncan at my side.

And his knee far too close to mine.

His explosive temper didn't terrify me.

But *that* did.

"Is this okay, Genny?" I heard him ask softly.

I was busy rescuing my napkin that had fallen out of my lap and onto the stone floor amidst my enforced bear hug.

I smoothed it in place and muttered, "Yes, yes. Please just sit," without looking at him.

"Sit, bud," he ordered low to his friend.

"Right," Harvey mumbled.

Heddy leaned deep into the table and whispered conspiratorially, "She gets attention. It's not like she isn't used to it, it just, you know, can be oppressive if there's too much of it. Dig?"

I aimed my gaze at her. "I can speak for myself, Heddy."

She leaned back and shot big eyes at me. "All right. Chill out, mama."

Someonekillmesomeonekillmesomeonekillme.

Duncan's knee brushed mine as he scooted in.

Frissons of electricity shot from there, up my thigh, straight between my legs.

SOMEONEKILLMESOMEONEKILLMESOMEONEKILLME.

"Right. Yeah. Cool. The ladies got their wine. Nut Brown, on tap. And while we're perusin' our menus, bring us some of those beef pinchos," Harv ordered.

I looked up to see the waitress standing by our table.

"And the fig with goat cheese," Heddy added.

"Is that good?" Harv asked her.

"Oh my *gawd*," she said as answer.

"Should we get two 'a those?" Harv inquired. "'Cause even though Bowie's mostly veggie, I think we should get two 'a the beef pinchos. Breakfast wore off at least an hour ago."

Heddy was about to answer, but I was so stunned at what Harvey said, I turned my head Duncan's way and asked, "You're a vegetarian?"

He opened his mouth.

But Harv answered.

"Mostly. Something about methane. I can coax him into a burger every once in a while. And chicken, if he's assured they're free range."

"I can speak for myself too, Harvey, and it's not just methane," Duncan said to Harv and turned to me. "It's the rain forest."

"Of course," I murmured.

"Since we got a veggie amongst us, we'll do the brie nachos and falafel too," Heddy decreed, then queried of Harv. "You down with that, big man?"

"For starters," he allowed.

"Liquid Amber," Duncan stated his drink preference when the waitress cast her gaze his way.

"I'll get those drinks in and your tapas out when they're up," she promised and took off.

Heddy instantly turned to me. "Speaking of the rain forest. Do you remember that dress you wore to that fundraiser to save it?" She didn't let me answer. She turned her attention to the gents. "She looked *beautiful*." She then homed in on Duncan. "And she gave, like, I don't know...*a bazillion* dollars to that charity."

"*Heddy*," I hissed.

When I received her gaze, it was all innocence. "What? You did."

I ignored her, turned to Harv and began to explore new territory in a desperate attempt to change the subject.

"So, Harv, what do you do?"

He jerked a thumb at Duncan. "Work with this guy. I'm his COO."

"Oh," I mumbled.

Perhaps we were in new territory.

But not the right territory.

"Best gig I ever had," Harv stated. "We were friends, see. Been friends *years*. Back then, I managed a pro shop. Made shit...'scuse my French, money. But that shop was in the shitter, 'scuse my French again, when I started there. Bitched, damn, 'scuse my French *again*, to Bowie the whole time about the hassle it was. He gave me a couple pointers, which were helpful. The story is longer, due to the fact the employees were a pack of hyenas, but makin' it short, after I turned it around, he poached me." Big grin. "The owners were *ticked*. The history of that shop was not good, they were finally turning a profit, and their manager is gone. Though, big risk for Bowie, seein' as there's a difference between managing one little shop and overseeing the operations of fifteen huge ones. Though that was then. Now we got seventy-five."

He turned to Duncan and gravely bowed his head.

And then kept talking.

"My wife thanks you, seein' as she's toolin' around in a shiny new GMC and not that crappy ten-year-old minivan. And my daughters thank you, seein' as they won't have to sell a kidney to go to college, and they found it embarrassing, being ferried around in that crappy ten-year-old minivan."

Duncan said nothing to Harvey.

He turned and said it to me.

"We have a River Rain here in Prescott. It's not far, though if I take you now to get you some waders, something I think we both need considering how deep it's getting out here, we'll miss the goat cheese."

It came out before I could stop it.

A rush of laughter.

This was something else I had not forgotten about Duncan.

How funny he could be.

And how much I'd loved I had a guy who could make me laugh.

I managed to get a handle on it as fast as I could.

But I would find it wasn't fast enough.

For when I was done, Heddy had a gleeful expression, Harv had a hopeful one...

And Duncan's eyes were soft and warm on me.

God.

"Okay, there's an elephant on the patio, and before that bastard sits on us," Harv started, attention on me, "he's my boy so I'm his boy and she's your girl so you're her girl and we all obviously know what's goin' on here so I'll just say it. Your dead friend was an asshole. He did you so dirty, it's killin' me he's dead so I can't track his ass down and choke the life outta him. But that said, I'm glad you two are gonna have the chance to talk things out."

"I, well—" I didn't quite begin.

"Me too," Heddy chimed in.

"You wanna give it a rest?" Duncan said words directed at his friend that seemed like a suggestion, but the tone in which they were spoken stated clearly they were not.

"I *am* giving it a rest," Harv replied. "Is Beth here?"

"Jesus Christ, if you call her—" Duncan clipped.

"I'm not above it," Harv stated. "The threat is real, my man. So get with the program." He lifted an exceptionally large hand and whirled it over the table. "Talk amongst yourselves. I'm sure me and Heddy got all sorts we can gab about."

He then went so far as to turn a mountainous shoulder to the table and lean toward Heddy, who did the same damned thing.

I huffed out a breath, reconsidering my dedication to remaining friends with Heddy.

Duncan turned to me.

"I'm sorry," he said.

"It's okay," I replied. Then asked, "Who's Beth?"

"Harvey's wife."

"Is she scary?"

"No. But if she wants something, she's single-minded about getting it."

"I think we've had enough of people being single-minded about things they want in regard to us, don't you agree?" I inquired.

"There's an important difference when it comes to Beth. She's only single-minded when she wants something for someone she cares about. And in this case, it would be me being happy."

I had nothing to say to that.

Though I was lamenting my choice of wine and wondering where our waitress was and if it would be gauche to order an entire bottle of gin.

He shifted a little my way.

I stiffened.

He shifted no farther.

But his voice lowered. "I would still like the chance to talk."

I caught his gaze. "And I still feel there's nothing to say."

"In discussing this with Harvey this morning, some things I wasn't admitting to myself came clear, and Gen, I'd like to share them with you, and I'd appreciate it if you'd listen to me."

"I know a few things about wishing someone would listen to what you have to say."

His lips tightened and his jaw popped under his beard.

Then his expression grew perplexed as he focused over my shoulder.

He returned that focus to me. "There's someone taking a picture of us."

I didn't bother to look.

I fluttered a hand between us. "It comes with the territory."

"Do you want that?"

"It doesn't matter what I want."

"And I can take from that response you don't want that."

"Again, it doesn't matter."

I barely finished the words, and he was pushing out of his seat.

We got Harv and Heddy's attention, but I moved quickly to grab Duncan's forearm.

"Duncan, sit down," I ordered.

He looked down at me. "I'll ask nice that they stop."

"Please sit down."

"I won't be a dick about it."

God, he was stubborn.

"Bowie, *please*, sit *down*."

His head cocked sharply.

Then he moved to resume his seat.

I removed my hand from his arm.

He then shifted into me and didn't stop until he was right in my face.

"They're gonna post that on social media," he declared.

"Yes, they probably will."

"I know you're used to that, Genny, but—"

"Duncan, it hasn't escaped me that you are no stranger to the media feeds."

"Yes, pictures taken at events, and rallies, and press shit we do for the stores. Not at a restaurant where I took my boys and their mother to eat, repeatedly, but now I'm sitting next to a beautiful woman who is not their mother. She's a world-famous actress who they don't know their dad once loved more than his own life."

I could feel my pulse beating hard in my neck.

He continued speaking.

"So it may be no big deal to you, just another thing you put up with because that's a part of your life, but it isn't part of mine."

I'd seen him.

But I hadn't researched.

I'd wanted to.

However hard it was (and it was *hard*), I wouldn't allow myself.

Thus, now he'd mentioned it, I had to know.

"You have boys?" I asked quietly.

"Yes. Two. Sullivan, we call him Sully, and Gage."

I wondered if they looked like him.

"And are they not over your divorce?" I queried.

"They were so relieved we ended it, I think Gage considered writing us each a thank you card. And he's never done that in his life without his mother riding his ass to do it."

So it wasn't a happy home.

"That doesn't sound very good for you or them or her."

"It wasn't. It was unhealthy, but I put an end to it before it became destructive. But they're good kids and they care about their mother. More, we're tight and they'd be pissed I was with a woman and they didn't know about her, at least before we were all over Instagram. And that would be even if you weren't who you are. But it goes without saying, it'd be worse that I didn't tell them because you are who you are, and more, you are who you've always been to me."

I didn't field that last part.

I wasn't even planning on thinking about it.

"We are not out together, Duncan."

"We're sittin' side by side, Genny."

I suspected my lips thinned at that.

I unthinned them to ask, "How long were you married?"

"Sixteen years, six divorced. And yes, it took me so long to find someone partially because no one was as good as you, but also because I was tryin' to make a go of my stores, because I wasn't gonna hook up with another woman and not be able to provide for her the way I needed to do that."

This was a refrain I knew *oh so well.*

And even now, it irritated the hell out of me.

Because of the reason behind it.

"The way your father made you *think* you needed to do that," I corrected.

"The way *I* needed to do that, Genny," he retorted.

"So he *is* actually stuck in your head," I deduced.

"No, honey, you dreamed of having your own trailer and making acceptance speeches. And I dreamed of not having to worry about money, being in a position my family would not worry about it either and living in a big house surrounded by nothing but trees and maybe a lake."

He didn't need to tell me that.

I knew his dream.

"So we both got what we wanted in the end."

"Yeah, but it would have been nice to have had the shot to do it together."

"Sadly, that didn't happen."

"We finally agree on something. Though 'sadly' for me isn't a strong enough word for it."

Time to resume our earlier topic.

"And why was your marriage unhealthy, Duncan?"

"Because Dora was great. She was fun. She could cook and she loved hiking and mountain biking and she had a beautiful smile and she had drive to make something of herself. In the beginning, and for a long time, she was light in the darkness. She also had two assholes cheat on her before she met me. I did not know this next part. She did not know it. Neither of us saw it coming. But they did a number on her. And for some reason somethin' twisted somewhere along the line and she got it in her head I was fucking everything that moved. No matter what I said, I could not convince her otherwise. No matter what I suggested to get her head straight and our marriage back on solid ground, it didn't work. It was frustrating. Then it got old. Then it got aggravating. Then it got crazy. And when that crazy was looking like it would infect our boys, I ended it."

This wasn't a fun story.

In fact, living it had to have been agony.

What it also was, however, was a perfect opening.

And in an attempt to guard my peace of mind, I strolled right through it.

"I know a little something about how you felt, Bowie," I said smoothly.

"And don't think that hasn't been the top thing on my mind since the instant I saw those 'I'm sorrys'," he returned. "That was my punishment, a thousand-fold, for what I did to you."

I felt my head twitch in surprise.

"So you knew what was coming when you saw those apologies?"

"It felt like I was on the gallows and they were putting on the noose."

"That's rather dramatic," I scoffed.

"That I knew in that moment I threw you away for nothing at the same time I personally understood your pain? That isn't dramatic?"

Understanding that pain, and only having the one incidence of it, not what sounded like a rather uncomfortable, heartrending and demoralizing amount of time in failing to protect a marriage from it, I couldn't argue that.

Duncan didn't make me try.

He said, "Though, I didn't throw you away for nothing. I did it because I was weak, and I was an asshole because I knew after I ended us in high school that we shouldn't get back together until I had something worthwhile to give you. But I saw you and I couldn't stop myself. That was the weak part *and* the asshole part."

God!

It was like being thrown back in time.

"I already had the something worthwhile I needed, Bowie," I told him something he knew.

"Yes, Genny, baby, and you said that a million times then and you coulda said it a million more. But honest to God, if I said I wanted no part of LA or New York, that to have me, you had to stay in Chicago, I would have taken something integral from you that you needed."

That made me angry.

"I wasn't holding you back, Bowie."

"I didn't say that."

"It sounded like that."

"What I meant was, we were too goddamned young to be able to handle how big what we had was. I had come nowhere near sorting out the harm my father inflicted on me. And I was all about you. Lost to you. And I was that at the same time I was not the man I needed to be for you. And I *needed* that, Genny. Whether you get it or not does not negate the fact I *needed* it."

Since this made sense, even though I didn't know precisely how in the context of how he'd ended us, I decided it was time to move back to an even earlier topic.

"Should we have this talk you wish to have, a talk we're not going to have, and it got past the beginning phase, which it wouldn't, then it would eventually get to the part where you would have to understand that people taking pictures of me, approaching me, even touching me, people I do not know, *is* a part of my life, Duncan. Everywhere I go, I do it ready to face something like that. It's automatic. It used to disturb me, but now I'm used to it. And anyone in my life would have to be used to it too."

His lips hitched before he said, "Not sure how you missed it, beautiful, but we just had the first, second and maybe even third parts of our talk. And just for the record, if you're used to it and don't care, it doesn't bother me as long as it won't upset my sons."

I blinked at him.

"Food's here, baby," he whispered.

Stiltedly, my head turned to the table.

Tapas were all over it.

The beers had been served.

Heddy looked gleeful.

Harv looked hopeful.

But Duncan?

He reached to grab a falafel.

And he was smiling.

CHAPTER 7

THE AFTERNOON

Duncan

Considering Chloe was hanging on his porch with Bettina as he drove up to his house after lunch, Duncan didn't head around back to the garage.

He parked out front.

She was keen, worried about her mother, so he wasn't out of his Tesla SUV before Chloe was skipping down the stairs in her ridiculously high heels.

And he hadn't quite rounded his vehicle, and he definitely didn't have a chance to tell her not to skip or she'd break her neck, though she appeared to wear heels like they were a pair of Chucks, before she was calling, "Well?"

"Let's go inside, honey. We gotta talk," he replied.

Her face fell.

"It didn't go badly," he told her quickly. "And because of that, we have to talk."

A light of excitement hit her brown eyes that was so Genny, he felt it like a punch in his throat.

She then skipped back up his steps.

Duncan followed more sedately.

He sent a glance Bettina's way, and his housekeeper was practically wringing her hands with worry mingled with enthusiasm.

This meant, although Duncan did not share, Chloe did.

He sighed.

Bettina had been with them since Dora and he split. Even before he'd built this house.

She didn't live with him, but she came every day to tidy, or clean on the rotation she had in her head, do his laundry (and the boys' when they were home), stock his kitchen and sundries, deal with any house issues that sprang up as well as normal maintenance and over-seeing Bill, the man who saw to the grounds.

And she took care of the horses, chickens and garden when Duncan wasn't around to do it.

This was not a full-time job.

For her what it was, was a job she could do on her own schedule that paid well and she'd be finished by one at the latest and then could look after her grandchildren when they were done with school. Because her daughter had to work a job that didn't pay enough for childcare and she also had a baby daddy who was a fuckwit.

"It's all good, you can go get the kids from school," he told her.

"You all right?" she asked.

He was tentatively fucking great.

"I'm fine," he answered.

She gave him a long look before she nodded.

He followed Chloe into his house.

Now Chloe…

She was temporarily living there.

Her decree, not his invitation.

The woman was a steamroller.

Not like her mother at all.

But Duncan found it cute, mostly because of why she was that way.

The afternoon before, Chloe had shared with him that she intended to stay close, but could not stay in town, lest her mother see her (and she'd used the word "lest") and cotton on to what was happening.

So with him it was.

But even if she'd given him a choice (which she hadn't, but he could have pressed it, something he did not do), he wouldn't have denied her.

The opportunity to get to know Genny's daughter?

No way in hell he was going to pass that up.

So there she was and had been since yesterday, late afternoon.

She had her father's more dominant features, dark hair, dark eyes.

She had her mother's extreme femininity. Heart-shaped face. Tall, slim frame. Graceful hands. Long, elegant neck.

Mostly, though, she was her own being, and the force of her personality proved it.

Unless her father was aggressive about getting what he wanted.

Duncan took over the situation when they both were inside, and he led her to his office.

This had to be more formal, because she was not going to like what he had to say, and he had to push it and not cave.

Not even a day with this young woman, and he was glad he hadn't had daughters at the same time he was feeling Harvey's pain.

In other words, he was a total pushover.

He had utterly no qualms about that.

But he could see it causing problems.

When they arrived at his office, he gestured to a chair in front of the desk as he moved behind it.

"Well, doesn't this feel like I'm going to get a talking to," she remarked as she sat across from him.

Duncan had a feeling she was no stranger to "talking tos."

He sat as well, eyes on her.

The clothes she wore were Genny too.

Even back in the day, when neither of them had any money, his girl did what she could to be a fashion plate.

And there, in the mountains, when no one in Prescott dressed like Chloe, but definitely not in a home a ways out of town that was large, and luxurious, if rustic, but in the end it was just a big log cabin, she was wearing slim jeans, a fancy blouse and pumps with death-defying heels that probably cost a quarter of a semester of Gage's college.

"Right, we had lunch. My friend Harvey went with me. And your operative Heddy was on the ball. She got us to the table and your mom didn't object," he opened it.

Chloe smiled smugly.

"I told Harvey what's happening, he's on board. And between Heddy and him, Genny and I had no choice but to chat."

Her smile got even more smug to the point it was triumphant.

Christ, some man or woman out there was in for one helluva wild ride.

"And now it's done," he stated.

Her expression faltered. "Done?"

"I'm going to the hotel tonight and coming clean about this plan we've been instigating."

Her big brown eyes grew enormous and she leaned forward, crying, "You can't do that!"

"Honey, listen to me," he said calmingly. "I'm a veteran of two spectacularly failed relationships. So trust me on this, because I know. You do not start something, whether it's important or not, but I think all involved know how important this is, so *especially* this, on a play. A lie. A deceit."

"It's not a deceit," she declared heatedly.

"Do you deny we're playing your mom?"

She said nothing.

Right.

He smoothed his voice even further before he shared, "I think I got in there, and if I don't waste any time, I can get in further. But whether I do or not, that has to be her choice and she needs to be in control of the process of making it."

"Someone has to right Uncle Corey's wrong—"

Fuck, but if it did not borderline enrage him that this sweet, if forceful, girl called that man "Uncle Corey."

He could not get hung up on that.

"And I'm all over attempting to do that."

"And I want my mom to be happy."

He felt that.

The thought he could give that to her mother, and she thought he could do that too.

He felt it warm and sharp, like a cut to lance a boil, releasing poison. It hurt, but still, the relief was sweet.

"And I'll be all over attempting that too," he said quietly. "If she'll let me. But she has to make that choice, not be manipulated into it."

She opened her mouth.

He raised his hand, palm to her.

She closed her mouth.

He dropped his hand and said, "We were both manipulated, Chloe, and I made a fatal decision during that. I understand your motives, and if I still know your mother, she will too. But we have to stop this before it gets any further. And now, you need to leave this to me."

"So you're going to just throw us all under the bus, and I'm not unaware, as the ringleader, the person farthest under that bus will be *me*?"

"Are you saying your mother doesn't know you well enough to know you'd pull something like this?"

She hesitated a second before she rolled her eyes.

As he suspected.

This was not out of character.

At all.

"I've got this," he assured her.

It took a second, she shifted in her seat during that, then she said, "My dad—"

"Don't, honey," he whispered. "You know, if this happens like we want it to, your mom has to give that to me."

She straightened her spine. "He's a good guy,"

That remained to be seen.

"And you have to know, they're still the best of friends," she continued. "They talk, like…every day."

"Again, this is for your mother to give me if it gets to that."

"It's going to get to that."

He hoped like fuck she was right.

He didn't say that or anything.

He just nodded.

"She's going to dinner with Trisha and Scott tonight," she informed him.

"I know, you told me that already. I'll head to the hotel after."

"That means I'm making us dinner."

"I just had more tapas than a man should ever eat."

"Well, I'm not serving it *now*."

He grinned at her.

Then he stated, "You don't have to do that."

She stood, retorting, "I totally do. I cook *French* and I *rock it*. Your taste buds will not know what hit them. But to do that, I need preparation, I need time. The French do not hurry anything."

"Have at it then, darlin'."

"I'll assess your larder, but I'll probably have to go to the grocery store."

"You need money?"

Another eyeroll and a drawn out, "Pu-lease."

"Right," he muttered, trying not to laugh.

"Though, I do want to drive your Tesla."

He could no longer hold back his laughter.

And through it, he said, "The fob is in it."

Yup.

Total pushover.

"*Merveilleux*," she replied before drifting an arm his way and swanning out.

He waited until she was gone to pull out his phone and engage the screen.

He'd texted both his boys before he drove home, telling them he wanted a call back as soon as they had a chance.

Sullivan was in Indiana, studying environmental engineering at Purdue.

Gage was in Tucson, studying beer pong at U of A.

He hadn't missed a vibration.

Neither had texted him back.

Duncan turned his gaze out the window to the lake, but he didn't see it.

He thought about lunch.

Like they were practiced tacticians who'd planned and synced their mission down to the finest detail, the moment Duncan and Genny had turned their attention to the table, Harvey and Heddy had taken over.

They commenced what was a poorly disguised "Friends of a New Couple Getting to Know You Better" session that culminated (unsurprisingly from the person she seemed to be) in Heddy demanding Harvey arrange a dinner so she could meet "my soon-to-be-new-bestest-bestie, I can feel it" Beth without delay.

In truth, this was them giving Genny and Duncan the opportunity to be in each other's company without having to deal with communicating with each other, either in meaningful, life-altering ways, or something less burdensome.

It worked.

Genny relaxed, not entirely, but enough that she joined the conversation, even if she rarely looked at Duncan when she did, or when he did the same.

However, he knew the woman who sat at his side during lunch.

And she'd been the way she'd been at that table before.

It was not distant.

It was shy.

And very aware of the man sitting next to her.

He knew this because that woman was the girl who, right along with Duncan, started to become aware that "The Three Amigos" they had always been was shifting to three friends, two of which were terminally into one another.

Well, it would seem, both of the male amigos were into her, one even more terminally, but even Duncan had been blind to that.

Then again, he'd confessed to Corey way before he'd ever said a word to Genny what his feelings were about their girl.

And Corey had—the lying, pissant, piece of scum maggot—been entirely enthusiastic.

His eyes fell to the letter that still lay on his desk that he hadn't touched since he'd dropped it, therefore he hadn't finished reading it.

He, like Genny, did not give one shit what else that asshole had to say.

But before he could nab the letter and do something like burn it in the fireplace, his phone went.

It was Gage.

He took the Facetime call.

And said not a word before Gage shouted, "Jesus Christ, Dad! You had lunch with *Imogen Swan?*"

Fuck, fuck, fuck.

"Gage—"

"My phone is blowing up. Some of my friends follow her. She's been tagged, like, a *billion* times. And so have you."

He really should get on social media.

He had an account, but he never looked at it. It was run by a professional social media manager that was contracted through River Rain.

Duncan did not personally engage as an attempt at self-preservation.

Sully would be smart. If he did it, he wouldn't announce it to the world, but the kid was so hyper-responsible, he probably wouldn't do it.

Gage, however.

If Duncan saw the shit he was certain Gage got up to, he'd consider chaining his son in the basement.

"Son—"

"Do you know her from knowin' that guy who makes Steve Jobs look like a pussy? And not in the physical sense, because…no shade, your old friend was a runt…in the 'I got enough money to buy an island, and that island is Australia' sense."

"I think we've had several conversations about your usage of the word 'pussy,'" Duncan growled.

Gage shut up.

"And yes. I know her because I grew up with her."

"What?" Gage asked. "That's *insane*."

His phone shook, a notification came up, and Sully wanted to Facetime.

Goddamn it.

"Why didn't you tell us?" Gage demanded.

"It's a long story and—"

"Yeah, it looks like a long story. You're practically kissing her."

Goddamn it.

"Listen—"

"And she looks like she wants to swallow you whole," Gage declared.

That had Duncan shutting up.

It also had him wanting to see this picture.

"Are you guys like…*seeing each other?*" Gage asked.

Sully had disconnected, only to try again.

"Okay, Gage, listen and don't interrupt, are you hearing me?"

Gage nodded.

"Like I said, it's a long story, and it's time you heard it. I wish I could tell you face to face when our faces aren't projected on screens, but that doesn't seem like it can happen. And now your brother is trying to connect, and I need for both of you to know. So even if this is not how I'd like to do it, the truth of the matter is, Genny was my high school girlfriend. I broke up with her after I graduated, but we got back together again a few years later. It was intense. It was forever. And then I made that not so for a variety of reasons I may share one day, but today is not that day. We both went our separate ways, but now she's back in my life and it remains to be seen *how* back in my life she's going to be. What I can tell you is, I loved her very much. She was my world. It killed, letting her go. But now is now and we'll just see."

Gage was silent a beat before he asked incredulously, "*Genny?*"

It'd be good when all the people in his life got over this.

"She *was* my girlfriend, bud."

"Does Mom know about this?"

He nodded. "I told her a long time ago. Though, I don't know if she knows that Genny's back. That said, we've both moved on, as you know. So I don't see it as an issue for your mother."

Something occurred to him, and as usual with Gage, he didn't hesitate to share it, no matter how inappropriate it might be.

"Oh my God, you've had sex with Imogen Swan. My dad has had sex with *Imogen Swan.*"

Duncan closed his eyes and tipped his head back.

"I don't know whether to think this is awesome or hurl," Gage shared.

He looked back to his son. "How about not thinking about it at all?"

"That's a good call," Gage muttered, his face twisted in disgust, then something else occurred to him and he got right on letting that out. "Holy shit, if you guys become an item again, everyone is going to know my dad is doing *Imogen Swan.*"

"Gage, let's get off this topic, yeah?"

"Totally," Gage agreed.

"Are you okay with this?" Duncan asked, feeling his neck muscles contract as the question came out, because the answer could change everything.

But Gage just looked confused.

"Okay with what? You hooking up with a movie star?"

"Yes, and should that become more," Duncan confirmed.

"Dad, serious." Gage now looked serious. "I mean, do I have to count this down?"

"Considering the fact you're my son, I love you, your thoughts and feelings matter to me, and this woman was important to me, that never really stopped being the case, even if we moved on with our lives, and I'm hoping that she'll be big part of my life again, which means yours, yes. You have to count this down."

"Right, but you can't get pissed about how I do it."

Fabulous.

"Just share, Gage," Duncan sighed.

"One, and you can't argue this, she's a MILF."

Jesus.

His son.

"I mean, seriously, she's gorgeous. Like, Gwyneth Paltrow gorgeous. I'd totally do Gwyneth Paltrow."

"Stop speaking," Duncan clipped.

Gage grinned, shameless.

"Second, my dad might be hooking up with a hottie. I agree, it's too bad we aren't doin' this face to face so I can't high five you."

Jesus.

His son.

"Third, if I'm reading this right, this might lead to Imogen Swan being my stepmom and that would totally not suck. I mean, everyone knows she's like, the coolest chick in Hollywood."

"She lives in Phoenix, Gage."

"Better, she probably has an awesome pad and lives next to Larry Fitzgerald or something and we can ask him over for a pool party and he and me could be buds."

The tension eased out of his neck as Duncan started chuckling.

It shot right back when he heard the tone of his son's voice and saw the change come over his features when he said, "I'm not sure I want the whole story, seein' as it obviously gutted you so much you didn't even tell us she was a part of your life. And you're all over getting her back when it had to be that guy dyin' that started this, and he offed himself, like, I don't know, maybe a week ago. So you aren't wasting time. But if she treats you right, Dad, without any crazy, I'll love her forever."

Jesus.

His son.

"Your mother isn't crazy," he said carefully.

"I know, but she was messed up for a long time, Dad, and it wasn't lost on Sully or me that you shouldered even more of it than she shoveled at you so we wouldn't feel it. I know she's got her shit together and I'm proud of her and I love her. But I love you too and it would far from suck, seein' you have it easy and good for a change."

Okay.

Maybe he hadn't shielded his sons from the damage.

"That's good to hear, bud. But not to get your hopes up, things are uncertain with Genny and me. But I'm hoping to change that, and I need you on board before I do."

"I'm on board."

"Thanks, son," he murmured.

"Dad?"

"Yup."

"Don't let the bright lights, glitz and glamor change you. I like you simple and no frills, just the way you are," he joked.

But it hid his true message.

He believed in his dad and he knew he had this.

That felt fucking great.

And Duncan hoped he was right.

"I'll try not to get a big head. Now go do something useful, like, I don't know, *study*. I need to call your brother."

"Later, Pops."

"Later, kid."

They disconnected and he went right to Sullivan.

Sully engaged immediately.

And while Duncan was in the process of saying, "Hey, son," Sully asked, "Does Mom know?"

"You've seen the picture with Genny," Duncan deduced.

"If you mean the one with Imogen Swan, yes. Does Mom know?"

"Your mother and I are past the point where we share about these kinds of things," he said cautiously.

"Yeah, when you were dating Betsy, even if that was getting serious, though it didn't go that way. But this is *her* and Mom knows about her."

Duncan went very still.

Of course Dora knew about Genny. He'd told her. She was his wife. He shared everything with her. And he did that before she was his wife.

What he did not know was how his son knew that.

Before he could ask after that, Sully stated, "And this is gonna mess her right up."

"Your mom is solid, Sul," he assured. "She's found a therapist she's connected with. She understands the obsessive paths her mind can lead her on. And she now has the mental tools to avoid them, and she uses those tools."

"It was her."

"What?"

"It started with her."

"What are you saying, Sullivan?"

"Imogen Swan. What kicked it all off. Ground zero. Her being yours. It's what kicked it all off. It was her."

Duncan's chest started burning. "How do you know this?"

"That time you were up in Oregon. Opening the store in Bend. Do you remember that?"

Shit.

That had been a particularly bad episode with Dora.

"Yes," he bit out.

"You asked her to come with you. You even begged her to come with you. I heard her. She said you had to go alone. It was a test."

There had been a number of tests with Dora.

He'd always failed.

"I remember this, Sully."

And he did.

He just hated his son had heard this and he had no idea, until then, that he had.

"Well, Gage was on that camping trip with Jack. And I was at a sleepover at Wyatt's, but Wyatt got to not feeling good and his mom brought me home. And when I came in, Mom was on the phone with you. And she was losing it with you."

Duncan said nothing.

He thought he was beyond the disappointment, and at times fury, other times frustrating impotence, and other times debilitating sadness, of what had become of his wife and their marriage.

But the fury was returning.

"I remember this clearly, Sully, and I didn't know you didn't have that sleepover," Duncan stated.

"Yeah, because she made me promise not to tell you because of what happened after she hung up on you."

Yes.

Fury.

"She made me lie to you, Dad. And that sucked. It really pissed me off. Because you never lied to us. You made a big deal of it. And there I was, Mom making me lie to you."

Mm-hmm.

Fury.

He could not deny he had guilt, feeling it, since Dora was unwell.

However, that was not news even back then.

But it couldn't be erased, the number of therapists she'd fired because "we don't connect." And his constant offers that she remain at his side, even when he was at work in his office in town, so he could show her whenever he left her, it was not about another woman. Offers she did not accept.

He was not a man who thought he'd allow any illness, no matter the cause of it, to end his marriage.

But as he'd have to face the consequences of a wife who decided to treat cancer with homeopathic remedies that had no hope of rooting out that disease, he faced the consequences of a wife who had lucid stretches of understanding something was terribly wrong, and deciding to take the path of denial and not treatment.

That was Dora's.

And eventually, she'd owned it.

Unfortunately, by the time she'd done that, not only was their divorce final—and it being further after he'd endured more abuse from her accusing him of picking up with "his women" after he "got done with her," when, for her sake, he hadn't started dating—she'd finally found a therapist who could reach her.

But it was too late.

Because he'd met Betsy.

He hadn't started anything with her, but he'd met her, and he intended to start something.

He did.

Betsy had since moved to Park City, a move that Duncan was not willing to make with her, and she was not willing to stay in Prescott, which told the tale of how committed they truly were, and that ended.

But now it was Imogen.

And he had no idea what Genny had to do with anything.

He'd told Dora about her before he'd even asked her to marry him.

And from that time on, it had never come up.

They'd opened their store in Bend eight years ago.

Sully had been thirteen.

And Duncan knew nothing about this.

"What happened after she hung up?" he asked tightly.

"She lost it, Dad. Totally destroyed the kitchen. Tore everything out of the fridge and threw it around. Ketchup everywhere. Tomato sauce. Salsa. Mayonnaise. Broken jars. Stuff came out of the pantry and mixed with it. Pasta. Flour. Spices. Bottles rolling around. Her slipping all over it. I stopped her before she got out the plates. But I had to do that physical. I had to lock her down. In the end, she threw back a pill and went to bed, but it took me, like, three hours to clean up that mess."

"Son, you should have told me."

The pain for his boy carved through his voice.

And his heart.

"Dad, what would *you* do? Seeing that and her coming to, you know, like she did, snapping into being with it, and then getting so worried you'd be mad and making me promise."

"I wouldn't have been mad. But I would have done something about it."

"Well, I was too young to know then. I see it now. It was her being, you know...*her*. How she'd get shady. Like, she fed off being sick. She got something out of it. You know, negative attention is still attention. That kind of thing. And she didn't want you to take it more seriously, how messed up she was. Maybe commit her or something."

Duncan drew a sharp breath into his nose and said nothing because they both knew all of this was true.

"And while she was throwing shit around, she was ranting about Imogen Swan. How you were trying to find her again. How all your 'other women' were blonde and blue-eyed and she was the love of your life. And you were longing for her. And since she was married to some tennis guy, you'd never have her back, so you were fucking a hundred Imogen Swans to get her back—"

"Okay, son," Duncan cut him off, not for himself, but because this couldn't be easy on his boy.

"I'm not done, Dad. She showed me a picture of you two. After she calmed down. To prove to me she wasn't crazy. She showed me a picture. And there you were, together. But she said you kept it in your wallet with you all the time. She found it there. In your wallet. She didn't seem to get that you were in Bend, we were in Prescott, and she went to the basement to get that picture, so obviously it wasn't with you all the time in your wallet. It was something in those old boxes of junk you said you'd get around to clearing out, and never did. And she found it and, well...it set her off. And that's it."

Duncan did not know what to say and he had no idea what to do.

Which brought back the feeling of frustration he thought he'd left behind, because he had spent a lot of the last part of his marriage not knowing what to say or do.

"Mom follows you on Insta, Dad," Sully warned.

"I don't know how that works, son," Duncan reminded him.

"You can follow a tag or a hashtag. And that pic with you and Imogen Swan has been both. By the way, you guys' hashtag is isit-gonnabeimoway."

"What?"

"Imoway. Imogen and Holloway mashed together. It's what they do with famous couples."

Fucking hell.

"Sully—"

"I saw that picture, Dad. And I'm not just talking the one on Instagram."

Duncan remained silent.

"I'm not saying Mom had any reason to say what she said or be how she was because of whatever you two had. I remember the good times, before she got sick. I know you loved her. You didn't hide it. You always told us not to bury our feelings or hide them and you were about tell, but also about the show. But I saw that picture, Dad, and it wasn't hard to see you two loved each other. I don't know why that didn't work, but you're available, and so's she, and it sucks, your old friend killed himself. But if that's how you two have reconnected, then I hope something good comes of it. And it isn't your problem anymore, but someone is gonna have to tell Mom. If you want that to be me, I'll do it. But I hate to say it, it probably should be you."

He was right.

And maybe Duncan wasn't going to be able to go visit Genny tonight to find some way to explain what they'd all been up to and hope her interest in his life and bashfulness at his side meant they were going to finish talking things through, find a way to let go of the past and explore a future.

Because he needed to deal with Dora.

And that might take a while.

"I'll call your mother," he agreed.

Sully tried to hide looking relieved, but he didn't manage it.

"And I don't know what's happening with Genny, son," he continued. "But I need to be clear that if something is happening, you're okay with that."

"Totally," Sully said. "Aubrey and Charlie had such a huge fight about whether or not she was robbed of an Oscar for her role in *It Wasn't Easy* that they made us watch it. And Aubrey was right. She was really good in that. But I, you know, avoided her, after the whole Mom thing. But Aubrey's a huge fan of hers and she talks about her sometimes and what she says, she seems really cool."

"I'm not sure what's gonna go down, Sul, but since you mentioned this, it's important to understand that her life is very different from ours."

"Yeah, like you going to El Gato for lunch and it being all over the world in matter of seconds?"

Duncan smiled. "Yeah. Like that."

"Dad, you're famous too. You're like the Ralph Lauren of outdoor gear."

"What?"

"I don't know. It's something Aubrey says. About how Ralph Lauren became the face of his company and lived the life he was trying to sell with his clothes and home stuff. She was watching a documentary. I wasn't paying attention. I had a test to study for."

"Well, I understand what Aubrey means, but I can go to El Gato and not have it all over the world in a matter of seconds."

"I'm just saying, it's a non-issue. If you like her and she makes you happy, who cares about anything else?"

In all that was going down, one thing he knew felt great.

He'd raised good boys.

"I'll handle your mom. Don't worry about it. Now go do something that might not involve cramming. Call Aubrey. Take your girl out. Have some fun. Live a little."

"No way to get summa living a little."

"Sul, there's more to achieve in life than achievements."

Sully grinned at him. "Epic, Dad. I was wondering what to get you for Christmas. I'm putting that on a coffee mug."

He shook his head but did it with his lips twitching.

"Okay, go study. I'll talk to you later."

"Love you, Pops."

"Love you too, kid."

They disconnected and Duncan was interrupted in pulling his shit together so he'd have the patience to deal with Dora if she was off the wagon due to Genny being back in his life, not to mention controlling himself from going over old ground neither of them could change with what she'd asked of their son that was the opposite of okay, when he saw the Tesla take off down the drive.

Apparently, his "larder" was not appropriately stocked.

That made him grin, but it faded when his eyes fell on Corey's letter again.

He was reaching for it when his phone chimed with a text.

He looked down at it, expecting something from Dora.

What he saw was a number he didn't have programed, but it had a six-oh-two area code.

And when he opened it, his smile was wide.

This is Imogen. You're right. We need to talk in order to have some closure. Do you have plans this evening? Could you meet me in the bar at The Queen at around 8:30?

No dicking around, he immediately texted back.

Yes.

It might not be right, but after getting that from Genny, it was what he was going to do.

So he opened up his text string with his ex-wife and asked, *Do you have time to talk tomorrow?*

He got a, *See you then.* from Imogen.

He was texting a, *Count on it.* back when he got a reply from Dora.

I saw. I'm fine. Don't worry about me. You've done enough of that.

He was staring at that in shock when another text came in from his ex.

Be happy, Duncan. We'll have lunch some time. If I'm not incarcerated after driving down to Tucson and holding my son at gunpoint to force him to study. Remain off Instagram. I'm deleting my account. He's killing me. Slowly.

It was not lost on him that when she found help that worked for her, Dora had come back. The woman he'd married and made a family with who he'd loved.

It was too late, what they'd had and built was gone, regrettably, but irrevocably.

But knowing she had this kind of lock on it, that she could joke and be real...

Again, for the first time in a long time, Duncan's breath was coming easier.

We'll do an intervention at Thanksgiving. He texted back.

If he survives that long. She replied.

He gave her a thumbs-up emoji and a smiley.

She returned an angry face and an eye-rolling emoji.

He was grinning when he went directly back to Genny's text and programmed her number in.

He was still grinning when he opened the Instagram account that he had not touched since his assistant had downloaded it on his phone.

It took him a minute, but he finally found it by searching #isitgonnabeimoway.

And when he found it, he could see it.

How they were bent toward each other, faces close, focus intense, no one in that restaurant but them.

They were having a deep, informative, but not entirely comfortable conversation.

The picture did not say that.

It looked like he was about to kiss her.

Hard.

And she wanted to swallow him whole.

Duncan was still grinning when he got up and walked out of his office.

Completely forgetting about Corey's letter.

CHAPTER 8

THE STEPS

Corey

Thirty-eight years earlier...

HE WAS SITTING on Duncan's back steps, waiting for him, when his friend strolled up.

As he did, Corey watched Duncan move, his body big and muscled, his shoulders wide, but all that didn't seem heavy or clumsy to Dun. He moved like he was born in that body.

Corey didn't know what it was, and it made him feel uncomfortable, and something else, something that seemed like he was kinda...*mad* that he knew Duncan would be that way even if his dad didn't make him play football.

Duncan just...*did stuff.*

It wasn't just all the hiking around.

He climbed trees to get better views. And he swam in the creek, saying swimming in a creek or some pond was "so much better than any swimming pool, *totally*." And his dad made him chop wood for the fireplace, and Duncan didn't mind that, because he was outside and he was moving and, "The smell of just cut wood, man, nothing smells that good." Or, "I could sweat forever, tackling a stupid dummy over and over. But this, *this* is the *good* kind of sweat."

Corey had never smelled just cut wood (or if he had, he didn't think about it because only Duncan would think things like that, everyone else knew that nothing smelled as good as cookies in the oven). Corey also had zero interest in tackling a dummy *or* wielding an ax.

Corey also didn't look like Duncan.

Nothing like it.

Oh, he'd gotten tall.

But as much as it sucked, he couldn't say they were wrong in calling him The Stick.

"So?" he asked, even if he didn't have to ask, what with that stupid look on Dun's face.

It was also that he knew.

He knew more than Duncan knew before Dun had gone off to do what he'd just done, kinda nervous, like he didn't already know it was *all good*.

Yeah, Corey knew. He'd been living this nightmare now for what seemed like *forever*.

Dun and Genny.

They were into each other.

Big time.

So before he even asked, before he'd even seen that fucking look on Dun's face, he knew she'd said yes to Duncan taking them out of the friend zone.

Asking her out.

Duncan sat on the steps beside Corey. He did this two steps down, and still, his big body seemed to take all the space.

Dun leaned back into his elbows and smiled at his backyard.

"We're goin' out on Saturday," he told the yard, not stopping smiling even when he was talking.

"That's fucking *awesome*," Corey lied, trying hard to sound like he was super excited, but that feeling was back.

The burn.

It was intense and it made him feel like he wasn't doing something he really, *really* needed to do.

Throw something.

Kick something.

Yell at something.

Hurt something.

Duncan dropped his head back and turned it so he could look at Corey.

And Corey braced at the happy look on Duncan's face.

God, he'd never looked that happy.

Maybe he'd never even *been* that happy.

"Kissed her, man."

Yeah.

Fuck yeah.

Corey needed to *hurt something.*

"Wow, whoa. Wow," was all Corey could think to say. Then he pushed out, "Cool."

Duncan's eyes moved again to the yard, real slow, like all drifty as he said, "She tastes like, I don't know, *fresh*. But warm. Like fruit, but not. Peach cobbler or something."

"Girls have lip gloss that tastes like that," Corey informed him of something he had absolutely no clue about seeing as he'd never kissed a girl.

Though he'd heard something like that.

Duncan turned back to him. "She wasn't wearing lip gloss and I wasn't talking about how her lips taste."

Corey was sickened.

Pissed.

And intrigued.

"You mean, you slipped her the tongue?" he asked.

Duncan nodded.

Then Corey watched as his friend shut down.

That was going to be it.

And he knew that before Duncan could say anything to draw that line.

That was all Corey was going to get.

This wasn't going to be his.

This was going to be *theirs*.

Duncan would kiss her more, and Corey would never know.

He'd touch her, and Corey wouldn't know that either.

Eventually, he'd have sex with her, and Corey also wouldn't know that.

Duncan wouldn't tell him when Genny sucked Dun's cock.

Or how she felt down...*there*.

But all that was going to happen.

It was going to happen.

Forever.

Forever it would happen.

Because nothing would break them up.

Not their three.

And now, not *their* two.

He knew that. Fuck, to his bones, he knew that with that look on Duncan's face.

How happy he was.

How *completely happy*.

Duncan had always been like this.

He always knew what he liked. He always knew what he wanted. He always knew how he wanted to be.

Now, he knew *who* he wanted to be with.

And when Duncan knew something, decided something, it just *was*.

Corey felt his palms get sweaty, his throat get hot, and he also felt his dick start to get hard.

Shit.

Shit, shit, *shit*.

That wasn't about Duncan.

It was about her.

Genny and her golden hair and her mouth that he now knew (but would never *know*) tasting like peach cobbler and thinking about getting a blowjob.

From her.

"Anyway, we're going out," Duncan said. "To dinner," he finished, like that was important.

And maybe it was.

"Not to the drive-in or something?" Corey asked, because that's where guys took girls on dates so they could make out and feel girls up. And it was cheap and dark and private, but not totally private. People could see them through the car windows, and they'd talk, and the guy could brag about how far he got, but others would *see it*, so they'd know, which was bonus points for a guy (obviously).

God, Corey didn't want that for Genny.

"No, the drive-in will be for like, when we're going together. Like, officially," Duncan declared.

Because that was going to happen.

Like…

Officially.

He could hear it in the sound of Dun's voice.

And that officially would be soon.

"Right," Corey mumbled.

"Do it proper-like, you know. Start with something fancy." He turned his head back to Corey. "It's Genny."

That said it all and Corey didn't have to force that nod, that agreement.

It was Genny.

Proper-like and fancy was the only way to go.

Duncan was just about to say something, but he didn't.

They heard the door behind them open before whatever Dun was going to say could come out and Corey felt his spine tingle.

In other words, he knew who was there before he even turned his head to look up.

"Jesus, what the fuck? You two bums got nothin' better to do?" Mr.

Holloway asked.

Another feeling shot through him.

And this feeling, Corey knew.

He knew it *real* well.

It didn't feel *like* anything. He knew exactly what it was.

He knew he wanted to get up, turn around and punch Duncan's dad in the throat.

"Boy, trash needs taken out, your mom's got dinner ready, and you better not have brought my goddamn car back without any fuckin' gas," Mr. Holloway said.

"There's plenty of gas, Dad," Duncan replied.

Mr. Holloway didn't even acknowledge Duncan spoke.

He looked at Corey like he was a pile of warm, steaming shit marring the broken concrete of his back steps.

"Don't you got homework or something to do?" he asked.

He didn't.

He'd already done it.

Corey never fucked around when it came to homework.

That was his way out of this shit town, his shit family, and his shit life.

So, no.

Hell no.

He didn't have homework to do.

Corey did his homework and then he did more of it to get extra credit because, just as well as he knew Duncan and Genny were into each other, he knew he was going to get out of this shit town, away from his shit family and say goodbye to this shit life.

"Yeah," he said, pushing up to his feet, glancing at his friend, muttering, "Later, Dun."

"See you tomorrow, Corey," Duncan replied. "Thanks for hanging and waiting for me."

"No probs," he mumbled, and took off.

It was no surprise that he didn't even get around the side of the house before he caught Mr. Holloway saying in a voice that begged to be heard, "Watch that kid, Bowie. I think he's a fag. And you're a good-lookin' guy. He's here all the time because he's pantin' after your ass. Even when he was young, always thought he was a little pervert. But he's older now and kids your age think with their dicks. Don't let him get a shot at yours."

That burn coming back, feeling like it would consume him, Corey stopped out of sight and listened.

"Corey's not gay, Dad," Duncan returned, voice firm.

Always.

Even with his huge freaking dick of a father.

Dun never let anyone shovel shit on Corey.

"Did I ask for your fuckin' opinion?" Mr. Holloway demanded.

"He's my friend," Duncan clipped out.

"If he's not a fuckin' fag, he's a fuckin' dweeb. Don't know why you waste your time with him."

"Because he's smart and because he's funny and because he likes football and basketball, but he knows there's a whole lot more in this world than just that. Like I do."

Corey didn't really like football and basketball.

He was just *supposed* to like them.

So he pretended he did.

"Whatever, the trash needs taken out. Get on that. I don't want to eat a cold dinner," Mr. Holloway ordered.

There it was.

That was what people like Mr. Holloway were like.

Duncan was sixteen years old, and Mr. Holloway was his dad.

But Duncan didn't back down.

After that whole hunting thing, Duncan stopped backing down.

Sometimes he'd be grounded, or Mr. Holloway would yell at him forever or make up stupid chores for him to do, but still, Duncan never backed down.

Corey had noticed when Mr. Holloway had started petering out and then he started doing it faster and faster.

He'd say shit, Duncan wouldn't eat it, and Mr. Holloway would shut up.

He heard the screen door slam, and he knew they'd gone in and

Duncan would be bringing out the trash, so Corey rushed away.

And he walked home thinking Genny and Duncan would look real good together. He was dark and she was light. They were both tall. They were both beautiful.

And okay, so he thought that about Dun, that didn't make him gay or anything.

It was just fact.

Corey felt safe in facts and that was a fact.

And those two liked each other, all the way back when, when they went to the fairy stream.

Maybe even before.

Maybe even when Dun threw that frog at her, he liked her.

And she liked him.

So they were going to date.

No surprise.

No biggie.

Whatever.

He wasn't going to lose either of them. He knew that for a fact too.

Genny would let Corey go when the sun exploded and took the earth with it. He knew it with the way she looked at his dad, all angry and her cheeks getting pink, when his dad was being a dick to him, and she was around.

He knew it.

No one looked at his dad like that when he was being a dick.

Not his mom.

No one.

Wait.

No one but Genny…

And Duncan.

So he wouldn't ever lose Dun either.

He'd never lose either of them.

No matter what.

Not ever.

He was safe in that.

Because that was a fact.

CHAPTER 9

THE DRINKS

Imogen

I sat at the bar, knowing this was a bad idea.

There were so many reasons it was a bad idea, it wasn't funny.

First, Cookie was upstairs, as delivered by Mary, who was already likely back in Phoenix, this as delivered by Rodney.

Chloe wasn't available to help her with getting my cat and car to me, so she did what Mary always did. Took the bull by the horns and got things done.

So now Cookie, her litter box, her food and water bowls, the placemat I kept under them and about a month's worth of cat food was up in my suite.

All of that along with the contents of four additional suitcases, including the huge ones I took when I spent time in Europe. Offerings, after I'd unpacked them, that I saw afforded me every possible wardrobe change (for an urban woman on the go, it should be noted, not a woman on a break in a casual mountain town), including accessories that did not stop at shoes and handbags.

I could not focus on why Mary was behaving like I was moving for half a year into the deluxe suite at The Queen.

I had a great many other things to focus on.

I'd managed to be able to spend about a half an hour with my cat in new surroundings before I'd had to go to dinner, and I didn't feel that was enough time.

She needed her mommy.

I'd been up to check when I returned from dinner, and okay, when I'd opened the door, I woke her up from napping.

But I still sensed the unease.

The second reason this was a bad idea was that, within seconds of sliding on my barstool, Matt had texted.

His text had included four words.

Who is this guy?

And a photo.

One of the ones taken of Duncan and I at lunch.

I'd had no choice but to text back, *An old friend of Uncle Corey's and mine. A long story. I'll catch you up later.*

Matt didn't reply.

Which was a concern, considering that photo looked like we were on a date, but one hundred percent not a first date.

More like the seven-hundred and fifty-seventh one.

Which, if it was a date with Duncan and me (and it wasn't), was maybe close to the right number.

But I thought making a big deal about it and pressing explanations on my son, when it was *not* a big deal *at all*, and would soon be easily explained away when I could get home and resume normal programming, was not a good idea.

Thus, I let it be.

The third reason was that I had a variety of wardrobe changes, and for some reason I could not even begin to understand, because this was *not* a big deal *at all*, I'd changed clothes to go to dinner with Trisha and Scott.

An outfit that Chloe brought over a couple of weeks ago.

Slightly faded dark-gray jeans. Slim black belt. Shiny, silky, blousy off-black top cut low. Stretchy black tank under it. And sexy red pumps that gave some serious toe cleavage.

I'd had a stylist, who Chloe fired, saying, "The woman dresses you like you're Betty White. You're fifty-two, not one hundred and two." And although this was not entirely true, including the fact Betty White was not that old (though she was close), it wasn't entirely false either.

Now Chloe was my stylist. And after self-appointing this role, she'd dumped half my closet (and by that I meant she auctioned it off for charity), declared my look was "edgy elegance" and then she proceeded to fill my closet with that.

I had to admit, since she took over, I'd made a lot of best dressed lists.

And wearing the clothes she selected for me, I felt like I'd somehow come back to myself.

But this was an issue now.

Because instead of looking like this was casual and it didn't mean anything to me, and thus I showed at drinks in the same outfit I'd been in at lunch, it looked like I'd made an effort.

Or I was up myself and I couldn't take Hollywood out of Prescott, which would be totally up myself.

I had a defense.

Mary had not packed a single thing that did not scream "Edgy Elegance!"

In fact, the only non-heeled shoes I currently had access to were the slides I'd packed myself.

But I could have worn those slides with this outfit.

Or I could have not changed at all.

And I did not do either.

The next reason this was not a good idea was that it was not lost on me that picture had made the rounds, and now there we'd be, at a public bar, Duncan and me.

If anyone took another snap, and it was a good possibility they would, it'd be a fan to a flame.

However, I felt it was less of a good idea to ask him to come up to my suite to chat.

No.

After the knee brush at lunch, I knew that was a very, very *bad* idea.

The last reason this was not a good idea was that I'd asked for this meeting with Duncan at all.

We did not need closure.

We'd had closure.

Twenty-eight years of it.

But did that stop me from asking Mary to get me his cell phone number?

No.

What was I doing?

"Genny."

I turned on my stool and looked up at Duncan.

And I didn't miss the casual plaid shirt he'd been wearing with faded jeans at lunch was gone and a nice button down with dark-wash jeans had taken its place.

He looked really, *really* good.

Oh hell.

We weren't going for closure.

We were both behaving like we were on a date.

"Duncan," I greeted.

He looked to the barkeep, who was coming our way, but he was unable to order.

Our attention was taken by a beautiful, impeccably dressed African American woman who was now at our sides.

Damn.

A fan.

"Ms. Swan, Mr. Holloway, I'm Sienna Sinclair."

Not a fan.

Or maybe still a fan.

But also the owner of the hotel.

"If you'd like to follow me, I think it'll be more comfortable for you to be seated in our brand-new VIP area," she finished.

Her gaze then slid to the side, and I twisted to look over my shoulder to see a rather cozy corner booth recessed in an alcove in the back, in front of which two members of staff were erecting an attractive, freestanding folding screen.

"If you'll give me your order, Mr. Holloway, I'll have it brought to your table," she said.

That cozy booth looked *cozy*.

But the way they were positioning that screen, someone would have to be very intent on getting a picture of us around it.

And it was much better than speaking with Duncan in my suite.

I grabbed my drink and slid off my stool.

Duncan ordered something that sounded like it was beer.

I expressed my thanks to Ms. Sinclair, who inclined her head before she led the way, and Duncan put his hand light to the small of my back to guide me to the booth.

I did not discourage this due to what it might look like if someone saw me doing it.

But I had no idea how I made it to that booth considering every iota of my attention was on the touch of his hand, no matter how light, so I wasn't sure how I managed to put one foot in front of the other.

Okay, just me asking for this meet was a very, very *bad* idea.

And that idea was getting worse by the second.

I slid in, put my drink on the small table, and Duncan slid in beside me.

Our hips were touching, and if I wanted to avoid that, I'd need to slide some more, which would put me on the floor.

I gritted my teeth.

Sienna Sinclair faded away after wishing us to enjoy our evening, and the staff closed us in with the screen, leaving only a small opening a human might, if they sucked in their tummies, get through.

I turned instantly to Duncan.

"I can't stay long. My cat is upstairs."

He blinked fast and asked, "I'm sorry?"

"My cat. My building has a sanitation problem and I can't return to my condo until it's sorted. So I'm staying here. And I'm close to my cat. I'm an animal lover, as you, well, um...*know*. So my assistant brought her up. She's a low maintenance cat, but she's still in new surroundings, so I don't want her up there alone for long."

"Your building has a sanitation problem?"

"I'm trying not to think of that, but yes, my building. I, uh...live in a condo."

"Right. Gen—"

"It's a really nice one. But it might be too big of one, because the kids are now gone."

"Okay. But, you see, Ge—"

"It's fancy though, not a hint of wood around. Lots of marble. Crystal chandeliers. No wood."

He didn't say anything, but he was now watching me very closely with an expression coming over his handsome face that was very, *very* dangerous.

Which meant I kept babbling.

"I've been there seven years. I love it."

"Do you now?" he murmured, his eyes falling to my mouth.

Ohmigod!

"Uh, yes. I have the most amazing view."

"Mm," he hummed.

My thighs started quivering.

My mouth kept blabbing.

"You should know that today is not normal. Maybe it's Prescott. But mostly it's you."

That got his eyes returning to mine.

"What's me?"

"Me being with, uh...*you*. And you being you. Well, me being me too, but you're also you."

There was silk in his deep voice, as well as humor, when he agreed, "I *am* me."

Why could I not stop talking?

I really couldn't because I kept doing it.

"What I'm saying is, I can go grocery shopping and everything without being recognized. At least, down in Phoenix."

"Is that right?"

I nodded, maybe fervently, and to stop doing that, I snatched up my drink and took a far-too-large sip.

The lime in the gimlet hit me hard with sour and it took a lot not to make a face.

Drink, bad.

I put it down.

"Excuse me," we heard from beyond the screen.

"Yeah?" Duncan answered.

A waitress squeezed around.

"Your drink, sir," she said.

His drink hit the table as did an elegant, cut crystal tall-sided bowl filled with a crisp bit of paper in which was tucked, to almost over-flowing, a bevy of seasoned chicharrones.

Yum.

"Would you like another drink, Ms. Swan?" she offered.

Absolutely not.

"No," I answered. "But thank you."

"I'll be around in a bit to check on you," she said, before she squeezed away.

I took a deep breath.

Duncan took a sip of beer.

I turned to him to get a firm hold on this conversation, which meant having it, and ending it, and walking away.

For good.

I didn't get that first word out.

"What's your cat's name?" he asked.

It came out automatically. "Cookie."

"I thought you were a dog person."

"I am. I travel too much for a dog. And my building doesn't let you have animals over a certain weight. So I've discovered my latent cat person."

"That sucks. The certain weight rule that is. Not you being a latent cat person."

"Yes."

He grinned at me and it was not lost on me it was all kinds of playful.

And woefully effective.

"I thought you rich, jet-set celebrities chartered planes and took your animals everywhere."

"Well, I might be a rich, jet-set celebrity, but I'm also a responsible pet owner, and I'm not certain dragging a cat, or a dog, all over the globe is good for the cat, or dog. Cookie notwithstanding," I hastened to add. "But only for this trip and only because she doesn't mind car rides…uh, much."

"What you're saying is, you didn't want to be without her, so you caved when you know she hated every second of being in the car on the way up here."

Cookie didn't seem worse for the wear.

In fact, she had found a cozy nook in the toss pillows on the bed to curl up in before I left for dinner, the very nook she was stretching out of when I returned.

Though Mary reported she'd been vocal the entire way up, and I didn't think Cookie was sharing her desire to get a better view out the windows.

"Well, *hated* is a strong word."

"Mm-hmm."

I wished he'd quit humming all deep and rumbly like that.

"Listen, Duncan—"

"I have five."

My head ticked. "Sorry? Five?"

"Animals." He reached for a chicharron. "Not counting the horses. Three dogs. A cat. And a rabbit."

He'd always loved animals.

All of them.

Even snakes.

So this did not surprise me.

Though I was probably more relieved than was healthy that he did not share he had a snake, since what would it matter to me if he did?

He started counting them down.

"Shasta, my rescue husky. Rocco, Sully's tripod silver receiver. Bounce, Gage's rabbit. Tuck, our cat. And my baby, Killer."

"Your baby?" I whispered.

"A Peekapoo. Pekingese, poodle mix. She weighs about twelve pounds. Could not believe that score at the shelter. Then again, they all were scores from the shelter."

He crunched into the chicharron.

"I thought you were a vegetarian," I noted.

"I avoid meat. I limit intake of products produced from animals, specifically cows and pigs, because cows cause an environmental issue, and the treatment of swine for consumption is unconscionable. Examples, I use almond milk and go for olive oil instead of butter. But I'm not a vegetarian."

Okay, well that explained that.

"Though, just to say," he continued, "as proved seconds ago, my conscious isn't exactly clear since I find it harder to say no to pork because...bacon, and well..." He dipped his head to the chicharrones with his lips twitching.

He'd always leaned toward pork. Even at restaurants, he'd go for a chop rather than a steak.

I didn't need this memory of how well I knew him.

"You have a twelve-pound girl dog named Killer?" I asked.

"My son Gage has an interesting sense of humor."

I could not get caught on thoughts of Duncan having a little dog he referred to as his "baby" or a son he spoke of fondly who had an interesting sense of humor.

What I needed to get caught on was guiding us to whatever closure we needed to achieve.

But curiosity got the better of me.

Because he'd always loved horses and always wanted to own one.

"How many horses do you have?"

"Three."

"Do you ride a lot?"

"Yes, seein' as I got three horses to exercise and the boys are at school."

"Where do you ride them?"

He crunched, chewed, swallowed, and said, "'Round my land. I managed to nab ninety acres, though it took me ten years of buying neighbors out."

"Oh," I mumbled.

"Most of that butts the National Forest, so we got plenty of space to ride," he shared.

"That's great," I muttered.

And I shouldn't ask.

I shouldn't want to know.

It shouldn't mean anything to me.

But I asked anyway.

Because it meant something to me.

"Your boys are at school?"

He nodded, took a sip of beer, set it aside and reached for another chicharron.

But he didn't take a bite.

He answered, "Sully's at Purdue. He's gonna save the world in ways his old man can't. He's studying to be an environmental engineer."

"Impressive," I said. And it was. "And Gage?"

"He's at University of Arizona, and I should have known things were going south when he majored in communications. Mostly, I think he needs to get the wild out of his system before he comes to work for me. They both had jobs at the store throughout high school. But Sully did it because his dad told him he had to. Gage did it because he liked to score chicks who were into hiking, climbing and trail running. But that's because Gage likes hiking, climbing and trail running. Sully does too, but he'd stop to dig in the dirt. Gage wouldn't stop until he reached the peak. But after Gage fails out of college, gets sick of being a river rafting guide or some shit like that, and gets serious, he'll come work for me."

"You're sure of that?"

He shrugged, ate his chicharron, and answered, "It doesn't matter. What matters is, whatever he chooses, he's happy."

So...

Duncan was not his father's son.

Duncan's dad was a plumber.

And I never sat a meal at their house—and I sat many meals at their house, both as a little kid hanging with her buddies, then as his girlfriend, times two—when Burt Holloway didn't mention in some form how someday Duncan was going to join him as a member of his union.

It was never fun, but the older Duncan got, the nastier the conversations became.

What, you too good to be a plumber, boy?

I like to be outside, Dad, and there isn't a lot of plumbing done outside.

Smart mouth. Always got a smart mouth. So...what? You're gonna be a park ranger, pussy shit like that? Glorified mall cop, hanging around feelin' like a big shot with nothin' to do.

Remembering this one particular conversation, which happened around the time Duncan was looking into what it would take to become a park ranger, and he'd made the mistake of mentioning that to his father, our conversation from lunch that day morphed over it and I wondered.

Because I got to LA, and what happened to me did not happen to hardly anybody.

I got an agent quickly.

A few commercial jobs.

I worked as a substitute teacher and had two roommates.

And I was cast in *Rita's Way* after only two other acting gigs, both as one-line, glorified extras, one on a sitcom, one on a gritty nighttime cop drama.

But then, I was off.

What would Duncan have done if he'd come with me?

I'd never heard of a River Rain store until *Rita's Way* signed off for good and I was starring in feature films.

A chain of stores didn't happen overnight.

And it didn't.

"Hey," Duncan called softly, and I focused on him. "You were a million miles away."

"I was remembering that dinner when your dad confronted you about being a park ranger."

He shook his head, took a sip of beer, but I stared at him with some surprise because his mouth didn't get tight, the skin around his eyes, nothing.

Nothing at all, when before, just the mention of his father could put him in a bad mood that it would take certain talents I'd honed to work out.

"He passed. Heart disease," he told me. "Five years ago. Mom's down in Goodyear. She should be up here, where I can keep a closer eye on her. But she has her women and her bowling club and whatever else she does, and she won't even discuss it. Not lost on me fifty years of marriage to Burt Holloway wasn't easy. It's like she's on perpetual vacation and I worry about her, but I can't find it in me to take it away from her."

I'd always liked his mom.

Ruthy Holloway was quiet, sweet, a great cook, a mom who loved her only son (and I had suspicions she kept it at one child deliberately, so Burt couldn't dig into another one) and a woman who was totally dominated by her husband.

"Goodyear isn't too far from me. I always liked your mom. I should go visit," I murmured.

"Baby," Duncan murmured back.

I snapped to, staring at him.

What was I thinking, telling Duncan I should go see his mom?

The expression on his face now was speaking volumes, and his mouth was opening to make them audible, and I was terrified what I'd do if he did.

"I have three," I announced.

He looked bemused, which was a far safer look than the one he'd been wearing the instant before.

"Three what?"

"Kids," I stated.

Again, he was opening his mouth.

But I kept speaking.

"There's Chloe, my oldest. She's a stylish, perfectly accessorized, never-ending trail of lit rocket fuel."

Something else moved over his face, I couldn't read it, but it didn't matter.

Yes, again, I kept talking.

"Then there's Matt. He came barely a year after Chloe. We...we...we..." I nearly pounded a fist on my chest in order to get out words that would indicate what any adult knew, children were the products of having sex, but somehow alluding to Duncan I'd had sex with another man, even if that man had been my husband for twenty-four years, had me regressing to a fourteen-year-old, "got pregnant again fast. He's in his second year of med school. At USC. We're very proud of him."

"Genny," Duncan whispered.

"Then there's Sasha. Our baby. We took a break after Matt. You have children so you know, they're a lot of work. Two babies that close together, I couldn't quit working, but I was very hands-on with my kids, so I was a walking zombie. This means Sasha is three years younger than Matt. She, like Chloe, elected not to go to college, and instead, is a 'student of the planet.' Her words. And I kinda wished this meant she was a sci-fi geek, chasing around the country, looking for UFOs. Which likely gives indication that I try not to be judgy, but I think it's been over a year since I've seen her when she didn't have fresh flowers woven into her hair and I'm not sure she owns a pair of shoes. Though, she does have a cell phone. And needless to say, I have concerns about all of that. Because she can use her cell for GPS, but she has no direction."

"Gen, I need you to listen to me."

No.

No no no no no.

He sounded serious.

Too serious.

I knew he didn't want to talk about closure.

He wanted to talk about the opposite.

But to get there, we had to talk about something else.

And I didn't want to talk about Corey. What Corey did to us. Who Corey really was and how vile that person turned out to be.

I didn't want to be reminded I put my faith in him, and years of life into our friendship, and he'd taken this magnificent man who was sitting beside me, who had a dream and worked hard to realize it, away from me.

I did not get to live his dream with him.

And he did not get to live my dream with me.

Because of Corey.

And maybe all of that would have turned into a disaster.

But it would have been *our* disaster.

Not Corey's.

So I didn't even want to think about Corey.

I wanted to talk about our kids and his acreage and his little dog called Killer.

"They're twenty-four, twenty-three and twenty, respectively," I blurted.

"Gen—"

"And I think—"

I cut myself off because my phone was ringing.

"A second," I said quietly, pulling it out of my back pocket, and seeing it was Matt.

My son never called.

Texts and emails and person to person, even if that person to person was over Skype.

That was Matt.

I didn't even know the last time I spoke with him on the phone, to such an extent, I was wondering if I'd ever actually spoken to him on the phone.

"I need to take this. It's my son," I told Duncan.

"Absolutely," Duncan replied.

I engaged, put the phone to my ear and asked, "Are you okay?"

"Right, Mom, don't speak and listen to me."

My eyes flew to Duncan and I knew the fear was there because our hips were touching, but then they became tight, the side of my thigh pressed to his, all because he'd wrapped his hand around the back of my neck and pulled me close.

"Matt—" I began.

"Listen, okay?"

"Okay, darling." My voice was wavering.

Duncan's fingers squeezed reassuringly.

"Now, I know you just lost him, but I can't sit on this anymore. Not with you getting your picture taken with one of his friends. And I know you're not going to like hearing this, but it's the truth. Dad felt the same way. And I think the girls did too, they just never said. But there was something not right about Uncle Corey. And I'm not real thrilled you're hanging out with one of his friends."

I fell forward, dropping my forehead to the tiny table, miraculously missing my glass.

And the chicharrones.

Duncan's hand didn't move through this, but his head did, and he whispered urgently in my unoccupied ear, "Baby, hey, hey, hey."

I sat up just as abruptly, did the *Phew!* gesture of fake swipe of forehead, and returned my attention to my son.

My protective son.

Who, even though his father was not entirely out of my life, had cast himself in the role of my protector because that was who his father taught him to be.

"Can you listen to me for a second now?" I asked.

"Yes, but—"

"No buts, Matt. Your dad and I spoke of this and he admitted you both felt that way. So I know. And what you said didn't upset me. Things have come to light where I'm fully aware that Corey had some significant issues, especially in regard to me. I'm fine. I can explain those to you the next time I'm in LA. But I can assure you that Duncan is no longer a friend of Corey's. He hasn't been for a very long time.

They haven't seen each other in decades. But we used to be friends, the three of us. And something Corey did drove me to seeing Duncan. So that's what's happening. Okay?"

"What'd Corey do?"

"Can we Skype about this later?"

"Only if you can assure me you're okay."

Now I was seeing Chloe's side of the argument in her lifelong debate that there was a place for little fibs.

"This is a lot, I can't deny it. But I'm fine. Truly. All right?"

"All right, Mom, but seriously. Who is this guy? You were practically making out with him."

"We weren't. It just looked that way. He's an old friend."

"An old friend?"

I gave Duncan big eyes.

His concern fled, his finger trailed my nape, but his hand disappeared.

Though he left his arm draped on the back of the booth.

And that nape touch shot all the way down my spine.

And farther.

Great.

"An old boyfriend," I admitted.

Duncan chuckled and nabbed his beer.

"Are you starting things up again?" Matt asked suspiciously.

"Matthew, my only son, I love and adore you. But can we not talk about this now, or maybe forever, please?"

"Holy shit," he whispered. "You're starting things up again."

"Don't you have some life-saving technique you should be studying?"

"I am currently incredibly grossed out, so no. I'm going to be looking into finding the nearest isolation chamber so I can lock myself in it and try not to think of my mother dating. But this conversation can be done."

"It's always so gratifying when you demonstrate how mature you are," I teased.

"Cut me some slack, Mom. I'm your only boy and no one will ever be good enough for you. And that includes Dad."

Uh-oh.

I dropped my head and said gently, "Matt."

"Nope. Not talking about that either, Mom. We'll Skype. Soon. Love you."

"Love you more."

He hung up.

I put my phone on the table.

Then I turned to Duncan. "I've recently learned that my son has never liked Corey. He thought he was a creeper."

"Sadly, your boy was very right."

Dammit.

There was nothing for it.

"We should talk about Corey."

The words were so tight, it was a wonder each didn't snap the both of us like rubber bands pulled too long.

"We need to talk about something else first, honey."

"I think—"

"Your daughter Chloe is right now stretched out on the sofa in my great room with a martini she ordered me to make her before I left, because I apparently make very good martinis, and my Amazon password, so she can order whatever she wants to stream."

I stared at him, unblinking.

"She came to me yesterday after you visited, and I know this won't come as a surprise to you, but she loves you very much and she wants to see you happy. It's my understanding you shared with her about you and me and she's decided what's going to make you happy is me. So it isn't coincidence Harvey and I were at El Gato today. And I haven't been let in on all the varied facets of her diabolical but ultimately loving plan. But I suspect your building is not having a sanitation issue."

I continued staring at him, unspeaking.

"She made me dinner tonight. Cheese soufflé followed by bouill-abaisse accompanied by a hearty loaf of bread and ending in chocolate mousse. All homemade. She told me this was her 'starter menu.' If I was lucky, she'd allow me to work my way up. Which blows my mind, considering what she made was the best thing to come out of my kitchen since it was built, and I do not suck as a cook. And neither does Sully."

That got me talking.

"I thought you said your ex-wife was a good cook?"

He seemed out-and-out astonished by this question.

And his answer was hesitant.

"Dora never lived in that house."

"You moved into a six-thousand square foot house after you divorced your wife?"

"No, I *built* a six-thousand square foot house after I divorced my wife. I had two sons who had a lot of friends and I hope like fuck they give me a ton of grandchildren."

I was out of questions.

Duncan said no more.

My mind remained a blank.

His didn't.

He touched my nape again.

I felt it down my spine again.

Then he asked gently, "Are you pissed at Chloe?"

To which, of course, I burst out laughing.

He waited until I was finished, and when I could focus properly again, I noticed that he seemed like he wanted to smile, but he wasn't sure it was appropriate.

"Can I take it that means you're not ticked at your girl?" he queried.

I shook my head, tsking, before I said, "Duncan, Duncan, Duncan. Although I'm sure in your fresh experiences with Chloe, this all feels rather unseemly. But I can assure you, this is downright tame. Now Chloe running the long con that lasted three years that meant her father and I allowed her to stay in France, not to mention paid for this extended stay. And yes, there was a boy. And yes, he was an *artist*. And yes, there are paintings of my naked, then nineteen-year-old daughter somewhere in France. And yes, this was not the only thing she got up to when she was over there, because she dumped that boy, and found other things to turn her mind to that made us pine for that boy. And yes, there was a period of time when I thought I might have to secretly sedate her father by slipping drugs into his beverages. So no, I'm not angry at my daughter for doing what my daughter does and being who she is. As long as you aren't angry at her for dragging you into it."

"I'm sitting here with you, your eyes are shining like they used to, so fuck no, Genny. I'm not angry at her. And just to say, she looks a little like you, but she's not one thing like you. But you should be warned, she's got me wrapped around her finger to the point she took my Tesla to the grocery store today and she has my Amazon password."

Oh God.

He liked my girl.

A lot.

"Duncan," I whispered.

His fingers were back around my neck and his face was again close, like at lunch.

And it was solemn in a way that both frightened and excited me.

"I want to explain to you what was fucking me up so much it made me believe Corey and let you go. And I want to get to know who you are now, Genny. Because I miss you like fuck. I have for twenty-eight goddamn years. And I wanna see if we can find something together again. I know it won't be what we had before. I also know, down to my bones, that if it's with you, it'll be amazing."

"I'm reeling that I read Corey wrong for so long and in doing so he made me lose so much," I admitted.

"Well, not that I wanna be in that club, but since we're the only two members, I'm probably the only one who can help you with that."

"There's also Sam," I pointed out.

"You wanna reach out to her?"

"I don't know. I'm not sure it'll make her feel any better, finding out Corey married her while in love with me and divorced her because he was in love with me, but he never cheated on her with me.

She's avoided me like the plague over the years, and when she couldn't, she wasn't very nice. But even if Corey wasn't close with his son, I was. He was a lost little boy and Corey practically ignored him during their visits. Corey eventually moved to LA, not long after I did, and now I understand why. So I found the schedule and made sure I was around for Hale. We formed a bond. We're still very close. And honestly, Tom's more a father to him than Corey ever was. But bottom line of that, Hale is also a member of our shitty little club."

"I do not find this surprising. Corey was seriously fucked up."

"Yes," I agreed.

"Come out and meet my animals tomorrow."

"Duncan."

It was shaky.

"At least come say hello to your daughter."

That made me crack a smile.

My smile fled when he pulled my face closer toward his and I thought he was going to kiss me.

And in that second, I wanted him to kiss me.

I wanted that very badly.

But he didn't.

I felt the swab of his thick beard across my cheek and his lips were at my ear.

"Please, Genny. It's quiet and there are no distractions and no cameras and you can have whatever reaction you want, including leaving. If that's what you decide, I'll let you go, and I won't bother you again. I'll hate it, but if that's what you need, I'll stand by it and that's a promise."

"They have delicious croissants here and amazing coffee and I like slow mornings. Can I come around ten?"

His forehead landed with a bang on my shoulder.

I shut my eyes tight and fought my chest heaving.

He wanted this chance.

He wanted it so very badly.

I allowed myself to press my jaw into his hair for just a moment before I took it away.

He lifted his head and looked into my eyes.

"You need me to pick you up?"

I shook my head. "Mary brought my car up today."

He nodded.

"Duncan?"

"Baby, until you decide you can't keep Cookie waiting a second longer, my ass is right here and not going anywhere. So...what?"

God.

God.

He really wanted the chance to get beyond our shit and get to know me again.

Me.

Genny.

I'd never be Imogen Swan to Duncan.

I'd always just be...

Me.

"Thanks for making my daughter a martini. I would say I don't know where she got that bossiness, but you've met my mom."

"Yeah," he said quietly. "I was thinkin' something was familiar."

"They were thick as thieves. Chloe was in mourning for over a year when she died. I had to get her counseling."

"Fuck, baby. How'd she go?"

"Dad died, and she threw a clot. It wasn't even a year after. She always got what she wanted, and she missed him so much. So I suspect she told her body to get with the program, it complied, making it quick and painless, so at least I'm thankful for that. And it got Chloe home from France, though I would have obviously preferred a different impetus."

That was indeed her impetus.

That and her father and I divorcing.

But that could wait for later.

Maybe.

"I always loved that dame," he muttered, letting me go and moving away.

But not far away.

"Mom *was* a dame, wasn't she?" I asked.

"I would say Marilyn Swan was the last of her breed, if I hadn't met your daughter."

I shot him a smile.

He watched me do it for a while.

And then he shot one back at me.

CHAPTER 10

THE OMELET

Chloe

She checked the clock on the microwave when she heard him coming.

And she was ready with a bright smile aimed his way when he strolled into the great room, headed her way, wearing pajama pants and a tee that was snug at his broad chest.

Yes, it'd be cool when her mom got to wake up to that.

The messy hair especially.

"*Bonjour!*" she cried.

His eyes were moving around the kitchen, taking in the various animals, three of whom were clamoring for his attention, those canine, one of whom was sitting on the counter where Chloe was, that one feline, and one that was bouncing around, that was leporidine.

What they were not doing was clamoring for food, since Chloe had already fed them.

He also checked out the coffeepot and the various bowls Chloe had on the counter.

"It's six o'clock in the morning," he stated.

"Yes," she agreed.

"I thought you young people slept until eleven," he remarked, moving to the coffee at the same time giving his dogs some rubdowns.

"I'll sleep when I'm dead and not before," she replied.

Duncan pulled down a mug and noted, "We try not to let Tuck up on the counters."

"I regret to inform you of the fact that Tuck has claimed me, and as his minion, I do as he says, and he wants up on the counter to observe my work and pass judgment. In his service, I cannot deny him."

Duncan was shaking his head, grinning and pouring coffee.

But he said no more on the issue of her new darling, Tuck.

She turned and winked at Tuck.

The svelte tuxedo cat with his upside-down triangle face and wicked eyes who currently owned her heart blinked at her languorously.

"I'm making omelets to order," she shared. "Your choices are cheese, chives, mushrooms, bits of turkey sausage patties and salsa."

"All of it," Duncan ordered.

"*À votre service*," she declared and turned to the skillet.

"Honey, you can calm down," he said in that deeper, richer gentle voice of his. "Your mom and I had a good talk last night and she's coming over today at ten to do more of it."

It seemed every muscle in her body released.

She made a mental note to take a bath in Epsom salts later.

For then, she just murmured, "Good." She pulled it together, swirling heated oil in the pan, and finished, "Though, I guessed that since you were home way past curfew."

He chuckled.

She wanted to start crying.

She pulled it together again and continued her work.

After a bit, he spoke.

"It's like this with us, Chloe. Genny and me. We're connected. But there's a lot to go over and we're both very different people now. And I'm telling you this because I don't want you to get hurt along this process should things take a nosedive."

And wasn't that just the killer?

That she'd hid it, had her back to him, and he'd sensed it.

"My friends call me Coco," she informed him.

"And my friends call me Bowie," he informed her right back.

She turned to him.

He was sitting at the island and Killer was in his lap.

Hot guy and little dog.

Man, she needed this to work.

"Why are you called Bowie?" she asked.

Coffee mug lifted to his mouth, he tipped his head at the range, and said, "Finish the omelets and I'll tell you. You need any help?"

She shook her head.

"You makin' one for you?"

She faked being utterly aghast.

"Food passing my lips before eight in the morning? That's positively barbaric."

He quirked a grin at her. "I see you're your mother's daughter in one way. She said she liked slow mornings. And back in the day, she was the same. Hated getting up early. Lived for the weekends when she could take her time."

"I suspect Mom hasn't changed much," she stated leadingly.

"I'm sensing you're right," he muttered.

So she wouldn't ruin it, she returned to the omelet.

She finished it up, plated it, put it in front of him with the fork, knife and napkin she'd already gotten out, then topped up both their mugs before she climbed up next to him.

Duncan had dropped Killer to the floor in preparation for eating.

Tuck jumped from the counter to the island and she cooed at him.

He gave her outstretched hand a sniff, but was more interested in sitting, swishing his tail, and watching Duncan eat.

For a moment, Duncan regarded the cat in his position that was verboten until Chloe arrived, before he sighed.

"All right, Bowie, tell me about being Bowie," she urged.

"I'm tellin' you this story 'cause you should know this story and what it says about me and what it says about the way I feel about your mom."

Her eyes grew wide. "Did she give you the nickname Bowie?"

He swallowed the bite he'd put in after he'd said that, shook his head and replied, "My dad gave it to me. The first time he took me hunting."

She was shocked.

She'd researched this man to within an inch of his life.

And although he was not a resolute opponent of that, he'd had a fair few things to say about hunters who did not follow fish, wildlife and game rules, and a fair few more things to say about poachers.

Especially the fat cat rich ones who flew to Africa and hired locals to drive animals from land that was designated protected game reserve to land that was not in order that they could shoot them.

Duncan Holloway had *lots* to say on *that* matter.

"Hunting?" she asked.

"I didn't want to go. Pitched one helluva fit. And he…was…*pissed*. He had a temper, but I kid you not, I thought he'd beat the snot outta me. He was that pissed. It terrified me."

"Did he beat you?" she asked quietly.

He looked her in the eye in a way she knew what he said next was important.

"Never once. Never laid a hand on me."

"Oh," she mumbled. Although glad, unsure, since the man didn't beat his son, why it seemed that important.

"But I thought he was gonna do it, so I went hunting with him. And he rode my ass in the car, and he rode my ass in the woods, and he didn't let up until he had to be quiet so he wouldn't spook the deer. I was twelve and a goddamn mess. He'd taught me how to shoot. I had the rifle. And I was scared as shit of that thing because I knew the power it wielded and I was shakin' so bad, I thought, once I got my finger near the trigger, I'd hurt him or me. But fear can also give you focus. Because when we saw that doe, and he told me she was mine, I downed her in a shot."

Chloe stared at his profile as he said this to his omelet, and even in profile, his pain was so obvious, so palatable, she felt it with him.

He was fifty-four.

Forty-two years he'd carried that pain.

Apparently unabated.

"He made me gut her where she lay. Handed me his bowie knife and made me gut her. I didn't get sick. Didn't even feel nauseous. I did what I was told with his hand on my shoulder, squeezin' so hard, I thought his thumb would break my clavicle. And he did this tellin' me from then on, my name was Bowie, and he'd never been so proud of me in his life."

He ate more omelet.

Chloe didn't say a word.

When he'd swallowed, he told his plate, "A father never so proud of his son in a moment of death he forced his son to create, a son who had no desire to do that. That was the only time I made my father proud. But I didn't make him proud. He *made* me make him proud."

"Duncan," Chloe said softly.

He turned his eyes to her.

"I never went hunting with him again. He grounded my ass at least two dozen times for what he called disrespect because I flat refused to do it."

"I'm glad," she whispered.

He nodded shortly to acknowledge her comment and kept going.

"It was about control. It took me a long time to realize it, well past losing Genny. Men like him don't make *men*. They make ignorant, mindless automatons who go on to create more of the same if the cycle isn't broken. I'm not saying at twelve years old I should have manned up and told my father to go fuck himself. I'm saying he was proud of me because he thought making me kill that deer, he was going to mold me in his image. And that was the meaning of his life. He did not create a child to nurture him and set him free on this world to find happiness and do good. He created a child in order to live longer, because it was all about him, not one thing to do with me."

"You're so right," she agreed.

"But that's beside the point."

"Okay."

"The point I need to make is, I did what I did to your mother, and the regret I feel for that is fierce. But you need to know, the thing I regret most in my life is that I had a choice that day. A possible beating for me, or the life of that deer. And I picked killing that deer. He'd never laid a hand on me, Chloe, and I still picked that deer. And every time he'd lose it and I'd think, 'now's the time, he's gonna whale on me,' and he didn't, I remembered that deer. I remembered I took her vitality to save my own ass. And to this day, I prefer to be called Bowie to remind me never to be that person again."

"I understand that," she said.

"Make no mistake, I wish like hell I'd done things differently with your mom."

"I understand that too."

"But if I had one thing in my life I was allowed to go back and change, I would not have killed that deer. It says nothing about how I feel about your mom or the pain I caused her. It says something about the man my father was trying to force me to be that I had to overcome before I could really be with her. But the truth of it is, mostly, it's about that deer."

She nodded. "And that's understood too. And it doesn't make me feel badly toward you. In fact, I get it. I've never killed anything. But if I did, I probably would wish that too."

"Okay, honey," he said in his lovely gentle tone. "Now I need to understand why it means so much to you, me being with your mom."

Sneak attack.

Yes.

She was pulling nothing over on Bowie Holloway.

"I want her happy."

"It's more than that. You're sharp as a knife, and you're lethally loving. But you do not strike me as a woman who focuses her formidable energy on a whim."

"Dad and her are never going to get back together," she blurted.

"Okay," he said.

He was going to say more, but she spoke fast.

"I'll let her explain why."

"I'd appreciate that."

"She needs someone strong to protect her."

He shot straight on his stool and practically barked, "*Why?*"

Yes.

She was right.

Oh, hell yes, she was.

Shewasrightrightright.

It was him.

"She doesn't have a stalker or anything," she assured quickly. "She's just..." she shook her head in short shakes, "She's just Imogen Swan."

"Your mom is strong and capable."

"It isn't about her."

"What's it about?"

She rolled her shoulders. "It's about me."

"What about you?"

"I just need to know she's looked after."

It dawned on him, what she wasn't saying, and the man she was coming to know, she should have known it would.

"Divorce sucks," he murmured.

"Yes, it does," she said bitterly.

"She's going to be okay, with or without me."

"I'd rather her be okay with you."

It took him a second, his hazel eyes concerned and warm on her.

And then he said, "Me too."

Chloe relaxed.

Then she declared, "No offense, Bowie, but your dad's a dick."

"He's dead."

"No offense, Bowie, but I'm kinda glad."

He grinned at her, shaking his head, and replied, "None taken, Coco."

"Though, well done you for breaking the cycle."

He kept grinning and shaking his head, but he said nothing.

"I'll vamoose after Mom shows so you two can have some privacy."

"That'd be appreciated."

"But be forewarned, I'm not leaving because this is the best vacation I've ever had."

He burst out laughing.

She watched.

Then she reached out and forced Tuck to endure the indignity of enjoying some chin scratches.

After that, she climbed off her stool to do some tidying.

CHAPTER 11

THE TOUR

Duncan

"*A*ren't you nervous?"

Chloe was standing at his side on the porch, both of them watching the black Cayenne roll up the drive.

Since breakfast, she'd morphed from pretty girl in pajama bottoms, cami and Sully's purloined flannel shirt to fashionista in jeans, slouchy sweater belted at the waist, and shoes he knew—and did not get why women did not find it funny and stop doing it—they called booties.

The heels again were high.

He was learning not to worry about it.

In fact, at this point, he'd probably be more concerned if she wore flats.

"With age, honey, you learn a lot of shit. One of the things you learn is that, in this world, there is absolutely nothing you can control, except your own actions and reactions."

He looked down at her noting, not for the first time, she was visibly nervous.

And one of many things she made clear about her personality, Chloe Pierce was not a nervous person.

Maybe she was thinking her mom was going to be ticked at her.

Mostly, he suspected, it was wanting what was to come to work.

"Don't get me wrong," he continued. "I want with all I am to carry on the good work Gen and me started last night. But I got one job in this and all I can do is do it right. I fully intend to do that. What comes of that is beyond my control and the only thing I can do is react when it happens in a way that's best for your mom."

"You know…" she hesitated and then, "I shouldn't say it."

He turned fully to her.

And he got down to it.

For him.

And for her.

Because whatever was going to happen was imminently going to happen.

And this had to be said.

"Whatever goes down with your mom, Chloe, you and me, we have what we have, and I want you to know, it means something to me. If things don't work out with Genny, I get I'll likely lose you. And you're an extraordinary young woman. So that will pain me. But I'll understand, and we'll have had our time. And I already know it's an honor that you gave it to me. But while we're having it, I don't want you to feel you can't say something to me."

She stared up at him, expression open and sweet, and yeah.

Someone was in for a helluva ride with Chloe Pierce.

But when that ride was over, life would be really fucking good.

"You remind me of my dad," she blurted.

It had not been lost on him, in coming home last night from Genny the way Genny had been at the bar, getting his laptop, and doing what he'd not once allowed himself to do: a deep dive into her life—that there were definite physical, and it would seem if he could believe what he read, other similarities between him and Tom Pierce.

Duncan was unusual because he didn't have a type. He enjoyed women. Height. Weight. Race. None of that mattered. He was attracted to a variety of things.

Which was evidenced by the fact Gen was tall, slender and blonde, Dora was just under average height, curvy and brunette and Betsy was tall, voluptuous and mixed race.

But they were all funny. They were all loyal. And they were all motivated.

But it was clear Genny had a type.

Something that didn't bother him, and not only because Chloe had openly, and not unwittingly, but perhaps not understanding how crucial it was, shared that Gen and her ex would never get back together.

Tom Pierce, as far as he could tell, was halfway to sainthood.

The public didn't know something, though.

And neither did Duncan.

Considering the fact that family still seemed very tight, he just hoped, if Genny gave that to him, he didn't lose his shit when he found out.

Onward from that, he'd discovered that neither of them had dated since the divorce.

It was just over a year old, but even so, they were both vital people, it was high time to move on.

Until Chloe had shared what she'd shared that morning, Duncan had found this concerning. Because it might be they couldn't move on because they were still hung up on each other.

Now, he just saw it as something else made clear at the bar.

Genny was out of practice with this shit.

Which was why, last night, sitting next to a man she wanted, she was cute, nervous and a babbling mess.

He'd seen her that way twice before.

When she was coming to terms with their mutual attraction in their teens.

And at Corey's wedding, before he'd taken her home, they'd torn each other's clothes off and had sex on the carpet five feet from her front door.

"I find that a compliment," he told Genny's daughter.

"It was meant as one," she replied. "And newsflash, Bowie, I love my mom loads. But I'm not the type of gal, and she isn't either, that would let anything stand in the way of something that means something. And it means something, you and me being *amies*. So my mission today is to find some boots so we can go riding tomorrow. And I'm leaving them up here because I have no use for riding boots in Phoenix. And because we're going to go riding again."

"Your wish is my command," he replied.

"As it should be," she stated.

Christ, he liked this kid.

He grinned at her.

She shot him a sassy smile then turned to the drive and cried, "*Ma mère chérie!*" and flung herself down the steps.

His body automatically jolted.

Nope.

He was still worried about her in those heels.

"My dastardly, nefarious daughter!" Genny, who was out of her car and rounding the hood, cried back.

But her face said she didn't mean it.

And Duncan started chuckling.

"You know you love me," Chloe stated, throwing her arms around her mom.

"She makes it hard. I best the mother of the year competition every year with all her varied tests, but I do it," Genny called up to Duncan, and he noted she was holding her daughter close.

Duncan watched, but he did it aware there were things he refused to see.

No.

Feel.

He'd unpack that later.

Maybe with Genny.

More likely with Harvey.

They broke apart only for Chloe to seize Genny's hand and start dragging.

"Come!" she shouted. "You must have *le grand tour*."

"Lead the way, my darling," Genny said unnecessarily, since her daughter was pulling her up the steps.

Duncan watched and noted their outfits weren't much different.

Gen's sweater was crewneck and fitted. She had a little scarf tied around her neck. And the heel height on her booties wasn't stratospheric.

Still not Prescott.

But at this point, he couldn't imagine either woman in anything less.

Chloe tugged her mother to a stop in front of him.

"Hello, Duncan," Genny greeted.

"Genny."

She looked nervous again and unsure what to do.

So he caught her by the side of the neck, pulled her in and up, and kissed her cheek.

The woman was blushing when he let her go.

"*Maman, vraiment?*" Chloe murmured teasingly.

"Shut up," Genny mumbled.

Duncan made note look up the word "*vraiment*."

"Tour!" Chloe exclaimed. "Then I'm vanishing so you old people can do boring things like chat over coffee. Come, Mummy. Come, Bowie."

And off Chloe went, again dragging her mother with her.

But Genny looked over her shoulder and mouthed, "Bowie?"

She knew.

He was steadfastly "Duncan" to outsiders.

He was "Bowie" to those he let in.

He shrugged.

She disappeared inside his house.

He followed but stopped a few steps in, even though Chloe was pulling Gen to the great room at the back of the house.

He then looked around.

He'd designed this place, came once a week to watch it go up and lived there for five years, but it was like he was seeing it for the first time.

The square entry was very large, open, and this feeling was increased by the upstairs gallery that ran the entire space. There were seating areas up there, one recessed in an alcove. The walls were covered in shelves that held books, things Duncan had picked up while traveling, framed pictures of the boys or their terrible, but cute and hilarious, artwork from when they were little and trophies his sons had earned.

The back of the house was a great room that had two-story, floor-to-roof windows and a view of the lake curving around the back of the property, the forest, and the mountains.

Off to the right of that, the open plan kitchen with a walk-in pantry, access to the four-car garage and wide doorway to the dining room. And to the left, hidden beyond the wall where the large stone fireplace was, was utility and laundry as well as a powder room.

The rest of the house, upper and lower floors, had two halls leading off each side of the entry (down) and gallery (up).

Downstairs there was his office. A den. The dining room. A room that held pretty much nothing but an antique pool and poker table, because Duncan and his buds liked to play poker and pool. A couple of guest baths, because there was a lot of space, and when you needed one, you didn't want to have to walk miles. And a game/media/TV room, because he didn't want his boys hogging the television with their game play, nor was he a fan of seeing them on their asses for hours, so since they dug that on occasion, he gave them space where he didn't have to look at it.

Upstairs were all bedrooms, each with their own en suite bathroom, and the master had a balcony and a pretty damn spectacular view of the lake, forest and mountains.

It was furnished in comfortable, sturdy furniture and decorated in family, west, old west and southwest with some mission and Native American thrown in.

It was masculine.

Already felt lived in.

And it was entirely overkill.

He felt a pang in his side at holding back the need to bend double laughing.

Sure, in his current, smug self-actualized state, he could admit this was a realization of a dream.

But it was also a massive, six-thousand-square-foot fuck you to his dead dad.

And last, it was a house Imogen Swan would feel comfortable in.

Because no matter the sturdiness of the furniture, it was top of the line, looked great and cost a whack.

And the west, old west, southwest and Native American stuff was mostly art, carvings, statues, weavings, antiques, and it had all cost a small fortune.

She wasn't even a dream, the idea of Genny coming back into his life. Until his assistant got a call from her assistant a few days ago, not even a possibility.

But he'd built this for her.

For Genny.

For the woman she was today and the man he'd always wanted to be for her.

And he could not deny that.

"You look amused," Genny noted, coming back into the entry.

"I am."

"Is it because my daughter, who does not live here, has commandeered guide duties and is giving me a tour of your home?" she asked.

"No," he answered.

She tipped her head to the side in curiosity.

Chloe ignored this exchange and pulled her to the stairs.

"I won't bore you with the rest of down here. It's all man stuff, outside the dining room, which you've seen. And the den, which has no purpose, since the entirety of the house is set up for men to do indoor manly things, and the den is no different. Therefore, that would be the room a woman could requisition and cover in floral wallpaper and chintz furniture. We'll save that for last. Now, we'll go to my bedroom. Which, if you don't poke yourself on the sharp things, *is divine*."

He didn't miss Genny glanced at him several times as she went up the stairs.

But he waited until she and Chloe disappeared down the hall before he went to his office, grabbed his laptop, took it to the kitchen, refreshed his coffee, and opened it up.

The room he'd put Chloe in was the room he'd designed for when his mom came to visit.

Ruthy Holloway loved her boys, but she also loved to read and have quiet times, and it wasn't lost on Duncan she savored these after living in a house with a man who claimed every inch of space as his own and demanded every second of attention for the same.

Duncan wouldn't describe the room as "divine," but for his mom, he'd made sure it was damned comfortable and designed to be relatively self-contained.

It included a larger walk-in closet than the other bedrooms had (save the master, which had two). It had a lounge area. It was the only room outside the master with a balcony, though it was much smaller. And it had a closed-away niche that had cabinets, a counter that held a coffeemaker and a wine-rack, and a small built-in fridge, all of this offering snacks, beverages, with not a small selection of wine.

It was a cool room.

But he sensed that was their current destination not because it was a cool room, but because mother and daughter needed some time, and he was down with giving it to them.

He was not wrong.

Twenty minutes later, he was standing at the island, replying to an email when they reappeared.

"May I liberate the hounds, warden?" Chloe asked.

He'd put the dogs in the utility so they wouldn't overwhelm Genny.

"Have at it," he invited.

Gen wandered his way.

Chloe went toward the utility room.

"My daughter has made a mess of your guest room," Genny shared.

Duncan had two boys. Duncan was a veteran of many messy rooms.

Therefore, Duncan shrugged.

"I'm glad you feel that way, because Tuck has nested in a cashmere sweater in a way I think he might be most annoyed if he was forced to give it up and Bounce has made a hutch of her suitcase," she remarked.

Duncan grinned.

The cacophony began, heralding the imminent arrival of "the hounds" which reminded him.

"Baby, Rocco's got some strength. Missing his front leg, he's developed muscle in a way other dogs don't. It can be surprising. Be aware. Yeah?"

She nodded quickly, turned, and then he lost her.

Because she squatted so low, he could only see the top of her head.

"Oh, my goodness. Oh, my darlings. Look at you precious beings," she cooed.

Shasta barked her greeting.

Killer scooted and whirled around.

And as suspected, Rocco tackled her flat on her ass.

She let out a cry and started giggling.

Duncan moved positions to get a better view.

They were all over her.

"You're not going to have any makeup left, Mother, if you keep letting them kiss you like that," Chloe warned.

Gen made not one move to stop them from licking her. "If I need to, I can touch up using your things."

"You are forbidden to get dog saliva residue in my Chanel cosmetics."

"I'll buy you more."

"Well, okay then," Chloe huffed.

Christ.

He loved these two.

He loved them.

He didn't question it; he just knew it.

With only half an hour in their combined presence, he knew to his gut and bones, Genny, the mother, and Chloe, her daughter had his love until the day he died.

And he suddenly wished he had daughters and wondered what Sasha was like.

But he refused to dwell on that.

"Well?" Chloe demanded.

Of him.

"Sorry?" he asked her.

She pointed at her mom. "Are you not going to rescue her from canine carnage, the canines perpetrating the carnage being yours?"

Duncan didn't get a shot to answer.

Genny did.

"Stop being dramatic."

"For the last time, that's never going to happen!" Chloe announced on an outraged cry. "Now, I'm leaving. I can witness this no longer."

On that, she stomped to the island, nabbed her bag, then stomped toward the door to the garage, smacking her leg and calling, "Come here. Come to Auntie Chloe. Come say goodbye. I'm going to be gone for a while, and you're going to miss me because I'm pretty sure Daddy doesn't give you full turkey sausage patties as treats."

Jesus.

She was right.

On two counts.

One, he did not do that.

And two, heading toward the door to the garage, so the dogs knew she was departing, they defected the woman who was a human-size dog toy on the floor for the woman who gave them turkey sausage as treats.

Duncan went to Genny and helped her up.

"Ta ta, *mon ami et ma jolie maman*. I'll text before I head back. Be good," Chloe called.

Then she was gone.

The dogs stared at the door in confusion.

"Is my makeup a mess?"

Duncan looked from his dogs to his Genny.

There was a smudge of black at the corner of her left eye, but otherwise, she'd come out unscathed.

"Not bad, though I don't know how important it is to you, so the powder room is through there."

He pointed across the room.

"Be back," she murmured, hustling that way.

The dogs chased after her.

"Stop!" he ordered. "Enough!"

They skidded, turned and raced to him.

And when they arrived at him, *he* nearly went down.

Gage was petitioning for another one.

Duncan's youngest had some asinine argument about how having five pets upset the balance of the universe because the number needed to be even. He was hoping for a cat, but Sully, who'd bought into this shit, was pushing for another dog.

Duncan's response was, "When you flunk out of U of A, you can get another animal because you'll be around to feed them and take care of them as well as the horses, chickens, and anything else I make you do to be all over your ass for flunking out of college."

That ended the discussion.

But right then, he gave orders for the ones he had to cool it, which Shasta and Rocco did, but Killer totally ignored him, and he ignored his baby girl doing that.

He then heard a noise coming from the garage and was still smiling when Genny came out of the bathroom.

"Now what's amusing you?" she asked on her way over.

"Your daughter took my car."

She stopped dead in the middle of the room, arched far back with her hands clenched at her chest, and called to God, "Please, *please* let there be a partner out there who can handle the handful she is or make her a woman who is perfectly fine in her own company *for eternity. Please.*"

"Babe?" he called.

She looked his way.

"That sedation you considered for your ex?"

She nodded.

"It wasn't because she's a handful. It was because *she's a handful*. He knows that. She's the reason shit like duels was invented. You should be praying for the guys, or gals, or whatever she's into. Because there's probably a pack of them she's already laid waste to in her wake. They're the ones who need your prayers."

"Now I think *I* need sedation," she said, finishing making her way to him.

"Sorry, I only got coffee."

She grinned and stopped at the island.

The dogs fanned out all around her, hoping she'd collapse on the floor and play.

Instead, she looked to his laptop and a hint of worry shadowed her face.

"Do you need to work?"

There was no denying it.

All that was happening, he was getting behind.

Gen in his house for the first time, there because she was ready to talk things through, no way in fuck he was working.

"No."

She nodded, biting her lip.

She started to say something, but he asked, "You wanna meet the horses?"

"I want to meet the horses and see the chickens, but Bowie, maybe we should talk."

He closed his laptop, kept his hand on it, rested his weight in his other hand on the counter, and queried, "Something new on your mind?"

But she was staring at his laptop.

"Genny, I don't need to work," he assured.

"You did that," she told his hand.

"Sorry?"

Her eyes came to his. "Even back then when things weren't..." she lifted a hand a circled it, "*heavy*, like they are now. If something was on my mind, you dropped everything. And listened."

"Genny," he said softly.

She drew in breath and let it out, saying, "I've had my coffee. I try to keep it at two cups, only in the morning. But I can hang if you want to make another cup and maybe we can go on the back porch and chat?"

He was a coffee fiend. Always had been. Drank it all day. Caffeine didn't affect him, or his sleep.

She knew that, but even if she didn't remember, it didn't matter.

It was time.

And he'd pushed for this.

But he was fucking dreading it.

He refreshed his cup. Led the way to the back porch.

Genny came with him.

She settled in an Adirondack chair that was angled to the lake.

He settled in standing and leaning against a roof post, facing her.

She didn't look at his view.

Her gaze was glued to him.

It was time to do this.

Then face the consequences.

"I'll start," he said.

"Please do," she replied quietly.

"I never felt good enough for you."

Pain slashed through her features and it took all he had to stay where he was.

But she whispered, "I know."

"It wasn't you."

"I know."

"It was my dad."

She nodded.

"And Corey played us both."

She nodded again.

"I let him because that was where my head was at. Yesterday, I realized, there was a part of me that nagged day in and day out since it happened that I knew to my soul you didn't step out on me. But I jumped on that excuse to let you go because I had to. Because I needed to set you free for you. But also, for me, because I had something to prove."

She rolled her head on her shoulders. Pressed her lips together.

But said nothing.

"To Dad and to myself."

She finally spoke.

Softly.

And it was a statement.

Not a question.

"But not me."

"Not you," he confirmed.

She got up and he had no idea what she'd do after he confessed that.

Confessed the rotten truth that it wasn't really Corey being a slimeball.

It was Duncan.

And in his head, her knowing that without doubt, even more than she had to know it before, he thought was worse.

She was too classy to just take off.

But with whatever goodbye she gave him, he had to stand there and take it.

And then let her walk into his house, get her bag, only to walk out of it, get in her car and leave.

He felt sick to his stomach.

But for her, he could not move.

So he didn't.

She stood for long moments, studying him.

Then she looked to the lake.

To his dogs who were pressing against the windows with their noses.

And back to Duncan.

She then walked to him and lifted her hands.

She didn't shove him into the post in fury.

She set them on his chest and pressed.

He held his breath.

Up.

And she pressed against his shoulders.

Up.

And she curled them around the sides of his neck.

Up.

And she cupped his jaw.

She watched her hands as they did this.

He watched her.

Not breathing.

Then she took her hands from his face, slid her arms around his middle, and fitted herself to his front, resting her cheek to his chest.

He let his breath go and closed eyes that were suddenly stinging.

"I couldn't have helped," she whispered to his shirt.

"No," he grunted.

"You had to take that journey yourself."

"Yeah."

"Corey still played you."

"Yes."

She let out a little sigh and melted deeper into him.

Good Christ.

Christ.

Genny.

He wrapped an arm around her, twisted his neck, and rested his jaw on her head.

"But you know I always believed in you."

He shut his eyes tighter and felt the wet slide over the bridge of his nose.

"Yeah, baby. I knew I always had you."

"Then as long as that's the case, let's figure out what's next."

Fuck.

Christ.

Fuck.

He had to open his eyes to put his mug on the railing, something he did and quick.

Then he curled his other arm around her shoulders and squeezed her tight.

She squeezed him back.

His voice was hoarse when he started, "I wasted—"

"Stop it."

"We lost—"

"Stop it, Bowie."

He shut up.

"It would have happened, you know, somewhere along the line," she said.

Yeah.

He knew.

"It could have been my career taking off as quickly as it did. It could have been you not liking LA, because I'm not sure you've been there, but it's not one thing like here."

A startled chuckle burst from his chest and he kept holding her tight.

"I've been there, Gen, and I'm not a fan."

"I bet not," she muttered.

They were silent.

She spoke first.

"It would have been something."

"Yeah."

"We weren't ready."

"You were. But I wasn't."

She tipped her head back. "You let me go and I let you let me go, Bowie. One could argue it isn't the place of a woman accused of something like that when she didn't do it to chase after her man. But you knew me better and I knew you did. And I didn't chase after my man."

"I'm not real comfortable with you takin' any of the blame for this, baby," he informed her.

"There are a variety of incidences where men and women fuck up and do hurtful things for no reason at all. Things that are avoidable, and if they do them, they're unforgiveable. This is not one of those cases. Trust me," she gave him a careful smile, "your fuckup was really, really *huge*. And I have no crystal ball to see what would have become of us if you didn't believe Corey. But something you said yesterday has stuck with me. We were too young for something that big. It was going to overwhelm us eventually. So, you know, wresting my rose-colored glasses from the gnarled, twisted, but deathly strong fingers of the hands of time and perching them back on my nose, what you did probably saved us so we could have whatever we're going to have now."

"Wresting your rose-colored glasses from the hands of time?" he teased.

She gave him a shake with her arms.

He got serious and said, "I'll take that view through those glasses, Genny. And we'll take it from here."

"Good," she stated firmly.

Christ, he needed to kiss her.

"But this does not let Corey off the hook," she declared.

Obviously, he did not kiss her.

"Baby—"

"If you're going to petition for my forgiveness of him, forget it, Bowie."

"No way in fuck I'd ever do that."

She stared up at him.

"And that's not totally about what he did to me and you. It's about what he kept doing to you all these years. Knowin' the lie he told and how it affected you and bein' close enough to you, your kids call him Uncle Corey. Which, by the way, makes me wanna throw something every time I hear Chloe say it."

Motherly concern washed into her face and she asked, "Do you talk about him a lot?"

"No. Mostly she bosses me while alternately feeding me and hiding the fact she's spoiling my animals so this house will never be the same if she's not in it, which I know is her goal. Chloe Pierce will never leave a place the same as it was before she arrived there. It's a singular gift. And Tuck is gonna hate me forever when I make it clear the counters are again off-limits."

She jostled him happily and set her chin on his chest, her eyes shining.

She was proud of her girl, as terrorizing as she was.

And he loved that.

"Gage is gonna have a massive crush on her," he muttered.

"How old is he?"

"Nineteen going on eleven."

She started giggling.

"And your older boy? Sullivan? How old is he?" she asked.

"He's twenty-one, and those hands of time you wrested your glasses from?"

"Hmm?"

"Those were his."

She giggled harder at that, so much, he felt it against his body.

Now was a better time to kiss her.

And he was going to do that.

God, Christ, tasting Genny again.

He couldn't fucking wait.

He started to drop his head.

Her laughing eyes grew wider then got serious right quick.

She was coming up on her toes…

"Well, hell."

They both froze.

"*Harvey!* I told you!"

Genny leaned to the side to look beyond him.

Duncan didn't have to look.

But he did anyway, holding her close and twisting his head to look over his shoulder.

Harvey and Beth were standing beyond the railing at the back corner of the porch.

"You didn't answer your doorbell," Harvey accused Duncan's way.

"Yeah, because he's necking with his girl on his back porch, you big dork!" Beth snapped, smacking her husband's arm and it looked like she did it hard.

"Woman! How was I supposed to know? Yesterday, she'd barely look at him."

"Omigod!" Beth turned and homed in on Genny. "He lives with four women and he *still* has no clue."

"I know about the three-day shampoo regimen," Harvey clipped.

"Well bravo for you," she shot back.

"You two wanna stop yellin' at each other long enough for me to make you both a cup of coffee, and Beth, I don't know, maybe before that, introduce you to Genny?" Duncan asked.

"We absolutely, one hundred percent, and I could not stress this more, do not want a cup of coffee," Beth decreed. "No offense, Genny."

"I could use some joe," Harvey said.

Before Beth's head could explode, Duncan threw out a compromise.

"How 'bout I fill a couple travel mugs for you."

"We're leaving," Beth decreed. And to Genny, "Genny, so nice to not quite but still meet you. I wish I could tell you we weren't these lunatics, but we totally are. Do with that what you will. If you take Bowie from us, we'll understand. God granted us more time with him than we deserved anyway."

"Speak for yourself, wife," Harvey bit out. And to Genny, "I am not a lunatic. You saw yourself yesterday, doll. I'm your average, everyday best friend to a man who shitty life circumstances tore from the arms of the love of his life and he needed my special guidance to get them back. Therefore, I'm taking total responsibility for this."

Harvey finished, jabbing his finger toward Duncan and Genny.

It didn't last long upraised.

Beth grabbed his wrist, yanked it down and started tugging it.

"You'll come over for dinner. Soon, a couple of days, I'll make something in the air fryer," Beth called as she moved, hauling Harvey with her.

"You and that air fryer," Harvey groused.

"You didn't complain about that air fryer when I was pulling homemade jalapeño poppers out of it. You were too busy shoving them in your gob."

They heard this even though Beth and Harvey had disappeared from sight.

"You were wrong."

At these words, Duncan looked down at Genny.

"She's scary," she decreed.

He burst out laughing.

She gave him a squeeze while he was doing it.

And even though he looked down at her and saw her smiling up at him happily, he stopped doing it.

Bent his head.

And took her mouth.

Genny gave him instant access.

So he took it.

She tasted warm and smooth and decadent.

Different and all the same.

But as ever, intoxicating.

And addicting.

He angled his head for more. She pulled her arms from around him to wind them around his neck and pushed up on her toes to give it.

She pressed deep.

He pulled her deeper.

But when his cock started stirring, he ended it, kissing her jaw, the downy skin in front of her ear, then resting his cheek against the side of her head and just holding her close.

"Okay, so, um…it seems we have no problems getting the hang of that again," she mumbled.

He smiled at his stables. "Nope."

"Are you going to introduce me to your horses?'

"Yup."

"And your chickens?"

"Yeah."

"Your dogs are about to break through the glass."

"We'll bring them with."

"Just so you know, I checked, and you were correct. My building has not had a sanitation emergency."

"I figured."

"Bowie?"

"Right here."

"Sam phoned Mary. She wants to sit down and talk."

Fuck.

CHAPTER 12

THE FIRE

Imogen

I stood, watching Duncan crouched before his gigantic fireplace in his great room, building a fire.

And I did it admitting I was a mess.

Because we'd scaled the mountain that was the heartache of our end.

But I'd come to realize what lay ahead was not a downward climb into a sunshine covered, lush, verdant valley of the promise of halcyon days.

It was another range of mountains we had to traverse.

Perhaps not as high.

But they were there.

Earlier, on the porch, after my announcement about Samantha, Duncan had freed his dogs while declaring, "I get it's gonna be on your mind, but how 'bout we make the rest of today a Corey's-bullshit free zone? We got plenty of time to worry about it tomorrow."

And having lived Corey's bullshit for what amounted to most of my life, I'd fallen on that suggestion like a woman overboard falls on a lifeboat.

Once I did, Duncan took me to visit his horses.

He then took me to see his very large, sophisticated, and protected "because of the kai-oats" chicken coop that offered a big area for them to range. A coop where he told me he housed thirty-five chickens "and me or Bettina collect the eggs, but it's Bettina who takes them to the shelter so they can make use of them."

After that, he took me to the surprisingly big patch of tilled, now fallow (since it was autumn) land where, "Me and Sul dink around. Use the horse dung. The chicken guano. A mixture of both. Household and land refuse we compost, shit like that, literally, to see what works the best. We had the same at the old house, and Dora keeps it for him, 'cause Sully's into it."

"And Gage?"

A grin and, "Not so much."

We then walked to the lake and he gave me a sense of how much was his land, and he did this with Killer curled in his arm (who was far from a killer, she was a snuggle puss), the other arm outstretched to point to landmarks of what was his.

Throughout all this, Shasta and Rocco were darting about, and it was cool to see how Rocco kept up with Shasta with absolutely no difficulty, even if he had one less leg.

However, Duncan warned me, "He gets tired quicker. He goes full-out with a quarter less capacity to carry the load. We keep our eyes on that."

And then my head was full of thoughts of how sweet it was he knew his dogs so well and took care of them.

Then he guided me back inside and gave me a proper tour of the house.

I already knew that my first assessment of it was perhaps unkind, but not incorrect.

Every inch of it, and there were a great number of them, with massive rooms and wide hallways (which also evidenced the overall theme, men tended to like to spread out and stake their claim), was decidedly masculine.

But it was in a way that was attractive, interesting, but most of all warm and inviting.

And the master, which Chloe did not show me (she'd only showed me her fantastic space upstairs), was a revelation.

A massive room with a big bed facing a huge arched window that started at the floor and provided an unobstructed view of the lake. That wall was covered in stone, the rest in rough wood planks. A comfy seating area sat before it. Two huge, well designed, walk-in closets, side by side, his and hers, even if there wasn't a "her." And I thought Duncan was smart to do that for resale value or if he left it to one of his boys, who would eventually have a partner.

There was also a not small, but not ostentatious terrace off to one side, and rounding out the interior, a fireplace on the wall next to the bed.

All this was incredible.

But the master bath was insane.

Three-side windowed shower smack in the middle of the room with the fourth wall made of stone. Floors an interesting mix of river rock and slate, the rock fashioned to make it look like a river was guiding you to the door of the shower. Rough-hewn planks on the walls, the same as the bedroom.

Amazing lighting, including what I considered the *pièce de résistance*, but a surprising one for Duncan to choose. A large, circular, free-standing soaking tub nestled under a window. So you could soak and look out at that view. The tub had a tri-globe falling chandelier in the corner next to it that wasn't exactly feminine, but it was gorgeous.

When we toured the master space, I knew I wanted to lie in that bed with a cup of tea and a book so I could look up at the view occasionally, and I wanted to soak in that tub and just take in that view.

And it was not lost on me that Duncan was not hiding he was keen to see my reaction to his home, but it came especially when he showed me his room.

Therefore, it was then it hit me his room should be one part of the verdant valley of the life we could be living.

But there was a hell of a mountain range still to climb.

He finished with the fire and came to me, and another sudden sense of awkwardness stole over me.

I knew this man biblically.

We'd been the best of friends and we'd been the best of lovers.

This was not taking anything from Tom.

I'd had two lovers, outside of Duncan and my ex-husband, and they had not been fun (which shared why there were only two).

Tom, as with everything he did, was about skill and results. There was passion, there was love, there was intimacy and affection, and there was an abundance of all of that, and sometimes even fun, and all of it worked on me greatly.

With Duncan, however, it was just hunger.

Corey had exaggerated in what he'd said in his letter. Out of necessity, considering we needed to sleep, and work, and eat, and talk, and share our life worries and annoyances and just share, we'd come up for air.

But Corey had not been far off base.

In the fourteen months we were together, outside that time I had a terrible cold, but through the time Duncan had thrown out his shoulder (we'd just compensated), morning and night (and if it was the weekend, we often spent it in bed), we were making love.

Without fail.

We couldn't get enough of each other.

I'd thought it would calm down.

It never did.

Not until the day he left.

I'd let only one guy go there in between Duncan in high school, and him again a few years later. I'd only had one man between him and Tom.

And no one since Tom.

And now, it was like I was fifteen again and had no idea what to do.

Which was one mountain we had to climb.

However, it had been a long time since it was Duncan who was that man who had my interest, and I'd forgotten.

But as he assessed me as he came my way, I remembered.

And then he demonstrated.

He could read me.

And he always knew what to do.

In this instance, he took my hand and shifted, so when he fell, he fell on his back to the couch and I went with him.

He then arranged us so I was on my side, back to the couch, front mostly on him, one of his legs stretched out on the couch, his boot on his other foot on the floor. He had an arm around me, and he did not hesitate to bring the other hand up to take control of a hank of my hair, move it forward, twist it around his fingers, and allow it to fall down my front.

"I dye it now," I whispered.

His eyes went from my hair to mine. "I do not care."

I dropped my forehead to his shoulder.

"Baby, who you are, I could not escape it. I watched you grow from who you were to the woman you are now. You are not frozen in time for me. And you cannot be unaware that you're still as gorgeous as you ever were."

I could deny that.

My career as it was essentially ending at age forty-five made that very apparent to me.

And I was one of the very few lucky ones.

I lifted my head.

"Duncan—"

"You know, we got shit to face with Sam and us catching up and our kids getting in the mix and you in Phoenix, me here, and the fact one photo of us on social media means we got a hashtag and some crazy mashup of a name. Do not focus on shit that is not an issue. I was attracted to you when you were fourteen and I was attracted to you when you were twenty-four and I'm a little shocked with the way I've been with you that you'd even doubt how attracted I am to you now."

He was making sense and I was being an idiot.

And there was a great deal of relief that I was not the only one who was aware that our vista was not without challenges.

"We need to tackle all of that," I pointed out.

He grinned playfully.

And heavens, did I like that grin.

He'd had it before, of course.

But maturity had made it *so much better*.

"Can't we just make out in front of the fire until your girl texts she's on her way home?'

I felt my lips curl up. "As tempting as that offer is, it would make me feel better if you knew what you were in for."

"And that would be?"

"Well, as you mentioned, we have a hashtag and have already earned a mashup. This will require my publicist getting involved."

He stared at me.

Then he asked, "Sorry?"

Yes, this was what I was afraid of.

He didn't understand.

I set about explaining.

"You see, there will be questions, and I've no doubt, there already are, and Mary is holding back the tide. We'll need to talk with our families, our friends, so they're aware and not blindsided, and then decide when we allow the statement to be released that yes, indeed, Imogen Swan and Duncan Holloway are an item. Then, I hope, there will come a time when we'll be 'official.' And the time where we declare we're 'serious.' And...uh, so on."

It took him a moment before he said, "How 'bout this? We do whatever we want, and your publicist, and mine, 'cause River Rain's got one, though she is not personal to me, she can be briefed, and when they get these requests, they can say, 'Ms. Swan and Mr. Holloway do not discuss their private lives.'"

"Darling," I whispered carefully, "that does *not* work."

"How does it not?"

"That feeds the fire."

"So what?"

"Bowie."

"Is it their business?"

"Well, no," I allowed.

"And is it gonna affect us? And I mean really affect us, Gen. People are gonna take pictures. They're gonna post them. You warned me they come up to you, and I can imagine they do. The touching part will stop, if I'm around, but you gotta take care of your fans as you see fit. That's part of your job. So all that's going to happen no matter what. But we pay these people, the publicists, to handle shit, and eventually, folks are just gonna get it. We don't have to spoonfeed them. We don't have to make decisions that are personal and private and then share how we feel. I've no doubt you got a lot of money and that makes your life very comfortable. These people gave you that life by watchin' your TV show and goin' to see your movies. So there is definitely a way that you owe them your kindness and attention. But you don't owe them your life."

"It's a little ridiculous how much sense that makes," I muttered.

He smiled smugly.

I wasn't feeling smug.

"We should talk about the other, Bowie."

"The other what?"

"You, well…me being in your face and not in your life and how that had to feel."

He turned into me, lifting his foot from the floor so he could tangle his legs with mine and wrapping both his arms around me.

"Right, I have not watched any of your movies or *Rita's Way*. I couldn't. It would have killed. And I didn't need my wife seein' that. And she knew about you."

"Oh boy."

I knew how that was.

I knew because Tom knew about Duncan too. I'd told him before we were married, when we were sharing about lovers past. And when

River Rain got bigger, and Duncan was the face of it, and Tom didn't miss that, he didn't handle it very well.

I didn't blame him.

They looked alike. They were both sporty, outdoorsy, even if in different ways, and they were both committed to causes that meant something to them.

Duncan, the environment.

Tom, the proper care and treatment of younger athletes in competition (suffice it to say, when the Larry Nassar scandal broke, Tom hit the roof, as anyone would, but Tom took it as almost a personal affront, but then, he had two daughters, and at the time Sasha was seriously into beach volleyball).

He got over his jealous spate toward Duncan, and it wasn't difficult for him to do so, but it was rocky for a spell.

"Yeah," Duncan grunted, bringing me back to our conversation. "And I did not know, until yesterday, that was an issue because she never told me."

I grew tense and repeated, "Oh boy."

He pulled me closer, not that there was much closer to get, but he managed it.

"She and I are done, baby," he said gently. "We are, and there's no going back. But just to say, if she had an issue, she should have told me. That's on her. A lot of it is on her, but how 'bout for now, we deal with stuff that involves you and me. Not Dora. Not Corey. Just where we are and where we're goin' and not try to tackle all of it, which is impossible, but it would be unsettling, and I don't wanna feel unsettled. I have a spell where I can feel good I got my Genny back in my arms. And that's all I wanna feel. For now. You with me?"

I knew a thing or two about a partner not sharing something they should share.

And now was not the time to get into that.

Now was the time to be happy I had Duncan back.

So I nodded exuberantly.

"Good," he murmured, his gaze dropping to my mouth.

I wanted his kiss.

However...

"Bowie," I called.

His eyes came back to mine.

"Right. Plan. Hear me out," he stated.

I nodded.

"We're gonna make out in a little bit, and I'm gonna warn you, I'm gonna feel you up. You're bein' shy, so I think it's fair you know what's coming."

I started giggling.

Duncan kept talking.

"Before that, I'm gonna ask you to give me the week. You don't have a sanitation problem at your place, but Cookie's already up here, and you clearly don't have plans that's messing with, so you can stay. Not here. Chloe has informed me she's using my place as her vacation destination and I don't know how long that's gonna last and her mom and her new, yet old man hooking up under the same roof, even if she's on the other side of the house, would not work for any of us. And more importantly, I'm sensing you wanna take this slow, and you're gonna need your space, so I'm gonna give it to you. So you stay at the hotel. During that week, we can get used to each other again, catch up our lives, and make a plan for after without any rush. Are you down with that?"

"What about your work?"

"I can't deny I'm getting behind, so I'm gonna have to hit the office. But you strike me as a woman who doesn't get bored easily, your girl is here, you got friends here, so I hope that's not gonna be a problem."

"It won't, but now I have to ask you to be honest, because I can assure you, I won't be offended. Are you okay with Chloe staying with you?"

"If she left me at this point without needing to go home and get on with her life, it'd gut me."

I stared at him, warmth (or more warmth) creeping around the region of my heart.

"Straight up, after Gage left, it took a while to get settled in this house without my boys and their mess and their friends and girlfriends in and out. I only had them every other week, but when they went away to school, no other way to put it, it fucking sucked."

"I so totally get that," I told him, and I so totally did.

"Yeah, and my boys, especially Gage, take up space. They're active. They had a lot of friends. Both were serial daters. So there was a lot of action around here. But your girl is one girl, but she seems like about five of them."

I started laughing and repeated, "I so totally get that."

"I don't have daughters," he went on. "Love my boys so much, really didn't think on it. Just happy with what I had, how great they were, and that was it. But bein' around your girl…" He paused, then continued cautiously, "This is for later, honey, but we woulda had beautiful kids, and you might have given me daughters, and that's not ever gonna happen, and that's a hole I discovered today that I got in me that's never gonna be filled. But all that's Chloe takes so much attention, I'm thinkin' I'm not gonna feel the empty too much."

His words made my head fall forward and it thudded against his chin.

He just shifted to kiss my forehead.

"We *would* have made beautiful children," I agreed.

"We didn't," he said gruffly. "But we got what we got, and we're all kinds of lucky."

At least with that, we were indeed all kinds of lucky.

I tipped my head back. "I love that you like her so much."

"She's the shit."

I smiled at him. "She is that. Your boys sound the same."

"They are."

"I'm scared of meeting them."

"Do you know Larry Fitzgerald?"

"Uh, no."

"Too bad. Though I figure Gage will like you anyway."

That made me giggle.

I was giggling a lot lately.

It felt nice.

"Can we make out now?" Duncan asked.

That made me giggle more.

I stopped when Duncan kissed me.

And it came back, just like on the porch.

What I'd lost, like it was a sense. Like I'd been flying blind. Moving deafened through the world. Unable to touch. Or taste. Or smell.

All that without Duncan and this and the freedom he gave me to just be me.

I knew Tom loved "Gen," not "Imogen Swan."

But in this, he took over. He guided things. And his alpha ways meant that was the only way.

And I could not say I didn't enjoy it. I did. To let go. To let someone steer that ship. It was a turn-on to give over control.

This was different.

Because Duncan took and he led, and he knew what he wanted, and he went after it.

But he let me have all that too.

Back then.

And now.

Like when I got so into our kissing, I yanked his shirt out of his jeans and started feeling him up before he got even close to the hem of my sweater.

That smooth, hot skin, the muscle underneath.

He groaned at my touch and shoved a knee through my thighs.

I pressed closer and tucked my hand down the back of his jeans, going for his ass.

He dipped his hand under my sweater and went right for my breast.

His thumb rubbing hard over my nipple meant I sucked his tongue deep into my mouth and pushed my hips into his.

He ground his hard crotch into mine in return and rolled me to my back.

"Duncan," I gasped when he released my mouth so he could work at my neck.

"Fuck, Genny," he growled, pulling the cup of my bra down and pinching my nipple.

Oh *yes*.

I had it *back*.

I arched into him, turning my head, nipping his ear and pulling my hand out of his jeans to round him, cupping his package.

"*Fuck, Genny,*" he grunted, surging into my hand.

He took my mouth and thrust into my hand and I caught his hair in a fist, rounding his thigh with one of my calves, pushing up in his rhythm with my hips.

Yes, like a sense coming back.

Essential.

My God.

How I'd *missed this*.

My phone chimed with a text, and maybe a second later, Duncan's did too.

He broke our kiss, pressed his forehead to the side of my neck and covered my hand at his crotch, pulling it around his back, muttering, "Fuck, shit, fuck, shit."

Both our breathing was labored.

But a double text indicated Chloe was on her way back.

He lifted his head. "I'm now sensing you don't need to take at least that part slow."

And again, I was giggling.

He held his weight in a forearm and used his other hand to stroke a line from the area under my eye down to the corner of my mouth.

"Times I knew I was good enough for you, whenever I made you laugh," he murmured.

I stopped giggling.

"You were always good enough for me," I murmured back.

"I know, baby. But you get it, yeah?"

I got it.

I didn't like it.

But I got it.

"I try not to hate. It's such an ugly emotion. And it says even more about the hater than it does about the hate-ee. But I hate your father, Bowie. I did then, and even dead, I do now."

"He's not worth that emotion, Genny. And understanding that was when I could let it go."

"I'm not there yet."

"We'll get you there."

"I'm not hopeful about that," I muttered.

He smiled at me. "You wanna know what I was thinking when you and Coco walked back into the entry earlier?"

I tipped my head to the side on his toss pillow. "Coco?"

"This morning, I got that she wants me to call her Coco. She got the Bowie story."

Oh boy.

"No wonder she's lost to you, if you gave her that," I remarked.

"I needed her to get who I was and who she was shovin' in her mother's path. I also needed to get why she was workin' so hard on that. I fear it'll affect my *ami* status, givin' you this, and it's somethin' else we gotta go over, both ways, how our exes became exes, though you know the bones of mine, but heads up. She's not over the divorce."

My heart hurt.

But I said, "I know."

He didn't ask me to expound on that.

He took us back. "So you wanna know what I was thinking?"

I nodded. "Please."

"I was seeing my home through your eyes and realizing, even though, for the most part, he's in my past in a way I get that's all he gets of me anymore. And don't mistake me, I built this for me and my boys and the work I hope they eventually do to make my brood bigger. Still, I also get that this house was a massive fuck-you to my father."

I smiled hugely at him. "It's a really impressive fuck-you, Bowie. Especially the master. And the master bath."

He smiled hugely in return. "I was noticing you had a thing for my room."

"You noticed correctly."

He kept smiling.

And then he said, "I also built it for you."

I felt my smile fade and I blinked.

"Sorry?"

"Left Dora in the house we raised the boys in and it's a nice house. Thirty-five hundred square feet. Great neighborhood up in the mountains. But it's not this. Not close. Now, I cannot say I did all I did in my life for you. I didn't. It was for me. And then it was for my family. But I can't deny, with this house, there was some part of me still striving to be the man for you, and you becoming Imogen Swan, famous actress. Well…"

He flung out an arm to indicate that gorgeous fireplace, the great room, the house, and beyond.

"Well, thank you, I accept that compliment as the grave tribute it was meant to be."

His body moved on mine with his deep chuckle. "You're totally welcome."

In all seriousness, I said, "And it really is a beautiful house, Bowie."

"Thank you, baby," he whispered.

"Now, do I have dry-humping-on-the-couch hair?" I asked.

"No idea, but you probably wanna make sure you don't before Coco gets back."

"I'll do that."

"And I'll see what I can rustle up for lunch for two fancy broads," he replied, angling off me and onto his feet, which caused a scattering of dogs.

He pulled me up to mine.

"I'm still that small-town Illinois girl, Bowie," I told him.

"Yeah, your publicists can feed that line to the drones who'll suck up anything, but marble and chandeliers and a Cayenne and an assistant that brings you your cat, you don't fool me, Genny. The thing it's important for you to get is, I'm proud as fuck you made the you that you are right now. I know it took work. And it probably took balls. And from what I've heard about that cesspool of an industry, you likely ate a lot of shit. But you came out on top, Gen. And that's fucking extraordinary."

One could say, unless his mouth was on mine, I felt timid about my body's reaction to his and definitely where that would lead, now that I wasn't twenty-four anymore.

But what he just said, I couldn't control it.

I jumped him.

We were back down on the couch, Duncan sitting, me straddling his lap, devouring his mouth, when he squeezed my ass with both hands, pulled his head back and said, "Babe, I'm hard again and honest to Christ, I'm fallin' in love with your kid, but even if I wasn't, I do not need to face her with a raging erection."

And there it was.

Another giggle.

"Climb off and fix your hair, because it's totally dry-humping hair. You do that, I'll get a shot to take a breath and try not to think of what I intend to do to you on this couch, in my bed, in my shower, in my bathtub, at The Queen..."

"Okay, Bowie."

I climbed off.

He stretched his arms out to either side of him on the back of the couch and I did my best (and failed) not to look at his crotch.

If luck had turned on me with falling in love with a man whose father's abuse and whose best friend's perfidy drove him from me, I was not unaware that that I'd lucked out very significantly in a variety of other ways.

To put a fine point on it, both the men who were important to me in my life were beautifully endowed.

Tom's cock was long and hefty and pretty.

Duncan's was all about girth and formation and it was gorgeous.

And I was going to get it back.

"Jesus, Genny, don't make me need to change jeans. You know better than me, Chloe will notice."

I tore my eyes from his crotch.

And it was my turn to have a smug smile.

I went to the bathroom.

By the time I came out, with an escort of Rocco and Shasta (Killer was sticking close to Daddy in the kitchen), Duncan called, "Check texts, beautiful. I'm thinking things are not all well in Chloe's world."

I went right to my phone that was lying on my bag on the island where I'd left it during the first part of the tour.

I checked texts.

There was an explosion of confetti effect, which did not share things were not well.

But I got it when I read the text.

Welcome to the first-ever Imoway family text string. Huzzah!

Now Bowie, you better have a martini ready for me or I'm going to kill somebody.

"Who would she want to kill?" I asked.

"No clue," Duncan, pulling plates out that we were going to use to consume what appeared to be a cornucopia of deli delights. "Far's I know, she went out to buy boots so she can ride. Has something like that ever led to homicidal tendencies before?"

"There was a limited edition Fendi clutch she decided to pass on, then changed her mind, and went back to get it, but it was gone and there wasn't another one available anywhere. Things were troubled for a while after that, and I know your acquaintance has been short, but my sense is, you understand that 'troubled' for Chloe is akin to 'apocalyptic' for everyone else. But she didn't threaten to kill anybody."

He was chuckling at the same time saying, "We'll find out soon enough."

We would.

He moved to and then came out of the pantry with four different bags of chips.

"I take it we're having sandwiches and chips," I noted.

"I can heat up some soup," he offered.

"This looks delicious, darling."

He jerked up his chin and went to the fridge for condiments.

"What can I do?" I asked.

"Give Kills a snuggle, she's dyin' and I got my hands full," he answered.

I went to get his dog and was seated at the island, giving her snuggles while she panted and watched her Daddy arrange slices of meat on a plate when I heard the garage door go up.

"Should I not be puttin' out meat and instead have been battening down the hatches?" Duncan asked.

Which meant I was laughing when Chloe came in.

She was carrying two large, handled paper bags, both that had a simple design of a river with some rocks through which were the words RIVER RAIN.

And she was not feeling in the mood to keep us guessing.

She started this with, "Where's my martini, Bowie?"

"Honey, I got a rule. Before the liquor comes out, food goes in the stomach. So tell me what sandwich to make you. You eat it, I'll pull out the vodka," Bowie replied.

"What's happening, Chloe?" I asked.

She dumped the bags and stomped to the island.

"I'll tell you what's happening, and prepare, Bowie," she said to Duncan. "You'll be needing to fire somebody."

Uh-oh.

I let Killer down (she wanted to greet Chloe anyway) because Duncan had had experience with Chloe. And he was a mature man and father of two sons. So he'd been trained to be aware and assessing of children, their moods and their words, no matter their age.

But Chloe was not yet a mother, nor had she had a long-term boyfriend, though she was an adult, but barely.

So she had not quite taken in all that made Duncan.

And therefore, intimating that she'd been done wrong by one of his employees was not the way to handle whatever bee was buzzing her bonnet.

Before I could intervene, she found out.

"*Who?*" Duncan barked, and Chloe jumped. "And what did they do?"

"Uh, Judge," she said uncertainly.

Duncan's head twitched in confusion.

"Judge was uncool with you?"

Whoever this Judge was, apparently, this was out of character.

"Okay, before this—" I tried.

"He made fun of me," Chloe shared.

"Judge? Judge Oakley?" Duncan queried.

Definitely out of character.

"I don't know his last name. I think he's kind of a higher up."

"Yeah, Chloe, he doesn't even work in the store. He's in charge of our Kids and Trails program."

"What?" Chloe asked.

"It's a nationwide thing we do. Along with some fundraising Judge does to build the program, River Rain pays for field trips, mostly for inner city kids in low-income areas. We bus them out to national parks and take them on hikes."

Oh wow.

I didn't know he had that program.

How lovely.

My daughter sniffed. "Well, I got the sense it wasn't his department when he butted into me buying boots."

"Corporate offices are attached to our Prescott store," Duncan explained.

"Oh," Chloe mumbled.

"And he was a dick to you?" Duncan asked.

"He made fun of my booties."

I sighed.

Duncan stared at her.

"They're Jennifer Chamandi," she stated, as if that meant anything to Duncan.

"Are you sure he wasn't teasing you or maybe flirting with you?" Duncan suggested.

"Well, yes, considering we got into an argument that I'm afraid to say was somewhat heated, on both our parts, and loud, on just my part, about how the cost of my booties would fund an elementary school lunch program for a year, which they would *not*. I'm very aware they're not exactly inexpensive, but they aren't covered in *diamonds*. Though I don't need some guy making me feel shitty because I'm privileged. I'm not unaware that I am and just because I don't take inner city school kids on hikes for a living, and instead, make women feel pretty for a living, I shouldn't be made to feel like crap."

Duncan was opening the bread, muttering, "I'll have a word with him."

"No, you won't," I said.

Duncan looked to me.

Chloe, who had picked up Killer and was cuddling her, looked to me.

"Mother," Chloe said.

I kept my eyes to Duncan. "She can fight her own battles."

"I don't pay my staff to have opinions about my customers' lifestyles," Duncan returned.

"Huh," Chloe huffed to Killer, then cooed, "So true, what your daddy is saying, googoo."

"Duncan," I said.

"What?" he asked.

I gave him a look.

His eyes moved over my face.

It took him a few moments, then he nodded.

"*Motherrrrrrr,*" Chloe whined.

I looked to her. "Is my daughter honestly standing beside me, after having an argument she should not have participated in at all, but who, let's face it, Chloe, you probably did something to set it off, and now you're all right with this young man's employer having a word with him because you're in a snit?"

"He was a jerk," she snapped.

"Rise above," I ordered.

"I try very hard not to rise above. It takes too much energy," she sniffed.

I couldn't stop myself from laughing.

Deeply.

"You're very annoying, and thus tonight, I'm not inviting you to my luxurious log cabin suite and opening a bottle of wine for us to make mother-daughter memories."

"That would be opening a bottle of *Duncan's* wine," I corrected. "Seeing as you're mooching off him."

"I am *not* a mooch," she bit out.

"Darling," I said softly.

She rolled her eyes, her indication it was a point she could not argue, and then stated, "Fine. You don't get the riding boots I bought *you* so you can ride because I *know* because I gave Mary very explicit instructions about the apparel she was supposed to bring that you don't have any suitable footwear to wear riding. And I also know you love riding, so you'll have to go *yourself* to get something or not ride at all."

"My beautiful daughter, you're acting about eight," I warned her good-naturedly.

"*Ma mère chérie*, please hear this and get it through your beautiful, well-coifed, but thick head, I am not *ever* going to act older than maybe...*twelve*. I will be a girl with a girl's delights and a girl's tantrums exercising a girl's prerogative to change her mind and be whatever she wants to be *until the day I die*."

Duncan chuckled low, which gave indication of his approval of my daughter's declaration.

Yes, he liked her.

And he might be a bit insane.

Chloe turned to him.

"And for the record, Bowie, I actually *don't* want you to talk to Judge because Mom's right. He's beneath my notice."

I had not said that.

I did not get the chance to correct her.

"But I *will* notice a turkey and swiss sandwich with a hint of mayo and some Bugles."

Duncan's "Coming right up," vibrated with humor.

He then got on making my girl's sandwich.

When he was done and passing her the plate, she declared, "Now, Killer and I are retiring to my balcony. Mother, you may attend me in thirty minutes whereupon you'll give me a detailed minute by minute breakdown of why I walked in on you and Bowie in what is apparently lovely domesticity with a romantic fire crackling in the background."

"That won't be happening, daughter mine, since Bowie and I are having lunch then we're going into town so I can introduce him to Cookie."

"Huh," she huffed.

Then she, and her plate, with Killer, walked out of the room.

And just to say, both Rocco and Shasta weren't far behind.

"Babe. Sandwich?" Duncan called my attention to him.

I gave him my order. He made it. He then got on making his own while I got on eating mine.

He did not skimp on meat or cheese.

It was fabulous.

We were both munching when his phone skidded across the island.

"Pic of Judge," he grunted, and then took a huge bite.

I picked up the phone, and on it saw a man wearing a River Rain tee, standing next to and laughing with a child, his hand curled around the back of the kid's neck.

Ash blond hair. High forehead. Brown eyes. Manly nose. Firm jaw. Great chin. Excellent stubble. Broad shoulders. Slim hips. Tall frame. Fantastic smile.

"Oh, dear Lord, it's Ryan Reynolds," I whispered in horror.

"She is absolutely not his type," Duncan declared.

With even more horror, my gaze shot to his.

He kept talking.

"Which means, when he got a load of her, and fell, he went up to her and picked a fight to prove to himself she was not the woman who was going to keep him from sleeping until he puts a ring on it. Even though this effort failed because every other woman he meets trips all over herself to do his bidding and he's not a fan of that. He didn't hike Machu Pichu to come home and find a woman who would fawn all over him."

"He hiked Machu Pichu?"

"Twice."

Oh boy.

"Chloe's had an exceptional education, but there is a good possibility she doesn't know what Machu Pichu is," I shared.

"She's gonna find out."

Oh *boy*.

"Is she going to chew him up and spit him out?"

"He'll hold his own."

I got to the harder part.

"Puts a ring on it?"

"He'll deny it but he's probably right now trying to figure out where he can run into her again, if only to have another fight."

"Oh my," I murmured. "She will, of course, have dropped your name."

"Which means we're going out to dinner since he's coming over tonight and I'm enjoying my day too much. I don't want to have 'the talk' with a man I respect about how he better treat Chloe right or I'll break his neck."

And again…

I was giggling.

"Eat up, Gen," he ordered, jerking his chin to my plate. "I wanna meet your cat."

He was going to love Cookie.

So I obliged.

CHAPTER 13

THE SEED

Corey

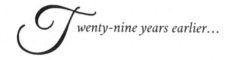 wenty-nine years earlier...

COREY WAS HAVING A MELTDOWN.

He had to get a handle on it.

But...

They'd fucked before they'd shown at his and Sam's condo.

Like they always did.

Jesus Christ.

Jesus *fucking* Christ.

Could they keep their hands off each other for *a minute*?

Just one goddamn minute?

Why, every *fucking* time, did Genny have to come over all glassy-eyed, her hair mussed, lips bruised and full from Duncan kissing them, and Duncan looking like he'd scaled goddamn Everest.

And this happened not only when they came over to his and Sam's place, but when he and Sam went to theirs.

Fuck, half the time, they were both still adjusting their clothes in some way when they opened their door.

And what *was* it with them *both* having to open the door as one? Like they were attached by some invisible thread and couldn't be apart for a minute. Like her going to work and him going to work was too much for them to bear, so when they were at home together, they were in each other's space constantly.

And Duncan was in Genny as much as he could physically pull that off.

Christ.

Corey had thought it was over after he and Dun graduated from high school and Duncan did the smart thing, the kind thing, and dumped her.

He thought it was totally over.

She was too damned good for him, and Duncan knew that.

She was *still* too damned good for him. And Duncan *still* had to know that.

Duncan was a mover, for fuck's sake.

Corey wasn't.

Six figures, fresh off an undergrad degree.

Six figures...*undergrad*.

He bought his first freaking condo—one he still owned and rented out, by the way—six weeks before his twenty-third birthday.

He wasn't even twenty-freaking-*three* and he owned *property*.

And then he'd traded up as a wedding present for Sam.

Did Genny give *that first shit* about him getting on the property ladder before she'd even graduated from college? Did she give *that first shit* that he'd offered to take her to Paris for a weekend?

No.

She'd laughed and said, "God, Corey, you're *so* funny."

He hadn't been joking.

A man could make a woman fall in love with him if he swept her away to Paris and kissed her under the Eiffel Tower.

But no, Corey suggests it, it's a joke.

Duncan, who doesn't even own a fucking suit, just stares at her wearing a pretty dress to a wedding like he wants to drag her to the nearest empty room, bend her over a table and fuck her breathless, and she's panting for it.

So.

Seriously.

The question needed asked.

What the fuck?

"Hey, you need any help out here?"

Corey jolted and turned from where he stood at the grill on their balcony to where Duncan was coming out the door, and swear to *fuck*, he nearly threw the tongs in his hand at his friend.

All that moving furniture around, Duncan no longer had a high school football player's body.

He was a powerhouse.

He was fucking Hercules.

"I don't have to be able to lift a couch by myself to be able to grill some chops without assistance, Duncan," he sniped.

Dun's head jerked and he slid the door shut behind him before coming toward Corey.

"What was that about?"

Yeah.

Corey had to get it together.

He turned back to the grill then looked to his view of the building next door.

He'd just bought this one, but he decided he needed a better condo.

He could afford it.

And he was *this close* to nailing down the investors.

So definitely, he needed a better place to sit them down, entertain, show them he was the man in whom they could put the faith that came in the form of their money.

He was the real deal. The whole package. OS, software, *and* hardware.

Also, he was the one who could bury himself in the work, come out of that, put on a suit, impress the board, bring on new investors, get more money, create more growth, innovate, more money, more growth, and the cycle repeating unending until he was dead, and everyone was very, *very* rich.

He was the man who would say, "I'll be the one making sure you buy your yacht," and if they already had one, buying the *bigger* yacht, and when he said that, he not only meant it...he delivered.

He couldn't do that in this 1200-square-foot condo in Wicker Park.

Wicker Park was the shit. Sam loved the neighborhood.

But it wasn't Michigan Avenue.

"Corey," Duncan called.

His friend was now standing beside him.

"You're not careful, you're gonna get her pregnant and you barely have insurance, Dun. Your apartment is shit, nowhere to raise a kid. And she wants to be a Broadway star, not a mom at twenty-two."

Oh yeah.

He got his digs in, for certain.

Corey had been doing that since they took off on his wedding day, Duncan his best man, for fuck's sake. Dun did his toast, they stayed for a couple of the dances, but Corey and Sam hadn't even cut their goddamn cake and Genny and Duncan were ghosts.

Since then, inseparable.

Again.

So yeah, he got his digs in.

Genny refused Paris but was in throes of ecstasy wherever Duncan installed her, just as long as his dick was close enough for her to suck.

But he could see his latest comment had taken it too far.

Not in Corey's estimation.

No, though he could see it was in Dun's with the look that was in Duncan's eyes.

Dun was *pissed.*

The important thing Corey had to determine was, *why* was he pissed?

Was he pissed that Corey was talking about shit that was none of his business?

Or was he pissed because Corey was right?

"I make that your business, Corey?" he asked.

Okay, it was that it wasn't his business.

Or was that it?

Corey modulated his tone to caring concern. Best bud to best bud referring to their other best bud, who happened to have a vagina one of them had the rights to eat out—and the other *did not*.

"You know I'm right, Dun."

Now it was Duncan looking at his not-so-great view of the building across the street because he absolutely knew Corey was right.

Corey watched him, wondering, leave it? Or dig deeper?

Corey pretended to give a shit about whether he burned the chops, and muttered, "Just, you know, I hope you're being careful."

"I'm not sixteen, and even when I was, and she was mine then too, I took care of her."

Corey didn't have to pretend anything when he turned squinted eyes at his friend and demanded, "You fucked her when she was fourteen?"

"No, Corey, Jesus," Duncan returned, getting even more pissed. "And just to say, this was one of the ways I took care of her. I let her decide when we went there, or *if* we went there. But this is none of your business either. Genny would not want us talking about it, that being the reason you and I never talk about it. And pointing it out when I probably don't need to, that's another way I take care of her."

That was a warning to back off.

It was also something for Corey to turn over in his head.

How would Genny react if she knew he and Duncan had talked about this?

"Since you got somethin' up your ass, I hate to point something else out, but still…you're burning the chops," Duncan noted.

Corey focused, and Dun was right.

The fat had sizzled onto the coals, the flames had risen, and suddenly, the idea of burning the chops annoyed him beyond reason.

This was because Duncan could man a grill like no other.

He'd never burn a fucking chop.

Corey shifted the meat around.

Duncan then went fishing, Corey knew he was when he asked, "Everything all right with Sam?"

His wife Samantha was very pretty.

However, not as pretty as Gen.

She was very sweet.

Though not as sweet as Genny.

She was exceptionally smart.

But although Genny was not as intellectual as Sam, she was far from dumb and far more talented than Sam could ever be.

He'd found Samantha and he'd liked her, been attracted to her, she was great in bed—a real go-getter, both career-wise and making Corey come harder than he'd even thought possible.

But he'd dated her in an effort to get Genny to notice he had a dick.

She didn't.

Then Corey pushed it to the limit, engagement, huge-ass wedding, the whole thing, all in the hopes that Genny would shake the blinders of "friendship" from her eyes and see him as the man who could give her everything.

Not only everything Duncan couldn't, but *everything*.

Like a new condo in a trendy neighborhood for her early wedding present.

That kind of everything.

She didn't see it, and then suddenly, Corey's ass was married, Gen was back with Dun, and Corey was in hell.

"Are you even alive in there?" Duncan asked, concern edging his tone, though it was also sharp because he was still pissed.

"Sam and I are great," Corey mumbled.

"Then what's up your ass?" Dun asked.

"I care about you and Genny, okay?" Corey snapped. "It's not only not a crime, you two are my best friends. *I* was the one caught in the middle the last time you didn't work out, remember? *I* was the one putting together the pieces after you broke her heart."

What he did not say was he loved every minute of it.

Until he realized he wasn't going to get anything out of it.

But what he said hit its mark.

Duncan appeared chastised.

Though, that was probably more his pain at breaking Genny's heart (something that had also gutted him back when he'd done it, mostly because he didn't want to do it) than his guilt that Corey had to pick up the pieces. Regardless of the fact there was no reason for the guilt since Corey looked at picking up those pieces as an opportunity.

Then.

And to be brutally honest, if only to himself, now.

"I hear you, Cor, but we're back together and it's all good. There's nothing to worry about."

"There's more to all good than using orgasms to blind her to the state of things."

Duncan was getting pissed again. "The state of *what* things?"

"She's not going to break into Broadway doing local commercials at the same time she's teaching fourth grade."

"She's thinking more LA," Duncan said, as if to himself.

Corey burst out laughing, and this was genuine.

Duncan in LA?

Hilarious.

Duncan mistook him.

"What's funny? And, man, careful how you answer that."

He thought Corey was laughing about the possibility of Genny making it in Hollywood.

Corey was quick to remedy that misunderstanding.

"I'm thinking about you in LA."

"Right then, what's funny about *that*?" Dun shot back. "I'll learn how to surf. Always wanted to do that. And they got parks. I'll look into becoming a ranger."

Corey allowed his lips to twitch as he feigned interest in the chops again.

It was low, and hurt, when Duncan pushed, "Now what's funny about that?"

And that was when Corey remembered.

Like he always did.

It was the hurt in Dun's tone that made him remember.

Though it was getting later and later these days whenever he thought about Duncan (and Genny, but also just Duncan), or had a conversation with Duncan.

He should be happy for them.

They were back together.

They loved each other.

God, so much.

Corey had never seen that kind of love, except for how Genny's mom loved her dad.

But with Duncan and Genny young and beautiful, what they had seemed...*alive.*

Their love seemed like an entity that existed with them, something they tended, something they nourished.

Something that, if it ceased to exist, *they* would too.

Not literally. They would carry on, but something—something important, maybe integral to them both—would be gone.

But more, hearing Duncan's hurt, his friend, *hurt* because of something Corey said...

Jesus.

What was the matter with him?

"Do you need time with yourself, man? Because Gen and I could go," Duncan offered when Corey again got quiet, and Corey fixed his attention on his friend.

"It's just, you know..." He tried to find a believable lie. And he went with a half-truth. "Being married, the wedding is great, and the honeymoon is great and then it's..." he shrugged, "tough."

Duncan looked confused.

Then again, he and Gen moved right in with each other and they didn't have that first problem.

"Are you guys fighting or something?" Duncan asked.

Corey returned to the chops, an entree, without thinking, he'd chosen and purchased for Duncan. Pork chops. His favorites. Thick, expensive ones.

He did not do this to shove in Dun's face that he probably couldn't afford to go to a proper butcher and get thick chops to grill, but because Duncan loved pork chops.

Corey had done that simply because...

Because...

This was Duncan.

God.

What the fuck was his problem?

"Brother," Duncan called softly, no longer pissed, it was total concern.

And that was his friend.

Corey was...all he was.

And Duncan was...

All the things Corey wasn't.

The things that were better.

The things he gave Corey without blinking, without thought.

He'd step in front of a bullet for Corey.

He'd lie, cheat and steal for him.

The only thing he wouldn't do was give up the woman they both loved.

And why should he?

He'd earned that love by being...*Duncan.*

He made her happy.

And more, she gave that back.

God, what the fuck was his problem?

Corey looked back at Duncan.

"We're not fighting. I just...we're adjusting."

"She's a good woman. Like I've told you before, I like her," Dun replied. "But if she's not for you, I know you just did the whole big thing, but, Cor…"

Dun's voice grew grave because what he was about to say was important to him, important that he knew his best friend had it, because Duncan wanted it for Corey.

Because his friend loved him.

"Buddy, you need to be happy."

Corey nodded and said quickly, "It's not that. I love her. I do."

And he did.

He really did.

Kind of.

"I just…you know," Corey went on, "I haven't had a real good example of how to be…*right*." He paused and thought it important to add, "For her."

Duncan immediately nodded. "Yeah. I hear that."

He did, and he thought he got it.

But he didn't.

Sure, Corey's father wasn't any kind of role model on how to be a good husband, absolutely not a good parent, and Duncan's dad wasn't either.

But it was more.

So much more.

And that was what Corey had in Duncan.

His friend didn't see any of that shit in Corey.

He saw Corey as Corey wanted to be.

Smart and driven and loyal and funny and loving.

Corey might be those first two things to his bones.

But the last three were just for Duncan.

And Genny.

If he let those go, he'd let go any good that was in him.

Good he gave to his friends.

Good he should be giving his wife.

"We'll find our way," Corey assured, lying now even to himself.

"She's a good woman," Duncan repeated, staring him straight in the eye. "And she loves you like—"

"Oh…my…*God*," Genny cried, both of them so into their conversation, they missed the sliding glass door opening.

She tackled Duncan from behind, wrapping her arms around his middle (and of course his hands went right to hers, where they linked fingers instantly).

She then tipped her head to the side to look at Corey, her golden hair falling in thick waves, her smile aimed Corey's way was radiant.

And yeah, seeing that, Corey loved his wife.

Kind of.

"What's taking so long? I'm starved!" Genny declared.

Duncan made a noise, it was low, you almost couldn't hear it, but Corey paid so much attention to the both of them, he heard it.

As she was who that noise was meant for, Genny heard it too.

She looked up at him, and when she caught Dun looking down on her, her face changed, and Corey could honest to fuck come in his jeans if he looked too long at her face staring up at Duncan with that expression on it.

So he turned his attention away.

They shared one of their many moments.

This one, remembering precisely *how* she'd worked up such an appetite.

And how much they enjoyed that memory.

That burn Corey had lived with since he was twelve made its presence known and he clenched his teeth.

Sam strolled out.

His wife.

He was married.

He looked to her.

Smiled at her.

She smiled back.

Yes, she was very pretty.

Smart.

His.

"Soon, we're eating soon," he promised Genny.

"Awesome. Sam, you need help with anything in the kitchen?"

Genny offered.

His wife answered and the women took off.

The men on the balcony got out of the heavy, and Corey hustled with finishing the chops, not quite allowing his brain to latch onto the fact he was doing it because Gen was hungry.

They served dinner, and Sam and Gen amused themselves, laughing and talking and lighting up the dining table. Though the truth of it was, Genny did most of that, the lighting up part, but Sam wasn't exactly a slouch.

Corey chimed in, because he might not have allowed his brain to latch onto the fact that his meaning of life became feeding Gen when she shared she needed food, but he did remind himself that these three people were the most important people in his life. Two of them had been since he was little. Those two being the only ones who stood at his side or had his back the entirety of his existence.

And they were at his table.

And they were all happy (of a sort).

So life was good.

However, it didn't slip Corey's notice that, as the night wore on, Duncan had begun to get subdued.

Duncan sat, a small smile on his face, watching Genny, giving Sam his attention when she spoke, also Corey.

But he'd grown quiet.

And eventually, it was not lost on Corey, Duncan grew reflective, and this was only when he was watching Genny.

From that, Corey knew, the seed had been planted.

And the feeling he felt having that knowledge was what he guessed people meant when they said they were beside themselves with glee.

At the very same time he hated himself completely.

So completely, if he let himself think about it, that feeling would well up in his chest, getting bigger, spreading wider, filling his throat...

Overcoming him.

Completely.

Until it drowned him on dry land.

CHAPTER 14

THE CELL

Imogen

*T*he next morning, I lay on my side in bed, Cookie curved into the crook of my body, and although I had a view across the room to the charming square, I wasn't looking at it.

Instead, I was scrolling up and down on my phone, reading the same thing over and over again.

Duncan: *You up, baby?*

Me: *Yes.*

Duncan: *Morning.*

Me: *Good morning.*

Duncan: *You going riding with Coco?*

Me: *If she gives me my boots.*

Duncan: [smiley face] *You girls ride Caramel or Streak. Don't get on Pistol. Gage's stallion only likes Gage on his back. You gotta be strong to control him.*

Me: *OK*

Duncan: *See you at lunch.*

Me: *You bet.*

And that was it.

When we were together before, cell phones had not yet been invented.

Why having a text string with Duncan meant so much to me, made me feel girlie and young and giddy, I didn't know.

And I didn't question it.

I just lay in bed, with what I knew had to be a silly grin on my face, going back and forth over the words.

There was a knock on the door and Cookie immediately moved to investigate.

I looked at the clock.

Apparently, I was so involved in that text string, I lost track of the time.

I had a standing order for breakfast delivery at nine o'clock.

And it was nine o'clock.

On the dot.

I pulled myself out of bed quickly, shrugged on my robe, tied it tight and went to the door.

"Good morning, Patrick," I greeted.

"Ms. Swan," the staffer replied. "Breakfast."

I stepped aside to let him in. "Thank you."

He rolled the food to the bistro table.

I went to my wallet.

I had his tip out before he was finished setting out my breakfast, and I took that moment, watching him, to remember that Duncan and I had spent the entire afternoon, and evening, in that room the day before.

In our Corey-free, ex-free, trouble-free zone, we still managed to talk about everything.

At least everything important.

His boys. What they were into. The girls they'd loved and left, and how much that had pained Duncan because he had liked them all (the man really needed a daughter...or two step ones). How River Rain came about. His work on his causes. The Kids and Trails program. My children. My work. The movies I was proud of. The ones that didn't turn out all that great. My semi-retirement where I might take a meaningful, but small part in a film, or an amusing cameo.

With years to catch up on, we were not wanting for topics of conversation.

Though, this was mingled with lots of touching, cuddling and kissing on the couch, then after dinner, more of that, but hotter and heavier on the bed.

And, of course, in the midst of that, Duncan fell for Cookie.

Then again, Cookie was a flirt.

And we called for room service and ate dinner right there at that table.

Honestly, at the end of the evening, I didn't want him to go home. I wanted him to spend the night with me.

But Duncan wouldn't hear of it.

"I know it might not seem like it," he said, "but this has happened fast. And I wanna leave like I wanna cut off a limb, but I think it's smart, at least for a while, we take it slow."

He was right, of course. Although it took twenty-eight years to get to that place, it had only taken a couple of days to get back to us.

"And anyway, I need to get my ass home to make sure Coco hasn't covered my den in florals and chintz," he finished.

This meant our goodbye kiss was through me laughing.

Now, Patrick had finished with my breakfast, and he was rolling out.

I gave him his tip and went to the bed to retrieve my phone.

I'd already fed Cookie (she was a love, but she didn't put up with delayed breakfast), brushed my teeth and washed my face.

Then, I'd gone back to bed.

Now, I was very ready for coffee.

So I grabbed my phone, and then settled in at the table with Cookie in what she'd decided was her place when I ate (and Duncan wasn't there).

Sitting on the seat next to me, peering over the table, watching me.

Sienna Sinclair definitely had it together. Not only was her staff professional, obviously discreet, and friendly, and every inch of her hotel that I had seen was amazing, the layout of my breakfast honest to God reminded me of the times I'd spent at the Ritz in Paris.

The butter was molded into flower shapes. The bowls of jam and little pitchers of cream were crystal. The coffee pot was silver. The china was, well...china. They covered the table with a fresh, crisp linen before placing the food, and they always included a little vase with a flower.

Today's was a cluster of pink sweetheart roses.

And the croissants were perfection. The jam homemade. And the bowl of Greek yogurt and blackberries, sprinkled with granola and striped with local honey was rich and delicious.

I tucked in and was through my first croissant, half the yogurt and pouring my second cup of coffee when my phone rang.

I looked to it and saw it was Stephanie. Stephanie Giron. My friend.

And agent.

Even if I rarely worked, we spoke often. Because now was the time when work was less, so after the fifteen years we'd been together, we could concentrate on being friends.

I picked up the phone. "Hey, Steph."

"You...will not...*believe this.*"

I tensed, thinking it might have to do with Duncan and me.

As far as I knew, no one had gotten another picture of us since El Gato, and I was no longer the hot topic I used to be, so I would assume that had died.

But you never knew.

"Teddy is putting together a new series. He's been shopping it around, and unsurprisingly with one of Teddy's vehicles, *two* networks and *three* streaming services are *very* interested. But they want to know what name is attached. And he wants it to be yours."

Frozen, I stared unseeing out the window.

Teddy was Theodore Mankowitz, the creator of *Rita's Way*.

He had, since then, done another long-lasting, popular, acclaimed series. And as such, now his name was synonymous with sensitive, thoughtful, high-quality television that tackled real-life, real-people issues.

Back in the day, we'd hit on unplanned pregnancies and cancer, but also homosexuality, including the ravages of AIDs through that community, mixed race relationships, addiction, and my favorite storyline, when Rita met a younger man.

Rita, whose character was only a few years older than the age I was now, met a man in his early forties. They fell in love. It was beautiful and so well portrayed by Maggie Mae, the actress who played Rita, and Gordon Fuller, the man who played her love interest, Troy.

However, it was unpopular.

So much so, it was the first time Teddy caved.

He'd intended them to mix families (Rita with full-grown children, Troy with early teenagers) and marry them off so Rita could finally have some happy.

In the end, Teddy broke them up because the public saw Rita as a cougar and was turning on this beloved matriarch who, by that time, for eight seasons had the adoration of our viewers.

It had infuriated me, and Maggie, not to mention Gordon, who was then written off the show.

But even though Rita's ex, Kenny, had married a woman in her freaking thirties (before he'd died in that terrible car accident), and they were okay with that, Rita could not have her man.

I always thought we'd all reacted poorly to that and it was one of the reasons the show wound down. Teddy felt like a failure that arc didn't work. And the rest of us were disappointed at the reaction of the fans.

"And before you start in," Steph said in my ear, "he sent me the pilot script, and Gen, it's *phenomenal*. Think *Thirtysomething* but with a fifty-somethings cast and *Sex and the City*."

Not a chance.

"That doesn't sound phenomenal, Steph. *Sex and the City?*"

"I know. But remember. This is Teddy."

I took a sip of coffee, because that was something to consider.

"I read the script, Gen, and would I honestly come to you with this if I didn't think you'd like it?" Steph asked. "It's funnier than his normal stuff, but just as deep. There isn't a character, male or female, under the age of forty-eight who is not ancillary. It's a female-driven show. It's sexy. It's smart. These characters are vital and *real*. And he told me, outside the networks he's pushing it to, he hasn't shown it to anyone, because he wants you."

That felt incredibly nice.

And it was a huge compliment, coming from Teddy.

However.

"Okay, Steph, I hear your excitement, honey. But we talked about this and that part of my life is over. Small gigs. A few days on the set. I live in Phoenix and—"

"Right now, it's set in northern Cali. But Teddy says he'd set it in Phoenix, do a lot of location shots there, and film it there. For you."

Oh my goodness.

"Seriously?" I asked.

"Yes. And the money they're talking is big budget. Even just for the pilot. Anti-ageism is a thing, it's heating up, and those that hold the purse strings have cottoned onto the fact that the people who have the most money are not the ones spending it on craft beer, in speakeasies and at nightclubs, and since they're out doing that, they're not at home, watching TV."

I took another sip of coffee, reflecting on this too.

"Which means the money we could negotiate for you is big budget too," she went on.

Although I didn't need it, money was money. It wasn't something you turned down, and when in negotiations, you went for as much as you could get.

And it would be a big win, at my age, in that industry, to demand what I was worth.

"Read the script, Gen," she urged.

"This could tank," I shared.

"Yes, it could. But then any of them could. But listen to me, *Outlander* is hugely popular, and the two leads go at each other all the time, and neither of them are twenty-three."

"Neither of them are fifty-three either."

"But they're closer to fifty-three than twenty-three."

"Just."

"It's still true."

She had me there.

"The last meaty role I was offered was playing the mother to an actor who's seven years younger than me," I reminded her.

"I was with you through that ridiculousness, Gen, I remember. And it was the highlight of my career when I got to tell them to go fuck themselves. But...*this is Teddy.*"

One could say I did not need this, considering it was very clear I was resuming a relationship with a man I had loved deeply, and there were no indications that feeling would not come back.

In spades.

And honestly, I wanted to focus on that.

And only that.

But I was drifting.

Chloe had her shop.

Matt had his school.

Sasha was dug in deep being a student of life.

Tom was two years into a five-year contract that had him in the booth, commentating on every grand slam tournament, not to mention the Davis Cup, year-end Finals, and when the Olympics rolled around. And when it was not those times, he was busy with a small, but demanding medical practice.

I was adrift.

And I knew it.

There was only so much reading to consume, phone app games to play, carefully selected charity functions to attend and Met Gala to prepare for a woman could do.

And I'd loved my job. My work.

It had been my dream.

I was not unaware that I had a shelf life. I was not Meryl Streep. I was not Helen Mirren.

But playing a mother of a man who was seven years younger than me?

Really?

"Send me the script," I said.

I could hear her excitement when she replied, "Teddy will be thrilled! But he's going old school on this. He's being so secretive about it, he couriered it to me. Hard copy. He says the digital is on his PC at home, not even in a cloud. And he's made me promise to do the same with you. So I'll have to FedEx it. But no one can read it. No one can touch the printed pages. Not even Mary."

"I'll let you know when I receive it, and we'll chat after I read it."

"Fantastic, Gen."

"Okay, Steph."

"I'll let you go. I need to get this out and call Teddy."

"Don't make any promises."

"Girl, who are you talking to?" she asked. But I didn't get the chance to answer. "We'll chat soon. For now, *ciao*."

"*Ciao*."

We hung up and I stared at my phone, uncertain what to feel.

Ten years ago, it would have been excitement.

But enduring what amounted to fifteen years of declining quality in the roles I was offered, culminating in that last offer...

An offer that came on the heels of having been asked to lunch by a longtime friend who was a studio head, who told me, "Darlin', you need to Lucy Liu. Get into directing and find a TV show where you can be smart, but sexless. Or find your Goop. You could sell the shit outta crystal-infused water bottles, or whatever the fuck. I know it's harsh, but it's the only way to go for talent like you."

I disagreed greatly that Lucy's role in *Elementary* was sexless.

It was smart, but just her wardrobe, intelligence and no-nonsense, with-it attitude made me want to jump her, and I wasn't a lesbian.

I also didn't have a dick.

And it was dick that drove that business.

In too many ways.

In my career, I had successfully avoided the casting couch.

And to this day, I carried some shame that I had not done this because I was a strong and willing to put myself and my peace of mind above my career.

I'd done it because my first real gig was with Teddy, and Teddy was absolutely not that man.

But I'd also done it because I quickly got involved with Tom, and when this was intimated by a producer who held the reins of a movie role I very much wanted, and I told Tom, he blew his stack and went to visit said producer.

I did not get that role.

But I did get a call from a friend who was an actress who said, "I don't know what Tommy did, girl, but thank him for castrating that prick."

What Tom had done was what I should have done.

Told him that if he didn't stop with that shit, "Bonnie is going in front the reporters and sharing what a schmuck you are in a way you'll never sell another ticket to a movie."

He was not wrong. The American public thinking that some creepy guy was going to make Bonnie from *Rita's Way* suck his cock to get a job?

He'd be finished.

But it should have been me who had done it.

Actually done it.

Gone in front of the reporters.

But then, I would never work again.

Never.

I knew it.

Every woman in my shoes knew it.

And the lasting gift those kinds of assholes gave us was the shame we carried that we blew it because, in order to continue in our chosen profession, we never did anything about it.

Somehow, it was *our* responsibility to put our necks on the line to put a stop to it, not *their* responsibility to be decent human beings.

And when things finally blew up, no matter how awesome that was, I was not surprised that the fingers were pointed.

Why didn't they say something?

No one really understood the power that was wielded and just how *over* you would be if you stood up against that power.

It was so easy to sit at home and cast judgment when you didn't understand most those actresses weren't living in nine-million-dollar homes in the Hollywood hills and their choice was work and eat…or not.

But we could just say, Tom doing that and me being with Tom for the next twenty plus years meant that never happened again.

At least not to me.

On this thought, my phone rang, and as if I'd conjured him, Tom's picture was on the screen.

Needing to get down to finishing eating, and then showering, then getting to Chloe so we could ride before I met Duncan for lunch, I hit the screen to take the call and put it on speaker.

"Hey, Tommy."

"Seriously, Imogen? I mean, fucking *seriously?*"

I was arrested by his enraged tone.

So much so, I couldn't speak.

He could.

"We had a deal," he bit out.

A deal?

I was scrambling to think about what deal he was talking about, when he spoke again.

"And him? *Him? Christ*, honest to fuck, you're starting it up again with *him?*"

My back-together-with-Duncan happy daze mingled with my am-I-really-going-to-get-to-work-again confused haze shifted and it hit me.

We had a deal, Tom and me.

If we started dating, even casually, we'd share.

I did not share.

Things were so crazy, I didn't even think about it.

But then again, no matter what that Insta picture showed, it had only happened yesterday.

"Tom, let's talk."

"Fuck you, Gen."

My body jerked violently at his words and his call disconnected.

Duncan had an explosive temper.

Tom did not.

He was an athlete, and even when he retired from professional tennis, he continued being very active, played all the time, and worked out daily. Not to mention, he had a lock on a variety of mental practices that he utilized to keep calm and focused and was rarely even stressed. He could lose his patience with our kids, but that didn't happen often, and considering Chloe (and I had to face it, Sasha), that was quite a gift.

He could definitely lose it.

But the only times I'd seen him do that was when someone he loved was hurt or taken advantage of or when he heard of things that angered him in the news.

He had never, not once, not even while we hashed out the issues in our marriage, coming to the conclusion it could not go on, lost it with me.

Even when I, who had advocated understanding the art of forgiveness to my children for years, could not find it in me to forgive him.

And yet again that morning, I had something on my mind that I didn't know what to do with.

Which meant, when my phone rang again, and I saw it was Mary, I did not want to answer it.

But Mary had a job to do and me being unavailable to give her my decisions in doing it made her job impossible. So I tried not to waste her time, because that would be frustrating, but also, I was paying for it.

"Hey there, honey," I greeted, my voice sounding strained.

"Yeah, well, that Insta shot, it was bound to happen."

She clearly thought I knew something I didn't.

"Sorry?" I asked.

"The Insta shot. And the Szabo connection. The media is putting together you knew Corey all the way back from when you lived in

Winston, Illinois. And it's on the River Rain website bio of Duncan Holloway that he grew up in Winston, Illinois. So some reporters hit up some folks from your hometown. And folks like to talk about famous folks. So now they know that you and Holloway were high school sweethearts who got together again when you were in your twenties, broke up, and now your hashtag is imowayreunitedanditfeelssogood."

Damn it.

"And just so you know, I've been holding Mindi back," Mary went on, referring to Mindi Leigh Russell, my publicist. "They're all over her to make you two official. She wants to know what you want to say."

"Well first, for you, my respected, adored and appreciated personal assistant, that is, when you're not roped into one of my daughter's capers..."

Mary and I had talked the morning before. And she'd admitted to being dragged into Chloe's plan.

I didn't reprimand her, as such.

Though I did make it clear that Chloe was not her employer, I was. And although I understood Chloe often made it difficult, if not impossible to say no, if I were anybody else, she'd be out on her ass, and if things had gone screamingly poorly with Duncan, I would have considered it.

Mary was very astute.

I said all of this in a nice way.

But she got it.

"...Duncan and I have decided to see where this goes."

She made a truncated noise of elation.

"Which means I'm staying here for the week, as planned, so we can begin exploring that."

"I'm really, *really* happy for you, Gen," she said, sounding really, *really* happy.

"As for the press, Duncan and I have had this conversation, and the statement Mindi can give is that Ms. Swan and Mr. Holloway do not discuss their personal life."

There was a moment of silence and then, "What? Genny, that *never* works. That's translated to 'we're hot and heavy and a *huge* item so get ready for reports of us tearing apart hotel rooms or adopting a kid from Africa.'"

"That's all they get."

"Gen, I'm no publicist, but I've been with you for five years, which means through the divorce and—"

"Mary," I interrupted her firmly. "That's what we're going to say."

"They're gonna go Team Tom and Team Duncan, Gen, and everyone loves Tom, especially with you. He's going to win."

Damn it.

"I'm far too old to tear apart hotel rooms, or, sadly, adopt children who need loving homes. Duncan is not that person either. And they'll eventually get used to it," I told her.

"You have to let Mindi spin the lovers reunited thing," she urged.

I really did.

"I'll speak to him about it."

"Thank God," she breathed.

"But for now, she can either remain silent or say what I said. Those are her choices."

"Right, I'll tell her."

"And there's going to be a script FedExed to me. You'll probably get it tomorrow. Can you courier it up here?"

"A script?"

"Don't get excited. And I can't talk about it. Don't open it either. Just please courier it up to the hotel."

"Righty ho, boss. Now you need to get on email. You've got your usual ton of invitations. And I know the nos, but I need answers on the maybes."

"Duncan's working today, and Chloe and I are riding this morning. I'll get on it this afternoon."

"Cool. Now I'll let you go. Have fun with Chloe and I really, *really* hope you enjoy exploring things with Duncan. And I really, *really* can't wait to meet him."

That made me smile. Not big, but at least it was a smile.

"Thanks, honey. Take care."

"You too. Later."

Then she was gone.

And I had no choice but to phone Duncan.

I would have liked our first-ever cell phone call in history, and our first-ever phone call after we were back together, to be about something like if he wanted me to make spaghetti and meatballs (his favorite from back in the day) for dinner that night.

At his house.

Because I was dying to cook in his kitchen.

He had an *amazing* kitchen, which wasn't a surprise, considering he had an *amazing* house.

But sadly, it had to be about other.

He picked up right away with a, "Hey, honey."

"Hi, uh, do you have a sec?"

"So you heard they made the connection with Corey."

This surprised me.

"You heard too?"

"Sheila, our publicist, has had her phone ringing off the hook. Before you worry, she's skipping through the office. She loves this. 'Because if I get another call about how you feel about fracking somewhere, when the answer is always, he's decisively against fracking, I'll scream,' her words. And she knows the response is, it's none of their business, not in those words, but she still thinks this is the shit."

"Well, there's that," I muttered.

"Is that why you called?" he asked.

"Well, yes, and no, since I have not spoken to my publicist. But she does have experience with this. And my PA is no fool. So she shared ahead of my publicist doing the same that this could get ugly."

"How?"

"Well..." God dammit! "Tom and I were really a favored couple, Bowie. And things can get nasty, and inappropriate, but there's no stopping it and—"

"Again, do I give a crap about this?"

"Well, when Team Tom wins in the race over Team Duncan, you might."

He burst out laughing.

I sat in stunned silence, listening to him.

When he got control of himself, he asked, "I get the sense you two salvaged things, so your kids don't have to deal with your garbage, like me and Dora did, but is it over?"

"I wouldn't start things with you if it wasn't."

"So I'll repeat, do I give a crap about this? Team Tom can win, but you're still about to ride my horses, have lunch with me, dinner at my house, you're gonna be in my bed, and we're gonna work it out so we're in each other's lives. Not that it's a competition. But still. I win."

I closed my eyes and turned my head, taking a minute, and not simply because I was glad he'd stated we were having dinner at his house.

"Gen?" he called when I said nothing.

I opened my eyes and said something.

"It means a great deal to me that you're taking this like you are, Bowie. Being Imogen Swan is a lot. That I can be Gen with you, hell, that I'm just Gen to you, means everything."

"Baby, you are not just Gen to me. You're Imogen Swan, famous actress. You're also Genny, the girl who didn't mind getting mud up to her knees and twigs in her hair when we went off trail on our hikes. And Gen, the girl who I looked to in the stands when I played football and could hear my father shouting over everyone else, coaching me from the sidelines. Also Genny, the hot piece I came home to who met my hunger, stroke for stroke. And now, Gen, a great mom, an interesting woman, and still a really hot piece I wanna sink into. Yeah?"

"You can't talk sex talk if you're going to slow things down, Bowie."

"I'm speedin' a few things up tonight, since Chloe just texted and told me she has to get back to her shop, which means she's returning here at some point, but we got a window. She's leaving after your ride. And you're spending the night at my place. So when you come over tonight, bring clean panties. And Cookie."

Oh my.

"Can I make spaghetti and meatballs?"

"You can do whatever you want."

"I need to get showered and go ride with my girl, Bowie."

"I'll let you go then. But Gen?"

"Yes?"

"It wasn't our time before. This is our time. Don't let outside shit fuck with your head. We're us. We always connect. We've got this."

"You're right, darling."

"I am, baby. Now go. See you in a few hours."

We said our goodbyes and hung up and I instantly thought of Tom.

Perhaps his jealous spate had not subsided.

He would feel no joy if Team Tom won out.

Because he'd know Duncan was the true winner.

And Tom had held up a number of shiny trophies to the cheering crowds.

So he was an excellent competitor.

And a very sore loser.

CHAPTER 15

THE MEAL

Duncan

*D*uncan probably broke a record, by a long shot, getting out of his car and hauling his ass to the door to the kitchen after he'd pulled into his garage and saw Genny's Cayenne there.

Clearly, Bettina had seen to things as he'd asked, giving her a remote.

He'd also instructed she give Genny a set of keys.

He doubted she failed in this endeavor.

He walked in and was accosted by dogs.

And the smell of garlic.

Last, his first vision of Genny, his old Genny, from back in the day, standing at his range.

Bare feet. Jeans. And a River Rain tee Chloe had stolen and given her to wear riding so she didn't sweat on her fancy duds.

She'd changed when she came to meet him for lunch but had admitted then that her daughter had light fingers.

He'd told her he'd already learned that, and he didn't care.

It was too big on her and she'd knotted it at the waist.

She looked amazing in it.

"I hope you don't mind, but you told me it was an old one, and you could always get more, and sauce splashes—"

She had not missed his eyes on her tee.

She also didn't finish what she said.

Because it was hard to talk when your man was squeezing the breath out of you and had his tongue down your throat.

When he broke their kiss, she stared fuzzily up at him and muttered, "I thought it was the little woman's job to welcome the man home like that."

"I'm enlightened. Totally equal opportunity when it comes to kissing you fuzzy."

"Fuzzy?"

"Baby, you can't even focus."

"I can see you clearly, Bowie."

To make her laugh, but only for that, he took one arm from around her and held three fingers in front of her face.

"How many fingers am I holding up?"

She took her arms from around his neck, pushed her hands between them, gave him a weak, totally-didn't-mean-it shove, and said, "Shut up, Bowie."

But she did it laughing.

He gave her a grin, a quick kiss, let her go and looked to the stove.

Genny's meatballs and red sauce.

Fucking hell.

He could almost convince himself he missed that more than he missed her.

Okay, not almost.

Not even close.

But he loved her spaghetti and meatballs.

Marilyn, Gen's mom, was a dame, but Marilyn's mom was Italian, and she'd taught Marilyn to cook.

As well as Genny.

Her meatballs were works of art.

And her baked ziti should have its own religion.

Thinking of Marilyn, and smelling his kitchen, and having Genny in it, cooking, Duncan couldn't stop himself chuckling.

"What's funny now?" she asked.

He grabbed the wooden spoon sitting on the spoon rest and looked at her.

"I was thinking of your mom. When we were hanging out on your back porch, and I wondered out loud how you got that blonde hair and those blue eyes, when your mom is dark and half Italian, and her answer was, 'My husband has superior sperm.'"

Genny giggled and leaned a hip against the counter. "God, I remember that. I was so embarrassed."

"You *were* only sixteen. At sixteen, boy or girl, no one wants to think their dad has sperm."

She snatched up a towel and slapped it against his arm, stating, "I *still* don't want to think of it, Bowie."

He shot her another grin and dipped the wooden spoon in the huge vat (Gen never skimped when she made her red sauce, but that made it better, because if, within a few days, a miracle had occurred and it wasn't eaten, it went into the freezer to provide future good times).

He brought the spoon to his lips, blew on it and then tasted.

Fucking *heaven*.

"Does it pass inspection?" she asked.

"Can we eat now?" he asked back.

She looked horrified. "We have at least twenty more minutes of simmering."

"Sorry, out of practice," he teased.

She rolled her eyes.

Now there...

That she gave to Chloe.

"You need to greet your dogs and give Cookie your stamp of approval," she ordered.

He bent to the animals gathered around his legs to do that, asking, "Is Cookie settling in okay?"

"Apparently, I can take her on my jet-set travels. She settled in swimmingly. But I'm not sure Tuck is a fan. I haven't seen him since she claimed the great room."

"He'll get over it," Duncan muttered, finishing with Shasta and Rocco, he straightened with Killer in his arms.

And Tuck would have to, since Gen was moving up there.

At least, she'd be there part time. When they weren't in Phoenix.

And if he got his way, that would be most-of-the-time part time.

"Beer?" she asked, heading to the fridge.

He looked around, saw she had a glass of wine on the counter, so he answered, "Yeah."

She ducked in the fridge.

He let Killer go, went in search of Cookie, and did this sharing, "Just to say, for the first time, Gage figured out a couple of days ago that his dad has sperm. He's entirely grossed out by this concept, but he figured it out because he further figured out it's been in you, it's gonna be in you again, and he's currently strategizing how he's going to handle all of his friends knowing this same thing."

By the time he found Cookie, who was curled up on the back of the couch (though she was a sweet kitty, and thus she uncurled to stretch and reach for some scratches from his hand), he turned and saw Gen was standing in his open fridge with a bottle of beer in her hand, staring at him in dismay.

"Further heads up on that my son has yet to clue into the basics of appropriate social discourse, and in some cases behavior, no matter how much his mother and I drilled it into him. So I take no responsibility for what comes out of his mouth, or noises from other orifices in his body," he finished.

Her eyes crinkled before her smile came and she was shaking her head as she shut the door on the refrigerator and went right to the drawer that held his bottle opener.

She'd familiarized herself with his kitchen.

He fucking loved that.

Having given Cookie his stamp of approval, or more to the point, having received the message she was done with it and she was jumping away, he returned to the island and slid onto a stool just as Genny slid the beer across to him.

She nabbed her wine and asked, "How was your day?"

"Lowkey, which is good. I had a shit-ton to catch up on. Email is like tribbles."

She laughed softly.

"Yours?" he queried.

"Well, um…" She turned from him and her wine to go to the stove and stir.

"Well, um, what?" he prompted, perplexed at her hesitancy.

They didn't have a lot of time in with their reunion, but unless she was being bashful, an obstacle it appeared she'd leaped right over, she'd always seemed totally open.

"Okay, there are things I didn't share at lunch," she told the pot.

Lunch was good. Light. What they'd had the day before when it was about them and they didn't let other shit drag on it.

He wasn't big on there being something dragging on her that she didn't share.

"Like what?" he asked, feeling a tenseness hit his neck, because they didn't have a lot of time in with their reunion, and although it seemed to be going great, at this juncture, it was very new.

Anything could fuck it up.

And that was something he couldn't let happen.

Not again.

She put the spoon on the rest, and returned to her wine, and him.

"Okay, well, the man who created *Rita's Way* is developing another series and he wants me for it."

The tension left and he smiled. "That's awesome."

She studied him. "Duncan, being a principle on a series is a lot of work."

"So?"

"He says, if I'm interested, and it's picked up, he'll film in Phoenix."

"Even better."

She studied him closer. "You really have no issue with this?"

Duncan was feeling something creeping up in him, and he didn't like it.

This being irritation.

"Why would I have an issue with it?"

"Well, depending on how long a season runs, I'd need to be down in Phoenix a lot of the time, and probably in LA on some occasions, to film it. And that doesn't include the travel I'd need to do to market it."

"Gen, I have seventy-five stores in fifty different cities and we're in the planning stages to open up five more. I'm also the official spokesperson for two very active charities. I'm a hands-on CEO. And I give one hundred percent to any commitment I make. I don't sit on my ass in Prescott watching TV when I'm not a drudge sitting behind a desk in the office."

"I didn't mean it like that."

"What did you mean?"

"It's just…different when it's so public."

"So you're saying Tom had an issue with you working and being out there."

"No, because Tom was a celebrity in his own right."

"So you're saying I won't get it 'cause I'm not famous."

"I'm saying it's something to get used to as it is, but if it takes off, as Teddy's shows have a tendency to do, it can get serious, invasive to life and stressful."

"And you don't think I can handle that."

She shot straight and her face set.

"What I think is I *don't know what to think*, Duncan," she snapped. "Don't keep telling me what I'm saying. I started a discussion about a possible job that might come out of a script I haven't even read yet. I'm not casting aspersions on you, your character, or your ability to handle life with me working. But we're doing this." She slapped a hand between them. "And as I'd expect a conversation from you if you were looking into taking on something that would take your time and especially take you away from me where you didn't, say, sleep in bed beside me, I'm doing that right now with you."

He was not irritated in the slightest anymore.

"Okay, Genny, you can cool it and thank you for that, and just to point out, if you wanna do this and it means something to you, I'll deal, and *we'll* deal. Dora's a salesperson. She sells software. Her area is a quarter of the US. She's good at it and she makes a load, and she travels a lot. She started that job after we split, and the boys were about ready to roll out. But she was in sales before that, she was successful then too, and to be that, you gotta work hard so she wasn't always in the kitchen baking cookies. It might not be the same scale, but it's not something I haven't dealt with."

"Okay, fine," she clipped.

"And I'm sorry I got irritated, honey, but you talk a lot about being Imogen Swan and all that shit and it might not have been casting aspersions on my ability to handle it, but it was feeling like that and it was getting annoying."

"I can see that," she bit off.

He stared at her.

And then he demanded, "Okay, what's actually the matter?"

She looked to her wine.

Then she nabbed it and threw a whole lot back.

She put it down and said, "Tom knows about us and I didn't tell him. We had a deal, if one of us started dating, we'd warn the other, no matter how casual. Tom also knows about you and who you are to me, and as such, he realizes this is far from casual. And you might have found out only recently that Dora had an issue with me, when you emerged as the CEO of an up-and-coming and very popular, which means very successful store, Tom knew who you were and there were issues. I thought he worked through them, but even if he didn't share the fullness of his feelings this morning, I got the drift and somehow he's seeing this as a betrayal. And he's *very* angry and Tom doesn't get angry. Not at me."

"Was he a dick to you?"

"Very much so, and that's not Tom."

"Trying not to lose it here, baby," he said softly in warning.

"You can't be mad. He's right. I should have told him. It should have come from me."

"You're divorced, he really does not get that, Gen."

She shook her head. "That isn't who we are."

That tension in his neck came back and his words were careful when he suggested, "Maybe you should share who you are."

She went to the stove.

Stirred the sauce.

He waited, not very patiently.

She came back to the island.

She put her hands to it, leaned into them, her head bent.

When she looked up at him, he knew to brace.

So he did.

And it was good he did.

"Okay, you see, when I lost the last man I loved, I lost my best friend."

Fuck.

"And when Tom cheated on me, and there was no question, because I smelled some perfume on one of his shirts that wasn't mine, and I honest to God thought it was Chloe's, but I teased him that he was stepping out on me, and he couldn't lie and say it was his daughter's. So he admitted it to me."

"Jesus, baby," Duncan whispered.

She nodded.

"It was not good. And although there is a part of me, in the months that came after, the endless talks, the counseling, that understands that, when my career dwindled, the roles I was offered were less interesting, less challenging, and then eventually simply insulting, I turned in on myself. Which means I tuned out my marriage, and him, and our sex life. Which I will admit, regrettably and with not a small amount of guilt, became nonexistent for a good length of time. It still was not okay for him to go out and fuck someone that was not me."

"No," Duncan said gently.

"But he did. And I couldn't get past that. I tried. But I couldn't. It was frustrating for us both. And harming what we had left. Which was still based in love, and respect, and history, and our family, and for me, very importantly, he was my best friend."

Tears were brightening her eyes, and it took a lot for Duncan to keep his seat, but he did and said, "I get that."

"So we made a deal to cut our losses with the marriage, and keep hold of the friendship. And so far, it's worked."

"And now there's me."

She nodded again. "And now there's you."

"And you don't wanna lose him in the way you have him," Duncan deduced.

She shook her head and looked away.

Now was the time.

He got off his stool and moved to her.

She didn't fight him when he pulled her in his arms.

Hers only loosely went around him and she shoved her face in his chest.

And he was right.

It was the time.

Because she lost it.

"I-I'm not c-crying because there's something there. It just died, Bowie. He killed it and he didn't mean to, but he did. I c-couldn't be intimate with him anymore. It was in my head. Did he touch her like that? Did he kiss her there? They'd fucked two times, and it was only her, and I believe that with the mess he was in sharing it, knowing what it was doing to us, and knowing it could have been fifty women and thousands of times, or just one just once, and it wouldn't matter. The damage was done."

She tipped her head back and her mascara was running a little.

"But I'd lost you and you were *gone*. We had a lot of sex, but you listened when I had a bad day, or we laughed when my mom was being crazy, or you unloaded on me when your dad was a dick. You were my go-to and then Tom was my go-to. I couldn't lose another go-to."

"Totally understandable," he said soothingly.

"And I can't now, even if I have my other go-to back," she admitted, then shoved her face in his chest again.

"I'm not ever gonna ask that, Genny," he assured, rubbing her back.

He said it. He meant it.

It was going to be tough, in the beginning.

But if this guy could get a lock on whatever was fucking with his head that made him be a dick to her, Duncan was willing to do it.

"Yeah," she snuffled. "That's how you get to be a go-to."

He grinned, bent, kissed the top of her head, and then asked, "So, he lost it with you this morning and what?"

"I've texted and told him when he gets a handle on it, he can call me, and we'll talk it out." She tipped her head back again. "He has not called me."

"You need to give him the go-to speech, beautiful."

"Wh-what?" she asked, blinking up at him and lifting a hand to swipe her cheek.

Mascara disaster.

He didn't say that.

"Gen, if he's the guy I think he is, and that's just what I know with you wanting to keep him in your life, then he'll hear the go-to speech and sort his shit. Give him time to get his head straight. And then call him. It'll be okay."

"I'm not making excuses for him, I'm saying, you live, you learn, and although I found I couldn't forgive Tom for sullying our marriage bed, Tom couldn't forgive me for not only not being able to forgive him, but also not turning to him, which was what sent him searching. You see, Bowie, he knew he was my go-to and that meant a lot to him. And when I hit that crisis, I didn't go to him. He saw that as a betrayal. The thing is, he turned right around and instigated the same thing, because honestly, he didn't try too hard to reach me. So I get we both fucked up, though it isn't immature to say his was a *way huger* fuckup. But we can't do that, you and me. We can't hit the skids and not talk about it. You can't coast in a marriage, a relationship. You have to keep your eye on the ball all the time."

"Okay, so I have this clear, if you clam up and get in your head, I got your permission to shake you out of it?"

She nodded vehemently. "Absolutely. I cannot even begin to tell you how ridiculous and pathetic I feel that my marriage ended because my husband and I didn't *talk to each other*. And then it was too late. Now you and I have found each other again. And that's an *impossibility*. And you mean so much to me, I honest to God don't know what I'd do if I threw you away because I didn't open my mouth and *speak*."

And you mean so much to me...

Yeah, he could be down with this guy in their life.

Totally.

"Well, just pointing out, seems like you're not havin' a lot of issues with that right about now," he teased.

Her body jerked.

Then she melted into him.

And did it laughing.

Thank fuck.

He tucked her even closer and held her through it.

When it was waning, it sucked, but it had to be done.

"I'm sorry you went through that. I'm sorry he did that to you. And I'm sorry you lost him. I also hope he gets it together so in the way you got, you can have him back."

Right.

He got that out.

Now the easy.

"But I'm glad you lived and learned it, honey. Because I honest to God don't know what I'd do if I lost you either. So let's both keep our eye on the ball and make sure that doesn't happen."

She burrowed in and muttered, "That's a deal."

"Now, I remember you'd rather cut off your own hand than serve meatballs that were not freshly cooked with your sauce, so by my estimation, the time is now to get frying. But I would not be doing my job if I didn't share with you that your mascara is a disaster so you probably should get on that first."

She lurched out of his arms and her hands flew to her face.

"Ohmigod!" she cried.

"Can I start frying while you're in the bathroom wiping?" he requested.

She nodded and took off, bossing, "Low heat, Bowie. Browned, not burned."

Like he'd forget that.

He'd had meatball duty a lot back in the day.

But he might often be veggie, there was one thing he agreed with his dad about.

A man knew how to cook meat.

The skillet was already out.

He found the meatballs in the fridge.

She didn't skimp on those either.

There had to be three dozen of them.

Jesus.

Gen re-joined him to look in on the sauce while he was putting them (or at least the first round of them) in the skillet.

She stayed close, probably to make sure he did it right.

So he curled an arm around her shoulders and held her there while he completed this task.

"Thanks for listening," she whispered.

He gave her a squeeze. "You're welcome."

"Thanks for knowing there was something wrong and pulling it out."

"You're welcome for that too."

"And thanks for sharing honestly I was annoying you with the Imogen Swan stuff. I'll back off doing that."

He turned and kissed the side of her head.

Then he said, "Do you. If I get irritated, we'll hash it out. But we *will* hash it out, Gen. Okay?"

"Okay," she mumbled, resting her weight into his side.

"When do the Cardinals get here?" he asked.

"What?"

"I'm only assuming, since you made enough to feed a football team."

She made a "puh" noise and pressed her hip into his.

He grinned at the meat.

He stopped grinning when he heard a door go up in the garage.

"Is Chloe coming back tonight?" Gen asked, because clearly, she'd heard it too.

"No, but regardless, she had the opener for your door, something you now have."

"You mean, my *daughter* had my spot before me?"

He shot her a smile as he moved to the garage door.

He opened it.

And sighed.

Because in Gage's spot in the four-car garage, folding out of his youngest son's orange Subaru Crosstrek hybrid was not only Gage.

But Sully.

It was Friday night so no class on the weekend.

But for fuck's sake, his oldest lived nearly two thousand miles away.

Apparently, Gage was up from Tucson.

And he'd swung by Sky Harbor on his way.

"Please tell me my eyes are deceiving me," he called.

"Whose Cayenne, Dad?" Gage called back, eyeing the Porsche.

"Did the global satellite network fail so you couldn't call me?" Duncan asked.

"Is she here...like, *now*?" Sully asked back, eyeing Duncan.

"*She* is but *you* weren't supposed to be," Duncan pointed out.

"Holy fuck, Sul, we're cock blocking Dad," Gage declared.

Duncan checked to see if the lock worked on the door.

"Thank God I fixed my mascara," Genny whispered from behind him.

From where he was still barring the door against his own flesh and blood, he looked over his shoulder at her.

She appeared as if she was in pain in an effort not to laugh.

"Are you gonna let us in, Dad?" Sul asked.

He was turning back to see them both right there, with their hulking bags, likely filled with laundry they were going to call Bettina and beg her to come on a Saturday to clean, when he heard Gage sniff.

"*Dear Lord in heaven, what is that smell?*" he demanded, then bowled through his brother and his father to achieve entry.

Sully came in behind him.

"Son two, or Gage, who fortunately thinks mostly with his stomach rather than other parts of his anatomy," he introduced.

Genny giggled.

Gage had forgotten about the smell of garlic and meat cooking and was staring at Genny with his mouth hanging open.

"He's also slick and real good with the ladies," Duncan joked.

"Holy cannoli," Gage breathed. "You're like, *seven thousand times* more beautiful than in the movies."

"Well, wow, thank you, Gage," Genny replied warmly.

"Dad," Sul said under his breath, elbowing Duncan in the ribs.

"And this is son one, Sullivan, or Sully," Duncan said.

Gen reached out a hand. "Nice to meet you, Sully."

He took her hand. "*Real* cool to meet you, uh..."

"Genny," Gen filled it in.

"Right, Genny," he said, pumping her hand.

Gage shoved him out of the way and stuck his hand at her. "Yeah. Genny. Hi. Gage."

She took it and shook. "Hi, Gage."

"I get it, people take pictures of you eating at El Gato. You don't even have to be famous. If I saw you at El Gato, I'd take a picture of you," he stated.

"And again, thank you. That's so sweet," Genny said, now not shaking, but Gage still was.

"Let her go, son," Duncan said low.

Gage did and popped back like a cat who'd been confronted with a cucumber.

"God, you are *such* a dufus," Sul said, again under his breath.

"Shut it, Sul," Gage bit out.

"Then cool it, Gage. Jesus. She's just a human."

"A gorgeous one."

"You've seen gorgeous women before."

"Not in our kitchen."

"All right, we're done with this," Duncan decreed.

"Good I made plenty," Genny noted, looking at him even as she skirted his sons to get to the meatballs, a twinkle in her eye.

"Yeah, good," he agreed, because his boys could pack it in, they loved food, and they'd love her (more, apparently, when it came to Gage) the minute they tasted it. He looked between his sons. "But, as much as I love you and pine for any time I can spend with you, I'd still like to be let in on the secret of why you two are here without you sharing that with me."

"We decided you needed, like, moral support," Gage said, having dumped his bag, he was following Genny like a puppy.

He turned to his eldest.

And got what he expected.

The honest story.

"We were worried," Sullivan said quietly. "That maybe you weren't saying something. Like, you know, it was clear she was real special to you. But then we didn't see anything on social media."

"Dad, have you ever had this much meat in the house *in your life?*" Gage called from hanging at Genny's side.

He ignored his second son.

"It isn't like every moment we share is going to be captured and disseminated on Instagram," Duncan pointed out to Sully.

"It also isn't like our dad is going to call and share he got his heart broken so he needs his boys around, is it?" Sul returned.

Fuck, they were nuts.

But he had good boys.

"Point taken, son, but as you can see, it's all good."

"Well, our crystal ball broke so we took a shot," Gage entered the conversation.

Genny started giggling again.

Then, before Duncan could make note he wasn't a fan of his son's smart mouth, when he actually was, seeing as his kid was hilarious, she waded in.

"Okay, we don't know each other at all, but we're at a crucial juncture with this meal so it's all hands on deck. I need water boiling. Spaghetti out. The oven needs turned on to pre-heat for the garlic bread. And we need dishes and cutlery. Then the salad has to be tossed."

And there was Gen being a mom in his kitchen.

He loved that too.

Gage saluted crisply and declared, "Aye, aye captain. I'm on water."

He then went to get a pot.

"What'd'ya need the oven set to, Genny?" Sully asked, now having dumped his own bag and he was heading to the oven.

"Four hundred, Sully. Thank you," Genny answered.

"Get on what Gen wants and then get these bags to the utility before the scent I'm sure that canvas is barely containing breaks free. And for Christ's sake, pay some attention to the dogs before they explode," Duncan ordered.

Shasta was actually beginning to keen.

The oven was on, but the water didn't get put in the pot before the boys focused love on the dogs.

But then they got down to it.

Things got sorted and Duncan was tossing Genny's homemade Caesar dressing on the romaine while the boys wisely got of the way and had taken seats at the now-set-with-plates-napkins-and-cutlery island and they were watching her.

"So, like, famous people cook food?" Gage asked.

Duncan looked to Sully who was staring at his brother like he wished he wasn't his brother.

"Not really, I have a cook as part of my entourage that travels everywhere with me, but she has the flu so needs must," Genny stated breezily.

"Wow, cool, a cook!" Gage exclaimed, likely thinking what that would mean to his eating habits when he was home.

"She's kidding, Gage," Sully spilled it.

Gage looked crushed. "You don't have a cook?"

She swirled pasta at the same time twisting to him and saying, "No, honey. I'm sorry. But if it'll make you like me, I'll hire one."

"If you haven't gotten it, Genny, he already likes you," Sully shared.

She winked at Sullivan and turned back to the stove.

"Are Harvey and Beth coming to dinner or something?" Gage asked.

Duncan looked to him. "No." And when he saw Gage turned on his stool to face the entryway, he knew it wasn't about the amount of food being prepared that he was asking. So he finished, "Why?"

"Because I saw lights. Someone is coming up the—"

The dogs rushed, barking, and in Killer's case yapping, to the front door.

He was already out of luck for their evening plans with his boys home.

But with them, he did not feel it would leave long-lasting marks if he took Gen back to the hotel and spent the night with her there at the same time his den was in no danger of being redecorated.

And he was happy to see his sons, especially Sully, who only came home for holidays, and in the case of spring break for the last three years, not even that.

Gen was going to have to get to know them eventually, she seemed relaxed and cool with them there, not nervous or awkward, so Duncan was seeing this as a good thing.

But if Harvey and/or Beth were adding themselves to the mix, he might just lose it.

"See who it is and send them away," Duncan ordered Sully.

"On it," Sul said, sliding off his stool.

"You need any more help, Genny?" Gage offered as Duncan dumped in the croutons and parmesan to mix that in.

"You can check the bread," Gen said.

"On it," Gage muttered the same thing his brother said, jumping off his stool.

Feeling Genny's eyes, Duncan looked from his boy to her.

She gave him a happy smile.

She liked his boys.

She liked family.

She liked cooking.

Yeah, this was a good thing.

Her face froze when a female's voice could be heard crying, "Oh! Look at you precious babies!"

And then dogs barking happily.

He then watched Gen's eyes get big as she whispered, "Sasha."

Sasha?

Her daughter?

Suddenly, Genny was racing out of the room.

Duncan looked at Gage. Gage looked at Duncan.

Then they both headed toward the front door.

"Momma!" they heard cried.

Dogs continued to bark excitedly.

"Baby girl!" was cried back.

And he rounded the corner just as Gen hit a body that was in the opened door, wrapped her arms around it, and swayed it side to side.

"Uh…" Gage prompted.

"Her daughter," Duncan muttered.

"Ah," Gage said.

Sully was standing off to the side, still and staring.

Too still.

Duncan would get why in a second.

Gen pulled away but kept her hands on a woman Duncan could not see.

"What are you doing here?" she asked.

"Chloe told me I *had* to meet this *Duncan*. And so, here I am, to meet Duncan."

Gen shifted aside and called to him, "Look, darling, Sasha's here."

Gage stopped dead.

Chloe had her father's coloring and her mother's style.

Sasha looked like her mother.

Long, blonde, beach hair, supremely ripped jeans, little satin cami, massive slouchy cardigan, tangle of two dozen necklaces, moccasins on her feet, and entirely makeup free, but healthy tan notwithstanding.

At least she had on shoes.

That'd be an additional item of clothing both his sons had to mentally take off.

Which was what they were doing.

"You're Duncan," Sasha said, coming forward, hand extended.

He was wrong.

She was taller than her mother. Slimmer. Willowy.

But she had Genny's blue eyes and bright, big smile.

"Yup." He put out a hand. "Sasha, really cool to meet you, kid."

She folded her fingers around his, cupped her other hand on top, and replied, "Right back at cha."

He let her go and she turned side to side, taking in his sons.

"My boys, Sullivan and Gage."

"Hi, guys!" she greeted excitedly, going to Sul first, who'd pulled it together to return her greeting and shake her hand. Then to Gage, who shook woodenly and couldn't stop staring. She then whirled and exclaimed, "God, Momma! Are you making meatballs?"

"Yes, darling," Gen confirmed.

"Have you had them before?" Sasha asked Duncan, whirling back to do it.

"A long time ago," Duncan answered. And then, when it looked like this information was a weight she could not bear, he quickly said, "And really lookin' forward to having them again. My boys having them. And having you at my table. Glad you're here. Come on in. You want some wine or a beer?"

Gen claimed her to bring her forward as Sasha answered, "Totes beer."

"I'll get it," Gage offered readily, and then hustled off.

"My God, this place is like…it's like…*rad*," Sasha declared, looking around as she moved. "I mean, this might be the coolest pad I've ever been in. Seriously."

"This is saying something, Bowie, since she's dined with several maharishis and the Dalai Lama in their I'm sure not-so-humble abodes," Gen called.

"I have not, Mom, stop being a goof," Sasha chastised. "I mean, not the Dalai Lama."

"I'll stop being a goof when you stop doing my head in by not letting me know where you are ninety-nine-point-nine-nine percent of the time," Genny retorted.

"Whatever," Sasha muttered, then asked. "Bowie?"

"If you are very lucky and win the heart of Bowie like Chloe did, you might learn the story."

"It's totally spiritual," Sully said.

And he meant that.

Gage handed her an opened beer.

"Thanks so much!" Sasha cried in delight.

"Don't mention it," Gage muttered, instead of saying, "I live to serve you."

"Sul, get Sasha a plate," Duncan ordered, heading to check the food on the stove. "Gage, look in on the bread."

Both boys moved.

"Chloe's won his heart?" Sasha asked her mother.

"Yes," Genny answered.

"*Chloe?*" Sasha didn't hide her shock.

Genny laughed.

Duncan chuckled.

"Who's Chloe?" Sully, sidling close, muttered to him.

"Genny's oldest daughter," Duncan answered.

"There's another one of *her?*" Gage was also close and sounding strangled.

Duncan chuckled again.

"So you've now met both of them?" Sully asked.

"Yup," Duncan answered.

"We have a brother too. Two of them, really, since we claim Hale."

Both his boys jumped because that was from Sasha and she was right there, holding her hair back and bending over the vat of sauce.

She sniffed, closing her eyes and emitting a long, "Ah."

Duncan heard Gage groan.

He looked to his boots.

He looked back at her when she said, "You guys are in for a treat. Mom's red sauce is *everything.*"

And with a sweet smile directed at them, she drifted away.

"Did I just hear a seagull call?" Gage asked.

Duncan felt pain in his middle from trying not to bust a gut laughing.

"And Mom, just a heads up, there's going to be news coming from that direction. And not from Hale."

That made Duncan look hard at Sasha, who was now looking at her mother.

So Duncan turned to Genny.

She looked freaked.

"What kind of news?" she asked.

"I should let Matt tell you," Sasha muttered.

"Oh no, baby girl, you cannot drop that morsel and not carry it through. What?" Genny demanded.

"Okay, so you can't lose it," Sasha started.

"Uh-oh," Sul mumbled.

"Holy shit," Gage said.

"Just spill," Genny ordered.

"He's dropping out of med school," Sasha declared.

"Uh-oh," Sul mumbled.

"Holy shit," Gage said.

Genny's face was getting red. "He…"

"Gen—" Duncan tried to get in there.

"*What?*" she shouted.

"Momma—" Sasha began.

But Genny was on the move.

To her purse.

Which undoubtedly was where her phone was.

"I really should have let him tell you," Sasha said urgently.

"Yes, you should have, but now it's out so there's no going back and…where's my goddamn phone?" Gen was digging irately through her bag.

"Is this it?" Gage asked helpfully, and glancing at him, Duncan saw he was holding up a phone.

Shit.

"Yes, darling, thank you." Genny headed to his boy.

When she got close, Duncan stepped in her way. "Babe, take a beat and get a lock on it."

"Yeah, Mom, chill," Sasha encouraged.

Gen didn't take her eyes from Duncan.

"My son is throwing away five years of education," she retorted.

"Right, this is why you need to get a lock on it."

"It's no biggie anyway, Momma. He's quitting so he can go to vet school."

Gen's body twitched and then she turned to her daughter.

"Sorry?"

"He got in at Purdue," Sasha shared.

"No shit? Righteous," Sully said.

"I know," Sasha replied. "I'm super proud of him. It's a really good school."

"I know," Sul told her. "I go there."

"Really?" she cried.

"Yeah," Sul confirmed.

Sasha turned to her mother. "Momma! Awesome! He'll know somebody!"

"They actually haven't met yet, Sash," Gen, visibly calmer, noted.

"So? We're all gonna be family, right?" Sasha returned.

The air in the great room went static.

But Gen looked to Duncan with an expression of *I'm worried this is too soon.*

And Duncan had to admit his expression was probably the same.

"God, stop being dorks," Gage broke it. "It's not like we're two and we don't know what's going on. She's cooking in your kitchen, Dad. And when we showed, you didn't hike our asses to the den to have 'a talk' about how we shouldn't read anything into this and to be nice to her. Genny cooking dinner was just happening and you started making the salad. And I don't know that cat," he pointed at Cookie, "but I do know it isn't ours and you didn't get another cat because you were being hardass about getting another pet, so it's obviously Genny's. And so there's the cat and you already know this Chloe chick and gave her the Bowie story so the mingling of families has happened. We're with the program so you can relax. Yeesh."

"Yeah, you can relax, yeesh," Sasha agreed and then, "Cookie!" and off she went to Cookie.

"Okay, I don't know about you all, but if I don't eat this food soon, I'm gonna die," Sul declared.

"Totally, there's, like, a hundred meatballs here and I feel like I could eat a hundred and five of them," Gage said.

Sully had the garlic bread out.

He also was intent to get control of the situation.

Which was what he did.

"Gage, get that meat off the heat. And Sasha, when you're done greeting Cookie, can you check the pasta?"

"I'm all over it," Sasha agreed.

Gage was already yanking off paper towel to put on a plate to drain the meatballs.

"Did I see stables?" Sasha asked, approaching the kitchen.

"Yeah," Sully answered, putting the bread in a basket Gen had ready.

"You have horses?" Sasha sounded excited, or more excited than what was apparently her resting state.

"Three of them," Gage answered.

"Rad!" Sasha cried.

"You ride?" Sul asked.

He felt a touch at his waist and looked down to see Genny closing in.

She moved in farther, her arm around him.

He slid his around her shoulders.

She dropped her cheek to his chest.

"Totes!" Sasha chirped.

"Take you out tomorrow. You can ride Streak. He's Dad's. Great horse," Sully told her.

"Cool!" Sasha exclaimed, fishing out a thread of pasta to test.

"Ready to eat?" Duncan murmured to Genny.

She tipped her head back.

He sucked in breath at the happy radiating from her face.

"Yes, darling," she replied.

With that happy, he couldn't stop himself

He bent and touched his mouth to hers.

When they made to get a move on, Sasha peeped, "You guys are *so cute!*"

"Gag," Gage muttered.

Sully started chuckling.

"Pasta's done!" Sasha announced.

And all was well in the world.

CHAPTER 16

THE NIGHTMARE

Corey

ne year earlier...

COREY SAT in Genny's couch, watching her as she stood at the windows, staring at north Phoenix.

"So it's over," she told the window.

Her voice was flat.

Dead.

As her eyes had been when, not half an hour before, she'd greeted him at her door.

In his seat on the couch, Corey didn't move, kept himself perfectly still.

He did this in an effort not to excuse himself, find some privacy, and then pull out his phone.

This was because, with a few well-placed calls, he could destroy Tom Pierce's life.

Obliterate it.

No more courtside commentary at Wimbledon.

Medical license revoked.

Publicly humiliated.

Financially decimated.

And he wanted to do just that.

Badly.

What was wrong with the man?

There she was, the most perfect female on the planet, Tom had his ring on her finger, planted his children in her womb, slept beside her at night, and he'd fucked someone else?

Lunacy.

Sheer lunacy.

"We've filed for divorce." She was still talking to the window. "A preemptive strike, doing it now, before our friendship ends as well as the marriage."

Jesus Christ.

"Are you serious?" Corey asked.

She turned to him, highball in her hand, the ice tinkling in the gimlet he'd made her from her drinks cabinet.

Genny could mix her own cocktails (and his).

Genny could do anything.

That said, when he was around, Tom insisted on doing it for her.

It was a thing. A good thing for them. A thing that irritated Corey no end.

It amused them both, some inside joke.

But it was more.

Corey could tell Genny thought it was gallant.

Because it was.

So now that Tom was gone, Corey had insisted.

However, earlier, when he'd handed her the glass, she tried, but she couldn't hide the wince.

Couldn't hide not only how little it meant Corey had made her a drink, but how badly it hurt that it wasn't her husband doing it.

Therefore, in the end, all he'd managed to do was make a hollow gesture which turned into an unexpected blow.

You're good at that.

"Sorry?" she asked back.

He repeated her words to her. "Before your friendship ends?"

"Yes," she answered.

"What friendship?"

"He's been my best friend since—"

Right.

No.

Corey could not listen to this shit.

Not again.

And especially not since he knew what came after her "since."

He couldn't bear it.

He couldn't be reminded of it.

He hadn't thought of it in years.

Liar. You think of it every day.

"*I've* been your best friend since you were *eight*," he bit off.

She shut her mouth.

"The man stuck his dick in someone who is *not you*," he kept at her.

She flinched, and the strength of that flinch wasn't just emotional pain. It was real pain. Physical. Like Corey had stabbed her with a knife.

But he couldn't stop himself.

"That is not a friend, Genny."

He saw her spine straighten, and fuck, he hated this shit.

Over the years—and he knew it sounded insane, but he didn't care —he'd learned that he would have vastly preferred her to be a weak woman.

That steel, it made her America's sweetheart. That steel, it earned her a brief but glorious period where she was the highest paid female actor in Hollywood, and she'd fucking deserved that (and she didn't deserve to lose it). That steel, it allowed her to put up with Chloe's bullshit, Matt being a proud, arrogant fuck and Sasha teetering off the rails.

Not to mention Sam's crap.

And Hale becoming…Christ.

His grown-ass son was a camp counselor, for fuck's sake (though, Genny and Tom thought it was fantastic, something Corey did not understand).

That steel also kept her from falling into Corey's arms the many times he'd opened them to her.

Corey could have practically any woman on the whole goddamned planet.

But not Imogen Swan.

And more importantly, not Genny.

"I don't mean to sound cruel," she said, her voice holding a hint of frost, "but you don't know where I'm coming from with this, Corey."

"I'll repeat, I've known you since you were eight. You have always had me. I have never treated you like shit. I have never fucked you over. Not once. Not fucking *once*."

Oh yes you have.

He ignored the voice in his head, the ability to do so being a gift he'd had his whole life.

A gift, of late, he was pretending was not slipping.

But it was.

He kept speaking.

"So I do know, Genny, sitting here, being the one who was always there for you, and listening to you telling me you're going to remain friends with a man who *fucked you over*."

"He's the father of my children."

"I haven't spoken to Sam in well over a decade," he retorted. "My assistants deal with her. And when that doesn't work, my attorneys do it. And through most of that time, our kid wasn't fully grown."

Her eyes flashed with anger, not simply at him, but also for his son.

"That is not something to brag about, Corey."

A million visions of Hale assaulted his brain.

Particularly ones of how his son looked at him.

And how he looked at *Tom Pierce*.

And how Hale reminded Corey of *someone else*.

God, fuck, God, fuck.

She was right.

With considerable mental effort, the kind it was only recently he'd had to expend, he pushed that aside.

He had to focus on what was important.

To him.

This was happening now, with Genny and Tom.

He couldn't think about his son.

Thus, to center his attention on Gen, he stood.

"What I'm saying is, your best friend is standing right here. I'm always here. I've always been here. I'll always be here. For you."

"I love you very much," she said softly, and it struck him softly, right in the gut. "But they held my heart."

They?

Oh no.

No, no, no.

No!

"I hate it you never had this," she kept talking, her voice sad, sweet, killing him.

Killing him.

"I always wanted it for you. Someone knowing...*you*," she whispered. "*You*. All of you. What makes you. What thrills you. What you can't stand. What you live for. What you'd die for. A glance in your direction, and they know your mood. Two seconds of listening, and they know if the start of a laugh will end in a fit of giggles, or just a wreath of smiles. The tone of voice on the first word sharing instantly you need to brace, because you're about to have words. There are things I can't tell you, things I can't give you, Corey, no matter how you've always been there, how much I adore you. Things... Important things. *Crucial* things. Things that Tom had. That Bowie had."

That name.

Bowie.

Duncan.

No.

No, no, *no.*

The bright hit her eyes, tears shimmering.

"And I've lost it again. Bowie..." she shook her head, "I nearly didn't survive that."

She hadn't.

He'd had to put her together.

You broke her apart, it was the least you could do.

Corey shoved that thought aside too, and it was easy, not only because he had so much practice, but because it didn't change the fact that he'd had to put her together.

And he did.

"I don't mean to hurt you, I love you to my soul, Corey," she kept talking. "But you don't get it. You don't understand what I lost. Now...twice."

Twice.

At that word, something slick sluiced through him, something he couldn't hold at bay.

A warning sign.

Because he did get it.

Stop looking at her.

He got it.

Look away!

He completely understood.

STOP LOOKING!

Because he took it from her.

Tell her.

Don't.

Tell her.

Never.

You should have told her years ago. Told *him* years ago. You know it. Excuses. Always making excuses.

You never got what you truly wanted, why should they?

Maybe because it was never his to have?

Anything is his.

SHE ISN'T. AND HE LOST HIM LONG AGO. HE HAD THEM ONCE. BOTH OF THEM. AND THEY WERE THE ONLY THINGS THAT MATTERED.

If it meant so much to them, why did they let it go?

THEY DIDN'T LET GO. HE DID.

He wasn't the one who walked away.

AND YET ANOTHER EXCUSE. HE KNOWS IT. HE KNOWS HE WAS THE ONE WHO *DROVE* HIM AWAY.

Corey actually shook his head to chase the competing thoughts from it before he opened his arms and murmured, "Come here, Genny."

She came to him, walked right into his arms, pressed her cheek to his chest and wept.

Corey folded her in, tucking her tight, held her, and listened to her grief.

It was then, he felt it, Genny held against him like that, trusting him, giving him something she'd never given to anyone else.

Not Tom.

Not Duncan.

Giving it only to him.

Giving him the grief of losing them.

The both of them.

That was just Corey's.

And holding her right then, he felt what he'd refused to feel for over forty years.

She and he…

They didn't fit.

You do.

She was tall, slender, but she had curves.

He was tall, still thin, not reed thin, like he'd been when he was younger, but slim.

But he was not significantly tall, as a tall woman would need.

Like Tom.

Like Duncan.

Stop thinking about Duncan.

Corey wasn't solid, fit, muscled.

Like Tom.

Like Duncan.

Stop it with Duncan.

She lived in a luxury condominium and was wearing twenty-thousand-dollar earrings, but she'd be just as at home and comfortable in a log cabin the mountains. Maybe *more* at home and comfortable in a log cabin in the mountains.

Corey owned five homes.

And not one of them was, or ever would be, a log cabin in the mountains.

She was not fragile.

She was not frail.

But it was the ones that were hard to crush that, when you eventually accomplished that feat, they were broken in ways that could never be fixed.

He'd learned that when he'd broken Sam.

When he'd broken Genny that first time.

When he'd broken Hale.

You didn't break Hale. He doesn't even know you.

Hale broke you.

Your son broke you.

By needing you.

AND LOVING YOU.

Corey closed his eyes, and unable to stop it as he had so many times in the past, another ability that was slipping from his grasp, he felt the sensation caused by his thoughts well in him, rushing into his chest.

His doctor said they were panic attacks.

His doctor was wrong.

Corey knew what they were.

You don't.

He did.

You don't.

He did.

He dreamed about it.

Christ, the nightmares.

The guilt.

You're one of the richest men on the planet. You don't become that...you don't get what you want in this world by playing nice.

AND HE GOT WHAT HE WANTED BY NOT PLAYING FAIR? OR INSTEAD, DID HE JUST LOSE EVERYTHING?

No answer.

Which was the answer.

Genny wept in his arms.

She'd lost the most precious thing to her.

Twice.

No, no, she hadn't.

She'd lost it once.

And he'd taken it from her the other time.

So it's over, she'd said.

So get in there.

TELL HER WHAT YOU DID.

It's over, she'd said.

With Tom.

It was over *with Tom.*

Now it's your turn.

TELL HER HOW YOU BROKE HER. HELP HER HEAL. GIVE HER BACK WHAT YOU TOOK FROM HER.

GIVE IT BACK.

It's over.

Yes.

It was over.

"I'm being an idiot," she sniffled into his chest.

He held on to her, and his voice was gruff when he replied, "You aren't. He was...you had a good marriage. He was a good man. A good dad. You had..."

It all.

She'd had it all.

All that was important.

She'd had it all once before too.

She was better than him.

But Duncan became a multi-millionaire on his terms.

She's still better than him.

NOBODY WAS BETTER THAN DUNCAN.

"Corey?"

He looked down at her face.

Red eyes, a mini-mascara disaster, nostrils still quivering.

She was gorgeous.

"You had it all, honey," he said gently. "It isn't easy to lose that."

She nodded, dropped her chin, pressed her forehead to his chest briefly, then looked up at him again.

"Thanks for coming to Phoenix. You didn't need…" A tremulous smile. "I won't finish that. You never need…but you're always there for me."

Of course, after it was me who crushed you, broke you in a way that even Tom couldn't fix, which was why, when Tom broke you, you wouldn't allow him to fix you both.

Where else would I be?

She studied his face, saw something there she shouldn't, and misinterpreted it.

"I'll be okay, Corey. Promise. I always am. You know that."

It was his turn to nod.

"Still, it means the world you'd fly out, be here." She shook him lovingly with her arms. "To listen to me. Look after me. You're a pretty busy guy."

That last was a tease, but the pride in her words ran deep.

Pride in him.

All he'd done.

What he'd become.

Guilt.

His chest flooded.

Was this what drowning felt like?

Suddenly very serious, her arms around him tightened. "It means the world, Corey, that you'd be here for me."

"Always, Gen," he murmured.

She forced a smile.

"Are you hungry?" he asked.

Shadows clouded her eyes.

But she forced her smile to broaden.

And her lie was nonverbal when she nodded.

Therefore, Corey took her out to eat.

It would be the last meal they shared alone together.

But even if Corey didn't know that at the time, he remembered every moment of that meal for months to come.

It was the most important, most treasured two hours of his life.

Corey, with his best friend Genny.

Precious.

Even if the pall was there, as it always was.

Because someone was missing.

IT TOOK months for Corey to be driven to silence the voices in his head.

And when he did, he was at his home.

Corey had learned a few things very well in his life, and one of them was how to be like Duncan always had been.

Decisive.

Therefore, when he decided to silence those voices, he didn't fuck around.

He went to the wall safe, opened it, and took out the file.

Except to tuck it away after adding to it, he'd never touched it. Never opened that ever-growing file.

Not a single page read.

Not one picture viewed.

But right then, he took it out, full to bursting, chronological with every new report shoved on top.

Twenty-five years.

Twenty-five years of a man's life.

Twenty-five years of his best friend's life.

Corey sat in a room with no view, a difficult thing to find in his sprawling oceanside home.

He opened the file.

And he started at the top, taking hours to do it, doing it thoroughly, studying every picture, and reading every word of what his investigators reported to him on the life of Duncan Holloway.

Seeing the risks Duncan took.

And the payoffs.

The friends he'd made, who had not fucked him over.

Garnering a deep understanding that even Duncan did not have a handle on how truly troubled his ex-wife was.

And an understanding Corey was utterly certain Duncan did have about how exceptional his two sons were.

Corey learned it all, and the way his mind worked, as he did, he fit them together along the way like a puzzle that had been put together, but was blown apart, some of the pieces still holding true, but other big, important chunks had been torn away.

And once the last piece was clicked back into place and that totality came into view, he saw with a clarity that obliterated him that they would have fit.

If Duncan had not been urged by Corey to falter in the understanding he was a good man, an ambitious one, a loving one, a loyal one, and one who knew not only who he was and what he wanted, but how to get it...

Yes, if Corey had not done that, and when that wasn't working fast enough, told him a lie that Duncan's love for Corey, his trust in him would make it the truth, they would have fit.

Genny and Duncan would have worked.

They would have built a life together.

But Corey took it away.

However, somehow, even with all of that, all he'd done, what haunted him the most was, if they had been as they should have been —together—they might have had a girl.

Duncan would have had a girl...

To teach how not to be afraid of frogs.

Corey, too, would have liked to have had a daughter.

Or two.

But he would have taught them about much more than frogs.

At least Corey got his chance, even if they weren't his girls.

Duncan...

Corey closed his eyes on that thought, images of Chloe and Sasha rushing his mind, and his heavy heart grew immensely heavier.

So he opened his eyes.

They would not have existed if he had not intervened.

Matt...

Duncan's boys...

But the bottom line, they weren't what was meant to be.

He'd altered what was meant to be.

Corey Szabo had it within his power to manipulate what man, or woman, was next elected president.

As such, he could fix this.

He had proved through his life that he could do anything.

And this was something he was going to do.

To that end, he destroyed that file.

However, the other ones he'd personally placed in capable hands, and then he gave very specific, exhaustive, meticulous instructions.

With that done, he spent the time it took going about seeing to every minute detail of fixing what he'd broken with Duncan and Imogen.

As well as fixing a few other things.

One vitally important thing in particular.

And then, ever the achiever, ever the man dedicated to accomplishing his desired result, leaving no stone unturned, no bet unwon, no success unattained, to make absolutely certain nothing got in the way...

Corey set in motion his plan to right the wrong.

And naturally, this culminated in his finger pulling the trigger on a brand-new gun.

CHAPTER 17

THE INTERVIEW

Imogen

*T*he next morning, I was mostly awake, just snoozing, when I heard the mug hit the nightstand.

So I opened my eyes and was thus able to see Duncan aiming his ass to the bed in the crook of my body.

I lifted my gaze to him.

"Hey," I whispered.

Something moved over his face, it was big, beautiful, profound.

Being in his bed, with him bringing me coffee and sitting right there, there was no doubt, I felt that something too.

"Hey," he replied.

I got up on an elbow.

"Animals are fed. Kids are fed," he stated. "They're already out on the horses. You do your slow morning. I'm going to get a shower in and hit some work. When you're sorted and the kids are back, we'll decide what's up for our day."

"Okay."

He bent and kissed my forehead.

Then he got up, murmuring, "Coffee on the nightstand."

I looked to the coffee, then watched Duncan stroll through his magnificent room to his even more magnificent bathroom.

I then aimed my eyes out the window to his resplendent view.

I was there, and not in the hotel, because of the kids.

This happened last night. After dinner. After Sasha asked if they had any games. After Gage and Sully took off to the den and came back with at least ten board games.

We'd started with Code Names. Moved on to Splendor. And then got serious with Ticket to Ride.

This through beer, wine, and after Sasha told them I was the Cookie Monster, the boys "throwing together" some sugar cookie dough that they dumped mini M&Ms in, which we all took turns getting out of the oven, or putting more in, and obviously eating them.

Warm.

The best.

In fact, the whole night was the best, with Duncan, his boys and my girl (and cookies).

What could only make it better was if we'd had Chloe, Matt and Hale.

But when it started getting late, Duncan announced, "Takin' your mom and Cookie back to the hotel, Sash. You can bunk there with her but want you to know you're free to use Chloe's room here."

This got a trio of, "Chloe's room?"

Sullivan's and Gage's were surprised. Sasha's was pouty.

"Sasha's room now, if she chooses to take it," Duncan corrected.

"I'm staying in *my* room. And Mom," she aimed at me, "you shouldn't be carting Cookie around like that. She's going to get stressed."

"She's fine," I said.

"She's going to get stressed," she repeated.

"Does she look stressed?" I asked.

Curled up in Gage's lap, purring, she did not look at all stressed.

"Well then, breaking the code you seem not to be able to decipher, we're all adults so don't be goofs. We won't get complexes because you two are sleeping together," she returned.

"Totally," Gage stated.

"Yeah, it's actually kind of weird you're taking Genny back to the hotel. Especially since her daughters stay here," Sully put in.

Duncan looked to me.

I was completely on board with staying in his beautiful room.

With him.

Tom and I had had a very active and fulfilling sex life, until I descended into my head. It wasn't like I hadn't carried on the intimacy with my partner with my children under the same roof.

Of course, the first time I connected like that with Duncan after our long absence from each other, I would prefer our children not to be in the house, even if they were all on the far side, which in this house, was *far*.

But we could sleep beside each other and wait on that (for the moment).

Most importantly, I didn't want to leave him.

I didn't want to leave my daughter.

I didn't want him to have to leave his sons.

And I actually did worry that Cookie would get stressed.

So I shrugged.

Duncan grinned.

That was his choice too.

We retired before the kids did and we did not reconnect in that way.

I'd brought a bag with a nightgown, a change of clothes and my toiletries.

So we both got ready for bed, taking turns in the bathroom.

And then we climbed under the covers, Duncan gathered me in his arms, and we whispered to each other with zero humility about how great our kids were.

Until we fell asleep.

Or at least I did.

And I'd slept *great*.

In bed in Duncan's arms, something peaceful and right and beautiful that I never thought I'd have again?

Oh yes, I'd slept like a baby.

Now was now.

The kids were riding.

We still hadn't talked about what to do about Samantha.

I needed to call my son to inform him that I was seeing a man, and it was serious, not to mention discuss other things with him.

And I needed to sort things out with Tom.

The shower went on.

I reached out, took a sip of coffee, and grabbed my phone, which Duncan had plugged in my charger so it could charge while we slept.

I texted Tom, *Just so you know, Sasha is here. And I understand why you're angry. You have a right. Now we need to talk it out. I'm here whenever you're ready.*

After I sent that, I set my phone aside, took another sip of coffee, tossed the covers from me and got out of bed.

It wasn't the time and it wasn't right.

Yet it was always the time and it was always right.

But bottom line, Duncan was naked in the shower and there was no way in hell I could lie in his bed, knowing that, picturing him there, without touching myself.

And I vastly preferred him touching me.

He'd closed the smoky-glassed double doors that led to the bathroom.

I opened one and went through, shutting it behind me.

The shower was pride of place.

Now it had droplets on the glass walls, and it was steamed a bit.

But there he was.

My Duncan.

I'd been right when I first saw him again, and I'd felt it in our makeout sessions (but not seen it), he carried a little weight around his belly.

But I liked it.

And *God*.

Those thighs? Those shoulders? That chest?

That cock?

He saw me just as I started pulling my nightgown up.

"Baby," he said.

I yanked it off, walked to the door of the shower and shoved down my panties.

"Babe," he growled.

I liked his cock a lot better like *that*.

I opened the door and stepped out of my panties when I slipped in.

He took hold of me, grasping my hips and pulling me to him, his back taking the spray, even as he said, "I wanted you first in my bed."

"Needs must," I replied, sliding my hands up his slick chest, the hair there damp, but still rough.

So nice.

"Genny—"

I lifted my hands and gripped his beard on either side.

"Kiss me, Bowie, and then fuck me," I ordered.

His hazel eyes flashed.

Then he did as told.

We were naked.

He was hard.

We were us.

And it had been a long, *long* time.

So this was never going to be sedate and lengthy.

Not even in a bed.

There was kissing and stroking and licking, he got my nipple in his mouth and tugged for about two seconds.

And I was ready.

"Bowie," I whimpered.

He knew.

He always knew.

And so I was up, slammed against the glass.

Oh yes.

I rounded him with my legs, he shoved a hand between us, then he yanked me down and I had him.

I had him.

I had him back.

My Bowie.

I fisted my hands in his wet hair and he pounded into me, both of our gazes locked.

"Harder," I begged.

"Genny."

"Fuck me harder, Bowie."

He fucked me harder.

I kissed him.

He held me with one hand on my ass, the other he trailed around my hip to go in at the front.

I broke the kiss. "No, just you."

"I want it to be big."

"No, just—"

He drove deep and there it was.

My head jerked back, hit glass, then fell forward and landed on his shoulder as I gasped at the beginning of my orgasm, then whimpered through the rest of it.

And those whimpers went on forever.

In other words, Duncan got what he wanted.

It was *big*.

As it floated away, I rounded him with my arms, trailing my nose, lips, tongue on the skin of his neck, his bearded jaw, his ear, tracing the hairline at his neck with my fingers, stroking his nape as I clenched and released with his thrusts.

I thrilled at his grunts and thrilled more when his control snapped, and he fucked me into the glass near to violently.

God, yes, I'd loved this with Duncan.

I still loved this with Duncan.

And I'd missed it so...fucking...*much*.

His release came on a deep groan that sounded so delicious, it caused my entire body to quiver, and he slammed inside me through it.

I took his harsh breaths on my skin that were better than winning an Oscar.

I hadn't won an Oscar.

But I knew that to be true down to my soul.

When he got a handle on it, he lifted his head.

And I whispered, "God, I've missed you."

Warmth and happiness and million other good things chased through his face before he settled on playful.

"You always did like a solid fucking."

I smiled at him, because I loved playful Duncan.

And then I said, "Yes. And that you knew my mom and dad when they were still young and vital, and you remember them that way. That you have stories to tell about Mom that dive deep in my history that no one else knows. That we had those times where Corey hung back, bitching and telling us to hurry up, when you took me off trail to show me some flower or a game trail you'd discovered. That I was there for you in those years you were beginning to understand the power your father had over you, and the time would come soon you'd have to decide to be him, or be you. And you could look at me, and I could ground you. I love how we connect, Bowie," I squeezed him in a variety of ways, and enjoyed watching and feeling the tremble of his body in reaction, "*all* the ways we connect. I missed it, and I'm ecstatically happy to have it back."

He did not reply.

Verbally.

He kissed me against the glass until I lost his cock and then he kissed me some more, until we had to come up for air.

Message received.

But he spoke anyway.

"You were right, honey, and I was wrong," he said, his voice hoarse and beautiful. "Havin' you right here was perfect. That's us. No holding back. And we should be us. Always."

I so totally agreed.

I gave him a quick kiss to communicate that.

And then I said, "Now I've had an orgasm, I need coffee and breakfast."

He set me to my feet but did it laughing.

That was us too, back then.

And what I was finding...now.

We laughed a lot.

He was funny. He thought I was cute.

If his dad didn't do something to mess with his head, we laughed and joked and teased all the time.

And boy, had I missed that too.

In the now, though, we showered, it got serious, there was touching, kissing, groping, but in the end, Duncan left me to finish up.

And by the time I got out of the shower, toweled off, lotioned up, put product in my hair and my panties, bra and robe on, he'd come back in with my mug and a plate that had a toasted bagel with whipped cream cheese.

"Threw out the old coffee, that's fresh. That do for food?" he asked, sliding everything on the counter by the basin where I was, which was not the one he used.

It was no croissant from The Queen.

But it was still perfect.

"More than do. Thanks."

He bent in to kiss my neck then said, "Take your time. Kids are still out. I'll be in my office if you need me."

Then he was gone.

I took my time in his awesome bathroom. Light makeup. Blew out my hair.

And I had on my jeans, was pulling on my sweater, when I heard Sasha screech, "*Mother!*"

Sasha did not call me mother.

And the tone of that screech set my blood to a chill.

I yanked down my sweater and went running.

At the gallery, I saw her at the bottom of the stairs looking like she was about ready to race up them.

Gage was hanging close.

Duncan was already there.

But she only had eyes for me.

"You have to get down here and *see this*," she declared.

And then she stomped off down the hall opposite the one where Duncan's office was.

"It's bad, Dad," Gage said. "C'mon."

And then he was off down the hall.

I looked to Duncan and started down the stairs quickly, asking, "What's down that hall again?"

"Game room. Dining room. Pool room."

"TV?"

He nodded even though I'd seen the room and it had a huge TV.

So I started running.

Duncan followed me (not running, but his legs were longer than mine) and we hit the room me first, him right after.

Sasha immediately started talking. "Sully's cueing it up on YouTube. But my phone blew up while we were riding. And so did the guys'. We watched it out there and came racing back. Because it's all over *everything.*"

I looked to the television and could not swallow my gasp.

Samantha was on it, kitty corner sofas, her on one side, Elsa Cohen, celebrity interviewer (or more to the point, gossip monger) on the other.

"I think that's the part, Sul. She was adjusting her skirt," Gage told him.

Sully went back and we listened to Sam saying some things, then it started.

"*And yes, this megalomaniacal behavior affected Duncan Holloway and Imogen Swan.*"

"Ohmigod," I breathed.

"I know," Sasha hissed irately.

Samantha: "*In fact, right now, they'd probably be celebrating their thirtieth anniversary if Corey hadn't been pathologically in love with Gen.*"

Elsa: "*Pathologically in love?*"

Samantha: "*Yes, because they were inseparable. Always were. The three of them, but mostly Gen and Dun. Star-crossed lovers with Corey in that mix. He broke them up. He told Duncan that he'd slept with Genny and that was it. Duncan trusted him like a brother. Gen didn't stand a chance.*"

"This fucking bitch is *whacked*," Sully bit off.

Elsa: "*Corey Szabo convinced Duncan Holloway that Imogen Swan had slept with him?*"

Samantha: "*You don't understand. I knew Gen and he told me the same thing so I would divorce him, and I believed him too and that is not the woman she was or is. As evidenced by the fact that she divorced Tom after he cheated on her.*"

"Oh my God!" I shouted.

"Motherfucker," Duncan clipped.

"I *know*, Mom," Sasha snapped.

"I need my phone," I said urgently.

"Where is it?" Gage asked.

"On the nightstand, darling," I answered.

Gage took off running.

Samantha: "*...and I cannot tell you how happy I am to see that they're back together. Obviously, his parting gift to them was the same as it was to me. To share he'd lied. As if that changes decades of tragedy. As if that erases the man he was and the things he's done. But it doesn't change a thing. And I am here right now to tell the world the kind of man he* really *was. That man does not get to start up a charity* a month before his death *when he did* nothing *good or kind with his billions* for years *and think he can rest on that legacy. So I'm making it my mission to share precisely what his legacy was. And it was nothing good. And all I can say, if Gen sees this,*" she looked into the camera and it instantly tightened on her, "*I'm sorry. I'm sorry I believed Corey's lies and lost you as a friend. I'm sorry you lost Duncan. And thank you for taking care of my son when that snake in the grass had him. If it wasn't for you, who knows what Hale would have turned out to be.*"

"Me and *Tom*, you bitch," I gritted at the TV.

The screen paused and Sully said quietly, "That was it about you guys."

I started to look at Duncan but turned my attention to my daughter instead when she said, "Hale? Yes, it's me! I'm with Mom and Duncan. What the fuck is wrong with your mother?" Pause then. "Right. Fine." She took the phone from her ear and jabbed it. "You're on speaker."

"Genny?" Hale's voice called.

Gage rushed into the room and handed me my phone while I replied, "I'm here, honey."

"I had no idea," he said. "I've called her ten times. She's blocked me."

"Why would she do this?" I asked.

"No clue. No fucking clue. Christ, I'm so sorry."

"It wasn't you, Hale," I told him.

My phone in my hand rang.

I looked at it.

It was Mindi, my publicist.

I put it on silent and returned to Hale. "Don't take this on."

"Fortunately, I'm a billionaire now, thanks to Dad remembering he had a son and leaving me everything. Including his jet. I'm on my way to the airstrip now to go to her directly and find out what she's playing at."

"She called Mary," I shared. "I...well, I got caught up in things and I didn't call back. Maybe she intended to warn me."

"Yeah, and maybe she actually shoulda *warned you* before she fucking sat on the couch across from that parasitic flea and shot her mouth off."

I could not agree more.

Hale's relationship with his bitter mother was not a lot healthier than the one he had with his absentee father.

And I'd had nearly thirty years of not only doing my best to give him what he didn't have between the two of them, but also running interference for them both with their son.

So it was ingrained in me to do what I did next.

"How about you change your flight plan and come here, to Arizona?" I suggested.

My phone vibrated in my hand.

This time, it was Tom.

Damn.

"No, Gen, sorry, I want answers for this," Hale decreed. "I don't give a fuck she washes Dad's laundry in public, but you and Tom?"

"I hear you, but I have to go. Tom's calling."

"Tell him I'm sorry and I'll call after we take off."

"Okay, honey, 'bye," I said in a rush, glanced at Duncan, he jerked up his chin, face hard as stone, and I walked out of the room and took Tom's call. "Hey, Tommy," I greeted softly.

"So, I guess Corey wasn't quite done fucking you over, leaving that bitter cow in his wake," he ground out.

"Tom, I'm so sorry."

"I fucked another woman not my wife, Genny. It really wasn't anyone's business but yours. But there are penalties to pay, and the lives we wanted that we worked to have, this is the price."

"Tom, that doesn't have to be true. Sam had no business doing what she did."

"She made passes at me."

Standing in the hall, I lifted my hand up to the wall and leaned into it.

"*Numerous* ones," he bit out.

"Samantha did?"

"Yes."

"Tom," I whispered.

"So I guess she's pretty pissed I turned her down but fucked someone else," he deduced.

"Why didn't you tell me?"

"Because she didn't matter, and honest to God, a lot of women did that, Gen, and you knew it. It never mattered. But with her, we needed to see to Hale and his life was already messed up enough. I couldn't avoid her and still be a part of his growing up, because *she* avoided *you*. So I just pretended it didn't happen. She stopped, and swear to Christ, I thought she forgot she'd done it."

I took the phone from my ear and squeezed it so hard, if it was made of anything else, it would have shattered in my hand.

Fucking *Corey.*

And fucking *Samantha.*

In one way or another, they both were constantly *fucking me.*

And worse.

Disappointing Hale.

I put the phone back to my ear. "We know what that was, and it was not about her. It was not about the woman you turned to. It was about us."

"You know, I was a world-class athlete. Won millions in purses. Earned more millions in endorsements. Have goddamn black-and-white photos that freaking Henry Gagnon took of my face with my wrist held up, wearing fifty-thousand-dollar watches, hawking that shit. Got my medical degree. And the greatest thing I ever did was win you."

I closed my eyes and my shoulder hit the wall.

I opened them and started, "Tom—"

"If you're happy, I'll eventually be happy. And I hate to ask this, I'll miss you and I know you still count on me, but I need a break. It won't be forever, honey. But I need to get used to a you with another man before I have you in my life when you're with another man."

"We need to be seen together," I said urgently.

"There's no spinning this," he replied.

I pushed from the wall. "Yes, there is. We'll lie."

Silence I could feel was stunned, even through the phone lines, then, "Lie?"

"I'm putting a statement out within an hour that Samantha Wheeler just lied her ass off to Elsa Cohen."

"Genny—"

"Fuck Elsa and fuck Sam."

"You forget, there's another person in this scenario," he said hesitantly.

"She comes forward, we'll say she lied too. And I'm goddamn Imogen Swan and you're fucking Tom Pierce, they'll believe *us,* and we'll *eviscerate them all* if we have to. No one does this to my goddamned family."

"Ge—" he started.

I cut him off. "How did she know?"

"Hale knows. I can only assume he told her."

"Hale would never do that to you."

"I have to admit, that's a part that was seriously gutting me, if he did that."

"You need to phone him. He's on his way to find out what's up his mother's ass. He's worried about you. You need to phone him and find out if he said anything. Because if he didn't, something fishy is going on and we need to get to the bottom of it."

"It wouldn't be her," he said quietly. "She's not the kind of person to do that."

He was talking about the woman he fucked.

"I'm sorry, Tom, but you need to get on the line with her too and find out. Or better, get our lawyer on her."

"She really isn't like that, Gen. I would not stick my dick in that."

"Tom, I'm about to press go on the first outright lie I've released to my adoring fans. And yours. We need everybody with this program."

"I'm not at one with you lying, Imogen. Everything you are is against that."

"Well, you've got five full minutes to become one with it, Tom, because if you're down with it or not, it's happening."

He was silent.

Not for five minutes but for at least half of one.

And then he said, "I'll get in touch with her and Hale. Don't let Mindi say anything until I do. I need an hour."

"You got it. But I'm starting her on it. She'll need that time anyway."

"I love you, and I will go to my grave regretting what I did to us."

Again, I closed my eyes tight.

Then I said, "I love you too, and I'll go to mine regretting you have that regret."

"Speak soon, honey."

"Of course, Tommy. Take care. And Tom?"

"Right here."

"You're my go-to guy, and even if I have another one, you'll always be that. Always. Even if you decide you need to take yourself away from me, that's the way I'll think of you."

His voice was guttural when he replied, "I love you, Gen."

"And I love you."

We rung off and I barely had my phone from my ear when I heard my daughter ask, "You're lying?"

I looked her in the eyes.

"Absolutely."

She stared into my eyes.

And then she said, "I love you so fucking much."

I smiled at her and ordered, "Call your sister and find out if she's okay and brief her. Then call your brother."

"Matt will—"

"Matthew will stick by his family."

She nodded, ducked her head to her phone and walked quickly down the hall toward the great room.

Duncan had clearly quarantined his sons away from our drama.

I walked back into the game room and announced, "I'm very sorry."

"I'm very sorry too. That bitch is a *bitch*. Laying you and Dad and your ex out like that. What the fuck?" Sully clipped.

I blinked because Sullivan had, thus far, seemed even keeled. Like his dad.

"Sasha is a mess and that is *not on*. I cannot freaking *imagine* knowing the world knows that shit about my dad when it's none of their fucking business. She's a c-word and I wish I could say it, but I don't even live with Dad, and he'd ground me until I was twenty-five if I did," Gage added.

Okay, I would love Duncan's boys just because they were his boys.

But now I just loved Duncan's boys because they were good guys.

I gave them both a weak smile and looked to Duncan. "I'm so sorry, darling."

"You got dick to be sorry for," he bit out.

"I'm lying," I told him.

"What?" he clipped.

"About Tom. I'm releasing a statement that he didn't do that."

"Good. It's nobody's fuckin' business. You need my office?"

I stared at him.

My Duncan.

Protective, almost to a fault.

Of me.

And mine.

And on this thought, it started happening.

Then he was there, his hands cupping my jaw, his face in mine. "Gen, fall apart in an hour. We got you. But now you need to keep your shit tight."

I nodded, fighting back the tears.

"I gotta call Sheila, baby. I'll need your statement so she can devise language around it if she gets questions."

I nodded again.

"Go to my office. I'll check in, in a bit. You finish your breakfast?"

I nodded yet again.

"You need more coffee?"

Totally gin.

I didn't say that.

I said, "Yes, please."

"Sul, get Genny a cup, cream and one sugar, take it to the office," he ordered.

"Got you, Dad," Sully replied, leaving.

"Gage, stick with Sash. Not close, but close enough she knows you're there if she needs you."

"On my way, Pops," Gage said and took off.

"Thank you for understanding," I whispered, my voice trembling.

"You're right, sometimes this Imogen Swan shit is a pain in the ass."

That made me smile, though it was trembling too.

He pulled me up as he came down, and he kissed me quickly.

When he pushed me back, he didn't let go.

But he did say, "We'll get through this. All of us. Now go take care of our families."

That made me get it together.

And I nodded one last time.

He gave my jaw a squeeze.

And I left the room to get on taking care of our families.

———

"THEN SHE WAS ALL, 'well, you've got five minutes to become one with it, Tom, because it's happening.'" Sasha relayed for the third time.

This time to Harvey and Beth, who were both over to provide moral support.

And yes, Beth brought her air fryer, because, from Harvey: "She's gonna take that goddamn thing on vacation with us." Which brought: "Yes, Harv, because we're camping in our RV and I have a kitchen, as such, and I also have a need to cook good food in a short time so I can *enjoy my vacation.*"

This was after Heddy showed.

I was currently on gimlet three, which Gage was feeding me, and at that moment I sure was glad I had the foresight to stock the ingredients for my gimlets when I went to the store the day before to get the stuff for my red sauce and meatballs.

Much earlier, Sienna Sinclair had left a message on my cell saying, "We'll be sorry to see you go, but we're sorrier about today's interview and will understand if that's your decision. I say this because we've had both phone and in person requests from journalists. We've shared that our policy is that we do not release information about any of our guests, but at no time have we had an Imogen Swan registered with us. And rest assured, all my staff are *very* aware that this is our policy. Please take care of yourself and thank you for staying at The Queen. It was a pleasure for us to have you."

And what she said wasn't entirely a lie, since I was registered there under Virginie Forbes.

Talk about a dame.

A classy one.

This meant Sasha and the boys had taken a brief trip to The Queen to pack me (and Cookie) up and move us to Duncan's.

And now was now, early afternoon, and Sasha, the boys, Heddy and Beth were in fits of glee watching the fallout of Mindi's strongly worded counter that Samantha Wheeler told grave falsehoods about Tom Pierce.

And yes, after warning Hale I was going to do it, and getting his approval, I threw that bitch *right* under the bus when she tried to do the same to the father of my children (this, after soothing his fury that his mother made passes at my husband and the dad of the only real family Hale had ever known).

Thus, I shared her interview was due to the fact she had frequently made advances to Tom Pierce, which were always rebuffed, we were taking her interview as an act of petty vengeance against Tom, and we could not stand silent about it considering what it meant to our family.

Duncan and I, Mindi and Sheila, on a conference call, decided the rest.

That the things Samantha said about he, Corey and I were "private matters and personal history that will not be discussed."

This, we knew, translated into "she did not lie about that."

But we didn't make that statement to protect Corey. We did it for the exact opposite reason.

The fallout of all of this was seeming to be that the world was Team Duncan all the way *and* Team Tom, since everybody loved him and wanted him happy. So now, if he was brought up, it was discussing potential women he should date.

So I guessed I had something to thank Sam for.

But I was not going to rush to my personalized stationery.

The feeds were clogged with a variety of unkind memes featuring Sam and even Elsa, taking stills from the interview or other photos to make fun of them.

I could not say this made me happy.

I could say that it I didn't care much that it probably would not take me long to get over it.

I was cuddled up with Duncan (and Killer) in his big chair, steadily becoming more and more inebriated.

But as yet this had not touched the fact that I was infuriated that a happy day that started with Duncan fucking me and should have carried on with us spending time with our kids, ended like this.

Even if Sasha was having the time of her life repeating the conversation I'd had with Tom in the hallway.

"And then there was the part where she shared Hale was off to find out what was up his mother's ass," Sasha said. "Though, my favorite was when she threatened to *eviscerate them all.*"

"Righteous, and I don't even know what 'eviscerate' means. Still sounds righteous," was Gage's reply.

"Baby, I don't know why you're in a bad mood. That *was* totally badass," Duncan whispered in my ear.

"Huh," I huffed Chloe's favorite refrain, and socked back more gin.

The dogs lost their minds (again) and raced to the door, including Killer, who took a flying leap from where she was lounging in both our laps.

This caused Cookie to scatter from where she'd settled in the crease of Gage's outstretched legs (she'd defected from me, but I wasn't too torn up about it, she'd come back) and Tuck to rush from his perch on Sasha's hip (he'd defected too, it was love at first sight, both ways).

Bounce, wisely, was hiding under a table.

"I'll see who it is," Sully sighed, and pushed up from his place on the floor.

"You do know, when everyone's gone or asleep, I'm shoving you in my car and driving you down to your condo, then barricading us in for at least a month, don't you?" Duncan asked.

I looked to him. "That's the second-best thing I've heard all day, behind the first-best thing which I cannot discuss in company."

He gave me a sexy smile.

"Yo!" we heard.

It was Sully sounding like he was calling out to someone.

In order to call them to a halt.

We looked to the entryway of the great room, and within seconds, Chloe stormed through it, Sul hot on her very high heels.

"Simmer down, hot guy," she snapped to Sully, then to me, "Are you okay?"

"Yes, darling," I replied.

To Duncan, "Are you okay, Bowie?"

"I'm fine, honey, are you okay?"

"I...am...*not*," she bit.

"You didn't have to drive all the way up here," I said. "We're—"

"I didn't?" she snapped. "Bitchface Wheeler declares war on *my* family and what? I'm supposed to head out to Straight Up at the Adeline and have a smooth whiskey?"

"Sullivan, Gage, Harvey, Beth, this is Genny's oldest. Chloe," Duncan introduced.

"Figures," Gage grunted.

"How do you do, kind people. And Heddy, love your face," Chloe stated and then to me, "*Motherrrr*, we need to be on Insta, riding horses and looking beautiful and being happy and rich and making that bitch squirm."

"I think I've made her squirm enough for one day," I said to my daughter, quite pleased that none of the words were slurred.

"Hardly," she returned. "But good call on the big fat lie. I approve."

I sighed.

She turned to Sasha. "What? You don't see me since Coachella and now I'm invisible?"

"I try not to get too close when you're in full snit," Sasha said, pushing up from her place on the floor and moving to her sister.

Chloe looked her up and down as she did and said, "My God, *please* let me style you. This Free People stint is lasting too long and it... is...*agony*."

"Shut up," Sasha replied, wrapping her sis in a big hug.

Chloe hugged her back, hard, and long.

"Have you talked to Dad?" Chloe whispered.

"Yeah," Sasha whispered back. "You?"

"Yeah."

"He okay with you?"

"He's pissed but hanging in there. You?"

"Same."

"You know, you're both insanely hot, but that's not the only reason we can all hear you," Gage shared.

The girls broke apart and they both looked to Gage.

But unsurprisingly, it was Chloe who spoke.

"Of course, you're Bowie's so you're impeccable."

"I'm what?" Gage asked.

"Impeccable. Flawless. Perfect. Sinfully handsome. A heartbreaker. Obviously, I'm going to have to get you in hand."

Harvey grunted in amusement.

Beth swallowed a giggle.

Heddy snorted.

Gage looked to his father, and he proved his instincts were sharp, because he didn't hide the fear.

"Honey," Duncan started while pushing out of our chair, "how 'bout I make you a martini and you sit and chill out and not terrorize my sons?"

At that, she turned her attention to Sully and said, "I haven't even fully taken *you* in yet. Good God, your father's genes are practically criminal. You're veritably illegal."

"Could say the same about you," Sul replied, strolling in to resume his lounge on the floor.

"*Touché*," Chloe murmured, lips quirking.

"Pretty sure Judge feels the same way," Harv chimed in.

Oh no.

Chloe's gaze snapped to Harvey.

But Gage got there first. "Judge?"

Harv jerked his head at Chloe. "Him and this gal practically shouted the shoe and boot display down at the store. Got that on camera. We've all watched it about a hundred times. And it's got no sound, it's still awesome."

"Her and *Judge?*" Sully asked, not hiding his shock.

"He's vermin," Chloe sniffed, picking her way through dogs and people to my chair so she could perch on the arm.

Killer came with her and perched on my lap.

"I *so totally* see him and you hooking up. I mean, Ryan Reynolds and Sandra Bullock were a thing, weren't they?" Gage asked.

"Dude, you're so right," Sul agreed.

"He does *not* look like Ryan Reynolds," Chloe stated, though she did not deny she bore resemblance to Sandra Bullock.

Gage ignored her. "And they say opposites attract. Right?"

"Oh my God, she's gonna send Judge around the bend. And he needs it. He just snaps," Sully snapped his fingers, "and the babes come running."

"*Ma mère bien-aimée*, make them cease speaking," Chloe demanded.

"Darling, Momma's had a bad day. Fight your own battles," I begged.

"Who is this Judge?" Sasha asked, excited, as ever, that her sister had a crush, and all that excitement centered around having fodder to give her sister stick about said crush.

"*You* are not to go anywhere *near* him," Chloe said quickly, then added as cover, "As I said, he's vermin."

"Don't worry," Sully put in smoothly. "She's gorgeous, but she's not his type. I think his last girlfriend did the weather or something. I don't remember. But she was on TV down in Phoenix. He goes for those swanky types." Pause, and then with faultless timing, "Like you."

Dear Lord.

Duncan was handing Chloe a martini.

Then he shoved in again beside me (and Killer).

Whereupon I whispered, "You didn't mention that part."

"Sorry, baby, don't keep track of Judge's love life. I didn't know that part. All I've seen is women throwin' themselves at him, not the ones he's caught. The boys, though, are tight with him. When they're not in school, they're both team leaders for Kids and Trails."

"Hmm," I hummed.

He grinned.

"No reply, Coco?" Sasha teased.

"I'm ignoring anyone who didn't bring me a martini, which means the only person in this room is Bowie," Chloe replied.

Sasha giggled.

Sully and Gage grinned at each other.

"I'll bring your next one, gal, 'cause you're a goddamned hoot and I wanna know you," Harvey said.

"All right, I'm not ignoring you either," Chloe allowed.

Harvey boomed with laughter.

"This is why I don't care," Duncan said in my ear.

I turned to him, and due to all the goings-on in that room, did it smiling.

"Sorry, honey?"

"This," he tipped his head to the room, "is why all that shit doesn't matter. Because we have this. In some form, we'll always have this. And your ex, he also has this, and when you guys sort shit out, he'll have this with us. So all that other, Genny, it doesn't matter."

He was very right.

I told him that by touching my mouth to his.

He got my message, if the sweet, warm look in his eyes I saw when I pulled away was any indication.

"I'm not sure I get this, Sash, you and your sister couldn't be more different, in looks and like, *everything*," Gage noted.

Before Sasha could answer, Chloe said in a dangerous tone, "*Sash?*"

My youngest looked to my oldest and crowed, "You got Duncan and the Bowie story. But *I* got the boys and the Bitchface Wheeler drama."

Chloe's eyes narrowed.

"Oh dear," I whispered.

Duncan chuckled.

Harvey had all daughters, so he knew precisely what to do.

"I could use me a jalapeño popper. What about you all? Could anyone use a popper?" Harvey asked.

"I can always use a popper," Gage stated.

"I'm guessing that's my cue," Beth said, also having all daughters, she didn't hesitate rising from the couch.

"I'll help!" Sasha cried, jumping to her feet.

"No offense, lovely lady who's about to feed me, but I'm enjoying my martini. *Bowie* makes *me* the best martinis I've had *in my life*. I'll help with dinner," Chloe chimed in.

Sasha threw her sister a look.

I sucked back more gimlet.

Duncan again chuckled.

Tuck followed Sasha to the kitchen.

"*Et tu*, Tuck?" Chloe asked the cat.

Tuck ignored her.

I grinned.

Duncan chuckled more.

"Babe," Heddy called.

I looked to my friend.

"I love your family," she declared.

"I do too, Heddy," I replied. "I totally do."

CHAPTER 18

THE DAY

Duncan

*D*uncan put the mug of coffee on Genny's nightstand, but he did it watching her face.

She pried her eyes open and aimed her eyeballs at him but otherwise didn't move.

So he was chuckling when he seated himself in the crook of her body.

"Mornin'," he greeted.

"Bluh," she moaned, rolling to her back with her forearm over her eyes.

He leaned over her, both hands in the bed at her sides.

"I think you're feelin' that fifteenth gimlet," he teased.

"*Bluh*," she repeated, blanching.

"Advice, honey, don't try to keep up with twenty-year-olds."

Shamelessly, she shifted blame. "Your boys are enablers."

"*My* boys? *Your* girls were with you drink for drink and eggin' that shit on."

"Don't say 'egg,'" she groaned.

He grinned. "As always, you're a cute drunk, but favor next time, baby. Put the kibosh on it *before* you get so hammered we can't have wild drunk sex because you've passed out."

She tossed her arm out to the side away from him and turned her head that direction. "Ulk, I missed wild drunk sex with Duncan."

"We'll reenact that scene without the celebrity drama and gimlet thirteen, fourteen and definitely fifteen, but probably eleven and twelve too."

"Ugh."

He started chuckling.

Then he kept giving her shit.

"Love your girls but you need to have a sit down with them."

She turned her head back his way and caught his eyes. "Why?"

"I like my house the way it is. I don't need them tearing it apart on a fight of whose name is attached to my guest room."

Her lips curved up.

"Though," he went on, "good to see they could make up and end up sharing it."

"Daughter lesson number one, Bowie," she started. "When they fight, you let them fight, because they always make up and do it by sharing a bed, talking and giggling all night, which was what they did last night. Or braiding each other's hair. Though Chloe has never allowed a braid to be plaited into her hair. She taught Sasha to use the straighteners when Sasha was seven, much to her mother's consternation, considering Sasha burned her fingers. But I think this time in your house is the longest I've known where Sasha *didn't* have braids in her hair somewhere."

He grinned and asked, "Can I kiss you?"

"My mouth feels like a cesspool so, absolutely not."

He grinned bigger and said, "Since their bodies can process alcohol seventy times faster than a mature adult, they're all downstairs, being bossed by Chloe who's making crêpes to order."

"You're talking about food again, Bowie."

He ignored her. "And they wanna head over to Goldwater Lake and dink around. I take it you're not up for that?"

"I am not missing a second of family time when we have both your boys and two of my three children in this house."

God, he loved this woman.

"However," she continued, "if I should need to take a personal break in order to vacate my stomach in a bush, none of you are allowed to share Imogen Swan does something as base as vomiting. I'll text Mary to have your NDAs sent to your phones. You can sign them online."

He burst out laughing.

But she was correct.

They had the kids, including the boys, for another two days.

Sul and Gage had fixed it with their professors to miss class on Monday (this meant Sully actually fixed it, and Gage was probably going to ditch) and neither had class until late on Tuesday.

So his sons were leaving at oh-dark-hundred Tuesday morning so Gage could get Sully to Sky Harbor to catch his flight, and then he'd drive down to Tucson.

Knowing this, and displaying an alarming competitive streak they had to have inherited from their father, Chloe and Sasha were in for that haul in order for them both to lavish attention, affection and their very different, but both endearing, personalities on Duncan and his sons.

In other words, he was looking forward to what would undoubtedly be a great two days.

"Give me fifteen minutes and I'll rally," Genny said.

"Take your time, babe. Goldwater isn't going anywhere."

He said this while her phone rang.

He looked to the nightstand and then told her, "It's Matt."

"Can you give it to me, please?"

He unhooked it from her charger and handed it to her.

He also intended to move so she had time with her son, but he didn't when her hand darted out and her fingers wrapped around his wrist.

"Hello, darling," she greeted, pushing up a little in bed. "Yes, I'm fine. I'm good. Are you?" Pause and, "I know, but desperate times." Another pause and in a sharper tone, "I understand that, Matthew, but to deliberately put a very fine point on it, I believe your father's debt is paid with losing his wife and having his son practically freeze him out of his life. Something, I would encourage you, this before begging you, to think very long and hard about ending."

She was staring at Duncan with an expression that warred between annoyed and worried.

She spoke again.

"I'm not defending him. I'm reminding you he's human and I'm telling you I love you very much. And since I do, I do not want there to be a time, and it will come, Matt, where you mess up, and you do it huge, and you hurt someone, that you look back with deep regret at the time you lost with your father when you were not allowing him to be something he cannot possibly stop being. Human."

Oh yeah.

He loved this woman.

Duncan reached out and stroked her jaw.

She turned her head into his touch.

"Yes, fine," she said. "Yes." A pause. "Yes, I know, and no, I'm not mad. I want you to be happy. And yes, Sasha shouldn't have told me. But Matthew, you know better than that. If you have something you want to keep a secret, you tell Chloe. She'll take it to her grave. You don't tell Sasha. She'll hold it quiet for precisely as long as it takes her to design the billboard she'll put up, broadcasting it."

Duncan chuckled.

Her worry faded as she watched him do it.

He took his hand from her jaw.

"Right," she kept going, "since you're taking a semester off, come visit your mother. I love and adore you. But I'm hungover, need a shower and one of Sasha's smoothies, because we're going hiking around Goldwater Lake." Pause then, "Yes, *hiking*. I used to hike all the time." Another pause, and, "Yes, I believe Chloe's coming with."

And then there was her laughter.

He bent and kissed her forehead and rose to leave her to it.

This time, she let him.

He left the room, and Sully was on his way from the hall to the great room when Duncan was heading down the stairs.

"Somethin' came for Genny, Dad. I put it on your desk," Sul said.

"Thanks, bud."

He knew what it was that was delivered on a Sunday.

The script.

He'd take it up to her.

"Is it okay if we pop into town and hit the store real quick?" Sully asked. "Sash is covered, but Coco says she's going to need some hiking gear."

Since it was Sunday, and Judge didn't work on Sundays, he figured this was safe.

"Ask her to get something for Genny. She's coming with," Duncan replied.

Sully smiled. "Awesome."

His son resumed his trek to the kitchen.

Duncan headed to his office, and as he did, his phone in his back pocket rang.

He pulled it out, didn't know the number, but considering all the shit that had been rising around them, and hoping this wasn't indication there was more, he took the call. Because, if it was, he wanted to deal with it and then they could go to the lake.

"Duncan Holloway," he said.

"Dun, don't hang up."

Two days ago, he would not remember that voice.

Now, he did.

Samantha Wheeler.

"How'd you get this number?" he growled, moving far more quickly toward his office and then closing himself in.

If this was going to be a drama, he was going to sustain it on his own.

His family had had enough.

"We still have mutual friends," she replied.

"Not friends any longer, they gave you my number."

"I told them I wanted to call to apologize."

"Not sure I care to have that."

"Please hear me out."

Damn it.

"You got two minutes, Sam, then I'm hanging up," he stated, glaring at the box of *I'm sorrys* from Corey that Bettina had tidied that he really wanted to burn, but he couldn't. That much paper wasted? It cut across the grain.

He was saving it to use as scrap.

He sat behind his desk.

"The world should know what he was like," she stated.

"I disagree. But I also don't care about that. I care about you dragging Genny and her ex into it."

"I guessed and I guess I guessed wrong."

That caught his attention.

"You guessed?"

"Yes."

"You guessed what?"

"About Tom. I mean, they were who they were. Nothing could break them up except Tom doing that. And he's *Tom Pierce*. Very attractive and successful and men like that do things like that."

Duncan was breathing deeply.

In and out.

"Dun?" she called. "Are you still there?"

"You *guessed*? You laid that man out like that on a *guess*?"

"Yes, that was Hale's response," she muttered. "Except louder and with a number of foul words."

"You know, Sam, I'm not certain what you were hoping to get from this conversation, but I'll tell you I'm not liking what I'm getting."

"I don't want you and Gen mad at me.'"

Was she insane?

He pointed out the obvious.

"You've failed in that endeavor."

"Duncan, we were once friends, and I'm sure that Gen told you she stepped up for my son. I haven't seen clearly since recently how much she did that, and I'm—"

"It's my understanding Tom Pierce is the only father he's really had."

She shut up.

"And this was exactly what we thought it was," Duncan said. "You made a play for him, he wasn't into that, and you struck out at him like you struck out at Corey."

"Dun, first, there are not many men like you. Or how you used to be. Men run the world, and if you haven't noticed with all your environmental work, they're running it into the ground. And not only when it comes to that. And they do it because they're *men*. Men like Corey. Who feel the need to prove how big their dick is when, at least with Corey, it wasn't that much to write home about."

He felt his lips twist before he said, "I do not need to know this shit and I don't really care about your philosophy on that other shit."

"I thought she'd slept with my husband," she spat.

There it was.

"So you made a play for Tom to get yours back," Duncan deduced.

Nothing to that.

She'd done it and that was why.

"And then you hung him out to dry when he wouldn't get with your program," he concluded.

"Men like him should not be able to get away with all their bullshit."

"If you're talking about Tom Pierce, I never met the guy, not yet. But what I know from seeing it with my own eyes is he has the abiding loyalty of two smart, together girls and his ex-wife. And hearing it with my own ears, the same from your own goddamned son. So I'm not sure how *a man like that* bought your bitter bullshit. Though I will point out something that clearly didn't cross your mind. Doing what you did to him meant doing what you did *to them*."

"As I said, I *guessed* and I *guessed wrong* and I'm calling to apologize. I'm calling Tom too."

"Can't speak for the man but you might wanna take a minute to think on that because, only *a guess*, he might be a helluva lot less inclined than I am to listen to you."

"Well, I need to apologize to Gen, because for years, I was not kind to her. I believed Corey's shit, I'll note, *the same as you*, and she was never anything but Gen to me. Not whenever we had to be around each other for Hale. And definitely not to Hale."

"I'll let her know your desires, Sam, but just to warn you, you are far from her favorite person right now so I wouldn't hold your breath."

"This was a mistake," she hissed.

"Recent days, Sam, you been making a lot of them."

"The first one being falling in love, genuinely *head over heels* in love with Corey Szabo."

That was her parting shot.

She disconnected.

And the fuck of it was, her parting shot was a good one.

No defense to what she'd pulled, but Duncan knew a thing or two about giving his love and trust to Corey Szabo.

On that thought, his eyes fell on the letter his closest, dearest friend from childhood had written at some point before he decided to eat a bullet.

Angrily, he snatched it up.

And read.

DUN AND GENNY,

I can't say it enough. I'm sorry. It was me. And it was me because I loved you, Genny. God, you never figured it out. I thought I was so obvious. But you never figured it out. And you picked him.

So I told him. I told you, Dun. I told you Genny and I slept together. And I told you because I knew you'd believe me. And I loved Genny so much, I was willing to sacrifice you to have her.

So I lied and told you we'd had sex.

And I was married.

God, what a fuckup.

I did it to myself, giving up on Genny and marrying Samantha.

Of course, both of you would come to my wedding. Of course, both of you would remember how into each other you were. And of course, you would hook up and be inseparable again. I couldn't even get either of you on the phone because, if you weren't working or sleeping, you were fucking. And every day it kept going on, turning to weeks, months, an entire year.

It was torture. It made me crazy.

I had to make it stop.

I told Sam the same thing so she'd leave me, and she did. I had no idea she was pregnant.

But that was the end. She didn't forgive me, and Dun, you didn't forgive Genny, and I got part of my way, you two were over. But then Gen, you moved to LA, and Duncan, you went to Utah, and all I managed to do was make certain no one had what they wanted.

I knew, way back then, I should say something. I knew way back then, I should come clean. I should tell you, Dun. Or you, Genny. Make it right, at least between the two of you.

But I didn't have the guts. I told myself I was working up to it, but then I always allowed something to get in the way.

Always, I allowed something to get in the way.

I had a million excuses as to why I was too busy to explain to the two people I loved the most in the world why I did the most unforgiveable thing in the world to them.

By now, if you're reading this, and I don't do something weak, make the wrong decision yet again, and change my mind about what I've decided to do, you'll know how much this has haunted me.

Gen, when you and Tom split, I knew. And yes, that's just what a puny fuck I am, that it's taken me this long to get there, knowing both of you are free, and I should finally do something about it.

Please, do not mistake that. I own this. I've finally come to terms with the life I bought being the man I became and doing the things I did.

And it's a life I can live no longer.

It is not about either of you. Or Sam, and all I put her through. Or Hale, and how, as what could only be some form of perfect punishment, I watched him grow up to be you, Duncan, and I could barely stand the sight of him because he was a constant reminder of what I did to my best friend.

It's about me.

I did this to me by doing the things I did to the people I should have protected and loved.

You know, I honestly considered filling a warehouse with paper covered in the words contained in this box, but I didn't, because I know how much that would piss you off, Dun.

Suffice it to say, there isn't enough paper in the world to contain the depth of my regret for what I took from the two of you and the selfish reason I did it.

But I hope, considering you both are who you are, that you give me something I don't deserve.

One of only two last wishes, and Gen, the other one is for Hale.

That being that you're standing in a room together, remembering who you are to each other.

And you'll find again what I took away and be what I also took away.

Happy.

I know I didn't show it, but I really did love you guys.

Corey

HAVING FINISHED THE LETTER, Duncan stared at it, Corey's precise, miniscule handwriting covering it from top to bottom.

His throat was closed.

His chest was burning.

His heart hurt.

Corey never once called him Bowie.

Not once.

Because his dad gave him that name.

And honest to Christ, sometimes Duncan didn't know who hated his father more.

Him.

Or Corey.

A knock sounded at the door and his head came up with a jerk when he saw Sasha had hers around the door.

"Hey!" she called. "I'm—" She stopped, stared, and asked in a much less vivacious tone, "Are you all right?"

He tossed the letter to the desk. "What do you need, honey?"

She slipped in and closed the door behind her. "I'm taking Mom up a smoothie and Sul said something came for her and I was going to take that to her too. But that was then. Now, what I need to know is if you're all right."

Astute.

Thoughtful.

Loving.

Genny's girl.

"We didn't finish it when we got it, but I just finished reading your Uncle Corey's letter."

She came in farther and leaned against one of the chairs across from his desk, saying, "Oh, man, did he lay some heavy on you?"

"Your mom hasn't seen it so I'd rather her see it before I share it with you."

She nodded. "I dig."

"I'll take the package up to her."

"Okay, wanna swing by the kitchen and get her smoothie?"

"Yup," he replied, pushing out of his chair then nabbing the letter and the thick envelope on his desk.

"Duncan?" Sasha called.

He looked to her as he rounded the desk.

"Don't take on Uncle Corey's shit. The dude was messed up."

At her simple, but profound advice, Duncan could not beat back his chuckle.

"I'll try to do that, honey."

She came to him and linked her arm in his, also shouldering some of her weight into his biceps to get even closer.

Yeah.

Genny's girl.

"Anyway, you know, I mean, life's weird," she said as they walked to and through the door, "I'm all over throwing shade on Uncle Corey, 'cause he's a dick. But if he hadn't done what he did so long ago, Chloe and me and Sul and Gage wouldn't be here. And if he didn't do what he did recently, we wouldn't have you guys. So, you know, fuck him, but at least he went out as not entirely a loser."

He grinned down at her. "Yeah, Sash, at least he did that."

She smiled brightly up at him and that, he was noticing, was all she had.

There were different nuances to the wattage, but they all blasted with the strength of the sun.

They went to the kitchen and then Duncan went upstairs.

He walked into his room to see Genny wearing her robe with her hair at the top of her head in a messy knot, standing in front of his window, staring down at her many suitcases.

When she caught sight of him, she declared, "I should have drunk fewer gimlets and unpacked."

"So you're movin' in now?"

Her body jolted. "Oh God, Duncan, I—"

He smiled at her. "Don't finish that, babe, and if this is shit you wanna leave up here," he gestured to the suitcases with the envelope in his hand, "leave it. But I think we both get, not only is that empty closet yours, but in some part of my head, I actually built it for you."

She giggled and said, "Did we just get through the difficult talk of what's up for our future with me in Phoenix, you here?"

"Pretty much."

She giggled more and shared, "Sorry, darling, but when Tom moved out, I gutted the condo and redid it entirely. I took the extra closet in the master to extend my own and add a steam shower. And Chloe was all in to fill my expanded closet and she got on that with all due haste."

He was not surprised at that.

Though he was intrigued about this steam shower.

"This does not come as a surprise, but I don't even own a suit, so you give me half a foot of hanging space and a drawer, I'll be good."

She was smiling, as bright as her daughter, when she said, "You mean the world to me and this is why I'm giving you a full week before I tell Chloe you don't own a suit."

As funny, and scary, as that was, all he could manage was forcing a tight smile back.

Because, fuck, he didn't want to lay more shit on her.

He knew she was still fighting the hangover when she didn't notice the state of his smile.

"Please tell me that's a smoothie á la Sasha," she begged.

"It is." He handed it to her.

She took it and then sucked back at least half of it.

"Holy shit, Gen," he muttered when she removed the glass from her mouth.

"Orange, ginger, banana, yogurt, vanilla and water," she declared.

"Hydration and electrolytes," he surmised.

She smiled. "Sasha was going to study to be a dietician before she took off to savor the world."

"We have ginger in this house?"

She held up the glass and looked at it. "It tasted a little gritty, so she probably used powder."

"Your script came."

"Cool." She smiled, looking at his hand.

"And Samantha got my number. She phoned to explain and apologize. You can also call off the dogs that you unleashed to get to the bottom of how she found out about Tom when Hale told you he didn't share. She guessed about the reason for your divorce."

The smile died. "Guessed?"

"Yup."

"Oh my God," she breathed.

Anger was suffusing her features.

Deserved, but they had more shit to get through before they could put it the fuck behind them and have the goodness of their day.

And then the rest of their lives.

"She also wants the shot to apologize to you. Your call. But I'll warn you of something that probably will come as no surprise. She's twisted. She loved Corey truly and he broke her heart and she's the kind of woman who never allowed herself to heal from that. So my advice, let her go spit."

"It is highly likely I shall take that advice, Bowie, unless Hale requests I go the other way."

He nodded.

And then he got into the worst of it.

"And I finished reading Corey's letter."

She paled.

Goddamn it.

"You should read it," he said quietly.

She stared at him a second before she downed the next quarter of smoothie.

She then raised her hand, and he gave her the envelope, on top of which was the letter.

She took both and sat, perched at the edge of one of the two big leather chairs in front of his window, and reached to set the glass on a table.

She tossed the script to the ottoman.

And she bent her head to read the letter.

When she was done, her hand fluttered down, and she twisted on her perch to stare at his view.

She didn't see anything; he knew that before she spoke.

"You know, Corey had a dad like yours."

He crossed his arms on his chest. "I know."

"Of course you know, that was what drew you two together."

She turned her head and her gaze came up to his. "But you were you, and he was a runt."

"Yes," Duncan forced out.

"His father was tall and lean and strong, like Hale. Like you."

Duncan said nothing.

"And Corey was not that."

Duncan remained silent.

"And even if he couldn't escape it with every time he looked in a mirror, or someone said something mean to him, his father never let him forget it."

"Nope," Duncan confirmed.

And yeah, back then?

Duncan had hated Corey's dad maybe more than Corey hated him.

"I see now, how jealous he always was of you," she whispered.

"Yes."

"And I see also, how much he worshipped you."

This was harder.

But he couldn't disagree.

"Yes."

"I forgive him," she whispered like she was confessing an ugly secret.

"Of course you do," he whispered back. "You're you. But, baby, I don't. He was my brother. Honest to Christ, it would be like Gage doin' that to Sully."

"I understand, Bowie."

They remained silent, holding each other's eyes.

Gen broke it.

"He killed himself because—"

"He killed himself because he made bad choices in his life that he couldn't live with. It had nothin' to do with us. And he made that plain in that letter, Genny."

Her voice was small on her, "I know."

"I need to hold you," he told her.

"Then why aren't you doing that?" she asked.

Good question.

In half a second, she was in his arms.

She didn't burst into tears or even weep.

She just lay her cheek on his chest, circled him with her arms and held him tight.

"I feel guilt, because, in truth, now that the shock of it all has worn off, I don't miss him. He was a lot of work," she confessed.

"Try to get that out of your head. It might be hard, but that also isn't on you."

She sighed.

Then she said, "Hale hasn't shared. He got everything, but I don't know if there was some letter, some wish—"

"If there was, would he tell you?"

"Yes, or Tom."

"Then brace, baby, because one thing we know, Corey was thorough. And systematic."

Her head tipped back, and she breathed, "Oh my God."

He nodded. "One down. One to go."

"He wanted you around to—"

"Yup."

"Oh my God."

They stared at each other again.

And then she asked hesitantly, "Will you do that?"

"Tell a man that his father was once a good guy? A good friend. Hilariously funny and whip smart and unceasingly loyal? Until he wasn't?"

"Bowie—"

"Yes, I'll do it. Any boy needs to know that his father had that in him."

That was when they came.

The tears.

She shoved her face in his chest.

He was just glad she hadn't gotten to the makeup part of her morning.

He held her while she wept, quiet and sad.

And he did this staring at his view.

Corey hated their hikes.

But he loved riding horses and being around water.

He would also love to be there, with Duncan, with Genny, their kids.

You fucked up, buddy, huge, he thought, staring at the clouds drifting in blue sky.

He took in a deep breath and let it go on his next thought, the one he'd need to remember when it was his time to give Corey to his boy.

But fuck, I missed you.

GEN ROLLED HIM.

Not a surprise.

His woman always liked the top.

Then she rode him, staring down at him, hot and hungry, and he had to concentrate on not coming just from that look on her face.

But it couldn't be avoided how she was pounding down on his cock.

Or how goddamned gorgeous she was.

His Genny.

Right there.

The look on her face got hotter.

So Duncan warned, "Don't you come, Genny."

She smiled, sultry and smug.

Then she started to gasp.

He grasped her hips, did an ab curl and rolled them again, him on top.

"Bowie!" she snapped.

He hitched a leg and went at her harder, coming around with a hand to go at her clit.

"Just you," she panted through an inward stroke.

"Clit," he grunted on another one, finding it and beginning to roll.

"I'll come too fast if you go at my clit."

"Baby, I didn't do that in the shower, and you came in two seconds."

"It wasn't two seconds," she snapped breathily, lifting her hips and clenching.

Christ.

Fucking ecstasy.

"All right, three."

She tried to glare, started to giggle and ended in a whimper.

"Yeah," he whispered.

She caught his hair in a fist.

"Yeah," he bit.

This was Genny. Always.

They could start slow and sweet.

But she always needed it to end with a hard, fast fucking.

The same as he.

He rolled his hips and went in.

And she was off, climaxing while puffing out cute, sexy little huffs of air, clenching him with all she had.

He kept at her clit and her pussy, until she went off again.

Then he concentrated on himself.

While he did, she engaged more than lips and tongue and fingers, also teeth and nails.

So it didn't take long before his mind blanked and he blew.

The best.

Best ever.

Always.

Absolutely.

Duncan nuzzled her neck, they kissed, then he slid out and rolled to his back.

She rolled with him, plastering herself down his side.

"You think the kids heard?" she whispered.

"This house is built solid, the doors are closed, and we left them outside around the firepit, swapping ghost stories. A competition which, I'm pretty sure, Chloe's gonna win. Though Sully will give her a run for her money. But even if one came in for something, they wouldn't hear." He grinned at her. "You're quiet anyway."

"You're grunty," she replied.

His brows went up. "Grunty?"

"You make a lot of noise. It's a massive turn on. But it's still a lot of noise."

He started laughing.

She was smiling down at him when he finished and said, "They didn't hear us."

"Okay," she whispered. "Good day."

No, it hadn't been a good day.

Genny and her kids and his hiking around the lake, the sun shin-

ing, Chloe's sass, Sasha's sweet, Sully's cool, Gage's goofy, coming
home, cooking dinner, throwing a few back, and then sitting under
the stars by a fire?

"Great day," he replied.

She started playing with his chest hair, her eyes watching, saying,
"I love having this back with you." Her gaze came to his. "The sex, I
mean."

"I love having *you* back, but also love having you back in my bed."
He gripped her ass. "Hottest piece I ever had."

She smiled at him, bent in to kiss him, but when she pulled away,
she said, "You don't have to say that."

"It ain't a line, darlin'," he replied.

She looked dubious.

Duncan wrapped both arms around her and pulled her up, so they
were face to face and chest to chest.

"Eye on the ball, honesty, out there, it was good with Dora, in the
beginning. Different from you. Though straight up, nothing against
her or what we had, it was not as good. But it worked. We worked. It
was fulfilling. Healthy. Because the emotion was there. We loved each
other. And then she turned. And it was not any of that. It was like I
was a show pony, performing for her, every move, every second,
aware that I was trying to convince her of something I shouldn't need
to. It got to the point, if I didn't get hard the second she looked at my
cock, she'd say shit like, 'That proves it. You're too tired from fucking
her to even get it up for me.' And we can just say, a man needs some
stimulus to perform, and that's not it."

"Oh, Bowie," she whispered.

"By the time we divorced, we hadn't had sex in two years. And that
was on me. In the end, the man she'd convinced herself I was, that she
could think that about me, I couldn't bear to touch her. Though,
unsurprisingly, she used that as an excuse to prove I was fucking
around on her."

"Oh, Bowie," she repeated, sadder, quieter.

"I'm not telling you this to put Dora out there." He lifted, rolled
again, so they were chest to chest but Genny was on her back. "I'm

telling you this, baby, because you need to know. Two years, and before that, shit was not great, and I did not stray. After I moved out, to prove something to her, and maybe to me, I didn't date, nothing, until well after the divorce."

Now the sad was dripping from her, "Darling."

"The point is, I will never step out on you, Gen."

She got what he was saying, he knew it when her body twitched under his.

"Bowie," she said softly, gliding her arms around him.

"Never," he told her. "And not only because you're a seriously great fuck."

Her eyes went huge.

And then she burst out laughing.

He grinned down at her while she was doing it and kissed her when it started waning.

She rolled him in the middle of it and then there was some groping, some licking, some sucking, before she took a bite of his beard then got in his face.

"I need to clean up, be back," she said, and slid off him.

He watched her ass as she walked to the bedroom.

And reclining on the pillows, hands behind his head, not too broken up about his attention being taken from the view of a moonlit lake, he watched her walk back.

She came right to him and then fell on him, teetering like a tree.

He grunted and curled his arms around her.

She put her face in his.

"It's almost more beautiful here at night than it is during the day. All those stars. The moon so bright. Crazy."

"Glad you like it, baby."

"You get Thanksgiving, but I get Christmas."

He was not quick on the conversational change uptake.

"Sorry?" he asked.

"I have a company that does my decorations and they are, as Gage says, *off the hook*. You and the boys have to come to the condo for Christmas."

"I do my own decorations, and they are *off the hook*, so your ass is here."

"Fifty-fifty," she haggled.

"Boys gotta give their mom time," he warned.

"Okay, we'll figure it out," she allowed.

"Tom?" he asked.

She bit her lip but let it go to say, "We still do holidays together with the kids."

"He's welcome here if he can handle it."

"God, God, *God*," she hissed fiercely, her sudden change in tone and expression taking him by surprise, not to mention, she'd grabbed hold of his beard, "I love you."

He stared at her.

Then he rolled her.

Before he kissed her, she said, "Please tell me we're fucking again."

"Genny, baby, I am no longer twenty-six."

"Then we'll make out and feel each other up," she declared. "For a long, long time."

"That I can do."

She smiled bright at him.

Christ.

There she was.

In his bed.

Genny.

"I love you too, Imogen, and I never stopped."

Her smile faltered as her eyes got watery.

That was when he kissed her.

And they made out and felt each other up.

For a long, long time.

CHAPTER 19

THE SETTLING

Duncan

"'Night, Bowie."

"'Night, honey."

After she gave him a smile, Duncan watched Sasha start toward the hall to her room.

Before he began to go the other way, though, she turned and said, "You know, I know you all let me win."

"You're bankrupting my boys, darlin'," he told her.

"Then you all should stop being cute dufuses and play for real," she replied.

He couldn't remember the last time he'd been referred to as cute, or a dufus, or if either had ever happened in his life.

But from Sasha, both felt like a compliment.

"I'll send out that memo," he told her.

She shot him another of her sunny smiles and a brief wave and then bounced down the hall.

Duncan didn't move until he lost sight of her, and he didn't move for a while after.

He had bi-monthly poker games at his house with his buds.

She'd sat in the last two, which were the only two since he'd had her mother back in his life, and Sasha in his life at all.

In that time, they'd been down to the condo on three occasions for short visits in order for Gen to show him her home, so Chloe could show off her shop, and for Duncan to attend his first event at Genny's side, a fundraiser for the Arizona Humane Society.

Which meant he now owned a suit.

And Chloe had not only selected it, she'd bossed the tailor at the shop to have it fit to perfection (or what she considered perfection) while he was trying it on.

Needless to say, there were a number more pictures of he and Genny together out there.

And without them making a statement, they were now "official."

And through this time, in her pale-yellow convertible Beetle, Sasha tended to wander back and forth between the cabin and the condo.

Though, she made a point to be at the cabin on poker night.

Duncan headed to where her mother made a point to be on poker night.

The bathtub.

When he got there, he felt the humidity in the air, and you could still smell the scent of the candles she burned, but she wasn't there.

So he turned around and retraced his steps.

He then went to her third favorite place in his home, outside his bathroom and his bed.

The den.

She hadn't had an army of designers come in and fill it with chintz and florals, or what he'd discovered was her aesthetic when he first saw her condo: glamour and wealth.

Genny liked it just as it was.

Big stone fireplace with an arch fashioned in the rocks and a deep hearth. Comfortable, deep-seated, leather chairs, throws over the back.

Several thin but colorful rugs overlaid on each other on the wood floors. Small, unobtrusive standing lamps that didn't give off light so much as warm glows. And rough-hewn tables close at hand to put down drinks.

Gen loved that room and had claimed it. She said it was small and cozy and it didn't have a TV, which was something he'd found she wasn't big on. A surprise, considering her profession. But she definitely preferred to read.

Or what he was seeing her doing now when he entered the room and saw her curled up in a chair with Cookie in her lap, the dogs around her chair jumping up to come greet him, and Tuck snoozing on a folded blanket on the hearth.

She was playing that game on her phone.

She glanced up at him, looking guilty.

"I need to clear the cursed forest," she told him.

He chuckled as he made his way to her with the dogs accompanying him.

She was not a morning person.

He was. Up early to face the day at least an hour before she cracked open her eyes. It would be an hour after that before she got out of bed.

Which meant she was a night person.

Duncan tended to hit the sack at around ten.

Gen hit it at around midnight.

They made this work sexually, because she woke him up when she got in bed, and with her there, he was all in to have a quick, or not so quick, fuck before passing out again.

And in the mornings, if she was going to be in bed for an hour anyway, he figured he might as well return to it and keep her busy.

So he did.

This meant he was usually in the office an hour later than his norm.

But he'd worked hard all his life.

He deserved this.

They deserved this.

So he was taking it.

And giving it to her.

"They've left," she said as he sat on the hearth by her knee and reached out to give Tuck some love.

"Yeah."

"Did you all let Sasha win again?" she asked.

He grinned. "Yeah."

She shook her head but did it also grinning.

She stopped doing that and asked worriedly, "They don't think it's rude I don't say goodbye?"

"Babe, you came in, said hi. Came back, checked in, refreshed the food. And came back again to say goodnight. Now, it's after midnight. It'd be rude for them to expect you to be at the door, waving at them as they drove away. I don't even do that shit."

This made her relax. "You have good friends, Bowie."

"Yeah."

"Harvey especially. I adore him."

"Adoration wouldn't be how I'd describe it, but he's the best friend I've ever had."

It was the wrong thing to say.

A shadow stole over her face.

"I'm glad you have that," she whispered.

"I am too. And I have it, Genny. And I've had Harv and Beth and their girls a long time. So it's all good."

Either that chased the shadow away, or the thought behind her next words did.

And a certain light hit her eyes before she said them. "You ready for bed?"

With her sleeping at his side, and other things they did there, always.

That said…

"We gotta talk about something first."

She instantly settled in, ready for that if he needed it, and that was always too.

She'd reminded him he'd given her that.

But she gave it back.

Then.

And now.

"What?" she asked.

"Sasha," he told her.

He had to say no more. She knew what he was thinking.

He told her anyway. "Honey, I now get what you were saying about direction. I'm of a mind too much pressure is put on kids to make decisions about the rest of their lives when they're seventeen, eighteen, about to graduate and go to college or find another vocation. They've no idea who they are and are clueless how the world works, so they're not at a place where they can make a decision about what they want to do with their life. If it was up to me, they'd all take time like Sash is taking, learn a little about the world and your place in it before you take it on. But I sense this is not what she's doing. She's..."

He didn't know how to describe it.

Gen did.

"Lost. Drifting. Aimless."

"Yeah," he agreed.

She rolled her head on her neck before she asked, "Do you think it might be the divorce?"

"I can't know, baby. I've known her a month and this is all I know of her. Sunny. Sweet. Lively. But directionless. Is that a change?"

She nodded.

"She was an athlete, like her dad, her brother. Matt played tennis. He was good. Not as good as Tom but few are. Sasha played beach volleyball. And she was great. Coaches talked to her and us about the possibility of her going pro and competing in the Olympics. She's a laidback kid. Chloe got all the drama in the family. But with that, Sash was driven. She loved doing it. After we moved to Phoenix, we spent a lot of time, shuttling back and forth so she could keep doing it. She was all in. And then she just...stopped."

"Before the divorce, during or after?"

"During," she whispered.

"You need to have a talk with her, Genny."

"I have, Bowie. And she tells me to chill out. She's all good. Just because she's not doing what everyone else is doing doesn't mean what she's doing is wrong. I tell her everyone else doesn't have a trust fund and rich parents to keep them in ripped jeans and embroidered tops. It isn't like she's scoring through the money we set aside for her to go to school and set up a life. She's low maintenance. It was far more expensive to have Chloe in France for three years."

He was not surprised about that.

"I shared in return you can't wander through life without *something*," she continued. "I agree with you, it's okay for a while. And even good. She's lucky she has that privilege when others don't. But I've told her it can't go on forever and Sash doesn't get angry easily, or impatient, but that sure makes her both."

"Can you cut her off, money-wise?" he queried.

She nodded but didn't look happy about doing it. "Tom and I have control of her trust. She can't get to the totality of it until she's twenty-six. But, Bowie, that's last ditch. It seems punitive. And she's not doing anything wrong...as such. She's just not doing, well, *anything*."

"Yeah," he muttered.

"I'll have a talk with her, after Christmas," Gen decided.

"How 'bout you corral Coco to have a talk with her?" he suggested.

"I think you can imagine that Sasha is the least inclined of anyone to do what Chloe tells her to do."

"Maybe. Chloe is also a big sister, has it together, and doesn't breathe unless she's doing it for someone she loves, and Sasha knows that. So it might not go down great in the beginning, but it also might get her thinking."

Gen was also thinking as she said, "I'll talk to Chloe about it. After the holidays."

"Good. Now, time for bed."

Her distracted expression fled, and her eyes came to his.

Then she gave Cookie a snuggle before she rose from her chair, dropped the cat on the seat and they walked, arms around each other, to their room.

DUNCAN DIDN'T KNOW what woke him, especially after poker, a number of Scotches, a late night, and a slow fuck that ended fast and hard.

But he woke.

To an empty bed.

Not even thinking about it, he sat up, ready to toss the covers aside and look for her.

But he didn't move when he saw her standing at the window, staring into the night.

Either she heard him move, or simply sensed he was awake, because she spoke.

"It snowed."

He could tell by the brightness coming into the room that wasn't just the usual from a moon that was not dimmed by the lights of humanity.

The theme of the planet: what they create doing everything from reducing to obliterating the beauty of nature.

"Come back to bed," he called.

"I hate that you lived the marriage you had," she told the window.

Shit.

Yeah, his comment about Harv being the best friend he'd had had gotten to her.

"Come back to bed, baby," he repeated.

"I hate that we didn't get the chance to make daughters. You're great with my girls. I love to watch you with them. A natural."

His voice was lower, rougher, when he reiterated, "Gen, please, come back to bed."

"I need to do this," she replied, also lower, throatier.

Hearing that, Duncan said nothing.

"Just this once," she went on.

Duncan remained silent.

Genny spoke on.

"I get that it wouldn't have worked. I get that it would have overwhelmed us. I get that, if it hadn't happened, I wouldn't have had my kids, and yes, Tom, and you wouldn't have had the boys, and the times that were good with Dora. I get all of that."

She stopped.

He waited.

She started again.

"But my mother loved you. There were times I thought she was more hurt than I was at how we ended. And my father never had a son. You were that to him. And he tried to hide it, so he could look after me, but I knew he was devastated. So I also hate that they didn't live to know what really happened, to see us together again, and to have you back in their lives."

That cut to the bone.

Even so, Duncan didn't move.

Nor speak.

"And I know it's useless to think, if we'd managed it, if we'd overcome it, if we'd stayed together, then what other ifs would there be? I know you would never have endured what you did with Dora. I would never have had the man I loved and trusted above all others in the world betray me. We would have made babies."

She stopped again.

Duncan held completely still, because he knew one move would drive him to her.

And he sensed she needed her space to get through this.

So he did what he was intent on doing for the rest of their lives.

He gave her what she needed.

"So just this once, between you and me, so it's just ours, I'm going to allow myself a moment I never allow because I think it's weak and meaningless."

When she didn't go on, he broke his silence to ask, "Allow yourself what, baby?"

"To hate," she said. "To hate what Dora put you through. And to hate what Corey did to us. Not to hate them. But to hate what they did."

"That's not only allowed, but understandable," he pointed out.

She turned to him at that. "I know. But you feel it and you let it go so it doesn't consume you, Bowie. You know that. You did it with your dad. Who, by the way, is the only exemption to the rule. I just straight up hate him."

That made Duncan chuckle.

He stopped when she declared, "Having you back is like having the breath reenter my lungs. And another thing I hate is that we have Corey to thank for that. So I'll only do that just this once. He'll only get that gratitude this once. Because in the end, it's about you and me and who we are and that we'd never quit each other. Not totally."

She had that right.

Before he could confirm, she kept speaking.

"Thank you for throwing that frog at me, Bowie. It's been a rough climb, and there are parts of that trail I wish neither of us had been forced to travel, but it was worth it to be right here...with you."

Right.

He'd given it to her.

Now he was done.

"Get back in this bed, Genny," he growled.

She came back to bed.

He gathered her close and kissed her hard when she did.

When he was done, she tucked her face in his throat and burrowed closer.

He pulled the covers up to her shoulder to keep her warm.

The room, bright with moonshine on snow, was quiet.

Gen broke it.

"Now, I can let that go and just concentrate on being with you."

"Good," he murmured.

"Are you at that place?" she asked.

"Baby, you anywhere near me, I'm at that place. Nothing on this earth means dick to me except my boys bein' good, now your kids bein' good, and me bein' with you."

She made no response.

Though she did.

And he loved what she had to say.

Without anywhere to go, she burrowed even closer.

"Now, go to sleep," he ordered when she was done.

"Okay, Bowie."

"Love you."

"And I love you."

Having gotten it out, Gen went right back to sleep.

With her giving it to him, Duncan couldn't find it.

So he was awake when the moon fell behind a cloud and he lifted his head to see snow falling again.

The roads up at that elevation were going to be a bitch in the morning.

So he'd work from home.

Gen, going out shopping now with Bettina, kept the kitchen stocked.

They were good.

Safe.

And settled in.

On that thought, Duncan finally drifted to sleep.

And the snow drifted down outside.

Blanketing a big log cabin next to an even bigger lake in peace.

CHAPTER 20

THE BEST FRIENDS

Corey

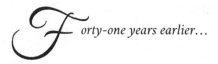 *orty-one years earlier…*

HE WAS IN BED, curled up, face stuffed in the pillow, even though he wasn't crying anymore. He kept it there, so in case he started up again, his father wouldn't hear him.

It would be bad if his father heard him.

Really bad.

It was usually *really* bad. Anything and everything at his house could range from not good at all to *really* bad with the line on that meter pointed most often to the right.

But him being awake and caught having done something as wimpy as crying would be seriously, really, *really bad.*

It was late and he was supposed to be asleep.

But he couldn't sleep.

Not after that day.

And that night.

Because, yeah…

It had been *bad*.

He heard the tap.

A tap on his window.

Ghosts?

Ghosts weren't corporeal, they couldn't tap.

Could they?

Maybe…

Zombies?

Oh man.

"Corey," he heard whispered urgently.

He turned swiftly in bed and saw Dun peering through the window.

When Dun caught his eyes, his friend grinned at him, and then Genny's head popped around at his side.

She grinned at him too.

What on…?

"Come on," Duncan whispered.

Quietly, he slipped out of bed and went to the window. Carefully, he shoved it open.

"What are you doing here?"

"Come on," Duncan repeated. "Mz. Swan is waiting."

Mrs. Swan?

What?

He looked to the alarm clock beside his bed.

Holy cow.

It was nearly eleven.

He not only was never up this late, he was supposed to be asleep two hours ago.

"Hurry," Genny urged.

"Jeans, buddy," Duncan said.

He had no idea what was going on, but today was what today was, and his friends were there (and so was Mrs. Swan).

So Corey nodded and rushed to get dressed as quietly as he could.

Then, with Duncan's help, and Genny's, he was out the window.

"Bucket," Duncan said, pointing at the big plastic paint bucket that was upended under the window. "For when you have to climb back in."

That was Duncan, always thinking of everything.

Corey grinned at him.

Then, like soldiers at war, they ran hunkered down through his side yard to the car at the curb.

Genny opened the front passenger door.

"Birthday boy gets front seat," Mrs. Swan declared.

Genny turned and smiled at Corey.

While Duncan and Genny shifted to get in the back, Corey climbed in the coveted front seat and looked at Mrs. Swan.

She was so pretty. *So* pretty. She didn't look like Genny at all, but man, she was pretty.

Especially as she was right now, all happy because they were being bad (Mrs. Swan was *the best* at being bad), smiling at him huge.

But her smile went funny as she caught his face under the car lights.

Dang.

She was a mom. You couldn't hide anything from a mom.

He'd stopped forever ago.

But he knew she knew he'd been crying.

Suddenly, the smile came back in full force, nearly as bright at Genny's, and she decreed, "We best get on, clock's running out. We have barely an hour left of your birthday, buddy boy. We gotta get crackin'."

And then, since the car was still running, she glided off, her headlights out, all covert and *everything*.

That was, until she turned the corner on the block and turned them on.

But her driving a whole half a block under cover of the night…

So cool.

He twisted in his seat to look back at his friends. "What do you have planned?"

"They better not tell you, or they won't get an extra scoop of ice cream with their birthday cake," Mrs. Swan warned, then, like she didn't intend to spill the beans, she said, "Whoops."

"Birthday cake..." Corey didn't finish because, all of a sudden what was happening hit him, and his throat closed up.

He looked front, right at the road, and he did it hard.

He also did it not thinking about what his birthday was like with his folks.

Or his *lack* of birthday.

No one in that car said anything, but they all knew.

He knew they did.

Especially Dun.

He knew how Corey's birthdays were.

He knew how Corey's everydays were.

But now...they had Genny.

Genny and Mrs. Swan.

They were at Genny's house in five minutes, and he'd gotten himself together by then.

Another couple minutes, he was at Mr. and Mrs. Swan's kitchen table, one of those awesome store-bought sheet cakes in front of him with all the big swirls of frosting all over it and lit candles, the perfect amount, the works!

"I can't even *begin* to imagine why this is your favorite cake, darlin'," Mrs. Swan said to him. "I would have made you anything you wanted. From scratch."

So *that* was why, *ages* ago, Genny had asked what his favorite cake was.

Mrs. Swan was good in the kitchen, her cookies were *the best*.

But—

"I can't even *begin* to imagine the level of loon I married, kidnapping her daughter's friend to give him a midnight birthday party," Mr. Swan said before Corey could say a word.

Corey got tense, but Genny didn't.

She grinned.

Because she did, Corey looked between Mr. and Mrs. Swan, and he saw straight out that Mr. Swan may have said those words, but he was all ready for cake.

And all ready to celebrate Corey's birthday.

Corey knew that when he looked from his wife, and saw Corey studying him.

So he tapped his knuckles on the table, lifted his hand, pointed at Corey, and then nodded to him.

What he did when Gen did something he was proud of her for doing, like a perfect cartwheel into an equally perfect roundoff. Or Duncan did something he was proud of him for doing, like when they found that fox in a trap and rushed back to tell Mr. Swan. And then Mr. Swan came out to the woods to help them get it loose, and Duncan worked close at his side to trap the thing in a nicer way and get it to the vet so they could get its leg fixed and then get it back into the woods.

Or when Corey did something Mr. Swan was proud of him doing, like when he showed Genny the trick he used to learn his multiplication tables.

Corey then turned back to Mrs. Swan. "You make great cake. But it's about the frosting, Mz. Swan," he told her.

When he said that, she shoved her finger right into his cake, scooping off a load of frosting and pushing it into her mouth.

She smacked her lips before she said, "I see what you mean."

She then tipped her head to the cake.

An invitation.

He couldn't.

He couldn't because he thought of what would happen to him if he did something like that at his house (not that they ever had cake at his house, birthday or other). With his dad watching (something he always did). And his mother frowning (something *she* always did).

But...

He looked hard at Mrs. Swan's face.

He...

Did it.

Shoving his own finger in, he scooped off a whole load of frosting and thrust it in his mouth.

Delicious.

Exactly what a birthday should taste like.

Which was what his birthday had not tasted even a little bit like. Not that day's.

Not ever.

Until now.

Mrs. Swan winked at him.

Then it was a free for all, Corey going back in, Gen and Dun going in, Mrs. Swan going in, and Mr. Swan muttering, "Good Lord. I got a pack of midnight hyenas on my hands."

That was, he muttered that before he went in.

They ate all the frosting and cake with their fingers.

And when it was decimated, cake crumbles and frosting smears all over the table (and Mrs. Swan *didn't even care*), Mrs. Swan said, "Well, would you look at that. No cake to put ice cream on." She clucked. "Guess I gotta make sundaes."

"Yesssssss," Genny hissed, bopping Corey in the arm happily then pumping her own.

He smiled at her.

"Gen, love, help me with the towels," Mrs. Swan said gently.

Corey felt that tone in a weird place in his stomach, like he always did when Mrs. Swan talked like that to Genny, or any of them.

He loved that for Gen. He knew Duncan did too.

How Mrs. Swan could be gentle, especially when she was telling her daughter what to do.

Mrs. Holloway could be like that when Mr. Holloway wasn't around.

But Mr. Holloway and Corey's folks?

Never.

Gen and Mrs. Swan gave them all their own damp kitchen towels so they had plenty of surface area to clean their hands and mouths, and after Mr. Swan had dropped a stack of dry ones on the table for them dry off, Duncan called, "Mr. Swan?"

At the way his voice sounded, Corey looked at him.

Corey's friend looked...strange.

"Right, right...before sundaes. We have to—" Mr. Swan started.

Mrs. Swan cut him off. "My dearest, darling husband, you know better than that. *Nothing* comes before sundaes."

"This does."

Her eyes danced and her lips twitched.

She then nodded.

With that, both Gen and Dun moved like lightning, jumping off their chairs and coming to Corey.

"C'mon!" Duncan practically yelled, tugging on Corey to get him out of his seat.

Corey went and they guided him through the house, to a place that was off-limits when they were hanging out.

Mr. Swan's study.

But they went right in.

And there was his desk.

And there was his reading chair.

And there was...

Another desk.

A much smaller one.

With a...

A...

Oh no.

He was going to cry again.

Because what that small desk had on it had a big, blue bow stuck to it.

So he knew it was for him.

"Duncan and Genny told us what you wanted, son," Mr. Swan said. "And we figure, well..." He cleared his throat. "You can say you're studying with Genny and you can come over and fiddle with it."

"It costs too much," Corey whispered.

And it did.

He knew exactly how much, and it cost *a whack.*

"Duncan and Genny saved up their allowances for a spell and... we'll just say me and Mrs. Swan chipped in a bit," Mr. Swan explained.

Corey stared.

And stared and stared at the thing with the bow.

"Hunh," Dun grumbled.

"Aren't you gonna go turn it on!?" Genny cried, all excited.

He looked to them.

"Dude, it's a *personal computer. No one has one of those,*" Duncan reminded him. "It's all you could talk about and..." He pointed. *"It's right there."*

Corey didn't move.

He stared at his friends.

Genny did chores around the house, a lot of them. Corey was always complaining about how she couldn't hang out because she had to do the vacuuming or polish her mom's silver.

But Duncan.

He never complained about Genny doing so many chores.

Also Duncan...

A whole long time ago, he got a paper route.

A *whole long time ago.*

Corey stared at his friends.

And he stared and stared.

"Aren't you gonna go turn it on, Corey?" Genny whispered.

He sensed movement and looked up, at Mr. and Mrs. Swan, who were standing together now. Mr. Swan had his arm around Mrs. Swan, and when Corey looked their way, she turned her head into her husband's shoulder.

But before she did, Corey saw the tears falling.

He turned back to his friends.

"You guys are the best," he said softly.

Duncan swallowed.

Genny bit her lip.

Then Duncan said, "We don't have all night. We have to get you home." He jerked his head at the computer. "Go turn it on, buddy. Give it a dry run."

He gave them one last look.

His best friends.

The best friends ever.

And then he moved to the computer and turned it on.

THEY HAD SUNDAES.

Because Mrs. Swan was Mrs. Swan.

And it was his birthday.

But it was Mr. Swan who took him home.

He was taking Duncan home too, but Genny insisted on coming with.

And Mr. Swan was Mr. Swan.

So even though now it was super-duper late, he let her.

Corey would get into a lot more trouble if he was found not where he was supposed to be, he figured Mr. Swan knew that, so he dropped him first.

"Turn your light on and off, son, real fast, so I know you're safe inside," he instructed as Corey was getting out. "Real fast, Corey, we'll be watching."

They'd be watching.

Watching out.

For Corey.

Corey bent down to nod at Mr. Swan behind the wheel then looked to the backseat at Genny and Duncan.

He smiled at them and said, "Thanks, guys."

"You're welcome," Gen chirped, totally on a midnight ice-cream-sundaes-and-cake high, but also, that was just Genny.

"No problem, buddy," Dun said, cool as ever, and that was all Duncan.

He nodded again, to them, shut the car door, and had jogged halfway across the yard before he stopped and jogged back.

He went right to the back door window of Mr. Swan's car.

Even though Genny could do it, she looked so worried, she was frozen with it as she stared at Corey, so Duncan leaned across her to slide open the window, and he stayed leaned into her as they both peered out at him, their heads super close, Gen's golden one, Dun's dark.

"Everything okay, Corey?" Duncan asked, like Mrs. Swan.

All gentle-like.

Corey took him in too.

Duncan was also worried.

"I..."

He couldn't get the words out.

"Do you—?"

He would never know what Genny was going to ask.

So he'd do it and not chicken out, superfast, he blurted, "I love you guys."

And then he didn't jog to his bedroom window that they'd left open.

He raced to it.

And he didn't look back.

EPILOGUE

THE HOLIDAY

Sullivan

"*Y*our dad's hung up, honey, something to do with the opening in Boise. He wanted to be here to get you, but he had to see to it. He's headed down as we speak."

"He texted and it's not a problem, Genny."

She smiled at him, watching him closely.

They'd just greeted outside the terminal and were walking to baggage claim.

He'd probably get used to people looking at her, some pulling out their phones, some of those not even hiding it, but for now, he wanted to chest butt all of them, get in their face and ask what they were looking at.

"So, a couple of days at the condo, and then we're all going up to the house," she said.

"Cool," he muttered.

"I'm excited to show you the condo. You haven't seen it yet. Gage loves it."

Yeah, he did.

Gage was there practically every weekend. Even when Genny and Dad weren't there.

Then again, Sasha was living there, and Chloe lived in Phoenix, and they'd all adopted each other, even Sully, who Sash and Coco texted all the time.

Coco had ironic gifs down to an art.

And daily, Sash sent him pictures of sunrises or starry nights or sandy beaches with the caption *Your Daily Moment of Zen.*

"Yeah, he's told me."

"You going to spend some time with your mom?"

Shit.

His dad, Sul could hide it.

He could do this because Sully lived far away, and emotionally his father was too close to it.

Genny was a mom.

You couldn't pull anything over on a mom.

Not one like Genny.

He knew this because he barely knew her, and still, he figured she'd called it.

"Yeah," he grunted.

They hit the display that told them where his bag was going to come out and she said nothing.

And they walked to the carousel and she still said nothing.

But he knew he was going to give his mom some time, more for Genny than for his mom.

It was getting to be a problem, him wanting to avoid his mother, and he should probably talk it through with Dad. He'd given him a little when Dad and Genny got back together, and his dad had taken it okay.

Though Sully didn't think the rest of it he would.

No, telling Duncan Holloway that the entirety of his son's high school years were fucked up because his mom decided he was going to be her ally with all her conspiracy theories about his dad fucking everything that moved, and she was up in his shit all the time (when

Dad wasn't around), wanting him to spy on his own father, babbling all her crap? This going on even after they split up and Dad moved out?

No.

Dad was not going to be okay with that.

Sully had hid it, and he'd lied.

For his dad and for Gage.

He didn't want her dragging Gage into her shit.

And he didn't want his father to end up hating her.

So it was on him.

And when they were done, decided to split, he was so relieved. He thought it'd be over.

But instead, he was supposed to be the honorable son, understanding his mom was sick and getting over it.

He did.

He understood she was sick.

And he hated that for her.

But it was hard as fuck to get over it.

Because everyone thought she was all right.

But all Sully saw was her playing more games.

So if it was his choice, he'd hang with Dad and Genny and maybe call her and say "Hey" and "Merry Christmas," sending his gift over with Gage.

But it was never his choice.

His phone binged and he looked at it.

Gage.

He'd had a late class and just made her house.

"Gage is at your place," he informed her.

"Wonderful," she murmured.

"I'm sorry, are you Imogen Swan?"

It felt like his entire body puffed out when he turned and got between her and the short woman who was talking to her.

"Sully, it's fine," Genny murmured, putting her hand on his forearm and coming around him. "He's protective," she explained to the lady who was staring up at Sully curiously, probably thinking he was a bodyguard or something.

"I'm her stepson and no offense to you, but I'm home for Christmas and I'd like my stepmom to be able to just be my stepmom," he bit out.

He could feel Genny's eyes on him, but he didn't take his from the woman.

"Oh my God, I'm so sorry to disturb you."

"Really, it's fine," Genny said.

"I wasn't going to ask for a selfie or anything. I'm just a big fan and I wanted to tell you how much I love your movies and *Rita's Way*."

"And thank you for that. Truly, it's fine," Genny replied. "It's just, I hope you understand, my loved ones are protective."

Her loved ones.

"Yes, I understand. And I'm glad you have that," the woman said to Genny. Then to Sully, "You look like your dad. Just as handsome."

"Thanks," he forced out. Then he forced out more, "Sorry I was rude."

"I get it. You probably have to deal with this kind of thing all the time. I'm sure it gets old." She gave him a small smile, another one to Genny and wandered away.

He looked to Genny. "Sorry, that wasn't cool. She's a fan and I overreacted."

"Totally worth it for you to call me your stepmom," she teased.

He felt some of the tension go out of him, and he replied, "You're probably going to get a ring for Christmas. So it's not official, but it will be."

She seemed intrigued. "Has your dad shared?"

"No, but he's a really good gift giver so I wouldn't be surprised because I figure that's a real good gift."

She wound her arm through his and leaned into him, saying, "Yes, that would be a real good gift."

And yeah.

Didn't that just cut it?

There he was, standing at a baggage claim with Imogen Swan leaning on him, and there was no baggage.

And he wasn't talking about the luggage kind.

He'd come back a couple of weeks after he met her for fall break, and she and the girls were there, and it was a blast. Just like the first time, except, thankfully, without some outside force fucking with it.

Then there was Thanksgiving, and it was awesome. Genny was a good cook, but Chloe rocked that shit.

And in between, he'd Facetime his dad, and sometimes she'd butt in to say hi, but she didn't take what little time he had blabbing at him and trying to make him like her.

She just said hi and asked how he was.

And made his dad happy.

Christ, he'd never seen his dad so laidback and at peace as he was with Genny.

And Dad was pretty laidback.

All that shit that started them off, and a couple months down the road, and there was this.

No fights or screaming and his dad all wound up, trying to pretend he was cool and handling things.

Just happy.

Just Genny.

They got his bag and she walked him to her car.

At it, she offered, "You want to drive?"

Drive a Porsche?

"Yes."

She handed him the fob.

He put his bag in her trunk and they got in.

"I've never been to the condo," he reminded her as he was backing out.

"You know Phoenix?"

"For the most part."

"Head to the Biltmore and I'll guide you from there."

"Gotcha."

It took her a while. But he figured it wasn't about lulling him into a false sense of security.

It was about giving him time.

However, before they were at her place and it was about Christmas and holidays and family, she did it.

Because she was Genny.

"I'm so sorry, Sully."

"Breakups happen," he grunted.

"I know, but they hurt."

She would know.

"Yeah," he agreed.

"Your dad told me you really liked her."

"Aubrey was the shit."

"Again, honey, I'm so sorry."

Okay, she was Genny and she was cool.

She was also a woman.

So he went for it.

"Why do they do that?"

"Do what?"

"Break up before Christmas? I mean, what the fuck, Genny? Is it because she didn't want to waste a gift on me? Couldn't she just wait two weeks and not spoil the holiday for me?"

"I don't know."

"She acted like it was my fault. Like I shouldn't be studying...*in college*. She told me she didn't want to break up, but unless I could give her more time, she couldn't see past it."

"I've never met the girl, so—"

"It's selfish."

"It sounds it."

"It doesn't matter. I shouldn't care."

"That's the bitch of it, Sully. Because you can tell yourself that, but the heart knows different."

Yeah, she'd know about that.

She'd loved his dad since she was eight.

Eight.

Forty-four years of love and he'd burned her bad, and they'd been apart forever, and there she was, sitting next to Duncan Holloway's son, listening to his post-breakup blues.

She knew what her heart wanted.

And he wanted that.

"I want that," he whispered.

"Sorry?"

"Nothin'."

"What'd you say, Sul?"

"Nothin'."

"Okay, honey."

And she let it be.

Because she was Genny.

And because she was Genny, he said, "I want what you give to Dad."

He knew she was looking at him even before she said, "Then that is not Aubrey. Your father could be on the moon for five years, studying rocks because that was his passion, and he'd come home to me."

"I know," he muttered.

She reached out. Touched his arm. Then pulled back.

"You're young. Wait for her, Sully. She's out there."

And she was not Aubrey.

She guided them to her place and told him to drive up to the front and valet, "Because the garage scares me. It's so tight. I only park down there when Bowie's driving. Before him, I always valeted."

Unsaid: or her ex did it.

Tom Pierce was now going to be in the mix.

He'd bowed out of Thanksgiving.

But this made Sash and Coco have to do the split (not Matt, he stayed with his mom and them up at the house).

And apparently, Pierce did not like that for his girls, or Genny, and not only because them doing the split meant them driving two hours between Thanksgiving meals.

So he was going to man up.

Sully didn't get this, and he figured it was going to be all kinds of awkward.

But it was also cool.

His mom and dad didn't avoid each other, but they didn't talk to each other at all that Sul knew. They were civil but not friendly.

His mom, because she was embarrassed, maybe still loved his dad a whole lot, and it made her sad she'd fucked that up so huge.

His dad, because he was over her before he divorced her and he'd moved on, dating and now Genny.

So yeah, not super close friends.

At all.

He'd barely stopped at the swank roll through in front of her high-rise when the valet was at her door.

"Good evening, Ms. Swan."

"Evening, Lucas," she replied.

Sully pulled himself out and moved to the back, where he'd popped the hatch.

"Good evening, Mr. Holloway."

He blinked at a guy who was probably older than him, but only by a few years.

"Uh, hey."

The guy smiled.

Then they both ran into each other going for his bag.

"I got it," Sully said.

Lucas backed off.

He started to hand him the fob, but Genny said, "They have one, Sully. That's mine."

So he handed it to her.

After being told to have a good evening, he followed her into a lobby that was all ritzy furniture, water features, real live plants, massive pots stuffed with poinsettias, and classy holiday decorations, including the fanciest menorah he'd ever seen sitting on the front desk.

And there were a lot of "Evening Ms. Swan, Mr. Holloway."

They didn't even fob themselves up.

The dude behind the desk hopped to and pressed the elevator button for them, outside and in, unlocking the security on the buttons with his own fob.

"Jesus," he muttered when the doors closed.

"Your brother got used to it really quickly."

At that, he looked to her and felt like a dick.

Because it was the first time he'd smiled at her since he got off the plane.

"Gage is feeling this luxury condo living," she shared.

And at that, he started laughing.

Her hall was just as posh, clean as a pin, deadly silent and a little eerie.

She opened one side of double doors and he got blinded by the light from a massive crystal chandelier.

And that was all he was able to take in.

"*Sully!*" Sash screamed, racing down a wide hall to him, her long hair flying, like he'd been off to war or something.

He dropped his bag before she hit which was a good thing, or they'd both go down.

She gave him a tight hug then jumped back and shouted, "God! I'm so glad you're here! Finally! If Bowie would just get here, *we can start Christmas!*"

Christmas wasn't for four days, but he didn't share that.

She was dragging him in.

All he caught was a lot of white, bits of black, gold and pops of bright pink, when Coco rounded a corner.

As usual, she looked right out of a fashion magazine, hair and shoes included.

Her fingers were wrapped around a martini glass that had some blue drink in it with white froth at the top, and she was smirking at him.

"Sullivan," she greeted.

"Cocoroco," he replied.

She rolled her eyes.

Gage had come up with the addition to her nickname.

She pretended to hate it.

It was cute.

He moved in and kissed her cheek.

She kissed his back, but when he went to move away, she caught him by cupping his jaw.

Her eyes moved over his face, soft, warm and concerned.

Then they caught his.

And honest to fuck, it was all better when she drawled, "She's a damned fool."

Christ, when Judge got his shit together about her, he was going to be the luckiest man on the planet.

Outside Dad.

And whoever earned Sasha.

She let his jaw go and lifted her drink. "You want a Snowman Jack?"

"I don't know, what's in it?"

"It is blue. It is pepperminty. And other than that, I have no clue, except it is *very* alcoholic and your brother made a pitcher of them."

"I'm in."

Her lips curled and she glided away.

"Dude! Look!"

Sully then looked.

Yes.

Lots of white.

And black.

Black floors. Black wood on some of the white-upholstered furniture. Mostly just white-upholstered furniture. So many crystal chandeliers, it was like there might not be any left in the world. Some gold accents.

And Genny's Christmas decorations were white, pearly-white and freaking *pink*.

There were a lot of them.

He looked to her. "Has Dad seen your decorations?"

"Of course," she murmured.

"And how much shit has he given you about them?" he asked.

"He detests them," Genny answered, her lips curling like her eldest girl's.

Sully shook his head but looked to Gage when he yelled impatiently, "*Sul*! Look!"

His brother was turned to face the back of the unit and his arms were expanded wide.

Sully looked.

The wall was all windows, and beyond a balcony, Phoenix was laid out before them like a blanket of urban-themed Christmas lights.

"Is that not...*the shit*?" Gage asked.

It was one-hundred percent the shit.

"Yeah."

"They call me Mr. Holloway. Did they call you Mr. Holloway?"

"Yeah."

"Sometimes I walk through the lobby just so they'll say, 'Good morning, Mr. Holloway.' Or 'Good afternoon, Mr. Holloway.'"

"Stop doing that," Sully ordered.

"I will when it gets old and it is *so not old* being rich and knowing someone famous," Gage returned.

"This is why I love and adore our brother," Chloe said, handing him a martini glass filled with white froth and blue liquid. "He understands what's important in life."

"Oh, Coco," Sasha landed with a bounce on her knees on a sofa that was so white, Sully was, frankly, scared to get near it. "Stop encouraging our baby bro."

"Lest he ever forget, I will drill this into him until my dying breath," Coco returned.

Grinning at this, Sully took a sip.

"Jesus, it's like Christmas in alcohol form," he said when he'd swallowed it.

"Gage Holloway, mixologist," Coco said like she was introducing him to Gage.

"I'm our self-appointed bartender. Last weekend, Googled holiday cocktails," Gage said. "Made a list. Coco went to Total Wine. And the valets had to carry up four boxes of booze."

"Yes, and you're all very lucky I'm rich," Genny stated. She had her own blue and white cocktail now and was aiming her ass into a chair at an angle to the couch. And once she was down, she crossed her long legs in her stylish slacks, still wearing her stiletto heels, and she looked every inch the movie star she was. "Because those four boxes cost me a thousand dollars."

"The fuck?" Sully asked then looked to Gage. "Does Dad know this?"

Gage shrugged.

"Allow me to translate," Chloe cut in. "What *ma mère* is saying, when she discusses something as gauche as money, is, you've done it once, which I will allow. Don't do it again." She leaned toward Sully. "This I learned upon the purchase of a thirteen-thousand-dollar Chanel evening bag. And I will note, I have only the one."

At this news, he nearly did a spit take since he was sipping.

"But truly, it is *that fabulous*," she finished.

"I'm not sure you're a real great influence on my brother, Cocoroco."

"*Our* brother, *mon magnifique frère*. And I know, isn't it perfect?" she asked.

Christ, he loved this chick.

He couldn't help smiling at her.

"Hey, where's Cookie?" Gage suddenly asked.

"We've decided to leave her up at the house when we're down. Bettina is looking after them. We've learned with the back and forth, it can't be one and not all, and she's bonded with Rocco," Genny told him.

"She's bonded with Rocco?" Sully queried.

"It's so cute, they *cuddle together*," Sasha shared.

Rocco loved everything and everyone, including cats, which Tuck wasn't a big fan of, and rabbits, which Bounce hid from.

Good he had Cookie now.

"Gage, darling, can you grab Sully's bag and show your brother your room?" Genny asked.

"On it," Gage said.

Gage beat Sully to the hall to get his bag.

Sully gave up on the ridiculous argument of who was going to shoulder it, let his brother do it, and Gage guided him to "their room."

It took a while. This pad was essentially an apartment.

But it was huge.

"She had it redone for us," Gage told him, dumping his bag on one of two queen beds that had padded head and sideboards in a gray tweed, matching benches at the bottom.

There was also a wall paneled in wood. Two nightstands for each bed that were boxy and clean-lined. The sleek lamps on them looking like they were made of brushed platinum.

And no white or pink in sight.

"I mean, like, we're grown, and we're gonna be like, on our own in a few years, at least me, next year for you, and she spent a fortune so we'd be comfortable in her place for a few days at Christmas or whenever we're visiting," Gage finished.

The tone of his brother's voice had Sully looking at him.

They both knew what they were thinking, and it was the same thing.

It wasn't about Genny being rich and redecorating a bedroom for them.

It was that they finally had the family they should have always had and they both knew it.

And appreciated it.

But they both wished they'd had it all along.

"Now I see why you come up here nearly every freakin' weekend," Sul noted.

"Nah, I come up here because Chloe buys me booze," Gage joked.

Sully grinned at him and then they joined the others in the living room.

There was general chitchat for a while.

And then the front door opened.

Sasha went flying, screaming, *"Bowie!"*

Sully got off a couch he hoped the blue of his jeans didn't stain to watch Sasha hit his dad like a bag of bricks, but when Genny came abreast of him on her way to greet Dad, he asked, "Where's Matt?"

"He's up at the house, he's…uh, decided to stay there and wait for us to join him," Genny answered.

"Sorry, Gen," Sully whispered.

He'd met Matt at Thanksgiving. Good guy. Nothing like his sisters. Mature, openly protective of the women in his life.

Sully approved.

Genny hadn't talked to Sul about it or anything, but he knew she wanted her son to patch shit up with his dad.

This had yet to happen.

And apparently, it wasn't going to happen anytime soon.

And this was something to think about.

Because he was, in a way, doing the same with his mom as Matt was doing with his dad.

Genny grabbed his biceps, squeezed, then moved away.

When she made it to Dad, she got a huge kiss where Dad actually bent her back over his arm a little bit, and honest to fuck, it was like some Hollywood photo.

Her in her swanky outfit and heels, hair shiny and pretty, holding her fancy drink aloft, bent over a man's arm, getting a snog from a tall, dark, handsome dude.

Dad finally had that.

And more, when they broke away, and Genny smiled at him like Sasha smiled all the time, and Dad's face got all tender and tranquil…

Dad had that too.

As far as he knew, Genny had driven down before Dad so she could be sure to get Sul in case Dad was further delayed, even though Gage could have done it. Or Sasha. Or Chloe.

That was not their way.

From the beginning when Gage and Sully walked into the house while they were cooking dinner, even if their kids were all grown, they were the parental units.

And even twenty-one and grown up, Sully could not say that sucked.

Still, they'd probably been apart three hours.

And they were kissing and looking at each other like that.

Then again, the last time they were parted, it had lasted twenty-eight years.

So he got it.

"Dad, I'm in protest at no pets. I can't be in a space without pets," Gage called.

"Get over it. Two of our animals don't meet HOA code," Dad returned, moving to Sully, his eyes glued to his oldest son even if he was talking to his youngest.

"Who cares about HOA. We can sneak 'em in," Gage said.

"I'm all for that!" Sasha cried.

Dad rounded the back of Sully's neck with his hand and squeezed, warm and tight.

"Sul."

"Hey, Dad."

"You good?"

"Yeah."

"Yeah?"

He knew what Dad was asking.

"Chloe says she's a fool."

"Chloe is always right."

"Now, *that* should go on a coffee mug," Chloe decreed.

Everyone laughed.

But for Sully, the rest of his tension slipped away.

Because Dad's hand was on his neck, Dad was there, Dad got that this sucked for him.

And when he was with Dad, everything was always all right.

His father let him go, looked at what was in Sully's hand, and around the room, and then asked, "Christ, what are you all drinking?"

"Snowmen Jack, would you like one?" Chloe offered.

Duncan Holloway didn't even bother.

He turned to his youngest and ordered, "Gage, get your old man a beer."

Everyone laughed at that too.

Gage took off to the open-plan kitchen, which was, yeah, all white. Even the counters.

And the counter appliances.

"So what do you think of a white tree with pink ornaments?" Dad asked him. "That is, the ornaments that aren't white."

"No offense, Genny," he said to her where she was standing in the curve of his father's arm, then to his dad, "I think it sucks."

Genny giggled.

Dad's eyes all crinkled, he caught him by the neck again.

"Now, that's my boy."

Yeah.

Everything was all right.

Tom

THE DOORBELL RANG, and he went to open it.

The man stood outside.

"Duncan," Tom greeted.

"Tom," Duncan returned.

He stepped aside. "Come in."

Duncan entered.

Tom closed the door behind him, led him to the living room, and asked, "You want a drink?"

"You got beer?"

He looked to the guy. "I was going to have a whiskey."

Duncan tipped up his chin. "That's better."

Tom went to the drinks cart, asking, "Ice? Water?"

"Straight."

Tom nodded and started to pour two fingers into two old fashioned glasses.

"Nice place," Duncan remarked.

He didn't look at the living room with the sunken seating area, the wall of windows that had a view to his lit pool, the stark but comfortable modern furniture.

It was the house he'd bought, and paid to have decorated, not giving much of a shit because he didn't think he'd be there very long.

"Thanks. Hear yours is pretty spectacular."

"Work hard, reap the rewards."

He couldn't argue that.

Though, he'd learned some rewards were more important than others, and if you didn't continue nurturing them, they slipped through your fingers.

He handed Duncan a glass and inquired, "Sit outside?"

"Sure."

Tom led him through the opened panel doors to the firepit right outside that had two chairs angled to it.

Phoenix was Phoenix, but in the winter the nights got cold.

He lit the firepit.

When he was done, he saw Duncan was still standing.

"Sit," he invited, going to his own seat.

They sat.

Tom started it.

"Decent of you to come here."

"Should be you and me first. Get over the awkward," Duncan replied. "Tomorrow is Christmas Eve and it starts."

"Right, yeah, but you didn't have to come all the way out here."

"You live in North Scottsdale, man, it wasn't that far."

Tom nodded, took a sip, stared at the fire. No more had to be said about that. Both men knew it was more than decent that Duncan agreed to meet for the first time on Tom's turf.

Neither of them said anything for a long time.

Too long.

Even if Tom had played in his head how he wanted this to go so they could move on and have...whatever it was they had to have for Genny and his kids.

Duncan broke the silence.

"Listen, we need to get past this so they can be good."

Tom looked to him. "I feel I need to explain."

Duncan shook his head. "That's not mine, that's Genny's."

"Not that," Tom returned. And he ignored the taste in his mouth when he had to say, "But she was yours when I was an ass to her, and that I have to explain."

Duncan looked surprised.

Tom kept talking.

"I thought we still had a chance. She wasn't dating, and to win her back, I wasn't about to look at another woman."

He watched the man hiss in a breath.

Quietly, Tom said, "I think you've proved she's not a woman you can get over."

"Yeah," he agreed.

"But I love her, and I'll always love her, and doing so, want what's best for her. And you make her happy. My daughters adore you. My son…"

He couldn't finish that by stating the truth.

His son liked Duncan Holloway, respected him and gave him his time.

None of which he gave his father.

"He'll come around," Duncan muttered.

Tom looked to the fire. "I taught him too well not to let anyone harm his mother."

"That's why he'll come around. 'Cause while you were teachin' him that, Genny was teaching him the importance of family."

Tom hoped he was right.

He took another sip.

"Your girls are amazing, your son is a good man," Duncan began. "Any other instance, I'd wanna know you, Tom. What's between us is big, but I figure I'm not wrong that we're both the type of men who can get beyond it."

"Because Genny wants that," Tom stated.

"Because Genny *needs* that," Duncan corrected.

Yes.

She did.

And Tom needed it too. For Genny. And for his kids.

"I went to one of your stores the other day," Tom told the fire, then looked to Duncan. "They're impressive. Interactive. The climbing wall. The mini-ski slope where you can test the skis. The dirt track you build around the perimeter where your customers can try out a mountain bike. It's like a store and a nature amusement park rolled into one."

"Gotta have something to draw the crowds," he said into his glass.

"Your Kids and Trails program is essential."

Duncan turned and looked him in the eye. "I agree. And it'd be a boost to fundraising if me and Tom Pierce took a pack of kids out and did a video."

A surprise.

Also a good idea.

And an olive branch that would work for them, their families and the public.

He did not underestimate this man, considering his accomplishments.

But he was impressed.

"I'm in," Tom replied.

"We can do this."

He didn't mean the Kids and Trails fundraising promo.

"We can."

"He chose to stay with you for Thanksgiving, but as you know, Hale's coming to the house for Christmas. I need to talk to him about his father. And I think it'd go easier on him if you were there."

"I'm already coming, Duncan."

"My friends call me Bowie."

They stared at each other again.

"Right then, Bowie," Tom said, "Chloe's force feeding us a rich-food French brunch tomorrow at Genny's. We all head up. I check into The Queen. Dinner at your house. And I'll be back Christmas morning. Warning to you, Sasha still wakes up at four and turns on the Christmas music loud to get everyone up, like she's still six years old. Gen loves her daughter, but she'll hold out until she's had at least some of her morning and can come down showered, her hair looking nice, and has applied a coat of powder and mascara. That's not about stardom, it's about vanity. She hates looking at pictures where she doesn't look put together. Even family ones. I'll aim to show around eight."

"Sounds like a plan."

He continued his warnings. "Matt will avoid me."

"My mom will be there. Hale. The girls. My boys. Genny. We'll make sure it's not awkward and you're both looked after. But I cannot guarantee Genny won't have a word with him. She's losing patience with this."

"Matt knows his own mind. We got that when he pretty much potty trained himself starting at two years old."

Duncan chuckled.

Because it was funny.

And because this was what they were.

Sharing stories.

Sharing life.

Family.

"We can do this," Tom said.

Duncan took a sip of his whiskey.

Then he looked at Tom.

"We can. And we will."

Tom took a breath.

Let it out.

And sat by the fire on a Phoenix night next to a good man and drank some more whiskey.

Imogen

"OH MY GOD, KILL ME," Matt groaned, head on the back of the sofa.

"Why? This is *radical!*" Gage shouted.

Matt looked to Gage and asked, "Did you hear the part about the sex scenes?"

"Yeah, but Genny said she wouldn't even show side boob," Gage returned.

Matt looked like he was going to throw up.

Needless to say, I'd just made the announcement that *The Next Life*, my soon-to-be starring vehicle, was a go.

And provided pertinent details therein.

"Sorry, Genny, I'm out. I'm happy for you that you got this gig, but no way am I watching you have sex...with anyone, even fake sex," Sully added.

"It's not *all* going to be sex scenes, Sully. You can close your eyes and chant *lalalalalala* and ask someone you're watching it with to tell you when it's done. That's what I do when I watch Mom do sex scenes," Sasha advised.

"I think this is all very exciting!" Duncan's mom Ruthy exclaimed. "Can I come on set?"

"Whenever you like," I offered.

"Oh my goodness. I've never been on a *television set*. This is unbelievable!" Ruthy cried.

"I know, Gram," Gage said to his grandmother, and then to me, "Can I come on set too?"

"Of course," I told him.

"Well, all I can say is that I'm proud to have a mother who has the courage to be out and proud as a mature female sexual being in a world where, for centuries, mayhap millennia, well before their ovaries have ceased producing eggs, they were deemed non-essential. This simply because they might be forming a crow's foot, had a single gray hair, or their tits were no longer perky," Chloe stated grandly.

"Rest assured, baby, your tits are still perky," Duncan muttered in my ear.

I elbowed him.

"And I love the fact your daughter can use the word 'mayhap' and own it," he kept going.

He got no elbow for that.

That made me smile.

"Well done you, *ma courageuse mère*," Chloe went on, lifting her champagne glass my way "Fight the power and all that."

"Hear hear!" Sasha shouted.

"Yes, hear hear!" Ruthy chorused.

I looked to Duncan, wedged in beside me in what had become "our chair," and saw he was now grinning ruefully and shaking his head.

He was doing this to Tom, who was accompanied by Killer (it had to be said, Killer had good taste in men) and doing the same.

Suffice it to say, Duncan had read the script.

And in the pilot, the female lead had sex three times.

I had signed on to be the female lead.

And the entire first season had been greenlit by a streaming service, which was what Teddy wanted, so we could be more "real life" visually and with language.

The first script was beyond exciting.

Teddy's ideas and the work he was sharing with me for the season even more so.

But before I'd committed, I'd asked Duncan.

His response was, "I don't pass by you which hiking boots I stock."

"Darling, you need to read the script," I replied.

"I will, Gen, but the point will remain."

He read the script.

It remained.

I could not say he was down with potentially millions of viewers watching a vital, interesting and sexual woman played by me lead her life.

But he was stalwartly supportive of me doing what I loved.

Tom had been the same.

Though sex scenes were never his favorite.

And it seemed this was going to continue to be a theme in my life.

A theme, but not an issue.

"Can we please stop talking about this and eat trifle?" Matt begged.

"Yes, let's finish the Christmas Eve food fest so we can introduce Bowie and Sully and Gage and Ruthy to our next Christmas Eve tradition after trifle. Christmas song lip sync!" Sasha announced.

"I'm in!" Gage said.

"Totally out," Sully said.

"I don't even sing in the shower, and I love you, honey," Duncan started, gaze on Sasha, "but that is not happening."

"Phooey! You and Matt and Dad. Killjoys. Hale sings!" Sasha returned.

"I was twelve lords a' leaping in *one* rendition of that song and you girls sang all the other parts," Hale reminded Sasha.

"I cannot even *begin* to imagine why singing emasculates men," Chloe drawled. "Mick Jagger sings, and my understanding is, he did not go wanting for pussy."

I dropped my head.

"Chloe! For God's sake," Tom bit out.

"Am I wrong?" Chloe asked her father.

"No, but your language in this company is not right," Tom returned.

"If you mean me, I always liked a girl who spoke her mind," Ruthy chimed in. "Should have done more of that myself in my time."

One could say *that* was the understatement of the year.

"More to say, *mon père?*" Chloe asked.

I looked to Tom to see him fuming, but not opening his mouth.

"Pretty sure ole Mick didn't sing 'Deck the Halls,'" Sul remarked.

"Whatever, Coco and I are starting it off with 'Christmas Wrapping' by the Waitresses," Sasha declared, jumping to her feet with her head bent to her phone, likely cueing up music.

Every family member was now hooked to Duncan's Sonos system, something that was connected to built-in speakers around the house. So you never knew what you'd get depending on which room you were in.

My favorite so far?

Duncan played Native American flute music throughout his entire home on Sunday mornings.

Peaceful.

Perfect.

Everyone loved that.

Even Chloe.

"I'm getting the trifle," Matt said, getting up from Duncan's couch. "The sooner this is over, the better. And for those uninitiated, eventually they get drunk and don't hand over the fake microphone and forget anyone else is even in the room so we can go about the rest of our night however we want. Though, we have to do it over them wailing out Mariah Carey."

"I am so very glad I do not have a penis," Chloe purred.

"Me too!" Sasha stated.

"Me too," Ruthy said.

"*I'm* glad you don't have a penis," Duncan whispered to me.

I looked in his beautiful, laughing hazel eyes.

And answered, "I am too."

———————

Duncan

"What's on your mind?"

Gen looked at him like he was crazy.

"Outside what's obviously on your mind," he added.

It was Christmas evening.

Post the unwrapping frenzy.

Post naptime (for Sasha and his mom), some board games and a communal watching of *The Christmas Chronicles* on Netflix.

Pre-late dinner, that was late because they wanted Sul and Gage to be there, and the boys were having a late Christmas lunch with their mom.

It was dark, they'd be home soon.

Tom and Hale were on the back porch, drinking hot buttered rum that Sasha had made.

And Gen and Duncan were heading out there with Corey's letter.

"Well, outside Christmas going well, and thank you for that, you just being you, and your mom being all grandmothery made it all seem really natural," Genny began.

He stopped them at the back door. "Grandmothery?"

"You know what I mean. Ruthy acted like a grandmother even when she was a mom."

He grinned.

"Corroborating evidence, she gave up her suite of rooms for the girls," she told him something he knew.

"Now, baby, you know no way my mom would take the good room when two kids not only could have it but wanted it."

"Yes, *grandmothery*."

He grinned at her.

She showed openly she enjoyed it.

Then she got serious. "Sullivan looked like he was headed to the execution chamber when he and Gage took off to spend some time with their mom."

With this comment, Duncan was thrown.

"Sorry?"

She studied him and asked, "You didn't notice?"

"They were having a good time here and didn't want to leave. But more, they're careful with their mom. She demonstrated for a long time she was fragile, and they handle her that way, even now, when she's got her shit together. It'll pass, the more time they have under their belt with her having her shit together."

"All right," she said, not meaning it.

"You think it's more?" he pushed.

"I think it's just that with Gage, and I think it's something else with Sully."

It was an understatement to say this did not make him happy.

"I'll talk to him," he said.

"I'm glad."

For now, they had something else they had to take care of.

He looked out the window. "Let's get this done."

She nodded, and she looked even less happy than he was about that news about Sully.

Both men outside were wearing fleeces, Hale's sportier and more casual than the smart one Tom was wearing.

But standing on his porch, with the moon shining on the lake behind them, they looked like a marketing picture from his website.

As they approached, Hale smiled at Genny.

Tom looked right at Duncan, query then worry hitting his face when Duncan dipped his chin to share now was the time.

Duncan turned his attention to Hale.

He could see some Sam in him.

But mostly, it was Corey.

Built-up and filled-out Corey.

Dusty brown hair. Pale green eyes. Features so fine, if his lifestyle out in the sun and weather and his personality didn't reflect on them, he'd be pretty.

That had been Corey's problem.

Corey was actually a good-looking guy.

But he was tall and painfully thin, so he was called "The Stick."

He was also a nerd, addicted to videogames and *Star Trek* reruns. The only time he got out and did anything physical was when Duncan made him.

So Corey was teased not only about being a nerd, but also about being gay or "a girl," even if he wasn't effeminate, kids were just assholes.

Duncan had spent time thinking about it, and back in the day, it was easy to convince himself Corey had latched onto Duncan to be his protector, his shield, because that shit didn't happen when Duncan was around.

But when he was honest with himself, he knew that wasn't true.

Because whenever they could get away with it, his ass was in a beanbag next to Corey's while they watched Kirk and Spock and

Bones and the rest of them boldly go where no man had gone before.

They were two kids with seriously shitty dads who made it clear they were disappointed in their sons, they shared common interests, they were only children...

And they both really dug hanging out with that girl Imogen.

When they arrived at the men, Hale claimed Genny with an arm around her shoulders, tucking her into his side, which was something Duncan noted he did with all the females. Even eventually, after getting to know her a little, Duncan's mom.

He was an affectionate guy. He communicated physically and nonverbally as well as with words.

Maybe it was the work he did with kids that were hard to reach.

Maybe it was just him.

"You guys don't have rum," he noted.

Genny made a face.

Hale started laughing.

Seeing that, truthfully, he wondered why neither Chloe nor Sasha had gone there.

Probably due to what had happened with his sons.

Hale was Matt, open to giving shit, taking it, teasing, cuddling, any and all brotherly duties, just without sharing the same blood.

When Hale quit laughing, he started to pay attention.

Mostly to the look on Gen's face and then the line of Tom's body.

Which made him ask, "What's up?"

"Okay, honey, your dad gave Duncan and I—"

That was all Genny got out.

He let her go and stepped away, saying, "No."

"Honey, let us—" she tried again.

"I got a box too, Gen," he said, his words curt. "After that Insta pic hit with you and Duncan."

Gen glanced at Duncan. He returned it and looked to Tom.

Tom caught it and sighed.

"Yeah, you all know his games," Hale stated. "His attorneys were instructed not to give it to me until he'd set up Duncan to make his play."

Okay, there it was.

Hale also got his father's smarts.

"Hale—" Tom began.

"Fuck him, Tommy. I'm all right with him coming clean with Gen and Duncan because he owed them that. But he doesn't get to try to be a dad to me after he blew the back of his head all over a priceless David Hockney."

Genny winced.

"Hale," Tom clipped warningly.

"Sorry, Gen," Hale muttered tersely.

"We'll give it time," Duncan said.

"Respect, Duncan, but there's not enough time in the world," Hale replied.

"Yeah, I thought the same thing and almost burned the letter he wrote to Genny and me before we finished reading it. Then a few days passed, and his games meant I knew her daughters and she my sons and that led to what you had today, Hale. And I'll share, even if his words affected me, I have not forgiven him. And I know myself enough, I won't. Not ever. But that does not negate the fact I'm glad I read them, even as it's upsetting that I read them knowing he felt compelled to write them before he took his own life."

He got closer and both Gen and Tom took his cue and they moved in too.

Not pushy, just supportive.

"And it *is* upsetting," Duncan went on quietly. "Because I don't forgive him, but I miss him. I loved him. And I hate that he was living in so much pain, and swimming in so much guilt, that was the only way he saw to end it. But none of that gives back what he took from me. And I mean Genny. But I also mean Corey. He was the only brother I had and what he did meant I lived without Gen for twenty-eight years, but I will live without Corey forever."

Hale swallowed.

Duncan didn't like it, but he had to keep at it.

"What I'm saying is, this isn't about forgiveness. This is about giving him the last things he wanted before he died. And at least for that, I'm glad I got the opportunity to give that to him."

Hale stared into his eyes before he turned his attention to Gen.

"Do you forgive him?" he asked.

"Yes," she answered.

"Of course you do," he muttered, and looked toward the stables.

"So we'll give it time," Duncan repeated.

Hale looked back to him. "At this very instant, he's very dead, and he's still playing you."

"Some games you don't wanna play. But still, it's important you play and do it to win," Duncan returned.

"Christ, too bad I hadn't heard that, or I'd have been in on the coffee mug gig."

Everyone, but Hale and Tom, had a new coffee mug with some saying on it they'd spouted to Sully or Gage.

And Tom and Hale had mugs too. Tom's said, I'M TOM PIERCE, AND I GOT A HELLA BACKSTROKE and Hale's said, BE GOOD, OR I'M INVITING YOU TO CAMP.

Chloe was drinking her hot buttered rum right then from a red mug with black words on it that said I'M GOING TO HAVE TO GET YOU IN HAND.

The boys gave joint gifts, always had, and this didn't have to do with the fact that the only money they had they got from their dad.

They were always in cahoots about "the perfect gift."

And this year, even with more people to come up with ideas for, they hadn't disappointed.

"Just not now, all right? It's Christmas," Hale gave in, somewhat.

"You leave tomorrow, darling," Gen pointed out.

"Just not now, Genny, okay?" he asked.

She thought about it for a moment and nodded.

"I need more rum," Hale muttered. "Excuse me."

Duncan moved out of the way, and Hale went into the house.

Sasha fell on him almost instantly.

But sweet, savvy Coco...

Her eyes were narrowed out the window at them.

And then she started to make her way to Hale.

"That went as expected," Tom said.

"I worry he thinks he can delay until we give up," Genny noted.

"In the end, it's his call if he wants it or not, honey," Duncan replied.

They all fell into unhappy silence.

Tom broke it, saying, "I need more rum too."

He touched Gen's arm, gave Duncan a chin lift and went inside.

Duncan moved to his woman.

"We shouldn't have done it on Christmas," she fretted.

"Stop worrying, baby. We had this window, and if he'd opened up, on Christmas, he'd have learned that his dad was more than he thought he was. He didn't and now he's in there with Sash and Coco and he'll be fine. We'll get another shot."

"Yes," she murmured, gazing into the house and slumping into his side.

Duncan pulled her close.

"Good call, building this huge log cabin," she said.

He turned his attention through the windows into his house and studied the goings-on.

Tons of presents, unwrapped, sitting in individually designated piles under the big, real tree.

Real garlands that made the place smell like a forest were swagged everywhere, fit with red and silver baubles, pinecones and bright red velvet ribbons.

Dogs and cats and a rabbit snoozing or mixing.

Chloe, Sash, Tom, and Hale in the kitchen, talking about something.

Matt and Duncan's mom playing some card game on the coffee table in the living room.

The fire was crackling.

Christmas music had been playing all day.

And his sons would be home soon.

Yeah, he'd rambled around that house alone whenever the boys were with their mom, and then after Gage went to school, and there were times, too many of them, that it wasn't fun.

But now, Gen was with him more than they were in Phoenix.

The girls came up whenever they wanted, like they were going to the mall and it wasn't a two-hour trek.

And every day he'd gone to work since she'd come back into his life, Genny had been home when he'd walked through the door.

Shooting for her new show started in February, so that would end soon.

But it didn't matter.

His boys' crystal ball may have broken, but his hadn't.

He'd built that house for his family and for Genny.

And that was who was enjoying it.

And he knew that was the best present he'd ever get every day for the rest of his life.

"Have I told you I love you today?" Gen asked, and he looked down at her.

And another present.

"You told me after I had Christmas breakfast, before I had the Christmas breakfast that involved food," he reminded her.

Her face grew soft and sexy with memories of her orgasm before she said, "Well, it bears repeating. I love you, Duncan William Holloway."

"And I love you too, Imogen Sarah Swan. And just so you know, that thing you opened this morning was a place keeper. Your real gift is up in our bedroom."

Her chin shifted back.

And then she stated, "First, I do not consider a Van Cleef and Arpels Alhambra pendant a *place keeper.*"

He smiled.

She kept talking.

"Second, sex with you *is* a gift, but since your mom is in a room on our side of the house, like I explained, we're refraining from the actual act, unless your mouth is engaged in some way, due to your gruntiness."

"First, your rule means sex for the next three days pretty much revolves around me going down on you—" he started.

"Well, if you'd let me suck you off at the same time, it wouldn't," she cut him off to proclaim.

He made the instant decision they were doing that later that night.

He didn't share that.

He got back to business.

"But I'm not talking about sex, Genny, I'm talking about the engagement ring that's upstairs that I'm giving you when we're alone."

Her eyes got huge.

Then they got wet.

Then she shoved him hard with both hands in his chest.

"Bowie, you're not supposed to *tell* a girl you're giving her a ring. You're supposed to just *give it to her* while asking her to marry you."

"Yeah, well, if I did that without warning, it'd lead to you making me grunty."

At that, she started laughing hard, then harder, then she collapsed into his arms, and she was making noises, but he didn't think she was laughing anymore.

"Baby?" he called into the top of her hair.

"We're getting married."

"Yeah, we are."

"Genny and Bowie are finally getting married."

He rested his cheek on the top of her head.

"Love you too, Gen."

"I know, Bowie," she squeezed him tight. "Boy, do I know."

And that right there?

Best present of all.

Chloe

CHLOE WATCHED her mom and Bowie out on the porch.

Her heart felt light.

Then she looked at her dad who was also watching them, until he realized he had his daughter's attention.

Then he gave her his eyes, a fake smile that was still sweet, and turned his attention to Hale.

And her heart felt heavy.

Chloe did not *do* a heavy heart.

She felt her sister sidle closer.

"We're gonna have to do something about that," Sasha said, *sotto voce.*

Chloe glanced at Sasha to see her expression was sad and her gaze was aimed at their father.

Chloe always took the flack, but quite often, it was Sash who was the instigator.

All right, perhaps "quite often" was overstating it.

"Operation Happiness Part One worked a treat. Now it was time for Operation Happiness Part Two," Sasha decreed.

"*Tout de suite, ma ravissante sœur, tout de suite,*" Chloe replied.

And then she took a sip of her hot buttered rum, knowing the expression on her face was at rest.

But in her head…

She was plotting.

The End

The River Rain series will continue…
With Chasing Serenity…
The story of Chloe and Judge.

POST SCRIPT

THE FIXER

Rhys

He reached into his sleeve, caught his cuff, and tugged it, his cufflink sparkling in the light.

Then he nodded to the men who were carrying away the paintings.

They'd been thorough, they'd gotten them all. The others, the ones that had been sold, had already been retrieved.

Now, once they dropped them where Rhys had instructed, their job was done.

Rhys's wasn't.

After the door closed behind his crew, he went about completing it.

Phone, computer, laptop, cameras, memory cards, clouds.

Wiped.

Clean.

Very clean.

Not unusable.

But data irretrievable, everything irretrievable. They were all set to default.

Though the memory cards, those he destroyed.

As for the clouds, well.

Those were just emptied, and then he downloaded and ran his program to clear all cloud caches on those directories so there was no option to restore.

He then searched the flat, methodically, though he was being impolite as he went about doing it, thus he didn't do it orderly, as he normally would.

He didn't simply because this...person didn't deserve the time it would take for him to do that.

He found two more older laptops, searched for their charge cords, plugged them in and then didn't bother to do any fixing.

He took the flash drive out of the inside pocket of his suit jacket, inserted it, one computer, then the next, and within seconds, both laptops were fried.

Now those...

Unusable.

He unplugged them, retrieved the flash drive, tucked it back into his pocket, and walked across the wood floors strewn artfully with threadbare rugs, the veneer of a struggling artist, when the man who lived in this flat had a trust fund worth seven million euros.

Rhys glanced around the space and saw something he missed.

Therefore, he went to the Xbox under the television and fried that too.

He heard a pained grunt.

Out of the side of his eye, he studied the owner of the apartment.

Dark, curling, longish, floppy hair. Slim nose. Tall frame. Muscles he honed for aesthetic purposes only, apparently.

In fact, Rhys had been embarrassed for him at how easily he'd neutralized him.

He was now on his ass, sniveling, snot running over the tape covering his mouth, but he wasn't fidgeting.

Any movement, and the ropes tied as they were would cause excruciating pain in one, or two, or all of his limbs.

The aspiring artist had learned that right away.

Rhys walked to the man and stood over him.

"It's my understanding that Chloe Pierce asked for the return of those paintings, and also requested you destroy all the photographs you took of her."

The man said nothing.

But of course, he couldn't.

Rhys bent and ripped off the tape.

The artist yowled.

Rhys straightened and stared down at him, lifting a dark brow.

"You didn't do that," he continued.

Jabbering, in French.

He understood it, of course, but he sighed.

The man switched to English, "They were mine."

"They were of her, how could they be yours?" Rhys inquired mildly.

"My cameras. My paints. My art. My vision."

"Her body."

The man sneered.

Rhys examined him.

Then he stated, "Tom Pierce offered you a great deal of money for those paintings, and for your assurance any images of his daughter would be destroyed. You refused him."

"They're mine!" the man snapped.

"Yes, you asserted this to Mr. Pierce. However, he requested you produce the paperwork where his daughter granted you permission to use her image for whatever your purposes may be..." his pause stated eloquently how he felt about the veracity of his next words, "your *art*, or other. You were unable to produce said paperwork."

The man had no reply to that.

"Ms. Pierce contends this is so because she never signed anything."

The man remained silent.

"I, myself, in a search of your space, have not found anything of the like."

The artist pushed out a breath.

"And then Mr. Szabo offered you five times what Mr. Pierce did," Rhys noted, his tone quieting significantly.

Sinisterly.

The man started trembling.

"A substantial amount," Rhys remarked.

Nothing.

"But you demanded he triple that offer," Rhys reminded him.

The artist looked to his threadbare rugs.

"You should have accepted Mr. Szabo's offer, sir," Rhys whispered.

The man's eyes darted back up to Rhys.

"Now, I've seen pictures of Ms. Pierce, she's lovely." He'd also seen pictures of her sister, but he didn't allow himself to think of Sasha Pierce. Her file was...later. "But a real man would accept a woman's decision about the end of their relationship, wish her well, and move on."

"She walked away as if I meant nothing at all. And she was the love of my life," the man spat.

"That is wholly untrue, for if she was, with her in your life, or without her, you would want her to have everything she desired, and you'd break your back to give it to her." Another pause. "Even if that meant you had to break your heart too."

Another sneer.

It should be enough that a man such as this would never truly know love.

But that wasn't Rhys's directive.

"We need to have an understanding, you and I," he said softly. "Just in case I missed something."

The artist was back to trembling.

Rhys then spent a bit more well-used time with him in his carefully fabricated studio.

Not long later, as he was walking down the hall, away from the artist's flat, he tugged at his cuff again, his eyes narrowing on it.

Not at the drop of blood now there.

But his cufflink had shifted.

Rhys stopped.

Adjusted it.

And then he strolled on.

Read on for a sample of the next in the River Rain Series...

SNEAK PEEK

CHASING SERENITY
River Rain Book 2
By: Kristen Ashley

PROLOGUE

THE LECTURE

Corey

*F*ifteen years ago...

GENNY WAS DOING something in the kitchen with a summer salad. Tom was off with Matt at their club, playing tennis, destined, from a recent call from Tom, to be home soon in order to eat the dinner Genny was preparing. Sasha was doing cartwheels on the beach.

And Chloe was on the terrace, arms crossed on her chest, ostensibly keeping an eye on her little sister, but mostly glaring at the sun glinting off the sea.

To Corey's mind, when it came to Tom and Genny's children, he thought Matt was okay. Too much like his father, a man who Corey put up with, but Corey had no patience for anyone, especially men, who got everything easy in life, like Tom Pierce had.

Life was not easy.

You suffered for what you earned.

Worked for it.

Cheated for it.

Stole for it.

Whatever you had to do to *get it*.

Tom, his looks, his talent on the tennis courts, his easygoing manner, sly smile, and inability to put up with any shit, it all fell in his lap.

Including Genny.

Sweet, beautiful, talented Genny. One, if not *the* most beloved actress in America.

Sasha, Genny's youngest, Corey simply did not understand. Although she had some of Genny's features, including her sunshiny blonde hair, she was not like either her mother or her father.

Or anyone Corey knew.

But Chloe, the eldest...

If she didn't so look like Tom, she could be Corey's child.

Smart as fuck.

Shrewd as hell.

Chloe Pierce calculated any situation she was in within seconds, deciphering what outcome would serve her purposes the best, and then she set about doing that.

And she was ten.

Corey adored her.

So now, seeing her seething about something, he went out to the terrace, and he did this not only because, as Genny's nearly life-long friend, Corey was there, as he often was, for dinner with the family, and Genny was busy with cooking, so he was bored.

He did it because he was interested in whatever was occupying Chloe Pierce's mind.

As he approached, Chloe sent him a ten-year-old's version of a look that said *fuck off*.

And he adored her more.

There were fair few people on that earth who had the courage to send him looks like that, considering he'd amassed the wealth, and thus the power, to buy and sell practically anyone.

Corey ignored the look and moved to the lounge chair next to where she sat at the end of hers, close to the sheet of clear glass set into the railing of a terrace of a house that rested above the cliffs of Malibu.

He sat on his chair's end too.

"Spill," he ordered.

"I don't wanna talk, Uncle Corey."

"*Want to*," he corrected, and heard her instantly suck her teeth in annoyance at the criticism.

Corey fought smiling.

"I'll repeat, spill," Corey pressed.

She didn't.

Corey waited.

She still didn't.

Corey continued to wait.

Chloe was no fool. In fact, there wasn't any vestige of that trait in any cell of her body.

She knew her Uncle Corey would have what he wanted.

So she didn't push it any further.

"There's…"

She trailed off, and Corey gave her more time.

She picked it up again. "Kids are bullying Matt at school."

This took Corey by surprise.

Matthew Pierce was the vision of his father.

At nine years old, already tall, dark, with boyishly handsome features. He was gifted in athleticism. He was clever.

Though what he also was, was introverted.

He was not a leader, like Chloe (and Tom).

He was not outgoing, like Sasha (and Genny)

He was perfectly happy doing his own thing.

To the point, even at his age, living in a house full of people, he was reclusive.

Like Corey.

The perfect target for jealousy.

The perfect target for bullies.

"And this is your issue because…?" Corey asked.

Her head whipped around to him, and now she was giving him a ten-year-old's look that said she thought he was stupid.

"He's my brother," she snapped.

"He can fight his own battles."

"Well, he isn't," she retorted.

Corey found this interesting, but not startling.

In all probability, Matt couldn't care less about the bullying.

Even at nine years old, his intellect was such (and his parents' lessons were as well) that he was not unaware that the fates had seen fit to grant him more of almost everything than most people received.

The boy had happily married, exceptionally successful, wealthy, loving parents.

Good looks.

Brains.

Not to mention, if Tom kept honing it, what would be Matt's version of physical excellence.

Matt Pierce didn't need anyone, and not only because he already had it all.

That was just him.

He just didn't.

"Has it occurred to you that your brother doesn't care?" Corey inquired. "I'm sure it hasn't escaped your notice that he's perfectly fine in his own company."

"It hasn't, Uncle Corey, but bullies shouldn't get away with being bullies. *One*," Chloe returned.

One.

She had a list.

Corey fought a smile.

"*Two*," she continued, "he's my brother, and no one messes with my brother."

He nodded and said nothing, because he knew there was a three.

"And *three*," she went on, "he's a Pierce. And *no one* pulls crap with *a Pierce*."

"You're right," he agreed. "So what are you going to do about it?"

That took her aback.

"What?"

"What are you going to do about it?" Corey repeated.

"They aren't bullying me," she pointed out.

Corey held her gaze in a manner that she did not look away.

Not that she would.

Another thing about the girl he liked.

Then he stated, "Do not ever, Chloe, *ever* let anyone harm someone you love."

A feeling welled up in his chest, instantly, overwhelmingly threatening to overcome him.

Used to this sensation, having experienced it for years, with little effort, Corey shoved it back down and kept speaking.

"It doesn't matter what you have to do, if you think it's bad, but it stops that harm, you do it. If you think it's naughty, and it stops that harm, you do it. Even if you think it's wrong, though it will stop that harm, *you do it*. No hesitation, no messing about. *Just do it*."

Chloe stared at him.

"The same with you," he carried on. "Do not let anyone walk all over you, Chloe Marilyn Pierce. Don't you *ever* allow that to happen."

She gave it a moment, and then she asked, "So you think I should...*do something?*"

"I think you've already waited too long."

Corey watched as Chloe considered this.

And he was unsurprised when, after she spent hardly any time in this contemplation, slowly, she smiled.

Chloe

Nine years later...

"Are you *mad?*" Pierre asked me.

I stared at him, for the first time wondering why I'd spent a single minute with him.

Was he cute?

Yes.

Did he have a good body?

Yes.

Did he give me my very first, not-given-to-myself orgasm?

Yes.

Was he an asshole?

Apparently...yes.

My voice was ice-cold, and I was pretty pleased with myself at the sound of it, when I noted in return, "You told me you'd never sell it."

"I'm an artist!" he cried.

The drama.

Boring.

In that moment, I made a pact with myself that I vowed to keep.

Only *I* would bring the drama to a relationship.

I modulated my voice and did not cut the tie between our gazes.

"You said it meant everything to you. You said you'd cease being you without it in your possession. You said you'd be ninety, and you would die in a room where, on the wall, that portrait you painted of me hung."

"I *do* need to feed myself, Chloe," he sniped.

No one, not a soul, disregarded money the way he did (unless not doing it served his purpose, like now), who did not have it in the first place.

Didn't grow up having it.

I was that person too.

But Mom did a lot of charity work, so did Dad, they made certain we understood that we were very lucky and many, in fact most others, were not.

Pierre and I had never discussed money (because, how gauche), and he didn't live in a fabulous apartment in a posh part of the city, though it wasn't rundown or seedy or anything like that.

Still…

I knew Pierre was like me.

So this whole thing was a big sham.

All of it.

Including his promises to me.

As I looked at his dark, loose, long locks, the perfection of his nose, the breadth of his shoulders, his gangly frame, for the first time I saw through him.

He was a sham.

A fake.

A pretender.

Maybe even worse.

A wannabe.

And I had to admit to more than a little concern that my affections for him shifted so quickly.

But they did.

I could walk away…

No.

I *was going to* walk away.

And what worried me was…

I didn't care.

I decided to think about this later and moved to begin packing, at the same time my mind swung to considering my next step.

Hotel for a few days while I found a flat to rent (and did the work it took to convince my parents I needed to rent a flat in Paris, and they needed to allow me the use of my trust fund to do that, or better, not allow me and instead, simply give the money to their darling daughter in order that she get the most out of her discovering-herself time in Europe).

One thing I knew, I wasn't leaving France.

Not on my life.

When I dragged out a piece of my luggage (there were three), Pierre was there.

"What are you doing?" he asked.

"Packing," I said in a bored tone, one that I didn't affect.

I was, indeed, bored.

Done.

Over this.

On to the next adventure.

"Packing? Just like that?"

I turned from unzipping and opening my suitcase to him.

"You need to get that painting back," I told him. "And you need to destroy the other one. You also need to give me all the pictures you took of me and erase any digital copies you have."

His mouth dropped open.

He then used it to say, "That is not happening."

"You don't have my permission to use my image, Pierre. It's illegal for you to sell those paintings or use those images for monetary purposes without my permission."

I was no Hollywood starlet rushing into the latest hip club, ripe for any paparazzo's lens, needing it at the same time feeling it wholly an invasion of my privacy.

I had posed for Pierre for the thrill of it. I'd done it because I had feelings for him. I'd done it because I loved his work and wanted to be a part of it. I'd done it because it was fun, and I thought it was cool. I'd also done it because I thought he wasn't going to sell them.

But bottom line, I'd acted as his model.

And first, he needed to pay me if he was going to make money off me.

Second, he needed my permission.

"That's rubbish," he bit out.

"Do you know who I am?"

It wasn't arrogant posturing.

But for God's sake, he knew I was Imogen Swan and Tom Pierce's daughter. America's sweetheart and one of the best tennis players ever to walk on a court.

They were two of the most famous people on the planet.

Of course I knew what I'd just said was far from rubbish.

And he knew it too.

"They are *my* paintings," he asserted.

"It's *my* body. *My* face," I fired back. "I own them, and you cannot use them unless I *grant you permission*. And I'll remind you, I posed for you because you said you were *never* going to sell the paintings you painted of me. 'Never' for you lasted less than three months. But the true meaning of never is *never*, Pierre. Which means you lied to me about your intentions when you took those pictures and did that work. Now, if you don't want to turn over or destroy all you have, you can give me a million euros. I think that's fair compensation."

His eyes grew huge.

And the French rolled off his tongue.

I was learning the language, but I didn't catch even half of it.

"English," I demanded.

"I am not giving you a million euros, Chloe. I am not getting that painting back. I am not destroying the rest. And you are not leaving."

"Oh, I'm leaving," I confirmed. "And I advise you rethink your course of action."

This time, his eyes narrowed. "Are you threatening me and leaving me at the same time?"

"Well, it's not exactly a threat, but for the most part, yes."

Now, as he took in my tone, actions, and demeanor, it hit him.

I was, in fact, leaving.

Suddenly, he appeared wounded.

Suddenly and genuinely.

This did not make me pause.

Truth told, I didn't care that he had pictures of me nude, or sold them. I had a great body, I was proud of it, and his work was *amazing*.

This was about something else.

Something far bigger.

It was the promise broken.

The betrayal.

Uncle Corey a lot of the time could be creepy (these times when he was around Mom).

But the man was a multi-billionaire tech czar.

Which meant he was no idiot.

So he gave great advice.

Every time he gave it, I stored those little gems so I could take them out and polish them when the time was nigh.

Obviously, with one of those gems, the time was nigh.

"Get that painting back and destroy the rest, or pay me, Pierre, those are your choices," I summed up. "Now, it'd be easier to do this," I motioned to the suitcase, "if you went off and got a coffee."

He stared at me, thrown, angry, hurt.

What he didn't do was go and get a coffee.

I sighed and then got down to business, taking my time and making perfectly sure I got everything because I wasn't coming back.

At the door, I decided it might be uncool just to sweep out, even if it would be dramatic and what I wanted to do.

Thus, I halted, turned to him and said softly, "It's been fun."

He stopped sulking (what he'd been doing the entire time I packed) and the hurt dug deep in his hazel eyes.

"Fun?" he whispered. "It's been *fun*? Chloe, *mon cœur*, you're the love of my life."

I studied him quizzically because that truly perplexed me.

"How can that be?" I asked, genuinely wanting to know.

"How can that...how can it... How can it be?" he asked in return. "Have you not been here," he tossed his arm out to indicate the flat, "with me for the last six months?"

"You lied to me," I stated flatly. "And you don't lie to someone you love."

His head snapped like I'd slapped him.

"Good-bye, Pierre," I said.

And with that, not looking back, not knowing that I'd never see him again, but even if I did, I knew I wouldn't care, I left.

And checked into The Ritz.

Judge

FIVE YEARS LATER...

"You have no direction."

Judge sat opposite his girlfriend of the last year and a half, Megan, and said nothing.

She did.

"I need a man with ambition. Drive. Who knows what he wants and goes after it, works for it, *fights* for it."

Judge remained silent.

"Judge, are you listening to me?" she asked, though she didn't wait for him to answer, probably because he was staring right at her, and he was doing it hard, so she had to know he was listening. She carried on, "I mean, I'm sorry. This is rough. But you always say we need to be honest with each other. And this is me being honest."

That got him talking.

"Right then, let's be honest, Meg. *Really* honest. What you're saying is, I'm not going in the direction *you* want me going. My life goals aren't what *you* want them to be. I know what I want, you know I do. I know who I am, you know that too. It's just that those things aren't what *you* want. Am I right?"

Her face twisted. "No man wants to hike for a living."

Okay.

Now he was getting pissed off.

"After all this time together, is that what you think I do?"

She shifted on her barstool.

She knew what he did, and she knew that was bullshit.

And...

Yeah.

Barstool.

They both lived in Arizona. But he lived in Prescott, she lived in

Phoenix, a two-hour drive from each other, so it wasn't like they were living together or even saw each other every day.

Though, they were exclusive and had been for over a year. He went out of his way to make time for her, get to Phoenix to see her.

Meg?

Not so much, but to be fair, her job didn't allow her to.

Still, not so much.

She was a reporter for a local station. She was aiming to sit behind the desk as an anchor, and after she achieved that, she wanted to move on to bigger and better things.

Or, he should say, stand on the set and talk at a camera, something he did not get why it was the thing. Judge thought when newscasters did that they looked like the awkward folks at a party, standing around not knowing who to talk to. It was his opinion, when you listened to the news, you needed to trust that the person giving it to you was taking it seriously, not gabbing while waiting for a tray of hors d'oeuvres to be passed around.

Needless to say, Meg did not share this opinion.

Judge ran an outreach program for a massive outdoor store that had over seventy locations in the US. A program aimed to get urban kids out into nature.

He hiked with the kids…a lot.

He also hiked by himself and did other things outside…a lot.

But most of his job was about raising money, ditto awareness of the issue, and the profile of the program, as well as managing the logistics that included hundreds of volunteers in dozens of cities doing hundreds of hikes a year.

He wasn't paid enough to afford a BMW. But even if he was, he wouldn't buy one.

He also wasn't homeless.

But they were here, at a bar, and Meg was ending things with him, when they'd committed to each other over a year ago. They regularly, if not all the time, slept at each other's sides. They'd gone on vacations together. And they'd met each other's families.

Or, she'd had dinner with his dad.

His mom?

Absolutely not.

"Though, a lot of men and women would want to hike for a living," he went on. "Around fifty million people in the US alone regularly hike."

"Judge—"

He wasn't done.

"You're not an outdoors person. That's cool. I don't care because you're smart as hell and goal oriented. You're interesting. You're funny. You're sweet. And you're beautiful. I want you to have what you want. I want to support you in your goals. I want you to be happy. What I *don't* want is for you to mold me into who you think I'm supposed to be to fit into your life."

Right.

The *real* honesty?

This had been an issue.

It being one right then, he wasn't blindsided by it.

She'd said some things. There had been more than a few looks when he'd been with her and shared with others what he did. She'd done some suggesting, urging and downright pushing.

He just thought she'd get over it when he didn't bend and definitely didn't break.

Her expression had softened when he'd told her all the things he found attractive in her, because Meg liked compliments. She told him her love language was words.

So he gave her words, because that was what she needed and she was upfront about it, even if he wasn't a flowery speeches kind of guy.

She also thought what he said opened a door for her, and even if it didn't, she tried to stroll through.

"You can get involved down here. In Phoenix," she said. "There are a lot of charities you can work for. On the whole, there are just tons more opportunities down here. And truly, Judge, you're wasted up there. You're whip smart, and when you talk, people listen to you. You're a natural leader. You *should* be with a bigger program. You

should be seeking new challenges. You *should* be reaching for something higher."

"Organizations that pay more, have advancement opportunities
and don't require me to travel," he filled in what she left unsaid.

She opened her mouth.

But this shit from Megan wasn't the only pressure Judge had about
this same subject.

And if he didn't put up with it from the other source, he was not
going to put up with it from his girlfriend.

"Meg, no," he cut her off before she could use it. "I love my job. I
love what I do. *I love it.* I've told you that. More than once. Does that
mean nothing to you?"

"Do *I* mean nothing to you?" she retorted.

Uh.

No.

"I could ask you the same thing," he returned. "And your answer
would be rougher, babe, because it isn't me breaking it off with you
because you're not what I want, and you won't adjust your life to
make yourself into that. So the only answer you could give me is, not
much. I don't mean much to you. You're seeing the wrong man. And
now, it's over because you've either figured that out, or you're cutting
your losses before you invest any more time with me."

She appeared insulted. "Judge, I love you."

Okay.

That *totally* pissed him off.

"And you're ending things not because I'm a dick to you. Not
because I lie or cheat or steal. Not because I flirt with other women in
front of you. Not because we fight. Not because we have differing
opinions we believe in strongly and we can't get around those differ-
ences. But instead, because *you* think I have no direction or ambition
when I do have direction *and* ambition."

He saw her start to intercede.

But he was far from done.

"I want, and I'll add that I work very hard, to get kids moving their
bodies. To show them how extraordinary nature is. Introduce them to

vistas that don't include concrete and asphalt. Where the air is fresher, and the stars shine brighter. I want to explain to them how important it is we guard these things, keep them safe and pure, and what it'll mean when we don't. Because they're going to be in the positions soon where they have no choice but to do something about it, and they need to start thinking about that now."

She again tried to say something.

But he hadn't even gotten to the most important part of it.

So he didn't shut up.

"And above all, just to let them know they aren't forgotten. There are people who give a shit about them and what they experience and want to broaden those experiences, their minds, and bottom line think they're worth spending time with. And I don't know, Meg, if that isn't good enough for you, then you're right. Though I wouldn't take you to a bar to dump you after we spent over a year of our lives together. But that makes no difference. You're right. We're wrong. And it's time to end it."

With that, and her staring at him, he slid off his barstool, pulled out his wallet, opened it and tossed enough money on the table to pay for their drinks and the food that had not yet been delivered.

"I gotta get home," he said. "Text me when I can come to your place to get my shit. I'll pack yours up and bring it when I do that."

He started to leave, but she caught his forearm.

"Are you really just walking away from me?" she demanded.

He stopped and looked down at her. "Sorry, did I steal your exit?"

She took her hand from his arm. "There's no need to be a dick."

Unh-unh.

No.

"Hang on a second, you told five minutes ago, *in all honesty*, that you thought I had no direction, no drive and that I didn't know what I wanted *or* how to go after it in a preamble to dump my ass. And I've given you what you want. We're through, and I'm walking away because I'm not real hip on sitting here after you've kicked me to the curb and watching you pick through a plate of tater tot nachos because eating two expends your allotment of calories for the day. And I'm being a dick?"

Right.

That was definitely dick-ish.

His sister (or that would be stepsister, but she'd been around so long, he didn't really think of her that way) said often that he looked like the Zen master. Mr. Outdoorsman. Mr. Easygoing. One with nature, one with humanity. But piss him off and all that was out the window.

And she did not lie.

"Maybe, when I said fight for something, I meant me," she suggested with not a small amount of hurt.

His stomach clutched.

It was not a good feeling.

"And how would I do that, Meg?" he asked quietly.

"Well, you could *not* live a hundred and thirty miles away."

Judge closed his eyes and dropped his head.

Because that meant *quit your job and move to Phoenix*.

"Judge," she called.

He opened his eyes and looked at her, what was happening fully registering.

This was it.

They were over.

And he wasn't okay with that.

Because he was in love with her.

"I want more of you, would you quit your job and move to Prescott?" he asked.

A hard shell slammed down over her eyes as she replied, "I know what you're doing, but there are far more opportunities *for both of us* in Phoenix."

"And then you get a job in LA, and I follow you there. And then New York, and I follow you there. Right?"

"There are programs for kids, in nature, for the environment, everywhere, Judge. You can't get away from any of them."

He'd been bending, because he'd been considering what she was saying and what was happening between them, because she was right, and he didn't want to lose her.

However, the last part of what she said struck him.

You can't get away from any of them.

Who exactly was "them"?

"Do you want kids, Meg?" he asked.

Her head twitched.

One of her tells.

"Of course," she lied.

Holy fuck.

She'd lied.

About wanting *kids*.

If he had it right, because this was so important to him, they'd had this conversation on their third date.

If it wasn't their third, it was their fourth.

And that wasn't the last time they'd talked about it.

"Do you want kids, Meg?" he repeated.

"We've talked about this, Judge," she snapped.

Another tell. She quickly got belligerent when she was called on something she couldn't defend.

"Yes, and you told me you did. Now, I'm not sure you were being truthful."

"Are you saying I lied?"

"I'm saying your hair shakes when you're hedging. And your hair just shook."

She knew not to challenge him on things like that. You didn't deal with children on a regular basis, not to mention donors, and not be hyper-attentive.

"I think I'm realizing I'm one of those later-in-life-for-a-family women," she admitted, like it was nothing.

But it was not nothing.

It was big shit.

And she knew it.

"You'd mentioned that, and I told you I wasn't real big on being in my fifties, and living the life with my family that I want, rather than being in my thirties or forties. And you agreed, saying you wanted the same thing."

"You'll be fit until you die, Judge," she scoffed. "You'll be hiking and biking and camping when you're eighty."

"Sure, but time doesn't discriminate. There's no arguing I'll be fitter in my thirties and forties. And when my kids are young, I want them to enjoy me when I'm also young."

"Judge—"

"This is a big shift, Meg, anything behind it?"

"Judge."

He didn't cut her off that time. She just didn't continue.

"Earlier, did you intend to end us or change us?" he asked.

It was slight, but she lifted her chin.

She had a dimple in it.

He'd thought it was cute.

He still did.

"I need a man who will fight for me," she declared.

"I get that, because I need a woman who will do the same for me."

It was impossible for him to put more meaning into those words.

And she knew precisely why.

She flinched.

Shit.

That said it all.

He remained standing, she sat there, and they stared at each other.

And suddenly, he got it.

He understood.

He understood where he was at.

And he understood where she was too.

This meant he got closer to the table, to her, because they both needed him to share it.

"Honest to Christ, this isn't meant to hurt you, Meg, but I'm in love with you."

Her expression warmed.

"But I don't love you," he finished.

Her face went blank.

"And if you're honest with yourself," Judge continued, "you'll see you feel the same way about me. We're great together. We're great in bed. We've had great times. But there's a reason neither of us is willing to give in order to have more of the other. We don't fit. We don't share the same goals. We don't find the same things important. There's nothing wrong with what you want or what you think is important. There isn't anything wrong with where I'm at with all that. They just don't go together, and I think we both knew it, you just got us on the road where we'd get it."

Her eyes were crazy, and as such, concerning as they moved over his face and she said, "I don't think I knew it. I think I just blew it."

"Give it some time, honey," he said gently.

"Judge—"

He cut her off then by leaning in and pressing a hard kiss on her mouth.

When he pulled away, he didn't go far when he said, "Bottom line, it's been fun, you're fantastic, and I'll never forget it, Meg."

Her mouth opened.

But so they could both get on with things, Judge walked away.

And he didn't look back.

Chasing Serenity
Available September 7, 2021

DISCUSSION & REFLECTION QUESTIONS

1. Corey eventually comes to the conclusion that Genny and Duncan would have worked, regardless that, when they were younger, they wished to take very different paths in life. Do you feel Corey was right? That, if he hadn't torn them apart, Gen and Bowie would have been able to find a way to make a life together?

2. These people live their lives under microscopes. How do you feel about the pressures the personal lives of famous people are put under? Do you think it's part of the price of success? Or do you think the general public erroneously feels entitled to these areas of celebrities' lives?

3. Many male actors have active careers, playing leading roles, deep into their 40s and 50s. How did it feel when you read about Genny's career stagnating simply because she'd reached a certain age—an age that is relatively young? Do you think this double-standard leaks into everyday life?

4. Statistics show that 81% of women report having experienced sexual harassment or assault in their lifetimes.* In this book, Genny

ruminates on the #MeToo movement and how the responsibility quickly was twisted to the females, laying blame on them that they didn't report incidences of sexual harassment and assault. Taking the risk in laying this blame, the possible fallout of that, and in some cases needing to be very public about it, even if their reputations and livelihoods lay in the balance.

How did you feel about the fact Genny expressed she carries some shame for not speaking up? How did you feel when she described how she was threatened with the casting couch, but it was Tom who came to the rescue? Do you feel it should have been Genny who dealt with that situation, even if it meant she might have been blacklisted and effectively her career would have been over?

5. Corey was clearly a troubled soul from the very beginning of his life. He hurt a lot of people whose only mistake was trusting and loving him. Does Corey deserve forgiveness from one or all of the people he wronged?

6. It's broadly hinted both Duncan and Corey had significantly dysfunctional upbringings, which produced the same (if still different) type of man: overachieving. As some insights into both men unfolded, did your thoughts turn to how these two chose to live their lives and how they went about making their fortunes? What affect did Genny's childhood, that was clearly loving and supportive, have on Genny? How she parents and lives her life? She, too, is highly successful. Did you feel her upbringing had any affect on the person she became and how she went about doing that?

7. Duncan being forced to hunt a deer altered the path of his life. It drove him to connect deeper with Genny. It informed the kind of father he'd become. And it formed the kernel of what would become his life's mission. How did you feel when he was telling this story? Did you think, ultimately, it was worthwhile that he went through this

trauma because it made him the man he'd become? Or did you feel he would become that man regardless?

8. Imogen and Duncan get their second chance after being brutally betrayed by someone they both trusted implicitly. After all the time they've missed together, what was your favorite part of their reconciliation?

9. Do you think Tuck will now ever stay off the countertops?

10. Speaking of second chances, do you think Tom will find his second chance at love? What sort of woman do you see him with and how do you think they will navigate the big shoes Imogen left behind?

11. Obviously, the next story is an enemies-to-lovers trope with Chloe and Judge. Do you enjoy enemies to lovers? What is your favorite part of that trope? How explosive do you think their relationship will be?

*Source: National Sexual Violence Resource Center

LEARN MORE ABOUT KRISTEN ASHLEY'S RIVER RAIN SERIES

Chasing Serenity: A River Rain Novel, Book 2

From a very young age, Chloe Pierce was trained to look after the ones she loved.

And she was trained by the best.

But when the man who looked after her was no longer there, Chloe is cast adrift—just as the very foundation of her life crumbled to pieces.

Then she runs into tall, lanky, unpretentious Judge Oakley, her exact opposite. She shops. He hikes. She drinks pink ladies. He drinks beer. She's a city girl. He's a mountain guy.

Obviously, this means they have a blowout fight upon meeting. Their second encounter doesn't go a lot better.

Judge is loving the challenge. Chloe is everything he doesn't want in a woman, but he can't stop finding ways to spend time with her. He knows she's dealing with loss and change.

He just doesn't know how deep that goes. Or how ingrained it is for Chloe to care for those who have a place in her heart, how hard it will be to trust anyone to look after her...

And how much harder it is when it's his turn.

Continue reading for an excerpt of Chasing Serenity.

CHASING SERENITY
Excerpt

Corey

Fifteen years ago...

Genny was doing something in the kitchen with a summer salad. Tom was off with Matt at their club, playing tennis, destined, from a recent call from Tom, to be home soon in order to eat the dinner Genny was preparing. Sasha was doing cartwheels on the beach.

And Chloe was on the terrace, arms crossed on her chest, ostensibly keeping an eye on her little sister, but mostly glaring at the sun glinting off the sea.

To Corey's mind, when it came to Tom and Genny's children, he thought Matt was okay. Too much like his father, a man who Corey put up with, but Corey had no patience for anyone, especially men, who got everything easy in life, like Tom Pierce had.

Life was not easy.

You suffered for what you earned.

Worked for it.

Cheated for it.

Stole for it.

Whatever you had to do to *get it*.

Tom, his looks, his talent on the tennis courts, his easygoing manner, sly smile, and inability to put up with any shit, it all fell in his lap.

Including Genny.

Sweet, beautiful, talented Genny. One, if not *the* most beloved actress in America.

Sasha, Genny's youngest, Corey simply did not understand. Although she had some of Genny's features, including her sunshiny blonde hair, she was not like either her mother or her father.

Or anyone Corey knew.

But Chloe, the eldest...

If she didn't so look like Tom, she could be Corey's child.

Smart as fuck.

Shrewd as hell.

Chloe Pierce calculated any situation she was in within seconds, deciphering what outcome would serve her purposes the best, and then she set about doing that.

And she was ten.

Corey adored her.

So now, seeing her seething about something, he went out to the terrace, and he did this not only because, as Genny's nearly life-long friend, Corey was there, as he often was, for dinner with the family, and Genny was busy with cooking, so he was bored.

He did it because he was interested in whatever was occupying Chloe Pierce's mind.

As he approached, Chloe sent him a ten-year-old's version of a look that said *fuck off*.

And he adored her more.

There were fair few people on that earth who had the courage to send him looks like that, considering he'd amassed the wealth, and thus the power, to buy and sell practically anyone.

Corey ignored the look and moved to the lounge chair next to where she sat at the end of hers, close to the sheet of clear glass set into the railing of a terrace of a house that rested above the cliffs of Malibu.

He sat on his chair's end too.

"Spill," he ordered.

"I don't wanna talk, Uncle Corey."

"*Want to*," he corrected, and heard her instantly suck her teeth in annoyance at the criticism.

Corey fought smiling.

"I'll repeat, spill," Corey pressed.

She didn't.

Corey waited.

She still didn't.

Corey continued to wait.

Chloe was no fool.

Chasing Serenity is available everywhere.

Taking the Leap: A River Rain Novel, Book 3

Alexandra Sharp has been crushing on her co-worker, John "Rix" Hendrix for years. He's her perfect man, she knows it.

She's just not his perfect woman, and she knows that too.

Then Rix gives Alex a hint that maybe there's a spark between them that, if she takes the leap, she might be able to fan into a flame This leads to a crash and burn, and that's all shy Alex needs to catch the hint never to take the risk again.

However, with undeniable timing, Rix's ex, who broke his heart, and Alex's family, who spent her lifetime breaking hers, rear their heads, gearing up to offer more drama. With the help of some match-making friends, Rix and Alex decide to face the onslaught together...

As a fake couple.

Continue reading for an excerpt of *Taking the Leap*.

Taking the Leap
Excerpt

Alex

It was happening.

He was flirting with me.

John "Rix" Hendrix, the coolest guy I'd ever met, the most interesting person I'd ever known, the most handsome man I'd ever seen, was flirting...

With...

Me.

And I was somehow managing to flirt back (kind of).

Okay, I might be relying on something from Moscow to do so (that something being their mules), but it was happening.

And I knew I wasn't making more of it than I should.

I knew that because Chloe and Judge were with us. We were out having drinks, celebrating the official beginning of our new Trail Blazer program (that day, Judge, Rix and I had signed on to new job titles with new responsibilities and new salaries with the expanded program—I got a promotion and a fifteen percent raise!—definitely worth sitting down to drinks with the man who terrified me most on this earth).

Chloe was giving Rix and me smug looks, but mostly me, and once, she'd even winked at me.

As an aside: Chloe Pierce, my boss Judge's girlfriend, was the coolest, most interesting, most gorgeous woman I'd ever met.

And even though (fortunately, so far, though maybe not now?) Rix had missed it, but although she hadn't said anything, I knew Chloe knew I was crushing on Rix...*big time*.

And I had been.

Crushing on Rix.

Big time.

She was happy for me.

I was happy for me!

Because Rix was *flirting with me.*

Me!

And the reason why this was crazy was not only because he was cool and interesting and handsome, and as yet, such a man had never shown any interest in me (no, the men who had shown interest in me lacked one or more of those qualities).

It was because I was, well…

Me.

First off, I was shy around cute guys (okay, I was just plain shy, but it got a lot worse around guys, and off-the-charts worse around cute ones).

Not to mention, I knew how to put on mascara, I just wasn't a big fan of wearing it (so, unless it was a super special occasion, or I was with my family, I didn't).

I had a little house up in the mountains (TBH, it was more like a big shack), but I was rarely in it because there were a lot better places to be (and my house was awesome, I just had a ton of interests and not a lot of them happened in my house).

I knew how to cook in a kitchen, but I cooked way better over a campfire (and in a hot coal pit).

There were Star Trek nerds, I was just a star nerd (that being, lying under them at night in the middle of nowhere and staring at them until I fell asleep).

I would rather snowshoe into a forest in the dead of winter, set up a tent and spend a couple of days in nature, reading by a headlamp at night cozied up in a one-woman sleeping bag in a one-person tent than sit by a fireside during a snowstorm with a mug of hot cocoa (though, that was nice too).

Many women didn't get me.

Men didn't either, and it was actually more men who didn't get me than it was women because I wasn't stereotypically womanly. Most women got there were lots of different kinds of women. Most men (in my experience) weren't that broad minded.

No, actually, it was more my family who didn't get me than anyone else.

My family didn't get me at all.

Which wasn't really surprising, seeing as I didn't get them either.

"Sexy as fuck," Rix was saying.

I came out of my musings to focus on his words.

Words he was aiming at me (me!).

Taking the Leap **is available everywhere.**

Making the Match, A River Rain Novel, Book 4

Decades ago, tennis superstar Tom Pierce and "It Girl" Mika Stowe met at a party.

Mika fell in love. Tom was already in love with his wife. As badly as Tom wanted Mika as a friend, Mika knew it would hurt too much to be attracted to this amazing man and never be able to have him.

They parted ways for what they thought would be forever, only to reconnect just once, when unspeakable tragedy darkens Mika's life.

Years later, the impossible happens.

A time comes when they're both unattached.

But now Tom has made a terrible mistake. A mistake so damaging to the ones he loves, he feels he'll never be redeemed.

Mika has never forgotten how far and how fast she fell when she met him, but Tom's transgression is holding her distant from reaching out.

There are matchmakers in their midst, however.

And when the plot has been unleashed to make that match, Tom and Mika are thrown into an international intrigue that pits them against a Goliath of the sports industry.

Now they face a massive battle at the same time they're navigating friendship, attraction, love, family, grief, redemption, two very different lives lived on two opposite sides of a continent and a box full of kittens.

Continue reading for an excerpt of Making the Match.

Making the Match
Excerpt

Corey

Decades ago...

He didn't think he'd gain entry.

But when he knocked, the door opened, and one of the groomsmen looked at him, then glanced over his shoulder, he heard the familiar deep voice call, "Let him in."

Corey entered and saw immediately that the groom had prepared for Corey's visit.

As, of course, he would.

He was not stupid.

Corey knew he'd prepared because, with a nod and a look, but not a word, all the groomsmen filed out.

Corey did not see joyous-wedding-day expressions on their faces when each man caught his eye as he left the room.

That wasn't about them having any apprehension about what was to happen that day or the woman their friend was about to tie the rest of his life to.

It was because they all detested Corey and perhaps knew why he was there.

Or they thought they did.

His face void of expression, Corey met every eye.

He was used to this, especially with the male gender. Men never knew what to do when another man was in their orbit who was smarter than them in a way they'd never equal him— and worse for them, richer just the same.

Especially ones with huge egos like these men had.

And on that thought, the door closed behind the last and Corey turned to Tom Pierce.

"I know," Tom started. "If I hurt her—"

"I will have her."

Tom's mouth snapped shut and his eyes, annoyingly always filled with wit and intelligence, turned shrewd.

Another annoying thing about Tom Pierce?

Not only was he the most talented tennis player on the planet—a player who turned that wit and intelligence against opponents so that he not only prevailed through physical prowess, he outthought them.

(As an aside, this was, to Corey's way of thinking, worse than someone humiliating you after serving an ace, then doing it again, and again, and then again, something Pierce did often—his serve was, as one of his rivals put it, like trying to return a bullet.)

He was also one of the most handsome men on the planet.

He was not built like a tennis player. He was built like a football player, his tall body packed with power. This being what made his serve so terrifying, not to mention his return.

Dark hair.

Dark eyes.

Classic looks, square jaw, strong chin, high cheekbones.

The first time Corey heard his name was overhearing office talk. Someone's assistant was talking about "that tennis guy, Pierce," who "looks like JFK, Jr., but more handsome."

When Corey saw a photo of him, he noted she was not wrong.

When Genny phoned him and said, "Corey, I think I've met the man I'm going to marry," and that man was Tom Pierce, Corey's heart cracked in two.

Last, when Corey had met Tom, he knew what Genny knew.

She would never truly be his.

But Pierce would always be hers.

And he'd be happy with that.

As to the matter at hand...

"You would not be the first to break her, or the best," Corey jibed.

Pierce, damn the man, didn't give him anything. Not a sneer, a flinch, or even an eye twitch, his ability to hold his own against Corey was something else he didn't like about the guy.

Corey carried on, "I put her together before, I'll put her together again."

At that, Pierce spoke.

"Let's not pretend that's what you're angling for."

"And what am I angling for?" Corey pushed.

It was a mistake.

His first for so long, he didn't realize it, not then.

"You hope this will crash and burn, like she and Holloway crashed and burned, because you hope she'll eventually give up on men she actually wants and settle for one she doesn't want, but he wants her."

Truly.

Corey hated this man.

Making the Match is available everywhere.

Fighting the Pull, A River Rain Novel, Book 5

Hale Wheeler inherited billions from his father. He's decided to take those resources and change the world for the better. He's married to his mission, so he doesn't have time for love.

There's more lurking behind this decision. He hasn't faced the tragic loss of his father, or the bitterness of his parents' divorce. He doesn't intend to follow in his father's footsteps, breaking a woman's heart in a way it will never mend. So he vows he'll never marry.

But Hale is intrigued when he meets Elsa Cohen, the ambitious celebrity news journalist who has been reporting on his famous family. He warns her off, but she makes him a deal. She'll pull back in exchange for an exclusive interview.

Elsa Cohen is married to her career, but she wants love, marriage, children. She also wants the impossibly handsome, fiercely loyal, tenderhearted Hale Wheeler.

They go head-to-head, both denying why there are fireworks every time they meet. But once they understand their undeniable attraction, Elsa can't help but fall for the dynamic do-gooder.

As for Hale, he knows he needs to fight the pull of the beautiful, bold, loving Elsa Cohen, because breaking her would crush him.

Continue reading for an excerpt of Fighting the Pull.

Fighting the Pull
Excerpt

Corey

Then...

It was not a good idea to roll up to his son's baseball game in a chauffeur-driven town car.

However, it was either that or miss another one of Hale's games.

No, that was incorrect.

It was either that or miss the entire season, since this was the championship, and until then, Corey hadn't been to a single game.

But weather had been atrocious in Minneapolis, where he'd been that morning. Their takeoff had been delayed for over three hours.

One of his assistants had made all the plans, and Corey should have had plenty of time to get home, get changed and drive to the field in one of his personal vehicles, all of which were high-performance, and thus expensive. But they weren't chauffeur-driven town cars.

Regretfully, after their late takeoff, that became impossible.

But he couldn't miss another game. Sam would be livid, and Corey would have to put up with her attitude.

And his son Hale would be...

Corey didn't finish that thought as he stood beside the bleachers in his ten-thousand-dollar bespoke suit trying to figure out what was happening on the field.

He'd never been into sports. However, since Hale played baseball, if Corey had more time, he'd look up the rules and regs, even read up on the history and watch a few games.

Although he didn't know much about baseball, he could see his son's natural ability. His focus. The ease with which he maneuvered his body, even at fifteen years old.

Watching him, Corey had a funny taste in his mouth because Hale reminded him of...

He didn't finish that thought either.

Nevertheless, Corey was a busy man. He didn't have time for much of anything, but work. If he had time, he'd have been at more than one of Hale's games and would have learned by being there, not reading a book about the history of baseball.

He stood where he was, not-so-easily ignoring the attention he got from both sides of the bleachers.

Yes, Corey was wearing a suit that no doubt cost months of their mortgages.

Yes, Corey was in a suit, rather than wearing something far more casual, like everyone else.

Yes, his chauffeur was also his bodyguard, and the man was not only sticking close to his charge, but also being obvious about it.

Yes, Corey was more famous than many in that town, and considering it was Los Angeles, that was no small feat.

And yes, he was by far richer than *any* in that town, and that was no small feat either.

What made the attention not so easy to ignore wasn't about any of that. Normally, he would have no issue with it. He was used to it. And in these instances, he could share it. Genny and Tom were in the bleachers watching Hale. As were their kids, Chloe, Matt and Sasha.

Or, as Corey understood it, but Sam did not, Hale's real family were watching Hale play baseball.

Now, *they* never missed a game.

Genny—or America's Sweetheart, Imogen Swan—wasn't richer than Corey, but she was far more famous. Tom, partly by association, was as well, considering he wasn't only Genny's husband, but many said he was one of the greatest tennis players ever to play the game.

And Corey could feel their censure, particularly Tom's.

Tom was a busy man too, but he'd cut off his own arm before he'd miss something important to his wife or one of his children. In fact, if the situation came up (and it had), Tom would fly from Australia to LA just to walk Genny down a red carpet, then fly right back in order to continue commentating the matches, which was what he did now that he'd retired.

Tom would find a way…and did.

Genny, the highest paid actor in Hollywood, would find a way…and did.

Corey showed up in the seventh inning, and he might not know much about baseball, but he knew there were only nine innings.

However, it wasn't only Genny and Tom being disappointed in him that was difficult to ignore.

Fighting the Pull **is available everywhere.**

DISCOVER MORE
KRISTEN ASHLEY

GOSSAMER IN THE DARKNESS:
A Fantasyland Novella

Their engagement was set when they were children. Loren Copeland, the rich and handsome Marquess of Remington, would marry Maxine Dawes, the stunning daughter of the Count of Derryman. It's a power match. The perfect alliance for each house.

However, the Count has been keeping secret a childhood injury that means Maxine can never marry. He's done this as he searches for a miracle so this marriage can take place. He needs the influence such an alliance would give him, and he'll stop at nothing to have it.

The time has come. There could be no more excuses. No more delays. The marriage has to happen, or the contract will be broken.

When all seems lost, the Count finds his miracle: There's a parallel universe where his daughter has a twin. He must find her, bring her to his world and force her to make the Marquess fall in love with her.

And this, he does.

WILD WIND: A Chaos Novella

When he was sixteen years old, Jagger Black laid eyes on the girl who was his. At a cemetery. During her mother's funeral.

For years, their lives cross, they feel the pull of their connection, but then they go their separate ways.

But when Jagger sees that girl chasing someone down the street, he doesn't think twice before he wades right in. And when he gets a full-on dose of the woman she's become, he knows he finally has to decide if he's all in or if it's time to cut her loose.

She's ready to be cut loose.

But Jagger is all in.

DREAM BITES COOKBOOK:
Cooking with the Commandos
Short Stories by Kristen Ashley
Recipes by Suzanne M. Johnson

From *New York Times* bestseller Kristen Ashley and *USA Today* bestseller Suzanne M. Johnson...

See what's cooking!

You're invited to Denver and into the kitchens of Hawk Delgado's commandos: Daniel "Mag" Magnusson, Boone Sadler, Axl Pantera and Augustus "Auggie" Hero as they share with you some of the goodness they whip up for their women.

Not only will you get to spend time with the commandos, the Dream Team makes an appearance with their men, and there are a number of special guest stars. It doesn't end there, you'll also find some bonus recipes from a surprise source who doesn't like to be left out.

So strap in for a trip to Denver, a few short stories, some reminiscing and a lot of great food.

(Half of the proceeds of this cookbook go to the Rock Chick Nation Charities)

Welcome to Dream Bites, Cooking with the Commandos!

WILD FIRE: A Chaos Novella

"You know you can't keep a good brother down."

The Chaos Motorcycle Club has won its war. But not every brother rode into the sunset with his woman on the back of his bike.

Chaos returns with the story of Dutch Black, a man whose father was the moral compass of the Club, until he was murdered. And the man who raised Dutch protected the Club at all costs. That combination is the man Dutch is intent on becoming.

It's also the man that Dutch is going to go all out to give to his woman.

QUIET MAN: A Dream Man Novella

Charlotte "Lottie" McAlister is in the zone. She's ready to take on the next chapter of her life, and since she doesn't have a man, she'll do what she's done all along. She'll take care of business on her own. Even if that business means starting a family.

The problem is, Lottie has a stalker. The really bad kind. The kind that means she needs a bodyguard.

Enter Mo Morrison.

Enormous. Scary.

Quiet.

Mo doesn't say much, and Lottie's used to getting attention. And she wants Mo's attention. Badly.

But Mo has a strict rule. If he's guarding your body, that's all he's doing with it.

However, the longer Mo has to keep Lottie safe, the faster he falls for the beautiful blonde who has it so together, she might even be able to tackle the demons he's got in his head that just won't die.

But in the end, Lottie and Mo don't only have to find some way to keep hands off until the threat is over, they have to negotiate the over-protective Hot Bunch, Lottie's crazy stepdad, Tex, Mo's crew of frat-boy commandos, not to mention his nutty sisters.

All before Lottie finally gets her Dream Man.

And Mo can lay claim to his Dream Girl.

ROUGH RIDE: A Chaos Novella

Rosalie Holloway put it all on the line for the Chaos Motorcycle Club.

Informing to Chaos on their rival club—her man's club, Bounty—Rosalie knows the stakes. And she pays them when her man, who she was hoping to scare straight, finds out she's betrayed him and he delivers her to his brothers to mete out their form of justice.

But really, Rosie has long been denying that, as she drifted away from her Bounty, she's been falling in love with Everett "Snapper" Kavanagh, a Chaos brother. Snap is the biker-boy-next door with the snowy blue eyes, quiet confidence and sweet disposition who was supposed to keep her safe...and fell down on that job.

For Snapper, it's always been Rosalie, from the first time he saw her at the Chaos Compound. He's just been waiting for a clear shot. But he didn't want to get it after his Rosie was left bleeding, beat down and broken by Bounty on a cement warehouse floor.

With Rosalie a casualty of an ongoing war, Snapper has to guide her to trust him, take a shot with him, build a them...

And fold his woman firmly in the family that is Chaos.

ROCK CHICK REAWAKENING:
A Rock Chick Novella

From *New York Times* bestselling author, Kristen Ashley, comes the long-awaited story of Daisy and Marcus, *Rock Chick Reawakening*. A prequel to Kristen's *Rock Chick* series, *Rock Chick Reawakening* shares the tale of the devastating event that nearly broke Daisy, an event that set Marcus Sloane—one of Denver's most respected businessmen and one of the Denver underground's most feared crime bosses—into finally making his move to win the heart of the woman who stole his.

Sign up for the Blue Box Press/1001 Dark Nights Newsletter
and be entered to win a Tiffany Lock necklace.

There's a contest every quarter!

Go to www.TheBlueBoxPress.com to subscribe!

As a bonus, all subscribers can download FIVE FREE
exclusive books!

DISCOVER 1001 DARK NIGHTS
COLLECTION NINE

DRAGON UNBOUND by Donna Grant
A Dragon Kings Novella

NOTHING BUT INK by Carrie Ann Ryan
A Montgomery Ink: Fort Collins Novella

THE MASTERMIND by Dylan Allen
A Rivers Wilde Novella

JUST ONE WISH by Carly Phillips
A Kingston Family Novella

BEHIND CLOSED DOORS by Skye Warren
A Rochester Novella

GOSSAMER IN THE DARKNESS by Kristen Ashley
A Fantasyland Novella

THE CLOSE-UP by Kennedy Ryan
A Hollywood Renaissance Novella

DELIGHTED by Lexi Blake
A Masters and Mercenaries Novella

THE GRAVESIDE BAR AND GRILL by Darynda Jones
A Charley Davidson Novella

THE ANTI-FAN AND THE IDOL by Rachel Van Dyken
A My Summer In Seoul Novella

A VAMPIRE'S KISS by Rebecca Zanetti
A Dark Protectors/Rebels Novella

CHARMED BY YOU by J. Kenner
A Stark Security Novella

HIDE AND SEEK by Laura Kaye
A Blasphemy Novella

DESCEND TO DARKNESS by Heather Graham
A Krewe of Hunters Novella

BOND OF PASSION by Larissa Ione
A Demonica Novella

JUST WHAT I NEEDED by Kylie Scott
A Stage Dive Novella

Also from Blue Box Press

THE BAIT by C.W. Gortner and M.J. Rose

THE FASHION ORPHANS by Randy Susan Meyers and M.J. Rose

TAKING THE LEAP by Kristen Ashley
A River Rain Novel

SAPPHIRE SUNSET by Christopher Rice writing C. Travis Rice
A Sapphire Cove Novel

THE WAR OF TWO QUEENS by Jennifer L. Armentrout
A Blood and Ash Novel

THE MURDERS AT FLEAT HOUSE by Lucinda Riley

ON BEHALF OF BLUE BOX PRESS,

LIZ BERRY, M.J ROSE, AND JILLIAN STEIN
WOULD LIKE TO THANK~

Steve Berry
Doug Scofield
Benjamin Stein
Kim Guidroz
Social Butterfly PR
Ashley Wells
Asha Hossain
Chris Graham
Chelle Olson
Kasi Alexander
Jessica Saunders
Dylan Stockton
Kate Boggs
Richard Blake
and Simon Lipskar

Made in the USA
Monee, IL
14 November 2023

46493390R00249